**Praise for *New York Times* bestselling author
JoAnn Ross**

"Ms. Ross knows just what romance is all about."
—*RT Book Reviews*

"[JoAnn Ross has a] talent for blending vibrant
characters, congenial small-town settings
and pressing social issues in a heartwarming
contemporary romance."
—*Booklist*

"Ross's insight into both romantic attraction
and family dynamics is striking."
—*Publishers Weekly*

Praise for Susan Meier

"Meier never ceases to amaze with
one-of-a-kind love stories."
—*RT Book Reviews*

"Meier's characters are realistic and likable in this
great story about dealing with life's blows."
—*RT Book Reviews* on *Nanny for the Millionaire's Twins*

JoANN ROSS

New York Times and *USA TODAY* bestselling author JoAnn Ross has been published in twenty-seven countries. A member of Romance Writers of America's Honor Roll of bestselling authors, JoAnn lives with her husband and three rescued dogs—who pretty much rule the house—in the Pacific Northwest. Visit her on the web, at www.joannross.com.

SUSAN MEIER

spent most of her twenties thinking she was a job-hopper—until she began to write and realized everything that had come before was only research! One of eleven children, with twenty-four nieces and nephews and three kids of her own, Susan has had plenty of real-life experience watching romance blossom in unexpected ways. She lives in western Pennsylvania with her wonderful husband, Mike, three children and two overfed, well-cuddled cats, Sophie and Fluffy. She writes for the Harlequin Romance line. You can visit Susan's website, at www.susanmeier.com.

New York Times Bestselling Author

JoAnn Ross

It Happened One Week

⬦ **HARLEQUIN**® BESTSELLING AUTHOR COLLECTION

Recycling programs for this product may not exist in your area.

ISBN-13: 978-0-373-18082-0

IT HAPPENED ONE WEEK
Copyright © 2014 by Harlequin Books S.A.

The publisher acknowledges the copyright holders of the individual works as follows:

IT HAPPENED ONE WEEK
Copyright © 1996 by JoAnn Ross

MAID FOR THE MILLIONAIRE
First North American Publication 2010
Copyright © 2010 by Linda Susan Meier

Printed in U.S.A.

Dear Reader,

I'm often asked, "Where do you get your ideas?" At such times, writers are tempted to invent some lofty, literary answer. I've decided to tell you the truth.

This story was conceived late one summer night in 1995 when I was having an after-dinner drink with a few of my foreign editors and Dianne Moggy—then a senior editor at Harlequin MIRA and now a VP of the company—in a Canadian karaoke bar. At the time, Harlequin had begun a new line of romances called Yours Truly, where the hero and heroine were brought together by some sort of written word. When the man behind the keyboard began playing "Love Letters in the Sand," Dianne looked up at the oversize screen and said, "JoAnn, look, there's a Yours Truly book you should write!"

My first thought was that I didn't have time to write another book. I was, after all, already committed to several novels for the Harlequin Temptation line and another mainstream novel for the MIRA line. But watching the video of the waves rolling up to wash away the words printed on the sparkling sand started my imagination stirring. By breakfast, I knew I had to write *It Happened One Week*.

This is one of my more autobiographical stories, drawing from my teenage days in Oregon and my own bittersweet summer romance. Fortunately, like my hero and heroine, we eventually got back together, went on to live mostly happily ever after and still visit the Oregon coast, where my husband proposed, often.

Happy reading!

JoAnn Ross

IT HAPPENED ONE WEEK

New York Times Bestselling Author

JoAnn Ross

To Dianne Moggy—who provided the inspiration

Prologue

Satan's Cove

The letters had been painstakingly carved into the shifting silver sands. Although she could see them from the top of the jagged cliff overlooking the Pacific Ocean, fifteen-year-old Amanda Stockenberg could not make out the message.

As she descended the stone steps to the beach, slowly at first, then faster, until she was nearly running, the words became clearer.

Dane loves Amanda.

Despite the fact that she'd spent most of last night crying, Amanda began to weep.

He was waiting for her in their secret, private place. Just as he'd promised. Just as she'd hoped.

Smugglers' Cave, carved by aeons of wind and ocean

out of the rocky seaside cliffs, had long been rumored to be one of the local sites where pirates had once hidden stolen booty before moving it inland.

Amanda wasn't interested in the legends about the pirates' nefarious behavior. And despite the violence that supposedly occurred here, to her, Smugglers' Cave was the most romantic place on earth.

It was here, on a star-spangled July Fourth night, while the glare of fireworks lit up the night sky, that Dane first kissed her. Then kissed her again. And again. Until she thought she'd literally melt from ecstasy.

"I thought you wouldn't come," she cried, flinging herself dramatically into his strong dark arms. Her avid mouth captured his. The kiss was hot and long and bittersweet.

"I told you I would," he reminded her, after they finally came up for air.

"I know." Her hands were linked together around his neck. Her young, lithe body was pressed against his so tightly that it would have been impossible for the morning ocean breeze to come between them. "But I was so afraid you'd be mad at me."

"Mad?" Dane looked honestly surprised by the idea. "Why would I be mad at you?"

"For leaving." Just thinking about her imminent departure caused the moisture in Amanda's sea blue eyes to overflow.

"You don't have any choice, sweetheart." With more tenderness than she would have imagined possible, he brushed her tears away with his fingertips. "We've both known that from the beginning."

"That doesn't make it any less awful!" she wailed.

"No." Despite his brave words, Dane's dark eyes

were every bit as bleak as hers as he traced her trembling, downturned pink lips with a tear-dampened finger. "It doesn't."

The tender touch left behind a taste of salt born of her overwhelming sorrow. "We could run away," she said desperately, grabbing his hand and holding it tightly between both of hers. "Just you and I. Somewhere no one could ever find us. To Wyoming. Or Florida."

"Don't think I haven't been tempted." His lips curved at the idea, but even as distressed as she was, Amanda noticed that the smile didn't reach his eyes. "But running away is never the answer, princess."

She was too desperate, too unhappy, to listen to reason. "But—"

"We can't." His tone, while gentle, was firm. "As attractive as the idea admittedly is, it's wrong."

"How can love be wrong?"

Dane sighed, looking far older, far more world-weary than his nineteen years. "You're only fifteen years old—"

"I'll be sixteen next week."

"I know." This time the reluctant smile turned his eyes to the hue of rich, warm chocolate. "But you still have your entire life ahead of you, honey. I'm not going to be responsible for ruining it."

"But you wouldn't!" she cried on a wail that scattered a trio of sea gulls. "You'd make it better. Perfect, even."

As much as she'd first resisted joining her family for this annual summer vacation on the Oregon coast, the moment she'd first seen Smugglers' Inn's sexy young bellhop, lifeguard, and all-around handyman, Amanda had changed her mind.

Over the past four glorious weeks, her life had been focused on Dane Cutter. He was all she wanted. All she would ever want. She'd love him, Amanda vowed, forever.

But now, she didn't want to waste time talking. Not when their time together was coming to an end, like sands falling through some hateful hourglass. Rising on her toes, she pressed her lips against his once more.

The morning mist swirled around them; overhead, sea gulls squawked stridently as they circled, searching for mussels in the foaming surge. Caught up in emotions every bit as strong—and as old—as the forces that had formed the craggy coastline, neither Dane nor Amanda heard them.

The ocean's roar became a distant buzz in Amanda's ears. For this glorious suspended moment, time ceased to have meaning. The hungry kiss could have lasted a minute, an hour, an eternity.

Finally, the blare of a car horn managed to infiltrate its way into Amanda's consciousness. She tried to ignore it, but it was soon followed by the sound of an irritated male voice cutting through the fog.

Dane dragged his mouth from hers. "Your father's calling." He skimmed his lips up her cheeks, which were damp again from the cold ocean mist and her tears.

"I know." She swiped at the tears with the backs of her trembling hands, looking, Dane thought, more like an injured child than the almost-grown-up woman she insisted that she was. Unwilling, unable to leave, she twined her arms around his neck again and clung.

For not the first time since her arrival in Satan's Cove, Dane found himself sorely tested. For not the first time, he reminded himself that she was far too young for the thoughts he kept having, the feelings he kept experiencing. But even as his mind struggled to hold on to that crucial fact—like a drowning man clinging to a piece of driftwood in a storm-tossed sea—his body was literally aching for fulfillment.

Dane was not inexperienced. He'd discovered, since losing his virginity to a sexy blond Miss Depoe Bay the summer of his sixteenth year, that sex was easy to come by. Especially during vacation season, when the beaches were filled with beautiful girls looking for a summer fling.

But he'd never wanted a girl as he wanted Amanda. What was worse, he'd never *needed* a girl as he needed Amanda. Accustomed to keeping a tight rein on his emotions, Dane wasn't at all comfortable with the effect Amanda Stockenberg had had on him from the beginning.

Finally, although it was nearly the hardest thing he'd ever had to do—second only to refusing her ongoing, seductive pleas to make love these past weeks—Dane gently, patiently, unfastened Amanda's hold on him.

"You have to go," he said again, prying her hands from around his neck. He kissed her fingers one at a time. "But it's not over, princess. Not unless you want it to be."

Distraught as she was, Amanda failed to hear the question—and the uncharacteristic lack of assurance—in his guarded tone.

"Never!" she swore with all the fervor of a young woman in the throes of her first grand love. "I promise."

Her father called out again. The van's horn blared. Once. Twice. A third time.

Giving Dane one last desperate kiss, Amanda spun around, sobbing loudly as she ran up the rock stairs. She did not—could not—look back.

He stood there all alone, hands shoved deep into the pockets of his jeans, and watched her leave, resisting the urge to call out to her. He heard the van drive off, taking her far away from Satan's Cove. Away from him.

Dane stayed on the windswept beach for a long, silent time, watching as the relentless ebb and flow of the tide slowly, inexorably, washed away the love letter he'd written in the drifting silver sand.

Chapter 1

Portland, Oregon
Ten years later

"This can't be happening. Not to me. Not now!"
Amanda Stockenberg stared in disbelief at the television screen where towering red-and-orange flames were engulfing the Mariner Seaside Golf Resort and Conference Center located on the Oregon coast.

"It *is* lousy timing," her administrative assistant, Susan Chin, agreed glumly. It had been Susan who'd alerted Amanda to the disaster, after hearing a news bulletin on the radio.

"That has to be the understatement of the millennium," Amanda muttered as she opened a new roll of antacids.

Hoping for the best, but fearing the worst, she'd left a meeting and run down the hall to the conference room.

Now, as the two women stood transfixed in front of the television, watching the thick streams of water prove ineffectual at combating the massive blaze, Amanda could see her entire career going up in smoke right along with the five-star resort.

She groaned as the hungry flames devoured the lovely cedar-shake shingled roof. The scene shifted as the cameras cut away to show the crews of helmeted firemen valiantly fighting the fire. From the grim expressions on their soot-stained faces, she sensed that they knew their efforts to be a lost cause.

And speaking of lost causes…

"It's obvious we're going to have to find a new site for the corporate challenge," she said, cringing when what was left of the wooden roof caved in with a deafening roar. Water from the fire hoses hit the flames, turned to steam and mixed with the clouds of thick gray smoke.

"I'd say that's a given," Susan agreed glumly. "Unless you want to have the group camping out on the beach. Which, now that I think about it, isn't such a bad idea. After all, the entire idea of this coming week is to present the creative teams with challenges to overcome."

"Getting any of the managers of *this* company to work together as a team is going to be challenge enough." Amanda sank into a chair, put her elbows on the long rectangular mahogany conference table and began rubbing at her temples, where a headache had begun to pound. "Without tossing in sleeping in tents on wet sand and bathing out of buckets."

Advertising had been a cutthroat, shark-eat-shark business since the first Babylonian entrepreneur had gotten the bright idea to chisel the name of his company onto a stone tablet. Competition was always fierce, and everyone knew that the battle went not only to the most creative, but to the most ruthless.

Even so, Amanda felt the employees of Janzen, Lawton and Young took the idea of healthy competition to unattractive and often unprofitable extremes. Apparently, Ernst Janzen, senior partner of the company that had recently purchased Amanda's advertising agency, seemed to share her feelings. Which was why the idea of corporate-management teams was born in the first place.

In theory, the concept of art, copy and marketing working together on each step of a project seemed ideal. With everyone marching in unison toward the same finish line, the firm would undoubtedly regain superiority over its competitors.

That was the plan. It was, Amanda had agreed, when she'd first heard of it, extremely logical. Unfortunately, there was little about advertising that was the least bit logical.

The agency that had hired her directly after her graduation from UCLA, Connally Creative Concepts, or C.C.C., had made a name for itself by creating witty, appealing and totally original advertising that persuaded and made the sale through its ability to charm the prospect.

Although its location in Portland, Oregon, was admittedly a long way from Madison Avenue, some of the best copywriters and art directors in the country had been more than willing to leave Manhattan and take pay cuts in order to work long hours under the tutelage of Patrick Connally. C.C.C. had been like a family, Patrick Connally playing the role of father to everyone who came for inspiration and guidance.

Unfortunately, two years ago Patrick Connally had died of a heart attack at the age of seventy-five, after a heated game of tennis. His widow, eager to retire to Sun City, Arizona, had sold the agency to another company. Eight months after that, the new owner merged the united agencies with yet a third creative shop.

Unsurprisingly, such multiple mergers in such a short span of time resulted in the dismissal of several long-time employees as executives trimmed excess staff. A mood of anxiety settled over the offices and morale plummeted as everyone held their collective breath, waiting to see who was going to be "downsized" next.

After the initial purge, things had seemed to be settling down until the advertising wars kicked up again. A six-month battle that played out daily in the newspapers and on the internet had resulted in an unfriendly takeover by the international mega-agency of Janzen, Lawton and Young, and those employees who'd been breathing at last, found their livelihoods once again in jeopardy.

Janzen, Lawton and Young had long had a reputation for the most artless and offensive commercials to run in America. But it also boasted the highest profits in the business. In order to keep profits up to the promised levels, a new wave of massive staff cuts had hit the agency.

Morale plummeted to new lows.

Unsurprisingly, the same creative people who had once been responsible for some of the most innovative—and effective—advertising in the business, turned on one another.

A recent case in point was today's client meeting. The creative group had been assigned to propose a new concept for a popular line of gourmet ice cream. From day one, the members of the recently established team had been at each other's throats like a pack of out-of-control pit bulls.

"I can't believe you seriously expect me to be a part of this presentation," Marvin Kenyon, the head copy-writer, had complained after viewing the animated se-quence proposed by award-winning art director Julian Palmer.

"It's a team effort," Amanda reminded him mildly. "And you *are* a valuable member of the team."

The copywriter, who'd won his share of awards him-self, folded his arms over the front of his blue oxford-cloth shirt and said, "I categorically refuse to share blame for something as sophomoric and static as that animation sequence."

"Sophomoric?" Julian Palmer rose to his full height of five feet five inches tall. What he lacked in stature, he more than made up for in ego. "Static? Since when are you an expert on visuals?"

"I know enough to see that if we present your idea, we'll blow the account for sure," Marvin retorted. "Hell, a baboon with a fistful of crayons could undoubtedly create a more visually appealing storyboard."

Julian arched an eyebrow as he adjusted the already perfect Windsor knot in his Italian-silk tie. "This from a man who creates—" he waved the printed sheets Mar-vin had handed out when he'd first arrived in the pre-sentation room like a battle flag "—mindless drivel?"

"Drivel?" Marvin was on his feet in a shot, hands

folded into fists as he came around the long, polished mahogany table.

"Marvin," Amanda protested, "please sit down. Julian didn't mean it, did you, Julian?"

"I never say anything I don't mean," the artistic director replied. "But in this case, I may have been mistaken."

"There, see?" Amanda soothed, feeling as if she were refereeing a fight between two toddlers in a kindergarten sandbox. "Julian admits he was mistaken, Marvin. Perhaps you can amend your comment about his work."

"I *was* wrong to call it drivel," Julian agreed. "That's too kind a description for such cliché-ridden rubbish."

"That does it!" Marvin, infamous for his quicksilver temper, was around the table like a shot. He'd grabbed hold of his team member's chalk-gray vest and for a moment Amanda feared that the two men were actually going to come to blows, when the conference-room door opened and the client arrived with Don Patterson, the marketing manager, on his heels.

"Am I interrupting something?" the longtime client, a man in his mid-fifties whose addiction to ice cream had made him a very wealthy man, asked.

"Only a momentary creative difference of opinion," Amanda said quickly. "Good afternoon, Mr. Carpenter. It's nice to see you again."

"It's always a pleasure to see you again, Ms. Stockenberg." The portly entrepreneur took her outstretched hand in his. His blue eyes warmed momentarily as they swept over her appreciatively. "I'm looking forward to today's presentation," he said as his gaze moved to the uncovered storyboard.

Wide brow furrowed, he crossed the room and began

studying it for a long silent time. Since it was too late to begin the presentation as planned, the team members refrained from speaking as he took in the proposed campaign. Amanda didn't know about the others, but she would have found it impossible to say a word, holding her breath as she was.

When Fred Carpenter finally did speak, his words were not encouraging. "You people have serviced my account for five years. I've dropped a bundle into your coffers. And this is as good as you can come up with? A cow wearing a beret?"

"Let me explain the animation," Julian said quickly. Too quickly, Amanda thought with an inner sigh. He was making the fatal mistake of any presenter: appearing desperate.

"Don't worry, the art can be rethought," Marvin interjected as Julian picked up the laser pen to better illustrate the sequence. "Besides, it's the words that'll sell your new, improved, French vanilla flavor, anyway." He paused, as if half expecting a drumroll to announce his message. "A taste of Paris in every spoonful."

"That's it?" the snack-food executive asked.

"Well, it's just the beginning," Marvin assured him. Moisture was beading up on his upper lip, his forehead. Another rule broken, Amanda thought, remembering what Patrick Connally had taught her about never letting the client—or the competition—see you sweat. "See, the way I envision the concept—"

"It's drivel," Julian said again. "But the team can fix that, Fred. Now, if we could just get back to the art."

"It's not drivel," Marvin exploded.

"Marvin," Amanda warned softly.

"I've seen cleverer copy written on rolls of novelty toilet paper," the art director sniffed.

"And I've seen better art scrawled on the sides of buildings down at the docks!"

Amanda turned toward the client who appeared less than amused by the escalating argument. "As you can see, Mr. Carpenter, your campaign has created a lot of in-house excitement," she said, trying desperately to salvage the multimillion-dollar account.

"Obviously the wrong kind," Carpenter said. "Look, I haven't liked how all these mergers resulted in my account being put into the hands of the same agency that handles my competitors. It looks to me as if you guys have been instructed by your new bosses to soften your approach—"

"The hell we have," both Julian and Marvin protested in unison, agreeing for once. Amanda tried telling herself she should be grateful for small favors.

"Then you've lost your edge," the self-proclaimed king of ice cream decided.

"That's really not the case, Fred," Don Patterson, the marketing member of the team, finally interjected. A man prone to wearing loud ties and plaid sport jackets, he was nevertheless very good at his job. "Perhaps if Julian and Marvin went back to the drawing board—"

"There's no point. We've had five great years working together, you fellows have helped make Sweet Indulgence the second-bestselling ice cream in the country. But, the team over at Chiat/Day assures me that they can get me to number one. So, I think I'm going to give them a try."

He turned toward Amanda, who could literally feel the color draining from her face. "I'm sorry, Ms. Stockenberg. You're a nice, pretty lady and I'd like to keep my account here if for no other reason than to have an excuse to keep seeing you. But business is business."

"I understand." With effort, Amanda managed a smile and refrained from strangling the two ego-driven creative members of the ill-suited team. "But Don does have a point. Perhaps if you'd allow us a few days to come up with another concept—"

"Sorry." He shook his head. "But things haven't been the same around here since all the mergers." His round face looked as unhappy as hers. "But if you'd like," he said, brightening somewhat, "I'll mention you to the fellows at Chiat/Day. Perhaps there's a spot opening up over there."

"That's very kind of you. But I'm quite happy where I am."

It was what she'd been telling herself over and over again lately, Amanda thought now, as she dragged her mind from the disastrous meeting to the disaster currently being played out on the television screen.

"You know," Susan said, "this entire challenge week isn't really your problem. Officially, it's Greg's."

"I know." Amanda sighed and began chewing on another Tums.

Greg Parsons was her immediate supervisor and, as creative director, he was the man Ernst Janzen had hand-selected for the job of instituting the team concept. The man who had moved into the executive suite was as different from Patrick Connally as night from day. Rather than encouraging the cooperative atmosphere that had once thrived under the founder of C.C.C., Greg ruled the agency by intimidation and fear.

From his first day on the job, he'd set unrealistic

profit targets. This focus on profits diverted attention from what had always been the agency's forte—making clients feel they were getting superior service.

Apparently believing that internal competition was the lifeblood of success, he instigated political maneuvering among his top people, pitting one against the other as they jockeyed for key appointments.

Although such intrigue usually occurred behind the scenes, one of the more visible changes in policy was the conference table at which Amanda was sitting. When she'd first come to work here, the room had boasted a giant round table, the better, her former boss had declared, to create the feeling of democracy. Now, five days a week, the staff sat around this oblong table while Parsons claimed the power position at the head.

Although it might not seem like such a big thing, along with all the other changes that had taken place, it was additional proof that C.C.C. had lost the family feeling that had been so comfortable and inspirational to both employees and clients.

Desperate to salvage his foundering career, Parsons had come up with the idea of taking the teams to a resort, where, utilizing a number of outward-bound-type game-playing procedures he'd gleaned from his latest management-training course, the various independent-minded individuals would meld into one forceful creative entity.

"The problem is," Amanda said, "like it or not, my fortunes are tied to Greg."

"Lucky him. Since without you to run interference and do all his detail work, he'd undoubtedly have been out on his Armani rear a very long time ago," Susan said.

"That's not very nice."

"Granted. But it's true."

Amanda couldn't argue with her assistant's pithy analysis. From the time of Greg's arrival from the Dallas office three months ago, she'd wondered, on more than one occasion, exactly how the man had managed to win the corporate plum of creative director. It certainly hadn't been on merit.

Then, six weeks after he'd moved into the expensively redecorated executive office, the question was answered when Susan returned from a long lunch with the other administrative assistants where she'd learned that Greg just happened to be married to Ernst Janzen's granddaughter. Which, Amanda had agreed, explained everything.

It was bad enough that Greg was frightfully incompetent. Even worse was the way he saw himself as a modern-day Napoleon—part dictator, part Don Juan. And although she'd deftly dealt with his less-than-subtle passes, her refusal had earned Amanda her superior's antipathy. He rode her constantly, belittling her work even as he routinely took credit for her ideas in upper-level corporate meetings.

It was no secret that the man was unhappy in Portland. He constantly berated the entire West Coast as hopelessly provincial. It was also common knowledge that he had his eye on a superior prize—that of national creative director and vice president. Along with the requisite increase in salary and numerous perks, the coveted slot also came with a corner-window penthouse office on Manhattan's famed Madison Avenue.

"I still don't see why you put up with the man," Susan said, her acid tone breaking into Amanda's thoughts.

"It's simple. I want his job."

"It should have been yours in the first place."

Once again, Amanda couldn't argue with the truth. While she hadn't specifically been promised the creative director's spot when she was first hired, there'd been every indication that Patrick Connally considered her on the fast track to success.

She'd worked hard for the past four years, forgoing any social life, giving most of her time and energy to the company.

The sacrifices had paid off; there had been a time, not so long ago, when the job of creative director had looked like a lock. Until Greg Parsons arrived on the scene.

"Blood's thicker than water. And unfortunately, Greg happens to be married to Mr. Janzen's granddaughter."

"Talk about sleeping your way to the top," Susan muttered.

"Unfortunately, family ties seem to have gotten Greg this far." Amanda frowned up at the oil portrait of the new creative director hanging on the wall. The ornate, gilt-framed painting featured Parsons in one of his dress-for-success chalk-striped suits, holding a cigar.

"But," she continued, "after the problems he's had instituting the team concept, he's stalled in the water."

Susan arched a jet eyebrow. "Are you saying you think he's on the way out?"

"Unfortunately, I don't think—unless Jessica Janzen Parsons wises up and divorces him—there's any chance of that. So, I've come up with a plan to get the guy out of my life—and out of town—once and for all."

"Please tell me it involves tar and feathers."

"Not quite." Actually, although she'd never admit it, Amanda found the idea of running Parsons out of town

on a rail—like in the good old days of the Wild West—
eminently appealing.

"Actually, it's simple. Or at least it was," she amended
with another bleak glance toward the television screen.
"Until the resort went up in smoke."

"Let me guess. You were going to lure the bastard
out onto the cliff behind the resort late one night, hit
him in the head with his precious new PING nine iron,
then shove him into the ocean. Where, with any luck,
he'd be eaten by killer sharks."

Despite all her problems, Amanda smiled. "As attractive as that scenario may be, the sharks would probably
spare him because of professional courtesy. Besides,
I've come to the conclusion that the easiest way to get
Greg out of my hair is to give him what he most wants."

"Don't tell me that you're going to go to bed with
him?"

"Of course not." Amanda literally shuddered at the
unpalatable idea. "Actually, I've decided to get him promoted."

A slow, understanding grin had Susan's crimson lips
curving. "To Manhattan."

Amanda returned the smile with a cocky, confident
grin of her own. "To Manhattan."

Amanda couldn't deny that losing the conference-
center resort to fire was a setback. After all, without someplace to hold the corporate challenge, Greg
couldn't prove that his idea had merit. Which in turn
would keep him here in Portland indefinitely.

But it wasn't the first challenge she'd overcome in
her rise up the advertising corporate ladder. Amanda
doubted it would be her last.

A part of her hated the idea of Greg Parsons getting

any more credit, when in reality, if the upcoming week proved a success, it would be her doing. A stronger part of her just wanted him gone. She would swallow her pride, along with her ego, if it meant getting the obnoxious man out of her life.

Now all she had to do was find some other location for the challenge. Which wasn't going to be easy, considering this was the high tourist season on the Oregon coast.

Could she do it? Amanda asked herself as she pointed the remote toward the television and darkened the screen.

You bet.

Satan's Cove

"We've got a problem."

Dane Cutter stopped in the act of nailing down cedar shingles and glanced over the steep edge of the roof. "So why don't you tell me something I don't know?"

He'd been the proud owner of Smugglers' Inn for two months. Well, if you wanted to get technical, he and the bank actually owned the century-old landmark building. Since he'd signed the final papers, Dane doubted a single day had gone by that he hadn't had to overcome some new catastrophe.

Having paid for an extensive professional inspection of the building that, because of competition from larger, fancier resorts catering to the corporate trade, had fallen into disrepair during his time away from Satan's Cove, Dane knew the problems he was taking on. And although they were considerable, he'd foolishly expected to have some time to do all the necessary renovations.

Thus far, he'd tackled the inn's ancient plumbing and electrical systems, evicted countless field mice and killed more spiders than he cared to think about.

He'd also replaced the ancient gas oven, replastered the algae-filled swimming pool, and was in the process of replacing the shingles that had blown away during last night's storm.

The next thing on his lengthy list—barring any further emergencies—was replacing the ancient gas heater, after which he planned to resand and seal the oak floors in the public rooms, then resurface the tennis court.

Since reopening last week, he'd reassured himself at least daily that it was just as well potential guests weren't exactly beating down his door. Although he admittedly needed all the bookings he could get to make the hefty mortgage payments, he also needed time to restore the inn to its former glory.

Reva Carlson grinned up at him. "Technically it's a bit of good news and some bad news. I suppose it's all in how you look at it."

"Why don't you give me the good news first?"

The way things had been going, after the storm and the burst pipe that had left the inn without water for twenty-four hours, Dane figured he could use a little boost. Hell, what he needed was a miracle. But he was willing to settle for whatever he could get.

"Okay." Reva's grin widened. "It looks as if we're going to meet this month's mortgage payment, after all."

"We got a booking?" If he'd had his choice, he would have kept the inn closed until all the needed repairs could be done. Unfortunately, his cash flow being what it was, he'd been forced to open for limited occupancy.

"We've sold out the entire place," Reva revealed proudly.

She was right. This was definitely a case of good and bad news. "Not including the tower room?" The last he'd looked into the hexagonal-shaped room that boasted a bird's-eye view of the Pacific Ocean, the wallpaper had been peeling off the walls.

"Of course not. You're good, boss, but you're not exactly a miracle worker. However, every other room, every bed, every last nook and cranny of Smugglers' Inn is going to be taken over by some Portland ad agency for an entire week."

Dane rapidly went over a mental list of repairs he'd have to accomplish in order to accommodate such a crowd.

"So, when are these ad people scheduled to arrive, anyway?"

"You could at least pretend to be pleased," she complained. "Besides, it's not that bad. We've plenty of time to get ready."

"What, exactly, do you consider plenty of time?"

"Three days."

"Three days?" He dragged his hand through his hair.

"Well, technically four. Including this one."

It was already four in the afternoon. "Damn it, Reva—"

"You're the one who's been bitching about needing bookings," she reminded Dane. "Well, now you've got some. Or would you rather me call the woman back and tell her that we're full?"

Reminding himself that the difficult could be accomplished immediately, while the impossible might take a bit longer, he said, "You did good, lady."

Another thought, beyond the necessary repairs, occurred to him. "You'd better warn Mom." He'd taken his mother out of a forced retirement and put her back in the remodeled kitchen, where she had happily begun stocking the pantry and whipping up recipes that rivaled those of any five-star resort in the country.

"I already did," she assured him, reminding him why he'd hired the former night manager away from the world-famous Whitfield Palace hotel chain. "Which reminds me, she told me to tell you that you'll have to drive into town for supplies."

"Tell her to make out a list and I'll do it as soon as I finish with the roof."

Dane returned to his hammering. And even as he wondered exactly how he was going to get everything done in time for the arrival of all those guests, he allowed himself to believe that things around Smugglers' Inn were definitely beginning to look up.

Chapter 2

Portland

"**Y**ou were right about every motel, hotel, resort and cottage up and down the coast being booked to the rafters," Susan reported to Amanda. "Every place with the exception of Smugglers' Inn, which, I'll have to admit, made me a little nervous. But the woman from the Satan's Cove visitors' bureau assured me that it's listed on the historical register."

"It is," Amanda murmured, thinking back to that wonderful summer she'd spent at Satan's Cove.

The memory was, as always, bittersweet—part pleasure and part pain. She'd never been happier than she'd been that summer of her first love. Nor more heartbroken than on the day she'd driven away from Smugglers' Inn—and Dane Cutter—back to Los Angeles with her family.

He'd promised to write; and trusting him implicitly, Amanda had believed him. For the first two weeks after arriving home, she'd waited for a letter assuring her that she was not alone in her feelings—that the kisses they'd shared, along with the desperate promises, had been more than just a summer romance.

When three weeks passed without so much as a single postcard, Amanda had screwed up enough nerve to telephone Dane at the inn. But the woman working the desk informed her that he'd left Satan's Cove to return to college. No, the woman had insisted, in a bored tone, he hadn't left any forwarding address.

She'd thought about asking to talk to his mother, who'd been the inn's cook. But youthful pride kept her from inquiring further. So, believing she'd simply been one more conquest for a drop-dead-gorgeous college boy who already had more than his share of girls throwing themselves at him, Amanda tried to write the intense, short-lived romance off to experience.

And mostly, she'd been successful. But there were still times, when she would least expect it, that she'd think back on that summer with a mixture of wistfulness and embarrassment.

"I'm surprised they could take us," she said now, recalling the inn's popularity. Her father had had to book their rooms six months in advance. "They must have had a huge cancellation."

"According to the reservations clerk, the place has been closed for several years," Susan revealed. "Apparently it's recently changed hands. This is the new owner's first season."

"I'm not sure I like the sound of that," Amanda muttered. Even in an industry built on ego and turf, the agency had become a nest of political intrigue and back-biting. The corporate team challenge week was going to be tough enough without them having to serve as some novice innkeeper's shakedown summer season.

"You can always call Popular Surplus and order up the tents."

Despite her concerns, Amanda laughed. The truth was, she really didn't have any other choice. She could put twenty people—none of whom got along very well in the best of circumstances—into tents on the beach, eating hot dogs cooked over an open fire, or she could trust the new owner of Smugglers' Inn to know what he or she was doing.

After all, how bad could it be? The landmark inn, located on one of the most scenic stretches of Pacific Coast, was pretty and cozy and wonderfully comfortable. She thought back on the lovely flower-sprigged wallpaper in the tower room she'd slept in that long-ago summer, remembered the dazzling sunsets from the high arched windows, recalled in vivid detail the romance of the crackling fires the staff built each evening in the stone fireplace large enough for a grown man to stand in.

"Smugglers' Inn will be perfect," she said firmly, as if saying the words out loud could make them true. "I don't know why I didn't think of it in the first place."

"Probably because you've had a few other things on your mind," Susan said, proving herself to be a master of understatement. "And although I have no doubt you can pull this thing off, I'm glad I'll be holding down the fort here while you lead the troops in their wilderness experience."

That said, she left Amanda to worry that this time she'd actually bitten off more than she could chew.

Never having been one to limit herself to a normal, eight-hour work schedule, Amanda remained at her desk long into the night, fine-tuning all the minuscule details that would ensure the challenge week would be a success.

But as hard as she tried to keep her mind on business, she could not keep her unruly thoughts from drifting back to the summer of her fifteenth year.

She'd fallen in love with Dane the first time she'd seen him. And although her parents had tried to convince her otherwise, she knew now, as she'd known then, that her feelings had been more than mere puppy love.

It had, admittedly, taken Dane time to realize they were a perfect match. But Amanda had steadfastly refused to give up her quest. She pursued him incessantly, with all the fervor of a teenager in the throes of a first grand love.

Everywhere Dane went, Amanda went there, as well, smiling up at him with a coy Lolita smile overbrimming with sensual invitation. After discovering that one of his duties was teaching a class in kayaking, despite her distaste for early morning awakenings, she showed up on the beach at six-thirty for lessons. Although the rest of the class was sensibly attired for the foggy sea air in jeans and sweatshirts, she'd chosen to wear a hot-pink bikini that barely covered the essentials.

And that was just the beginning. During Dane's lifeguarding stint each afternoon, she lounged poolside, wearing another impossibly scant bikini, her golden skin glowing with fragrant coconut oil. Grateful for childhood diving lessons, she would occasionally lithely rise from the lounge to treat him to swan dives designed to show off her budding female figure.

She tormented him endlessly, pretending to need his assistance on everything from a flat bicycle tire to fastening her life jacket before going out on a sight-seeing boat excursion.

Adding local color to the inn's reputation had been the legend—invented by a former owner—that it was haunted by a woman who'd thrown herself off the widow's walk after her fiancé's ship was sunk by pirates off the rocky shoals. One night, Amanda showed up at Dane's room, insisting that she'd seen the ghost.

It would have taken a male with inhuman strength to resist her continual seduction attempts. And, as Dane later confessed, he was, after all, only human.

Which was why, seven days after Amanda Stockenberg's arrival at Smugglers' Inn, Dane Cutter succumbed to the inevitable. However, even as they spent the star-spangled nights driving each other insane, Dane had steadfastly refused to make love to her.

"I may be too damn weak where you're concerned, princess," he'd groaned during one excruciatingly long petting session, "but I'm not reckless enough to have sex with a minor girl."

She'd sworn that no one would ever know, promised that she'd never—ever—do anything to get him in trouble. But on this point, Dane had proved frustratingly intractable.

And although, as the years passed, Amanda begrudgingly admitted that he'd done the right and noble thing, there were still times, such as tonight, when she was sitting all alone in the dark, that she'd think back over the bliss she'd experienced in Dane Cutter's strong young arms and wish, with all her heart, that he hadn't proved so strong.

Satan's Cove

The day before the group was due to arrive at Smugglers' Inn, Dane was beginning to think they just might make it.

The roof was now rainproof, the windows sparkled like diamonds, and every room in the place—with the exception of the tower room, which he'd written off as impossible to prepare in such short time—was white-glove clean. And although the aroma of fresh paint lingered, leaving the windows open another twenty-four hours should take care of that little problem.

His mother had definitely gone all out in the kitchen. The huge commercial refrigerator was stuffed with food and every shelf in the pantry was full. Kettles had been bubbling away on the new eight-burner stove nearly around the clock for the past two and a half days, creating mouth-watering scents.

Using the hefty deposit Reva had insisted upon, he'd hired additional staff and although the kids were as green as spring grass, they were bright, seemingly hardworking and unrelentingly cheerful.

He was passing the antique registration desk on his way to the parlor, planning to clean the oversize chandelier, when the sound of a stressed-out voice garnered his instant attention.

"I'm sorry, ma'am," Mindy Taylor, the nineteen-year-old cheerleader, premed student and local beauty queen he'd hired, said in an obviously frustrated voice. "But—"

She sighed and held the receiver a little away from her ear, indicating that it was not the first time she'd heard the argument being offered on the other end of the line.

"Yes, I can appreciate that," Mindy agreed, rolling her expressive eyes toward the knotty-pine ceiling. "But I'm afraid it's impossible. No, it's not booked, but—"

Dane heard the renewed argument, although he couldn't make out the words.

"It's a woman from that Portland advertising agency." Mindy covered the mouthpiece with her hand to talk to Dane. "She's insisting on the tower room, even though I told her that it wasn't available."

Dane held out his hand. "Let me talk to her."

"That's okay." Perfect white teeth that Dane knew had cost her parents a fortune in orthodontia flashed in the dazzling smile that had earned Mindy the Miss Satan's Cove title two years running. As this year's Miss Oregon, she'd be competing in the national pageant, which made her a local celebrity.

"It'll be good practice for Atlantic City. I need to work on my patience," she admitted. "Sometimes I think if I'm asked one more stupid question by one more judge I'm going to scream.

"I understand your feelings," Mindy soothed into the receiver as she tried yet again. "But you see, Ms. Stockenberg, Smugglers' Inn has been closed for the past few years, and—"

"Wait a minute," Dane interrupted. "Did you say Stockenberg?"

The name hit him directly in the gut, reminding him

of the time he'd been standing behind the plate and his cousin Danny had accidentally slammed a baseball bat into his solar plexus.

"Excuse me, but could you hold a moment, please?" Mindy put her hand over the mouthpiece again and nodded. "That's right."

"Not Amanda Stockenberg?" It couldn't be, Dane told himself, even as a nagging intuition told him it was true.

"That's her." Mindy appeared surprised Dane knew the name. "The guest list the agency sent along with their deposit lists her as an assistant creative director.

"I put her in the cliff room, but she's insisting on being moved to the tower. Something about it having sentimental meaning. I explained that it was impossible, but—"

"Let her have it."

"What?" Eyes the color of a sun-brightened sea widened to the size of sand dollars.

"I said, book Ms. Stockenberg into the tower room." His tone was uncharacteristically sharp and impatient.

Mindy was not easily cowed. Especially by a man she'd been able to talk into playing Barbie dolls back in his teenage baby-sitting days, when their mothers had worked together at this very same inn. "But, Dane, it's a terrible mess."

She wasn't telling him anything he didn't already know. "Don't worry," he said, softening his voice and his expression. "I'll take care of it."

Mindy eyed him with overt curiosity. Then, as the voice on the other end of the phone began talking again, she returned her attention to the conversation.

"It seems I was mistaken, Ms. Stockenberg," she

said cheerfully, switching gears with a dexterity that had Dane thinking she'd ace her Miss America interview. "As it happens, the tower room is available after all. Yes, that is fortunate, isn't it?"

She turned to the new computer Dane was still paying for. Her rosy fingernails tapped on the keys, changing Amanda Stockenberg from the cliff room to the tower suite.

"It's all taken care of," she assured Dane after she'd hung up. Her expressive eyes held little seeds of worry. "It's none of my business, but I sure hope you know what you're doing."

"If I knew what I was doing, I wouldn't have bought the inn in the first place." His crooked grin belied his complaint. After years of traveling the world for the Whitfield Palace hotel chain, there was no place he'd rather be. And nothing he'd rather be doing. "If you see Reva, tell her I had to run into town for some wallpaper."

"Ms. Stockenberg mentioned little blue flowers," Mindy said helpfully.

"I remember."

And damn it, that was precisely the problem, Dane told himself two hours later as he drove back to Smugglers' Inn from the hardware store in Satan's Cove with the newly purchased wallpaper. He remembered too much about Amanda Stockenberg's long-ago visit to Satan's Cove.

The only daughter of a wealthy Los Angeles attorney and his socialite wife, Amanda had come to the Oregon coast with her family for a month-long vacation.

Pampered and amazingly sheltered for a modern teenager, she'd obviously never met anyone like him.

Unfortunately, during his years working at Smugglers' Inn—part-time while in high school, then summers and vacations to put himself through college—Dane had run across too many rich girls who considered him along the same lines as a summer trophy.

Dane's own father, scion of a famous Southern department-store family, had been a masculine version of those girls. Rich and spoiled, he'd had no qualms about taking what he wanted, then moving on after the annual Labor Day clambake, leaving behind a young, pregnant waitress.

Although Mary Cutter—a quiet, gentle woman who'd gone on to be a cook at the inn—had brought Dane up not to be bitter about his father's abandonment, he'd decided early on that it was better to stick with your own kind.

Which was why he'd always avoided the temptation of shiny blond hair and long, tanned legs. Until Amanda Stockenberg arrived on the scene.

She pursued him endlessly, with the single-mindedness of a rich, pretty girl accustomed to getting her own way. She was part siren, part innocent; he found both fascinating.

When she showed up at his door in the middle of the night during a thunderstorm, swearing she'd seen the ghost reputed to haunt the inn, Dane took one look at her—backlit by flashes of lightning, clad in a shorty nightgown—and all his intentions to resist temptation flew right out the window.

Being male and all too human, he allowed her into his room.

"That was your first mistake," he muttered now, at the memory of the sweet lips that had kissed him senseless. His second mistake, and the one that had cost him dearly, had been letting Amanda Stockenberg into his heart.

They did not make love—she was, after all, too young. And even if he'd wanted to—which, Lord help him, he did—he knew that by legal standards Amanda was jail-bait. And from the no-holds-barred conversation Stockenberg had with Dane when even he could no longer ignore his daughter's outrageously flirtatious behavior, Dane knew the attorney would not be averse to filing statutory rape charges on any boy who dared take Amanda to bed.

Dane's mother, remembering her own youthful summer romance, had worried about his succumbing to his raging hormones and blowing his chances at finishing college.

"Don't worry, Mom," he'd assured her with the cocky grin that had coaxed more than one local beauty into intimacy. "I won't risk prison for a roll in the hay with a summer girl."

With that intent firmly stated, he'd managed to resist Amanda's pleas to consummate their young love. But drawn to her in ways he could not understand, Dane had spent the next three weeks sneaking off to clan-destine trysts.

Dane and Amanda exchanged long slow kisses in the cave on the beach, forbidden caresses in the boathouse, passionate promises in the woods at the top of the cliff overlooking the sea, and on one memorable, thrilling, and terrifying occasion, while her parents slept in the room below them, they'd made out in Amanda's be-loved tower room with its canopied bed and flower-sprigged walls.

Although he'd tried like hell to forget her, on more

than one occasion over the past years, Dane had been annoyed to discover that her image had remained emblazoned on his mind, as bright and vivid—and, damn it, as seductive—as it had been a decade ago.

"It's been ten years," he reminded himself gruffly as he carried the rolls of paper and buckets of paste up the narrow, curving staircase to the tower room.

And, damn it, he'd dreamed about her over each of those ten years. More times than he could count, more than he'd admit. Even to himself.

"Hell, she's probably married."

It took no imagination at all to envision some man—a rich, suave guy with manicured fingernails and smooth palms that had never known the handle of a hammer, a man from her own social set—snapping Amanda up right after her debut.

Did girls still have formal debuts? Dane wondered, remembering a few he'd worked as a waiter during college—formal affairs in gilded hotel ballrooms where lovely rich girls donned long elbow-length gloves, their grandmothers' pearls and fancy white dresses that cost nearly as much as a semester's tuition, and waltzed with their fathers. He'd have to ask Mindy. The daughter of a local fisherman, she'd certainly met her share of society girls at various beauty pageants. On more than one occasion she'd complained to Dane that those rich girls only entered as a lark. Their futures, unlike hers, didn't depend on their winning the scholarship money. The fact that Amanda still had the same name as she had that long-ago summer meant nothing, Dane considered, returning his thoughts to Amanda Stockenberg's marital status. Married women often kept their maiden names for professional reasons.

His jaw clenched at the idea of Amanda married to some Yuppie who drove a BMW, preferred estate-bottled wine to beer, bought his clothes from Brooks Brothers, golfed eighteen holes on Saturday and sailed in yachting regattas on Sundays.

As he'd shopped for the damn wallpaper, Dane had hoped that he'd exaggerated the condition of the tower room when he'd measured the walls after Amanda's telephone call. Unfortunately, as he entered it now, he realized that it was even worse.

He wasn't fixing it up for sentimental reasons, Dane assured himself firmly. He was only going to the extra trouble because he didn't want Amanda to think him unsuccessful.

He pulled the peeling paper from the walls, revealing wallboard stained from the formerly leaky roof. Water stains also blotched the ceiling, like brown inkblots in a Rorschach test. The pine-plank floor was badly in need of refinishing, but a coat of paste wax and some judiciously placed rugs would cover the worst of the damage.

A sensible man would simply turn around and walk out, close the door behind him and tell the lady, when she arrived, that the clerk had made a mistake; the tower room wasn't available.

For not the first time since he'd gotten the idea to buy Smugglers' Inn, Dane reminded himself that a sensible man would have stayed in his executive suite at the New Orleans home office of the Whitfield Palace hotel chain and continued to collect his six-figure salary and requisite perks.

I'll bet the husband plays polo. The thought had him snapping the plumb line with more force than necessary, sending blue chalk flying. Dane had not forgotten Amanda's father's boastful remarks about the polo ponies he kept stabled at his weekend house in Santa Barbara.

What the hell was he doing? Dane asked himself as he rolled the paper out onto a board placed atop a pair of sawhorses and cut the first piece. Why torture himself with old memories?

He slapped the paste onto the back of the flowered paper and tried not to remember a time when this room had smelled like the gardenia cologne Amanda had worn that summer.

When something was over and done with, you forgot it and moved on.

Wasn't that exactly what she had done?

After promising him "forever," Amanda Stockenberg had walked out of his life without so much as a backward glance.

And ten years later, as he climbed the ladder and positioned the strip of paper against the too-heavy blue chalk line, Dane was still trying to convince himself that it was only his pride—not his heart—that had been wounded.

Although many things in Amanda's life had changed over the past ten years, Smugglers' Inn was not one of them. Perched on the edge of the cliff overlooking the Pacific Ocean, the building's lit windows glowed a warm welcome.

"Well, we're here, folks," the driver of the charter bus announced with a vast amount of cheer, considering the less-than-ideal circumstances of the trip. A halfhearted round of applause rippled down the rows.

"It's about time," Greg Parsons complained. He speared Amanda a sharp look. "You realize that we've already lost the entire first day of the challenge."

Having been forced to put up with her supervisor's sarcasm for the past hour, Amanda was in no mood to turn the other cheek.

"That landslide wasn't my fault, Greg." They'd been stuck on the bus in the pouring rain for five long, frustrating hours while highway crews cleared away the rock and mud from the road.

"If we'd only left thirty minutes earlier—"

"We could have ended up beneath all that mud."

Deciding that discretion was the better part of valor, Amanda did not point out that the original delay had been caused by Kelli Kyle. The auburn-haired public-relations manager had arrived at the company parking lot twenty-five minutes after the time the bus had been scheduled to depart.

Watercooler rumors had Kelli doing a lot more for Greg than plotting PR strategy; but Amanda's working relationship with Greg was bad enough without her attacking his girlfriend.

She reached into her purse, took out a half-empty roll of antacids and popped two of the tablets into her mouth. Her stomach had been churning for the past twenty miles and a headache was threatening.

Which wasn't unusual when she was forced to spend the entire day with Greg Parsons. Amanda couldn't think of a single person—with the possible exception of Kelli Kyle—who liked the man.

The first thing he'd done upon his arrival in Portland was to prohibit staffers from decorating their office walls and cubicles with the crazy posters and wacky decorations that were a commonplace part of the creative environment at other agencies. When a memo had been sent out two months ago, forbidding employees even to drink coffee at their desks, Amanda had feared an out-and-out rebellion.

The hand grenade he kept on his desk and daily memos from *The Art of War* also had not endeared him to his fellow workers.

"Let's just hope we have better luck with this inn you've booked us into," he muttered, scooping up his crocodile attaché case and marching down the aisle. "Because so far, the corporate challenge is turning out to be an unmitigated disaster."

Unwilling to agree, Amanda didn't answer. The welcoming warmth of the fire crackling in the large stone fireplace soothed the jangled nerves of the challenge-week participants, as did the glasses of hot coffee, cider and wine served on a myrtle-wood tray by a handsome young man who vaguely reminded Amanda of Dane Cutter.

The young girl working behind the front desk was as pretty as the waiter was handsome. She was also, Amanda noticed, amazingly efficient. Within minutes, and without the Miss America smile fading for a moment, Mindy Taylor had registered the cranky, chilled guests into their rooms, handed out the keys and assigned bellmen to carry the luggage upstairs.

Finally it was Amanda's turn. "Good evening, Ms. Stockenberg," Mindy greeted Amanda with the same unfailing cheer she had the others. "Welcome to Smugglers' Inn."

"It's a relief to be here."

The smile warmed. "I heard about your troubles getting here from Portland." She tapped briskly on the computer as she talked. "I'm sure the rest of your week will go more smoothly."

"I hope so." It sure couldn't get any worse.

"You're in the tower room, as requested." Mindy handed her the antique brass key. "If you don't mind waiting just a moment, Kevin will be back and will take your suitcases up for you."

"That's not necessary," a male voice coming from behind Amanda said. "I'll take care of Ms. Stockenberg's luggage."

No, Amanda thought. *It couldn't be!*

She slowly turned around, taking time to school her expression to one of polite surprise. "Hello, Dane."

Although a decade had passed, he looked just the same. But better, she decided on second thought. Dark and rugged, and so very dangerous. The kind of boy— no, he was a man now, she reminded herself—that fathers of daughters stayed awake nights worrying about.

His shaggy dark hair was still in need of a haircut, and his eyes, nearly as dark as his hair, were far from calm, but the emotions swirling in their midnight depths were too complex for Amanda to decipher. A five-o'clock shadow did nothing to detract from his good looks; the dark stubble only added to his appeal.

His jeans, white T-shirt and black leather jacket were distractingly sexy. They also made her worry that standards might have slipped at the inn since the last time she'd visited.

"Hello, princess." His full, sensual mouth curved in a smile that let her know the intimacy implied by the long-ago nickname was intentional. "Welcome to Smugglers' Inn." His gaze swept over her. "You're looking more lovely than ever."

Actually, she looked like hell. To begin with, she was too damn thin. Her oval face was pale and drawn. Her beige linen slacks and ivory top, which he suspected probably cost as much as the inn's new water heater, looked as if she'd slept in them; her hair was wet from her dash from the bus, there were blue shadows beneath her eyes, and sometime during the long trip from Portland, she'd chewed off her lipstick.

Dane knew he was in deep, deep trouble when he still found her the most desirable woman he'd ever seen.

Amanda struggled to keep Dane from realizing that he'd shaken her. All it had taken was his calling her that ridiculous name to cause a painful fluttering in her heart.

How could she have thought that she'd gotten over him? Dane Cutter was not a man women got over. Not in this lifetime. Her hand closed tightly around the key.

"Thank you. It's a relief to finally be here. Is the dining room closed yet? I know we're late, but—"

"We kept it open when it was obvious you'd gotten held up. Or, if you'd prefer, there's room service."

The idea of a long bath and a sandwich and cup of tea sent up to her room sounded delightful. "That's good news." The first in a very long and very trying day.

"We try to make our guests as comfortable as possible."

He scooped up both her cases, deftly tucked them under his arm and took her briefcase from her hand. It was biscuit-hued cowhide, as smooth as a baby's bottom, with her initials in gold near the handle. "Nice luggage."

She'd received the Louis Vuitton luggage from her parents as a graduation present. Her mother had been given a similar set from her parents when she'd married. And her mother before her. It was, in a way, a family tradition. So why did she suddenly feel a need to apologize?

"It's very functional."

His only response to her defensive tone was a shrug. "So I've heard." He did not mention that he'd bought a similar set for his mother, as a bon voyage gift for the Alaskan cruise he'd booked her on last summer. "If you're all checked in, I'll show you to your room."

"I remember the way." It had been enough of a shock to discover Dane still working at the inn. Amanda didn't believe she could handle being alone in the cozy confines of the tower room with him. Not with the memory of their last night together still painfully vivid in her mind.

"I've no doubt you do." Ignoring the clenching of his stomach, Dane flashed her a maddening grin, letting her know that they were both on the same wavelength. The devil could probably take smiling lessons from Dane Cutter. "But someone needs to carry your luggage up and Jimmy and Kevin are tied up with other guests."

"There's no hurry." Her answering smile was as polite as it was feigned. Although she'd never considered herself a violent person, after the way Dane had treated her, dumping her without a single word of explanation, like he undoubtedly did the rest of his summer girls, her hands practically itched with the need to slap his face. "I'll just go on up and they can bring my bags to the tower whenever they're free."

"I have a feeling that might be a while." He nodded his head toward the doorway, declaring the subject closed.

Not wanting to create a scene in front of the avidly interested young clerk, Amanda tossed her damp head and marched out of the room.

This was a mistake, she told herself as she stood beside Dane in the antique elevator slowly creaking its way up to the third floor. The next few days were the most important in her life. Her entire career, everything she'd worked so hard to achieve, depended on the corporate challenge week being a success. She couldn't allow herself to be distracted.

Unfortunately, Smugglers' Inn, she was discovering too late, held far too many distracting memories.

"I'm surprised to find you working here," she murmured, trying to ignore the familiar scent of soap emanating from his dark skin.

He chuckled—a low, rich tone that crept under her skin and caused her blood to thrum. "So am I." He put the bags on the floor, leaned against the back wall and stuck his hands in his pockets. "Continually."

Amanda thought about all the plans Dane had shared with her that summer. About how he was going to get out of this isolated small coastal town, how he planned to make his mark on the world, how he was going to be rich by his thirtieth birthday.

She did some rapid calculations and determined him to be twenty-nine. Obviously, if his unpretentious clothing and the fact that he was still carrying bags for guests at the inn were any indication, if Dane hoped to achieve even one of those goals, he'd have to win the lottery.

"Looks as if you've done all right for yourself." His measuring glance swept over her. "Assistant creative director for one of the top advertising firms in the country. I'm impressed."

"Thank you."

"Tell me, do you have a window office?"

"Actually, I do." Realizing that he was daring to mock her success, she tossed up her chin. "Overlooking the river."

"Must be nice. And a corporate credit card, too, I'll bet."

"Of course." She'd been thrilled the first time she'd flashed the green American Express card granted only to upper-level management personnel in an expensive Manhattan restaurant. It had seemed, at the time, an important rite of passage. Having been born into wealth, Amanda wanted—needed—to achieve success on her own.

"High-backed swivel desk chair?"

Two could play this game. "Italian cream leather."

She refused to admit she'd bought the extravagant piece of office furniture for herself with last year's Christmas bonus.

Of course, the minute Greg Parsons had caught sight of it, after returning from a holiday vacation to Barbados, he'd rushed out and bought himself a larger, higher model. In jet leather. With mahogany trim.

Dane whistled appreciatively. "Yes, sir, you've definitely come a long way. Especially for a lady who once professed a desire to raise five kids in a house surrounded by a white picket fence, and spend summers putting up berries and long dark winters making more babies in front of a crackling fire."

How dare he throw those youthful fantasies back into

her face! Didn't he realize that it had been *him* she'd fantasized about making love to, *his* babies she'd wanted?

After she'd been forced to accept the fact that her dreams of marrying Dane Cutter were only that—stupid, romantic teenage daydreams—she'd gone on to find a new direction for her life. A direction that was, admittedly, heavily influenced by her father's lofty expectations for his only child.

"People grow up," she said. "Goals change."

"True enough," he agreed easily, thinking how his own life had taken a 180-degree turn lately. "Speaking of changes, you've changed your scent." It surrounded them in the enclosed space, more complex than the cologne that had haunted his dreams last night. More sensual.

"Have I?" she asked with feigned uninterest. "I don't remember."

"Your old cologne was sweet. And innocent." He leaned forward, drinking it in. "This makes a man think of deep, slow kisses." His breath was warm on her neck. "And hot sex on a steamy summer night."

His words, his deep voice, the closeness of his body to hers, all conspired to make her knees weak. Amanda considered backing away, then realized there was nowhere to go.

"I didn't come here to rehash the past, Dane." Her headache was building to monumental proportions. "This trip to Satan's Cove is strictly business."

"Yeah, I seem to recall Reva saying something about corporate game-playing stunts."

Her remarkable eyes were as blue as a sunlit sea. A careless man could drown in those wide eyes. Having succumbed to Amanda Stockenberg's siren call once before, Dane had no intention of making that mistake again. Although he knew that to touch her would be dangerous, he couldn't resist reaching out to rub the pads of his thumbs against her temples.

Amanda froze at his touch. "What do you think you're doing?"

Her voice might have turned as chilly as the rain falling outside, but her flesh was warming in a way he remembered all too well. "Helping you get rid of that headache before you rub a hole in your head."

He stroked small, concentric circles that did absolutely nothing to soothe. One hand roamed down the side of her face, her neck, before massaging her knotted shoulder muscle.

His hand was rough with calluses upon calluses, hinting at a life of hard, physical work rather than the one spent behind a wide executive desk he'd once yearned for. It crossed Amanda's mind that in a way, she was living the successful, high-powered life Dane had planned for himself. Which made her wonder if he was living out her old, discarded dreams.

Was he married? Did he have children? The idea of any other woman carrying Dane Cutter's baby caused a flicker of something deep inside Amanda that felt uncomfortably like envy.

"You sure are tense, princess." His clever fingers loosened the knot even as they tangled her nerves.

She knew she should insist he stop, but his touch *was* working wonders on her shoulder. "Knotted muscles and the occasional headache come with the territory. And don't call me *princess*."

Dane knew the truth of her first statement all too

well. It was one of several reasons he'd bailed out of corporate life.

"How about the occasional ulcer?" He plucked the roll of antacids from her hand, forestalling her from popping another tablet into her mouth.

"I don't have an ulcer."

"I suppose you have a doctor's confirmation of that?"

She tossed her head, then wished she hadn't when the headache stabbed like a stiletto behind her eyes. "Of course."

She was a liar. But a lovely one. Dane suspected that it had been a very long time since Amanda had taken time to visit a doctor. Her clothes, her title, her luggage, the window office with the high-backed Italian-leather chair, all pointed to the fact that the lady was definitely on the fast track up the advertising corporate ladder.

Her too-thin face and the circles beneath her eyes were additional proof of too many hours spent hunkered over advertising copy and campaign jingles. He wondered if she realized she was approaching a very slippery slope.

He was looking at her that way again. Hard and deep. Just when Amanda thought Dane was going to say something profound, the elevator lurched to a sudden stop.

"Third floor, ladies' lingerie," he said cheerfully. "Do you still wear that sexy underwear?"

She wondered if he flirted like this with all the female guests, then wondered how, if he did, he managed to keep his job. Surely some women might complain to the management that the inn's sexy bellhop brought new meaning to the slogan Service With a Smile.

"My underwear is none of your business." Head high,

she stepped out of the elevator and headed toward the stairway at the end of the hall, leaving him to follow with the bags.

"I seem to remember a time when you felt differently."

"I felt differently about a lot of things back then. After all, I was only fifteen." The censorious look she flashed back over her shoulder refused to acknowledge his steadfast refusal to carry their teenage affair to its natural conclusion.

"I recall mentioning your tender age on more than one occasion," he said mildly. "But you kept insisting that you were all grown-up."

Not grown-up enough to hold his attention, Amanda thought grimly. As she climbed the stairs to the tower room, she decided she'd made a major mistake in coming to Smugglers' Inn.

Her focus had been clear from the beginning. Pull off the corporate challenge week, get the obnoxious Greg Parsons promoted out of her life, then move upward into his position, which should have been hers in the first place.

Awakening old hurts and reliving old memories definitely hadn't been part of the plan.

And neither had Dane Cutter.

Chapter 3

The first time Amanda had seen the tower room, she'd been entranced. Ten years hadn't lessened its appeal.

Delicate forget-me-nots bloomed on the walls, the high ceiling was a pale powder blue that had always reminded her of a clear summer sky. More blue flowers decorated the ribbon-edged curtains that were pulled back from the sparkling window and matched the thick comforter.

"The bed's different," she murmured.

"Unfortunately, during the time the inn was closed, it became a termite condo and had to go."

"That's too bad." She'd loved the romantic canopy. "But this is nice, too." She ran her hand over one of the pine-log posts that had been sanded to a satin finish.

"I'm glad you approve."

He'd taken the bed from his own room this morning. Now, watching her stroke the wooden post with her slender fingers, Dane felt a slow, deep ache stir inside him.

"I'd suggest not getting too near the woodwork," he warned. "The paint's still a bit sticky."

That explained the white specks on his jeans. A pang of sadness for lost opportunities and abandoned dreams sliced through Amanda.

"Well, thank you for carrying up my bags." Her smile was bright and impersonal as she reached into her purse.

An icy anger rose inside him at the sight of those folded green bills. "Keep your money."

All right, so this meeting was uncomfortable. But he didn't have to get so nasty about it. "Fine." Amanda met his strangely blistering look with a level one of her own. "You realize, I suppose, that I'm going to be here at the inn for a week."

"So?" His tone was as falsely indifferent as hers.

"So, it would seem inevitable that we'd run into each other from time to time."

"Makes sense to me."

It was obvious Dane had no intention of helping her out with this necessary conversation. "This is an important time for me," she said, trying again. "I can't afford any distractions."

"Are you saying I'm a distraction?" As if to underscore her words, he reached out and touched the ends of her hair. "You've dyed your hair," he murmured distractedly.

"Any man who touches me when I don't want him to is a distraction," she retorted, unnerved at how strongly the seemingly harmless touch affected her. "And I didn't dye it. It got darker all on its own."

"It was the color of corn silk that summer." He laced his fingers through the dark gold hair that curved beneath her chin. "Now it's the color of caramel." He held a few strands up to the light. "Laced with melted butter."

The way he was looking at her, the way he kept touching her, caused old seductive memories to come barreling back to batter at Amanda's emotions.

"Food analogies are always so romantic."

"You want romance, princess?" His eyes darkened to obsidian as he moved even closer to her.

As she tried to retreat, Amanda was blocked by the edge of the mattress pressing against the backs of her knees. Unwilling desire mingled with a long-smoldering resentment she'd thought she'd been able to put behind her.

"Damn it, Dane." She put both hands on his shoulders and shoved, but she might as well have been trying to move a mountain. He didn't budge. "I told you not to call me *princess*."

"Fine. Since it's obvious that you've grown up, how about *contessa?*"

It suited her, Dane decided. *Princess* had been her father's name for a spoiled young girl. *Contessa* brought to mind a regal woman very much in charge of her life, as Amanda appeared to be.

The temper she'd kept on a taut leash during a very vexing day broke free. "You know, you really have a lot of nerve." Her voice trembled, which made her all the more angry. She did not want to reveal vulnerability where this man was concerned. "Behaving this way after what you did!"

"What I did?" His own temper, worn to a frazzle from overwork, lack of sleep, and the knowledge that

Amanda was returning to Satan's Cove after all these years, rose to engulf hers. "What the hell did I do? Except spend an entire month taking cold showers after some teenage tease kept heating me up?"

"Tease?"

That did it! She struck out at him, aiming for his shoulder, but hitting his upper arm instead. When her fist impacted with a muscle that felt like a boulder, the shock ran all the way up her arm.

"I loved you, damn it! Which just goes to show how stupid a naive, fifteen-year-old girl can be."

What was even more stupid was having wasted so much time thinking about this man. And wondering what she might have done to make things turn out differently.

His answering curse was short and rude. "You were too self-centered that summer to even know the meaning of the word *love*." Impatience shimmered through him. "Face it, contessa, you thought you'd get your kicks practicing your feminine wiles on some small-town hick before taking your newly honed skills back to the big city."

He would have her, Dane decided recklessly. Before she left Smugglers' Inn. And this time, when she drove away from Satan's Cove, he'd keep something of Amanda for himself. And in turn, leave her with something to remember on lonely rainy nights.

"I loved you," she repeated through clenched teeth. She'd never spoken truer words. "But unfortunately, I was stupid enough to give my heart away to someone who only considered me a summer fling."

Thank heavens she'd only given her heart. Because

if she'd given her body to this man, she feared she never would have gotten over him.

Which she had.

Absolutely. Completely.

The hell she had.

The way he was looking at her, as if he couldn't decide whether to strangle her or ravish her, made Amanda's heart pound.

"You were a lot more than a summer fling." His fingers tightened painfully on her shoulders. His rough voice vibrated through her, causing an ache only he had ever been able to instill. "When I went back to college, I couldn't stop thinking about you. I thought about you during the day, when I was supposed to be studying. I thought about you at night, after work, when I was supposed to be sleeping. And all the time in between."

It was the lie, more than anything, that hurt. All right, so she'd misinterpreted their romance that long-ago summer. Amanda was willing to be honest with herself. Why couldn't he be equally truthful?

"It would have been nice," she suggested in a tone as icy as winter sleet, "if during all that time you were allegedly thinking of me, you thought to pick up a pen and write me a letter. An email. Hell, one of those postcards with the lighthouse on it they sell on the revolving rack downstairs next to the registration desk would have been better than nothing."

"I did write to you." He was leaning over her, his eyes so dark she could only see her reflection. "I wrote you a letter the day you left. And the next day. And for days after that. Until it finally got through my thick head that you weren't going to answer."

The accusation literally rocked her. The anger in his

gritty voice and on his face told Amanda that Dane was telling the truth. "What letters? I didn't get any letters."

"That's impossible." His gaze raked over her snow-white face, seeking the truth. Comprehension, when it dawned, was staggering. "Hell. Your parents got to them first."

"Apparently so." She thought about what such well-meaning parental subterfuge had cost her. What it had, perhaps, cost Dane. Cost them both.

"You know, *you* could always have written to *me*," Dane said.

"I wanted to. But I couldn't get up the nerve."

He arched a challenging eyebrow. But as she watched reluctant amusement replace the fury in his eyes, Amanda was able to breathe again.

"This from a girl nervy enough to wear a polka-dot bikini horseback riding just to get my attention?" The ploy had worked. The memory of that cute little skimpily clad butt bouncing up and down in that leather saddle had tortured Dane's sleep.

The shared memory brought a reluctant smile from Amanda. She'd paid for that little stunt. If Dane's mother hadn't given her that soothing salve for the chafed skin on the insides of her legs, she wouldn't have been able to walk for a week.

"It was different once I got back home," she admitted now. "I kept thinking about all the older girls who worked at the inn, and went to college with you, and I couldn't imagine why you'd bother carrying a torch for a girl who'd only just gotten her braces off two weeks before coming to Satan's Cove."

Damn. He should have realized she might think that. But at the time, he'd been dazzled by the breezy self-confidence he'd assumed had been bred into Amanda from generations of family wealth.

Oh, he'd known she was too immature—her passionate suggestion that they run away together had been proof of that. But it had never occurred to him that she wasn't as self-assured as she'd seemed. She had, after all, captured the attention of every male in Satan's Cove between the ages of thirteen and ninety. She'd also succeeded in wrapping him—a guy with no intention of letting any woman sidetrack his plan for wealth and success—around her little finger.

Looking down at her now, Dane wondered how much of the girl remained beneath the slick professional veneer Amanda had acquired during the intervening years.

"I did work up my nerve to call you once," she said quietly. "But you'd already gone back to school and the woman who answered the phone here said she didn't have your forwarding address."

"You could have asked my mother."

Her weary shrug told him that she'd considered that idea and rejected it.

Dane wondered what would have happened if his letters had been delivered. Would his life have turned out differently if he'd gotten her call?

Never one to look back, Dane turned his thoughts to the future. The immediate future. Like the next week.

"It appears we have some unfinished business." His hand slipped beneath her hair to cup the back of her neck.

"Dane—" She pressed her palm against his shirt and encountered a wall of muscle every bit as hard as it had been when he was nineteen. There was, she decided recklessly, definitely something to be said for a life of physical work.

"All this heat can't be coming from me." His fingers massaged her neck in a way that was anything but soothing as his lips scorched a trail up her cheek. "The sparks are still there, contessa." His breath was warm against her skin. "You can't deny it."

No, she couldn't. Her entire body was becoming hot and quivery. "Please." Her voice was a throaty shimmer of sound. "I can't concentrate when you're doing that."

"Then don't concentrate." His mouth skimmed along her jaw; Amanda instinctively tilted her head back. "Just feel." When his tongue touched the hollow of her throat, her pulse jumped. "Go with the flow."

"I can't," she complained weakly, even as her rebellious fingers gathered up a handful of white cotton T-shirt. "This week is important to me."

"I remember a time when you said *I* was important to you." The light abrasion of his evening beard scraped seductively against her cheek as his hands skimmed down her sides.

"That was then." She drew in a sharp breath as his palms brushed against her breasts and set them to tingling. In all her twenty-five years Dane was the only man who could touch off the fires of passion smoldering deep inside her. He was the only man who could make her want. And, she reminded herself, he'd been the only man who'd ever made her cry. "This is now."

"It doesn't feel so different." He drew her to him. "*You* don't feel so different."

He wanted her. Too much for comfort. Too much for safety. The way she was literally melting against him made Dane ache in ways he'd forgotten he could ache.

"This has been a long time coming, Amanda." His hands settled low on her hips. "We need to get it out of our systems. Once and for all."

She could feel every hard male part of him through her clothes. He was fully, thrillingly aroused. Even as she tried to warn herself against succumbing to such blatant masculinity, Amanda linked her fingers around his neck and leaned into him.

"I don't know about *your* system," she said breathlessly, as his tongue skimmed up her neck, "but mine's doing just fine."

"Liar." His lips brushed against hers. Teasing, testing, tormenting.

Desire throbbed and pooled between her thighs. Flames were flicking hotly through her veins. She'd never wanted a man the way she wanted Dane Cutter right now. Worse yet, she'd never *needed* a man the way she needed him at this moment.

Which was why she had to back away from temptation. When, and if, she did make love to Dane, she wanted to make certain she knew exactly what she was doing. And why.

She needed to be certain that the desire coursing through her veins was not simply a knee-jerk response to the only man who'd ever made her burn. She had to convince herself that she wasn't succumbing to the seduction of the romantic setting, old memories, and sensual fantasies.

After suffering the resultant pain from her impulsive, teenage behavior, Amanda had acquired a need for an orderly, controlled life. Unfortunately, there was nothing orderly or controlled about the way Dane Cutter made her feel.

"I need to think," she protested weakly. "It's been a long and frustrating day and I'm exhausted, Dane."

"Fine." He'd give her that. There would, Dane told himself, be other times. "But before I go, let me give you something to think about."

Amanda knew what was coming. Knew she should resist. Even as she warned herself to back away now, before she got in over her head, another voice in the back of her mind pointed out that this was her chance to prove she was no longer a foolish young girl who could lose her heart over a simple kiss.

Since the second option seemed the more logical, Amanda went with it. She stood there, her palms pressed against his chest, as he slowly, deliberately, lowered his mouth to hers.

It was definitely not what she'd been expecting.

The first time he'd kissed her, that long-ago night when she'd come to his room, clad in her sexiest nightie, Dane had been frustrated and angry—angry at her for having teased him unmercifully, angry at himself for not being able to resist.

His mouth had swooped down, causing their teeth to clang painfully together as he ground his lips against hers. He'd used his mouth and his tongue as a weapon and she'd found it shocking and thrilling at the same time.

Later, as the days went by, Dane had grown more and more sexually frustrated, and it had showed. Although his kisses were no longer tinged with anger, they were riddled with a hot, desperate hunger that equaled her own.

Although the attraction was still there a decade later,

it was more than apparent to Amanda that the years had mellowed Dane, taught him patience. And finesse.

He cupped her face in his hands and she trembled.

He touched his mouth to hers and she sighed.

With a rigid control that cost him dearly, Dane forced himself to take his time, coaxing her into the mists by skimming kisses from one side of her full, generous mouth to the other.

"Dane—"

Ignoring her faint protest, he caught her bottom lip in his teeth and tugged, causing a slow, almost-languid ache.

Prepared for passion, she had no defenses against this exquisite, dreamy pleasure. Amanda twined her arms tighter around his neck and allowed herself to sink into his kiss.

"Oh, Dane…"

"Lord, I like the way you say my name." His breath was like a summer breeze against her parted lips. "Say it again."

At this suspended moment in time, unable to deny Dane anything, Amanda softly obliged.

"Your voice reminds me of warm honey." He soothed the flesh his teeth had bruised with his tongue. "Sweet and thick and warm."

He angled his head and continued making love to her with his mouth. The tip of his tongue slipped silkily between her lips, then withdrew. Then dipped in again, deeper this time, only to withdraw once more.

Every sense was heightened. Every nerve ending in her body hummed.

His clever, wicked tongue repeated that glorious movement again and again, each time delving deeper, seducing hers into a slow, sensual dance. The rest of the world drifted away. Until there was only Dane. And the pure pleasure of his mouth.

Damn. This wasn't going the way he'd planned. The rich, warm taste of her was causing an ache in his loins far worse than the teenage horniness he'd suffered the last time he'd been with Amanda like this. Sweat broke out on his forehead as he felt the soft swell of her belly pressing against his erection.

Her throaty moans were driving him crazy and if she didn't stop grinding against him that way, stoking fires that were already close to burning out of control, he was going to throw her down on that bed and rip away those travel-rumpled clothes.

He imagined sliding his tongue down her throat, over her breasts, swirling around the hard little nipples that were pressing against his chest, before cutting a wet swath down her slick, quivering stomach, making her writhe with need; then lower still, until he was sliding it between her legs, gathering up the sweet taste—

"Hell."

Jerking his mind back from that perilous precipice, Dane literally pushed himself away from her. For his sake, not hers.

It had happened again! Ten minutes alone with Amanda and he'd nearly lost it. What was it about this woman? Even at nineteen he'd been far from inexperienced. Yet all it had taken then—and, apparently, all it took even now—was a taste of her succulent lips, the feel of her hot, feminine body pressed against his, to bring him to the brink of exploding.

Her head still spinning, her body pulsing, Amanda stared at Dane and watched as his rugged face closed up.

He jammed his hands into the pockets of his jeans with such force that her eyes were drawn to the brusque movement. Heaven help her, the sight of that bulge pressing against the faded denim caused something like an ocean swell to rise up from her most feminine core.

Realizing what she was staring at, Dane again cursed his lack of control. "I'm not going to apologize." His voice was distant, and amazingly cold for a man who, only moments earlier, had nearly caused them both to go up in flames.

"I wouldn't ask you to." She dragged her hair back from her temples, appalled by the discovery that her hands were shaking. "I'm no longer a teenager, Dane. You don't have to worry about my father showing up at the door with a shotgun."

Dane almost laughed. He wondered what she'd say if he told her that he found the idea of an irate father far less threatening than what he was currently feeling.

"You're tired." And she had been for some time, if the circles beneath her eyes were any indication. "We'll talk tomorrow. After you've had some rest."

"There's no need to—"

"I said, we'll talk tomorrow."

Amanda stiffened, unaccustomed to taking such sharp, direct orders from any man. Before she could argue, he said, "Just dial three for room service. The cook will fix anything you'd like. Within reason."

With that, he was gone. Leaving Amanda confused. And wanting.

As he descended the narrow, curving stairway, Dane assured himself that his only problem was he'd been taken by surprise. Initially, he hadn't expected Amanda to show up from the shadows of the past. Then, when

Chapter 4

Amanda was not in a good mood the following morning, as she went downstairs to prepare for the kickoff meeting. Her headache had returned with a vengeance and her stomach was tied up in knots. She'd spent the night tossing and turning, reliving old memories of her days—and nights—at Smugglers' Inn.

And then, when she had finally fallen asleep shortly before dawn, her dreams had been filled with the man who had, impossibly, become an even better kisser. The sensual dreams had resulted in her waking up with an unhealthy curiosity about all the women with whom Dane had spent the past ten years practicing his kissing technique.

After a false turn, she found the conference room Susan had reserved. Ten years ago, the room had been a sleeping porch. The oversize green screens had been replaced with glass, protecting occupants from the un-predictable coastal weather without taking away from the dazzling view, which, at the moment, was draped in a soft silver mist.

It was absolutely lovely. Greg would find nothing to complain about here. The only problem would be keeping people's minds off the scenery and focused on the challenge.

Drawn by the pull of the past, she walked over to the wall of windows and gazed out, trying to catch a glimpse of the cave where she and Dane had shared such bliss.

Both relieved and disappointed to see the fog blocked the view of that stretch of beach, she turned her back on the sea and crossed the room to a pine sideboard where urns of coffee and hot water for tea had been placed. Beside the urn were baskets of breakfast breads, and white platters of fresh fruit.

Amanda poured herself a cup of coffee and placed some strawberries onto a small plate. When the fra-grant lure proved impossible to resist, she plucked a blueberry muffin from one of the baskets, then set to work unpacking the boxes of supplies.

As she separated T-shirts bearing the team challenge logo into red and blue stacks, Amanda wondered what Dane was doing.

Although she remembered him to have been an early riser, she doubted he'd have arrived at the inn. Not after the late hours he'd worked yesterday. Which was just as well, since she still hadn't sorted out her feelings. All the agonizing she'd done during the long and sleepless night had only confused her more.

Last night, alone with him in the tower room that

had been filled with bittersweet memories, it had felt as if no time at all had passed since that night they'd lain in each other's arms, driving each other to painful distraction, whispering tender words of love, vowing desperate promises.

This morning, Amanda was trying to convince herself that stress, exhaustion and the surprise of seeing Dane again had been responsible for her having responded so quickly and so strongly to him. To his touch. His kiss.

Memories of that enticing kiss flooded back, warming her to the core. "You have to stop this," she scolded herself aloud.

It was imperative that she concentrate on the difficult week ahead. If she allowed her thoughts to drift constantly to Dane Cutter, she'd never pull off a successful challenge. And without a successful challenge, not only would she lose her chance for promotion, she could end up being stuck with Greg Parsons for a very long time.

"And that," she muttered, "is not an option."

"Excuse me?"

Having believed herself to be alone, Amanda spun around and saw a woman standing in the doorway. She was casually dressed in navy shorts, a white polo shirt and white sneakers. If it hadn't been for her name, written in red script above her breast, Amanda would have taken her for a guest.

"I was just talking to myself," she said with embarrassment.

"I do that all the time." The woman's smile was as warm and friendly as Mindy Taylor's had been last night. "Sometimes I even answer myself back, which was beginning to worry me, until Dane said that the time to worry was if I began ignoring myself."

She crossed the room and held out her hand. "I'm Reva Carlson. And you must be Amanda Stockenberg."

Having observed the frenzied activity that had gone into preparing the tower room, then hearing how Dane had insisted on carrying Amanda's bags last night, Reva was more than a little interested in this particular guest. As was every other employee of Smugglers' Inn.

"You're the conference manager Susan spoke with," Amanda remembered.

"Among other things. The management structure around this place tends to be a bit loose."

"Oh?" Amanda wasn't certain she liked the sound of that. One of the advantages of the Mariner Seaside Golf Resort and Conference Center had been an assistant manager whose sole function had been to tend to the group's every need.

"Everyone's trained to fill in wherever they're needed, to allow for optimum service," Reva revealed the management style Dane had introduced. "Although I'm embarrassed to admit that I've been barred from the kitchen after last week's fire."

"Fire?" After having watched her first choice of resort go up in flames, Amanda definitely didn't like hearing that.

"Oh, it wasn't really that big a deal." The shoulders of the white knit shirt rose and fell in a careless shrug. "I was merely trying my hand at pears flambé. When I poured just a smidgen too much brandy into the pans, things got a little hot for a time." Her smile widened. "By the time the fire department showed up, Dane had things under control."

When even the sound of his name caused a hitch in her breathing, Amanda knew she was in deep, deep trouble. "Dane was working in the kitchen?"

"Sure." Another shrug. "I told you, we're pretty loose around here. And Dane's amazingly handy at everything. He shot the pan with the fire extinguisher, and that was that. But in the meantime, I've been banned from any further cooking experiments, though Mary did promise to let me frost a birthday cake for one of our guests tomorrow."

"Mary?" At the familiar name, Amanda stopped trying to picture Dane in an apron, comfortable in a kitchen. "Mary Cutter?"

"That's right." Reva tilted her head. "Sounds as if you know her."

"I used to." Amanda couldn't quite stop the soft sigh. "I came here with my parents on a vacation ten years ago."

"Mindy mentioned something about that." Reva's friendly gaze turned speculative. "I guess Dane must have been working here at the time, too." Her voice went up on the end of the sentence, turning it into a question.

It was Amanda's turn to shrug. "I suppose. It was a long time ago, and there was quite a large staff, so it's hard to remember everyone."

From the knowing expression in the convention manager's eyes, Amanda had the feeling she wasn't fooling her for a moment. "I do remember his mother made the best peach pie I've ever tasted." She also, Amanda had discovered this morning, baked dynamite blueberry muffins.

"Mary's peach pie wins the blue ribbon at the county fair every year." Returning to her work mode, Reva glanced around the room. "Do you have everything you need?"

"I think so." Amanda's gaze took another slow sweep around the room, trying to seek out any lapses Greg might catch.

"If you think of anything—anything at all—don't hesitate to call on any of us. I have to run into town on some errands, but Dane's around here somewhere."

"I'm sure we'll be fine," Amanda said quickly. Too quickly, she realized, as Reva's gaze narrowed ever so slightly.

"Well, good luck." Reva turned to leave. "With everything."

Matters taken care of to her satisfaction, Reva Carlson returned to her own work, leaving Amanda with the feeling that the woman's parting comment had little to do with the upcoming challenge exercises.

After she finished unpacking the boxes, Amanda headed down the hall to the kitchen, to thank Mary Cutter for the superb Continental breakfast, when she heard her name being called.

Believing it to be someone from the agency, she turned, surprised to see two familiar faces.

"Miss Minnie? Miss Pearl?" The elderly sisters had been guests the last time Amanda had stayed at the inn.

"Hello, dear," one of them—Minnie or Pearl, Amanda couldn't remember which was which—said. Her rosy face was as round as a harvest moon and wreathed in a smile. "We heard you'd come back. It's lovely to see you again."

"It's nice to see you, too. It's also a surprise."

"I don't know why it should be," the other sister

said. "With the exception of the three years the inn was closed—"

"A terrible shame," the other interrupted. "As I was telling Dane just yesterday—"

"Sister!" A scowl darkened a sharp, hatchet face. "I was speaking."

"I'm sorry, sister." There was a brief nod of a lavender head that had been permed into corkscrews; the pastel hue complemented the woman's pink complexion. "I was just pointing out to Amanda how sad it was that such a lovely inn had been allowed to fall into disrepair."

"You'd never know that to look at it now," Amanda said.

"That's because Dane has been working around the clock," the thinner of the two sisters huffed. It was more than a little obvious she resented having her story sidetracked. "As I was saying, with the exception of those three unfortunate years, we have been visiting Smugglers' Inn for the last sixty-four years."

"I believe it's only been sixty-three, sister."

A forceful chin thrust out. "It's sixty-four."

"Are you sure?"

"Of course. I remember everything that happened that year," the other snapped with the certainty of a woman who'd spent forty-five years as the research librarian for the Klamath County Library in southern Oregon.

The term *sibling rivalry* could have been invented to define Minnie and Pearl Davenport. Recalling all too well how these arguments could go on all day, Amanda repeated how nice it was to see the women again and escaped into the kitchen.

This room, too, was as she remembered it—warm and cheerful and immensely inviting. Fragrant, mouthwatering steam rose from the pots bubbling away on the gleaming stove; more copper pots hung from a ceiling rack and the windowsill was home to a row of clay pots filled with fresh green herbs.

An enormous refrigerator that hadn't been there the last time Amanda had sneaked into the kitchen for a heart-to-heart talk with Mary Cutter was open.

"Hello?"

A dark head popped out from behind the stainless-steel door. "Amanda, hello!" Dane's mother's expression was warm and welcoming. She closed the refrigerator and opened her arms. "I was hoping you'd get a chance to escape those boring old business meetings and visit with an old friend."

As she hugged the woman, Amanda realized that Mary Cutter had, indeed, become a friend that summer. Even though, looking back on it, she realized how concerned Mary had been for Dane. As she would have been, Amanda admitted now, if some sex-crazed, underage teenage girl had been chasing after her son.

"They're not that bad." Amanda felt duty-bound to defend the group.

"Oh?" Releasing her, Mary went over to the stove and poured two cups of coffee. She put them on the table, and gestured for Amanda to sit down. "Then why do you have those dark circles beneath your eyes?"

Amanda unconsciously lifted her fingers to the blue shadows she thought she'd managed to conceal successfully this morning. It was bad enough having to deal with Dane and their past, which now seemed to be unsettled. By the time the corporate challenge week was over, she'd undoubtedly be buying concealer by the carton.

"I've been working long hours lately."

"You're not sleeping very well, either, I'd suspect. And you have a headache."

"It's not that bad," Amanda lied as Mary reached out and rubbed at the lines carving furrows between her eyes.

The older woman's touch was gentle and more maternal than any Amanda had ever received from her own mother. Then again, the Stockenbergs never had been touchers. The Cutters—mother and son—definitely were.

Mary's smile didn't fade, but the way she was looking at her, hard and deep, made Amanda want to change the subject. "I just ran into Miss Minnie and Miss Pearl," she said. "But I couldn't remember which was which."

"Minnie is the one with white hair and an attitude. Pearl has lavender hair and hides Hershey's Kisses all over the inn."

"Why would she do that?"

"Because the poor dear has an enormous sweet tooth. And Minnie has her on a diet that would starve a gerbil." Mary flashed a quick grin that was remarkably like her son's, although it didn't have the capability to affect Amanda in such a devastating manner. "I feel so sorry for Pearl. She's been sneaking in here for snacks ever since they arrived last week."

"Well, I can certainly understand that. I had a muffin that was just short of heaven."

"I'm so pleased you enjoyed it." Mary's eyes skimmed over Amanda judiciously. "You're a bit thin, dear. We'll have to see what we can do about fattening you up a little."

"A woman can never be too thin," Amanda said, quoting one of her sleek mother's favorite axioms.

"Want to bet?" a deep voice asked from the doorway.

Amanda tamped down the little burst of pleasure brought about by the sight of Dane, clad again in jeans. Today's shirt was faded chambray; his shoes were high-topped sneakers.

Mary greeted him with a smile. "Good morning, darling."

"Morning." He crossed the room on a long, easy stride and kissed his mother's cheek. "Do I smell sugar cookies?"

"It's my new cologne," Mary said with a laugh. "The saleswoman said it has vanilla in it." She shook her head in mock regret. "She also said men would find it impossible to resist. I'm afraid I was oversold."

"Never met a man yet who didn't like sugar cookies," Dane said agreeably. His grin slipped a notch as his attention turned to Amanda. "Good morning."

Amanda had watched the way he brushed his finger down his mother's cheek in a casual, intimate gesture that was as natural to him as breathing. Once again she was reminded how different the Cutters were from the Stockenbergs. It would be wise to keep those differences in mind over the next several days.

"Good morning." Her tone was friendly, but cool. She could have been speaking to a stranger at a bus stop.

"Sleep well?" His tone was as studiously casual as hers.

"Like a baby," she lied. She pushed herself up from the table. "Well, I really do have to get back to work. I just wanted to stop in and say hi," she told Mary. "And to thank you for the lovely breakfast."

"It's been lovely seeing you again, dear." Dane's mother took Amanda's hand in both of hers. "I realize you're going to be extremely busy, but I hope you can find time to visit again."

"I'd like that." It was the truth.

Without another word to Dane, Amanda placed her cup on the counter, then left the kitchen.

"Well, she certainly has grown up to be a lovely young lady," Mary said.

"Really?" Dane's answering shrug was forced. "I didn't notice."

Mary poured another cup of coffee and placed it in front of him. "Reva says she has a very responsible position at that advertising agency."

This earned little more than a grunt.

"I couldn't help noticing she's not wearing any ring on her left hand."

Dane's face shuttered. "No offense, Mom, but I really don't want to talk about Amanda."

"Of course, dear," Mary replied smoothly. But as she turned to the stove and poured pancake batter into an iron skillet, Mary Cutter was smiling.

Despite instructions that they were to meet at eight o'clock sharp, the team members straggled into the conference room. By the time everyone had gotten coffee, fruit and pastries and taken their seats, it was twenty-eight minutes past the time the kickoff had been scheduled to begin.

"Well, this is certainly getting off to a dandy start," muttered Greg, who was sitting beside Amanda at the pine trestle table at the front of the room. "Didn't you send out my memo letting the troops know I expected them to be prompt?"

"Of course." Amanda refrained from pointing out that if one wanted troops to follow orders, it was helpful if they respected their commanding officer. "We arrived awfully late last night," she said, seeking some excuse for the tardy team members. "Everyone was probably a little tired this morning."

His only response to her efforts was a muttered curse that did not give Amanda a great deal of encouragement.

Greg stood and began to outline the week's activities, striding back and forth at the front of the room like General Patton addressing the soldiers of the Third Army. He was waving his laser pointer at the detailed flowchart as if it were Patton's famed riding crop. The troops seemed uniformly unimpressed by all the red, blue and yellow rectangles.

As he set about explaining the need for consistent process and implementation, even Amanda's mind began to wander, which was why she didn't hear the door open at the back of the room.

"I'm sorry to interrupt," one of last night's bellmen, who bore an amazing resemblance to Brad Pitt, said. "But Ms. Stockenberg has a phone call."

"Take a message," Greg snapped before Amanda could answer.

"He says it's urgent."

"I'd better take it," Amanda said.

"Just make it quick. I intend to get on schedule."

"I'll be right back." Amanda resisted the urge to salute.

The news was not good. "But you have to come,"

she insisted when the caller, the man she'd hired to conduct the physical adventure portion of the weekend, explained his predicament. "I understand you've broken your leg. But surely you can at least sit on the beach and instruct—"

She was cut off by a flurry of denial on the other end of the line. "Oh. In traction? I'm so sorry to hear that." She reached into her pocket, pulled out the antacids she was never without and popped one into her mouth.

"Well, of course you need to rest. And get well soon." She dragged her hand through her hair. "There's no need to apologize. You didn't fall off that motorcycle on purpose."

She hung up the phone with a bit more force than necessary. "Damn."

"Got a problem?"

Amanda spun around and glared up at Dane. "I'm getting a little tired of the way you have of sneaking up on people."

"Sorry." The dancing light in his eyes said otherwise.

"No." She sighed and shook her head. "I'm the one who should apologize for snapping at you. It's just that I really need this week to go well, and before we can even get started on the kayak race, my adventure expert ends up in the hospital."

"That *is* a tough break."

She could hear the amusement in his voice. "Don't you dare laugh at me."

"I wouldn't think of it." He reached out and rubbed at the parallel lines his mother had smoothed earlier. "I don't suppose a hotshot businesswoman—with her own window office and fancy Italian-leather chair—would need any advice?"

The soothing touch felt too good. Too right. Amanda backed away. "At this point, I'd take advice from the devil himself." Realizing how snippy she sounded, she felt obliged to apologize yet again.

"Don't worry about it. People say things they don't mean under stress." Which he knew only too well. Dane had found it enlightening that the temper he'd developed while working for the Whitfield Palace hotel chain seemed to have vanished when he'd bought the inn, despite all the problems refurbishing it had entailed. "How about me?"

"How about you, what?"

"How about me subbing for your kayak guy?"

Remembering how he'd taught her to paddle that double kayak so many years ago, Amanda knew it was the perfect solution. Except for one thing.

"Don't you have work to do?"

Dane shrugged. "It'll keep."

"I wouldn't want you to get in trouble."

"Why don't you let me worry about that, contessa? Besides, we all kind of pitch in where needed around here."

That was exactly what Reva had told her. And Amanda was grateful enough not to contest that ridiculous name. "Thank you. I really appreciate your help."

"Hey, that's what we're here for." He grinned and skimmed a dark finger down the slope of her nose. "Service With a Smile, that's the motto at Smugglers' Inn."

The knot of tension in her stomach unwound. It was impossible to worry when he was smiling at her that way. It was nearly impossible to remember that the man represented a dangerous distraction.

Relieved that she'd overcome the first hurdle of the

week, and putting aside the nagging little problem of what she was going to do about the rest of the scheduled adventure exercises, Amanda returned to the conference room and began handing out the challenge-team shirts.

"What the hell are these?" Don Patterson, the marketing manager, asked.

"They're to denote the different teams," Amanda explained. "Reds versus blues."

"Like shirts versus skins," Marvin Kenyon, who'd played some high school basketball, said.

"Exactly."

"I wouldn't mind playing shirts and skins with Kelli," Peter Wanger from the computer-support division said with a leer directed toward the public-relations manager, who was provocatively dressed in a pair of tight white jeans and a thin red top. The scoop neck barely concealed voluptuous breasts that, if they hadn't been surgically enhanced, could undoubtedly qualify as natural wonders of the world.

"Watch it, Peter," Amanda warned. "Or you'll have to watch that video on sexual harassment in the workplace again."

"Oh, Peter was just joking," Kelli said quickly, sending a perky cheerleader smile his way. "It doesn't bother me, Amanda."

That might be. But it did bother Greg. Amanda watched her superior's jaw clench. "Amanda's right," he growled. If looks could kill, Peter would be drawn and quartered, then buried six feet under the sand. "Just because we're not in the office doesn't mean that I'll stand for inappropriate behavior."

It sounded good. But everyone in the room knew that what was really happening was that Greg had just stamped his own personal No Trespassing sign on Kelli Kyle's wondrous chest.

"Talk about inappropriate," Laura Quinlan muttered as Amanda handed her a red T-shirt. "My kid's Barbie doll has tops larger than that bimbo's."

At thirty-six, Laura was a displaced homemaker who'd recently been hired as a junior copywriter. Amanda knew she was struggling to raise two children on her own after her physician husband had left her for his office assistant—a young woman who, if Laura could be believed, could be Kelli Kyle's evil twin.

Secretly agreeing about the inappropriateness of Kelli's attire, but not wanting to take sides, Amanda didn't answer.

"I can't wear this color," Nadine Roberts complained when Amanda handed her one of the red shirts. "I had my colors done and I'm a summer."

"This week you're an autumn." Amanda tossed a blue shirt to Julian Palmer.

"You certainly chose a graphically unsatisfying design," he complained.

"We should have come to you for help," she said, soothing the art director's easily ruffled feathers. Personally, she thought the white Team Challenge script just dandy. "But I knew how overworked you've been with the Uncle Paul's potato chip account, and didn't want to add any more pressure."

"The man's an idiot," Julian grumbled. "Insisting on those claymation dancing barbecue chips."

"It worked for the raisin growers," Kelli reminded everyone cheerfully. Despite all the rumors that had circulated since the woman's arrival two weeks ago, no one could accuse her of not being unrelentingly upbeat.

Amanda had been surprised to discover that beneath that bubbly-cheerleader personality and bimbo clothing, Kelli possessed a steel-trap mind when it came to her work. Which made it even more surprising that she'd stoop to having an affair with a man like Greg.

Not that there was actually any proof, other than gossip, that they were sleeping together, she reminded herself. However, given Greg's Lothario tendencies, along with all the time the pair spent together in his office with the door closed, Amanda certainly wouldn't have bet against the possibility.

Julian stiffened and shot Kelli a look that suggested her IQ was on a level with Uncle Paul's. "Potato chips," he said, "are not raisins."

No one in the room dared challenge that proclamation.

"Wait a damn minute," Marvin Kenyon complained when Amanda handed him a blue shirt. "I categorically refuse to be on *his* team." He jerked a thumb in Julian's direction.

Amanda opened her mouth to answer, but Greg beat her to the punch. "You'll be on whatever team I tell you you're on," he barked from the front of the room. "In case I haven't made myself clear, people, challenge week isn't about choice. It's about competition. Teamwork.

"And effective immediately, you are all going to work together as teams. Or at the end of the week, I'll start handing out pink slips. Do I make myself clear?"

He was answered by a low, obviously unhappy mumble.

Smooth move, Greg, Amanda thought.

The worst problem with mergers was their effect

on the employees. Even more so in advertising, where people were the agency's only real assets.

The rash of changeovers had caused dislocation, disaffection, underperformance and just plain fear. Which explained why more and more accounts were leaving the agency with each passing day. It was, after all, difficult to be creative when you thought you were going to be fired.

There were times, and this was definitely one of them, when Amanda wished she'd stuck to her youthful dreams of creating a family rather than an ad for a new, improved detergent or a toothpaste that supposedly would make the high school football quarterback ask the class wallflower to the prom.

When the idea of home and children once again brought Dane to the forefront of her mind, she shook off the thought and led the group out of the room, down to the beach where the first challenge activity was scheduled to take place.

Chapter 5

"Oh, my God," Laura said as the group reached the beach and found Dane waiting. "I think I'm in love."

While Greg had been harassing the troops and Amanda had been handing out T-shirts, Dane had changed into a black neoprene body glove. The suit somehow seemed to reveal more of him than if he were stark-naked.

His arms, his powerful legs, his chest, looked as if they had been chiseled from marble. No, Amanda decided, marble was too cold. Dane could have been hewn from one of the centuries-old redwoods found in an old-growth forest.

"That man is, without a doubt, the most drop-dead-gorgeous male I've ever seen in my life." Kelli was staring at Dane the way a religious zealot might stare at her god. "Oh, I do believe I'm going to enjoy this week."

"We're not here to enjoy ourselves," Greg ground out. "It's not a damn holiday." He turned his sharp gaze on Amanda. "That's the guy you hired to lead the adventure exercises?"

Call her petty, but Amanda found watching Greg literally seething with masculine jealousy more than a little enjoyable. Less enjoyable was the realization that Kelli's and Laura's lustful looks and comments had triggered a bit of her own jealousy.

"Not exactly."

Blond brows came crashing down. "What does that mean?"

"I'll explain later." She cast a significant glance down at her watch. "You're the one who wanted to stay on schedule, Greg. Come with me and I'll introduce you."

The introductions were over quickly, neither man seeming to find much to like about the other.

"The plan," Amanda explained to Dane, "as it was originally laid out to me, works like a relay race. Team members pair up, two to a kayak, paddle out to the lighthouse, circle it, then return back to the beach where the next group takes their places in the kayak and follows the same course. The best combined times for the two out of three heats is declared the winner."

Dane nodded. "Sounds easy enough."

"Easy for you to say. You haven't seen this group in action."

Seeing her worried expression and remembering what she'd told him about this week being vastly important to her, Dane understood her concern.

"Don't worry, Ms. Stockenberg," he said in his best businesslike tone, the one that had served him well for all those years in the big city, "before the week's over, you'll have turned your group into a lean, mean, advertising machine."

"That's the point," Greg Parsons snapped.

Amanda, who'd detected the sarcasm in Dane's tone, didn't respond. Instead, she introduced Dane to the others, then stood back and ceded control to the man she hoped could pull it off.

He didn't raise his voice above his usual conversational tone, but as he began to explain the basics of kayaking, Amanda noticed that a hush settled over the suddenly attentive group. Even the men were hanging on every word.

It was more than the fact that he was a stunningly good-looking male specimen. As amazing as it seemed for a man who'd been content to stay in the same job he'd had in high school, Dane Cutter definitely displayed leadership potential, making Amanda wonder yet again what had happened to sidetrack all his lofty career goals.

Perhaps, she considered, once this week was over and she'd earned the position of Northwest creative director, she'd offer Dane a job in management. After all, if he actually managed to pull this disparate, backbiting group into cohesive teams, helping him escape a dead-end life in Satan's Cove would be the least she could do.

Then again, she reminded herself firmly when she realized she was thinking too much like her autocratic father, there was no reason for Dane to be ashamed of having chosen a life of manual labor. It was, she admitted reluctantly, more honest than advertising.

Dane gave the teams a brief spiel about the versatility of kayaks, demonstrated forward and bracing strokes, explaining how the foot-operated rudder would help steer in crosswinds or rough seas, and skimmed over the wood-paddles-versus-fiberglass argument.

Amanda was not surprised to discover that despite the introduction of high-tech models, Dane remained an advocate of wood. The fact that he obviously felt strongly about a century-old inn proved he was a traditionalist at heart.

When he asked for questions, Kelli's hand shot up. "Shouldn't we be wearing wet suits like yours?" she asked.

"It's not really necessary," Dane assured her, making Amanda extremely relieved. She figured the sight of Kelli Kyle in a neoprene body glove could easily cause at least two heart attacks.

"But what if we get wet?"

"One can only hope," Peter murmured, earning laughter from several of the men and another sharp glare from Greg. At the same time, Amanda worried that Kelli in a wet T-shirt could be even more distracting than Kelli in a snug neoprene suit.

"Hopefully that won't prove a problem," Dane said with an answering smile.

"I've seen kayaking on the Discovery channel." This from Nadine Roberts. "And they always tip over."

"That technique is called an Eskimo roll. And you don't have to worry about learning it for this exercise," Dane told her.

"What if we don't intend to learn it? What if we roll anyway?" An auditor in the accounting department, Nadine was not accustomed to letting things slide.

"Never happen." Dane's grin was quick and reassuring. "You're thinking of the Inuit cruiser style, which is designed for speed and minimum wind interference.

You'll be in double touring kayaks, which are extremely stable. Think of them as floating minivans."

"My minivan is a lot bigger," Laura argued.

"People," Greg interjected sharply, "we're wasting valuable time here." He turned toward Dane. "As fascinating as all this might be," he said, his sarcastic tone indicating otherwise, "we don't have all day. So, if you're through with the instructions, Cutter, it's time to get this show on the road."

"It's your show," Dane said agreeably. But Amanda could see a simmering irritation in his dark eyes. "I'll need a volunteer for a demonstration." His seemingly casual gaze moved over the group before landing on Amanda. "Ms. Stockenberg," he said, "how about helping me with a little show-and-tell?"

Every head on the beach had turned toward her. Knowing that refusal would garner unwanted interest, Amanda shrugged. "Fine."

She took the orange life jacket Dane held out to her and put it on over her challenge T-shirt.

"Need any help with that?" he asked, reminding her of the time she'd pretended to need him to fasten the ties for her.

"I'm fine, thank you."

"Actually," he murmured, for her ears only, "you're a helluva lot better than fine, contessa."

Her temper flared, predictably. Remembering where she was, Amanda tamped it down.

"You'll need this." He handed her a helmet not unlike the one she wore when rollerblading or biking. "There are a lot of rocks around the lighthouse."

"I thought you said there's no risk of capsizing," she argued as she nevertheless put the white helmet on.

"Good point. But it never hurts to be prepared."

Good point, she echoed mentally as she watched him drag the kayak toward the water. If she'd been prepared to discover Dane still working here, she wouldn't be suffering from these unsettling feelings.

Within minutes of being afloat, she began to remember the rhythm he'd so patiently taught her that long-ago summer. Holding the blade of the wooden paddle close to her chest, her hands a bit more than shoulders' width apart, she plunged the blade in cleanly, close to the hull, pulling back with her lower hand, using torso rotation rather than arm strength, punching forward with her upper hand at the same time. When the blade of the paddle reached her hip, she snapped it out of the water and stroked on the other side.

Stab, pull, snap. Stab, pull, snap. Behind her, she could feel Dane moving in concert. *Stab, pull, snap.* "Not bad," Dane said. "For someone who probably considers the rowing machine at the gym roughing it."

Since his remark hit close to the truth, Amanda opted not to take offense. "I can't believe it's coming back so fast." *Stab, pull, snap. Left, right, left, right.* Although the touring kayak was built for stability, not speed, they were skimming through the surf toward the lighthouse. "I suppose it's like riding a bicycle."

"Or kissing," Dane suggested. *Stab, pull, snap.* The paddles continued to swish through the water. "We always did that well together, too. Ten years ago. And again, last night."

His words stopped her cold. "I don't want to talk about last night." Unnerved, she forgot to pull the paddle out until it had drifted beyond her hip. When she did, she caused the boat to veer off course.

The brisk professional ad executive was back. Dane was tempted to flip the kayak just to teach her a lesson. And to cool himself off. Didn't she know what she'd done to him last night? Didn't she realize how all it had taken was the taste of those succulent lips and the feel of that soft body against his to cause time to go spinning backward and make him feel like a horny, sex-starved teenager again?

"Tough," he deftly corrected, setting them straight again. Didn't she know that showing up this morning in that soft cotton T-shirt and those shorts that made her legs look as if they went all the way up to her neck was like waving a red flag in front of a very frustrated bull?

When he felt his hand tighten in a death grip on the smooth wooden shaft, he flexed his fingers, restraining the urge to put them around her shoulders to shake her.

"Because I have no intention of spending the next five nights lying awake, thinking about might-have-beens."

His tone was gruff, but Amanda was no longer an easily cowed fifteen-year-old girl. She began to shoot him a glare over her shoulder, but the lethal look in his eyes had her missing yet another stroke.

"You agreed to teach the kayaking just to get me alone with you, didn't you?"

"I could see from that schedule you and Mr. Slick have devised for the week that having you to myself for any decent length of time was going to be difficult, if not impossible," he agreed without displaying an iota of guilt about utilizing such subterfuge. "Fortunately, I've always prided myself on managing the impossible. Like resisting making love to a painfully desirable teenager."

"Dane…" Words deserted her as something far more dangerous than anger rose in those dark eyes.

They were behind the lighthouse now, out of view of the challenge-team members waiting for them back on the beach.

Dane stopped stroking and laid his paddle across the kayak. "I've thought about you, Amanda. I've remembered how you felt in my arms, how you tasted, how my body would ache all night after I'd have to send you back to your room."

"Don't blame me. *You're* the one who didn't want to make love."

"Wrong. What I wanted to do and what I knew I had to do were two entirely different things, contessa. But just because I was trying to do the honorable thing— not to mention staying out of jail—doesn't mean that I haven't imagined how things might have been different. If we'd met at another time."

"It wouldn't be the same." It was what she'd been telling herself for years. "That summer was something apart, Dane. Something that belongs in its own time and its own place. It doesn't even seem real anymore. And it certainly doesn't fit in our real lives."

She wasn't saying anything Dane hadn't told himself innumerable times. The problem was, he hadn't bought the argument then. And he wasn't buying it now.

"Are you saying you haven't thought about me?"

"That's exactly what I'm saying." It was the first and only lie she'd ever told him.

"Never?"

"Never."

He considered that for a moment. "All right. Let's

fast-forward to the present. Tell me you didn't feel anything last night, and I'll never mention it again."

"I didn't mean for that to..." She shook her head. "It just happened," she said weakly.

"Tell me."

She swallowed and looked away, pretending sudden interest in a trio of dolphins riding the surf on the horizon. There was a tug-of-war going on inside her. Pulling her emotionally toward Dane, pushing her away. Pulling and pushing. As it had done all during the long and lonely night.

"Tell me you haven't thought about how it could be," he continued in a low, deep voice that crept beneath her skin and warmed her blood. "Tell me you haven't imagined me touching you. You touching me. All over. Tell me that you don't want me."

Amanda knew that the easy thing, the safe thing, would be to assure him that the kiss they'd shared had been merely pleasant. But certainly nothing to lose sleep over. Unable to lie, she did the only thing she could think of. She hedged.

"You're certainly not lacking in ego." She tried a laugh that failed. Miserably.

"Tell me." His soft, gently insistent tone, touched with a subtle trace of male arrogance, was, in its own way, more forceful than the loudest shout. Once again Amanda wondered why Dane was wasting such talents here, at a small inn in a small coastal town, miles from civilization.

"I can't." She closed her eyes and shook her head.

Dane let out a long relieved breath that Amanda, caught up in the grips of her own turmoiled emotions, did not hear. So he'd been right. She wanted him, even as she didn't want to want him. He knew the feeling all too well.

"Have dinner with me tonight."

Was there anyone in the world who could resist that deep velvet voice? She certainly couldn't.

"I can't." Her voice shimmered with very real regret. "Greg and I have to go over today's results at dinner. And try to come up with substitutes for the bike race, backpacking trip and rock climb, now that we've lost our adventure leader."

"That's no problem. I'll do it."

The part of her who was desperate for the challenge week to be a success wanted to jump at his offer. Another, even stronger part of her, the part she feared was still a little bit in love with Dane, could not put his job in jeopardy on her account.

"I can't let you do that."

"I told you, it's no big deal."

"You won't think so if you lose your job."

Dane shrugged. "Jobs are easy to come by." His smile, while warm, was unthreatening. "Now, dinner with a beautiful woman, that's well worth throwing caution to the wind for.

"I'm volunteering for purely selfish reasons, Amanda. If I help out with the rest of the challenge week, you won't have to spend so much of your evenings with that cretin you're working so hard to get promoted back East, so I can be with you."

Her eyes widened. "How did you know I was trying to get Greg promoted to Manhattan?"

Amanda desperately hoped that he hadn't overheard any of the team members discussing such a possibility. She hadn't wanted anyone but Susan to know about her plan to win Greg Parsons's job. The job, she reminded herself, that should have been hers.

He watched the fear leap into her eyes and wondered if she realized that the goal she was chasing was not only illusive, but not worth the struggle.

"Don't worry. It was just a wild shot in the dark." He wanted to touch her—not sexually, just a hand to her cheek, or her hair, to soothe her obviously jangled nerves. "It's you city folks who are big on corporate intrigue. Out here in the boonies, we tend to spend more time trying to decide whether to take our naps before dinner or afterward."

Amanda still hadn't gotten a handle on Dane. But she knew he wasn't the country bumpkin he was pretending to be.

"I'd love to have you take over leading the corporate challenge. Of course, the agency will insist on paying you."

The figure she offered would pay for the new furnace the inn needed if he wanted to stay open year-round. Pride had Dane momentarily tempted to turn it down. He remembered just in time that the money would not come out of Amanda's pocket, but from the corporate checkbook of a very profitable advertising agency.

"That sounds more than reasonable. It's a deal."

"Believe me, Dane, you're saving my life."

He watched the worry lines ease from her forehead and wished that all her problems could be so simple to solve. He also wondered how bad those headaches would become, and how many cases of antacids she'd have to chew her way through before she realized that advertising wasn't real life.

"So, now that we've solved that problem, what about dinner?"

"I honestly can't."

She paused, running through a mental schedule. Now that they didn't have to come up with new activities, she and Greg didn't have all that much to cover. Besides, he'd undoubtedly want to get away early in order to sneak off to Kelli's room. Which, she'd noticed, conveniently adjoined his.

"How about dessert? We have to get together," he reminded, "so you can fill me in on the rest of the activities the leader you originally hired had planned for the week."

Telling herself that she'd just have to keep things on a strictly business level, Amanda said, "With your mother in the kitchen, how can I turn down dessert?"

"Terrific." His smile was quick and warmed her to the core. "I'll meet you down by the boathouse."

The boathouse had been one of their secret meeting places. Amanda knew that to be alone with Dane in a place that harbored so many romantic memories was both foolhardy and dangerous.

"Something wrong with the dining room?"

"It's too public."

"That's the idea."

"Ah, but I was under the impression that part of the corporate challenge agenda was to keep the teams off guard. So you can observe how they respond to unexpected trials."

Amanda vaguely wondered how Dane knew so much about corporate game-playing strategy. "So?"

"So, if we go over the events you have planned in

any of the public rooms, some of the team members might overhear us."

He had, she admitted reluctantly, a good point.

"There's always my room," he suggested when she didn't immediately answer.

"No," she answered quickly. Too quickly, Dane thought with an inward smile. It was obvious that they were both thinking about the first time she'd shown up at his door.

"Okay, how about the tower room?"

Not on a bet. "The boathouse will be fine."

"It's a date."

"It's not a date." Amanda felt it important to clarify that point up front. "It's a business meeting."

Dane shrugged. "Whatever." Matters settled to his satisfaction, he resumed paddling.

As Amanda had suspected, other than complain about the outcome of the first challenge event, Greg was not inclined to linger over dinner. Forgoing appetizers, he got right to the point of their meeting as he bolted through the main course.

"Today was an unmitigated disaster." His tone was thick with accusation.

"It wasn't all that bad," she murmured, not quite truthfully. The race hadn't been as successful as she'd hoped.

Unsurprisingly, Julian and Marvin had not meshed. They never managed to get their stroking rhythm in sync, and although each continued to blame the other loudly, their kayak had gotten so out of control that it had rammed into the one piloted by Laura and Don at the far turn around the lighthouse. Fortunately, Dane was proved right about the stability of the craft. But although neither kayak overturned, once the four were back on the beach, the three men almost came to blows.

Needless to say, Greg's subsequent cursing and shouting only caused the friction level to rise even higher. The only thing that had stopped the altercation from turning into a full-fledged brawl was Dane's quiet intervention. Amanda had not been able to hear what he was saying, but his words, whatever they were, obviously did the trick. Although their boatmanship didn't improve much during the second heat, the combatants behaved like kittens for the remainder of the afternoon.

"It was a disaster," Greg repeated. He pushed his plate away and took a swig from the drink he was never without. "I don't have to tell you that your career is on the line here, Amanda."

She refused to let him see how desperately she wanted the week to be successful. If he knew how important it was to her, he might try to sabotage her participation.

"If I remember correctly, this entire scheme was *your* idea."

"True." He turned down a second cup of coffee from a hovering waitress, and declined dessert. "But my job's not in jeopardy so long as *I'm* the one who eats a family holiday dinner with Ernst Janzen every Christmas." He placed his napkin on the table and rose.

"Make it work, Amanda," he warned, jabbing a finger toward her. "Or you'll be out on the street. And your assistant will be pounding the pavement, looking for a new job right along with you."

She felt the blood literally drain from her face. It was

just an idle threat. He couldn't mean it, she assured herself. But she *knew* he did.

It was one thing to blow her plans for advancement. She was also willing to risk her own career. But to be suddenly responsible for Susan's job, six months before her assistant's planned wedding, was more pressure than Amanda needed.

"I expect tomorrow's exercise to be a model of efficiency and collaboration," he said. "Or you can call Susan and instruct her to start packing both your things into boxes."

With that threat ringing in her ears, he turned on his heel and left the dining room.

The long day, preceded by a sleepless night, had left Amanda exhausted. Her dinner with Greg had left her depressed. And although she'd been secretly looking forward to being alone with Dane, now that the time had arrived, Amanda realized she was more than a little nervous.

Butterflies—no, make that giant condors—were flapping their wings in her stomach and she'd second-guessed her agreement to meet with him at least a dozen times during dinner.

Admittedly stalling, she was lingering over dinner when Mary appeared beside the table, a small pink bakery box in her hand.

"How was your meal?"

Amanda smiled, grateful for the interruption that would keep her from having to decide whether or not to stand Dane up again. Which would be difficult, since they were scheduled to spend the remainder of the week working on the challenge together.

"Absolutely delicious." The salmon pasta in white-wine sauce had practically melted in her mouth. "I'll probably gain ten pounds before the week is over."

"From what Dane tells me, with the week you have planned, you'll undoubtedly work off any extra calories." Mary held out the box. "I thought you and Dane might enjoy some carrot cake."

For ten years Amanda had been searching for a carrot cake as rich and sweet as Mary Cutter's. For ten years she'd been constantly disappointed.

"Make that twelve pounds," she complained weakly, eyeing the box with culinary lust.

Mary's look of satisfaction was a carbon copy of her son's. Although not as direct as Dane, in her own way, Mary Cutter could be a velvet bulldozer. "As I said before, a few extra pounds couldn't hurt, dear."

Running her hand down Amanda's hair in another of those maternal gestures Amanda had never received from her own mother, Mary returned to the kitchen, leaving Amanda with two pieces of carrot cake and a date for which she was already late.

She was on her way across the front parlor when someone called her name. Turning, she viewed the gorgeous young woman who'd been on duty last night, standing behind the desk.

"Yes?"

"I hate to ask, especially since you're a paying guest and all, but would you mind doing me a favor?" Mindy Taylor asked.

"If I can."

"Could you tell Dane that the furnace guy promised to begin work on Friday?"

Two things crossed Amanda's mind at nearly the same time. The first being that her meeting with Dane seemed to be common knowledge. The second being the fact that along with his other duties, Dane appeared to be in charge of maintenance.

"If I see him," she hedged.

"Great." Mindy flashed her dazzling Miss Satan's Cove smile. "Isn't it great how things work out?"

"What things?"

"Well, if the Mariner resort hadn't burned down, your advertising agency wouldn't have come here in the first place. Then, if your adventure leader hadn't spun out on his Harley on that rain-slick curve, you wouldn't have needed to hire Dane to fill in, and the inn would have to close after Labor Day."

Last night, Amanda had been impressed with Mindy's seeming combination of intelligence and beauty. Tonight she wondered if she'd made a mistake in judgment.

"I don't understand what hiring Dane to lead the challenge week has to do with Smugglers' Inn being able to remain open after Labor Day."

"Without a new furnace, we would have had to shut down for the winter."

"But what does that have to do with Dane?"

It was Mindy's turn to look at Amanda as if she was lacking in some necessary intelligence. "Because he's using the check from your agency to buy the new furnace."

"But why would Dane..." Comprehension suddenly hit like a bolt of lightning from a clear blue summer sky. "Dane's the new owner of Smugglers' Inn."

"Lock, stock and brand-new gas furnace," Mindy cheerfully confirmed.

Chapter 6

A full moon was floating in an unusually clear night sky, lighting Amanda's way to the boathouse. At any other time she might have paused to enjoy the silvery white path on the moon-gilded waters of the Pacific Ocean, or stopped to gaze up at the millions of stars sparkling overhead like loose diamonds scattered across a black velvet jeweler's cloth.

But her mind was not on the dazzling bright moon, nor the silvery water, nor the stars. Amanda was on her way to the boathouse to kill Dane Cutter.

He was waiting for her, just as he'd promised. Just as he had so many years ago. Unaware of the pique simmering through her, Dane greeted her with a smile that under any other conditions she would have found devastatingly attractive.

"I was getting worried about you."

She glared up at him, a slender, furious warrior with right on her side. "I got held up."

"So I see." Lines crinkled at the corners of his smiling eyes. "I hope that's Mom's carrot cake."

She'd forgotten she was still carrying the pink box. "It is." She handed it to him. Then reached back and slammed her fist into his stomach.

He doubled over with a grunt of surprise, dropping the cake box. "Damn it, Amanda!"

He gingerly straightened. She was standing, legs braced, as if intending to pound him again. He waited until he was sure his voice would be steady.

"You get one free shot, contessa. That's it. Try another cheap stunt like that and I'll have no choice but to slug you back."

"You wouldn't dare!" He might be a liar, but the man she'd fallen in love with ten years ago would never strike a woman. Then again, she reminded herself, apparently there was a lot she didn't know about the man Dane Cutter had become.

"I wouldn't risk putting it to the test." His dark eyes were hard. Implacable.

Dane saw her hand move to her stomach and damned himself for having caused another flare-up of her obviously touchy nerves.

But damn it, he hadn't started this. His plans for the evening had been to start out with some slow, deep kisses. After that, he'd intended to play things by ear, although if they ended up in bed, he certainly wasn't going to complain.

The worst-possible-case scenario was that they might waste valuable time together actually talking about her damn challenge-week events. One thing he hadn't planned on was having a fist slammed into his gut.

"You know, you really ought to see a doctor about that."

She frowned, momentarily thrown off track. "About what?"

"You could have an ulcer."

Following his gaze, she realized that the way her hand was pressed against the front of her blouse was a sure giveaway that she wasn't as much in control as she was trying to appear. "I don't have an ulcer."

"You sure? They can treat them with antibiotics, so—"

"I said, I don't have any damn ulcer."

Dane shrugged. "Fine. Then I'd suggest you work on your attitude."

"My attitude?" Her hands settled on her hips. "How dare you question *my* attitude. After what you've done!"

"What, exactly, have I done? Other than to offer to pull your fat out of the fire? Corporately speaking, that is."

Physically, she didn't appear to have an ounce of fat on her—one of the things he was hoping his mother's cooking could change. Amanda's society mother had been wrong; there was such a thing as a woman being too thin.

"That wasn't exactly the act of pure selflessness you made it out to be at the time," she countered with a toss of her head. "Not when you consider the new furnace for the inn. Which is scheduled to be installed Friday, by the way."

"Ah." It finally made sense. "Who told you?"

Amanda didn't know which made her more angry.

That Dane had lied to her in the first place, or that he appeared so cavalier at having gotten caught.

"That doesn't matter," she said between clenched teeth. "What matters is that you lied to me."

Now that he knew what all the storm and fury was about, Dane found himself enjoying the murder in her eyes. It spoke of a passion he had every intention of experiencing before this week was over.

"I'd never lie to you, Amanda."

She folded her arms and shot him a disbelieving look. "I don't recall you telling me that you were the new owner of Smugglers' Inn."

"I don't recall you asking."

Frustrated and furious, Amanda let out a huff of breath. "It's not the sort of question one asks a person one believes to be a bellman."

Her words were dripping icicles. Although hauteur was not her usual style, having been on the receiving end of her mother's cool conceit for all of her twenty-five years, Amanda had learned, on rare occasions, to wield the icy weapon herself. Tonight was one of those occasions.

Dane revealed no sign of having been fatally wounded. "You know, that snotty attitude doesn't suit you, contessa." Ignoring her warning glare, he reached out and stroked her hair. "It's too remote." Stroked her cheek. "Too passionless." Stroked the side of her neck. "Too untouchable."

That was precisely the point, damn it! Unfortunately, it wasn't working. Seemingly undeterred by her fury, he was jangling her nerves, weakening her defenses. Re-minding herself that she was no longer a naive, hope-

lessly romantic young fifteen-year-old, Amanda moved
away from his beguiling touch.

"You let me think you were still just an employee."
Although his touch had regrettably cooled her ire, the
thought that he might have been laughing at her still
stung.

Just an employee. He wondered if she knew how
much like her rich, snobbish mother those words
sounded. "I suppose I did." Until now, Dane hadn't realized that he'd been testing her. But, he admitted, that
was exactly what he'd been doing.

"Does it really make that much of a difference?
Whether I work at the inn? Or own it?" Her answer
was suddenly uncomfortably important.

Amanda had worked long enough in the advertising jungle to recognize a verbal trap when she spotted
one. "That's not the point," she insisted, sidestepping
the issue for the moment.

He lifted an eyebrow. "May I ask what the point is,
then? As you see it?"

"You were pretending to be something you weren't."

"We all pretend to be something—or someone—we
aren't from time to time."

Like that long-ago summer when she'd pretended to
be the Lolita of Satan's Cove. She hadn't fooled Dane
then. And she didn't now. Although he had no doubt
that she was more than capable of doing her job, he also
knew that she wasn't the brisk, efficient advertising au-
tomaton she tried so hard to appear.

"I don't." She jutted her chin forward in a way that
inexplicably made Dane want to kiss her. Then again,
he'd been wanting to kiss her all day long.

Thinking how ridiculous their entire situation was turning out to be, Dane threw back his head and laughed.

"I hadn't realized I'd said anything humorous," she said stiffly.

Her vulnerability, which she was trying so hard to conceal, made him want to take her into his arms. "I'm sorry." He wiped the grin from his face. "I guess you've spent so many years perfecting your career-woman act that you've forgotten that it really isn't you."

His accusation hit like the sucker punch she'd slammed into his stomach. The familiar headache came crashing back. "It isn't an act."

"Of course, it is." As he watched the sheen of hurt, followed by a shadow of pain, move across her eyes, Dane damned himself for putting them there. Laying aside his romantic plans, he began massaging her throbbing temples, as he had last night.

"I don't want you to touch me," she complained.

"Sure you do. The problem is you don't want to *want* me to touch you." His fingertips were making circles against her skin. Igniting licks of fire, burning away the pain. "Would it make you feel any better if I promised not to seduce you tonight?"

"As if you could," she muttered, trying to ignore the delicious heat that his caresses were creating.

Dane didn't answer. They both knew there was no need.

He abandoned his sensual attack on her headache, sliding his hands down her neck, over her shoulders, and down her arms. Amanda did not resist as he linked their fingers together.

"For the record, I think you're intelligent, creative,

and ambitious. You believe you think you know what you want—"

"I do know," she insisted.

"And you're not going to stop until you get it," he said, ignoring her firmly stated correction. "Whatever the cost."

"I have every intention of becoming Northwest regional creative director of Janzen, Lawton and Young." Determination burned in her eyes and had her unconsciously lifting her chin. "Once I get rid of Greg Parsons, just watch me go."

He smiled at that, because tonight, despite the change in plans, was not a night for arguing. "Believe me, I have no intention of taking my eyes off you."

Alerted by the huskiness in his tone, Amanda blew out a breath. "Am I going to have trouble with you?"

His answer was a slow masculine grin. "I certainly hope so." He moved closer. "Lots and lots of it."

She pulled a hand free and pressed it against his shoulder. "Damn it, Dane—"

He touched a finger against her mouth, cutting off her weak protest. "If you can forget what we had together, Amanda, you're a helluva lot stronger person than I am."

With effort, she resisted the urge to draw that long finger into her mouth. "It's over. And has been for years."

"That's what you think." He lifted the hand he was still holding and pressed his lips against her knuckles. Their eyes met over their linked hands—his, hot and determined; hers, soft and wary. "It's just beginning, Amanda. And we both know it."

Those words, so quietly spoken, could have been a

promise or a threat. Needing time to think, not to mention space in which to breathe, Amanda tugged her hand free and backed away. Both physically and emotionally.

"I only came down here to discuss the challenge."

Frustration rose; Dane controlled it. For now. "You're the boss," he said agreeably.

"Not yet," Amanda corrected. "But I will be." Because her unpleasant conversation with Greg was still in her mind, her shoulders slumped. "If I'm not fired first."

He wondered if she had any idea how vulnerable she could appear and decided that bringing it up now, after what even he would have to admit had not been the most successful of days, would serve no purpose.

Dane wanted to put his arm around her, to soothe more than seduce, but knew that if he allowed himself to touch her again, all his good intentions would fly right out the window. That being the case, he slipped his hands into the pockets of his jeans to keep them out of trouble.

"I can't see that happening."

"Believe me, it's a distinct possibility." She hadn't thought so, before today. Oh, she'd considered herself so clever with her little plan to get Greg promoted. Caught up in the logistics of getting the horrid man out of Portland, she hadn't given enough thought to the inescapable fact that half the challenge team actively disliked the other half. "After what happened today."

She dragged her hand through her hair. "Speaking of which, I suppose I ought to thank you."

"And here I thought you wanted to knock my block off."

"I did. Still do," she admitted. "But, as angry as I am at you for not being entirely honest with me, I can't overlook the fact that you were probably the only thing standing between me and the unemployment line today."

She sighed and shook her head as she stared out over the gilded sea. "From the way Julian, Marvin, Don, and Greg were behaving, you'd think we'd all come here to play war games."

"Business is probably as close to war as most people get," Dane said. "Other than marriage."

His grim tone suggested he was speaking from experience. A thought suddenly occurred to her. "You're not married, are you?"

Dane swore. Annoyance flickered in his dark eyes, and drew his lips into a hard line. "Do you honestly believe that if I had a wife, I'd be planning to take you to bed?"

"Planning is a long way from doing." As she'd learned, only too well. She'd had such plans for this week!

"That may be true for some people. But I've developed a reputation for being tenacious." He cupped her chin between his fingers, holding her gaze to his. "I'm going to have you, contessa. And you're going to love it."

The last time she'd allowed him to bait her, she'd ended up kissing him as if there were no tomorrow. Afraid that the next time she wouldn't be able to stop with a mere kiss, Amanda jerked her head back, folded her arms across her chest and reminded herself that it was important at least to pretend to remain cool.

"You may be accustomed to women succumbing to your seduction techniques, Dane. But I have no intention of joining the hordes. I'm also a tougher case than you're obviously accustomed to."

"Victories are always more satisfying when they

don't come easily. And you haven't answered my question."

Discounting his arrogant male statement about taking her to bed, despite the fact that he was also confusing, beguiling, and distracting her, Amanda sensed that Dane was a caring, compassionate individual. And although he had misled her, she knew, from past experiences, that he was also an honorable man. Most men would have taken what she was literally throwing at him ten years ago without a backward glance when the summer was over. But Dane was not most men.

"I suppose I can't imagine you committing adultery."

"Well, I suppose that's a start. Perhaps I ought to have someone write a reference letter. How about my mother? She'd love an opportunity to sing my praises."

"That's not the way I remember it."

"Ten years ago she was a single mother concerned her son was about to repeat her own romantic mistake." Because he could not continue to stand this close to Amanda without touching, he reached out and twined a strand of her hair around his finger.

"These days, she's a mother who's begun to worry that her son isn't ever going to provide her with the grandchildren she's so eager to spoil."

That was yet another difference between the Stockenbergs and the Cutters. Amanda's mother refused even to discuss the possibility of becoming a grandmother anytime in this century. While her father had warned her on more than one occasion of the dangers of falling prey to the infamous "baby track" that would hinder her success.

"How do you feel about that?" she asked.

"Actually, I think it's a pretty good idea. With the right woman, of course."

She couldn't help thinking of a time when she'd dreamed of having children with this man. She also had no intention of asking Dane what type of woman fit his criteria. Deciding that the conversation was drifting into dangerous territory, she opted to change the subject.

"May I ask a question?"

"Shoot."

"What did you say to Greg and the others today? To stop them from brawling on the beach?"

Dane shrugged. "Not that much. I merely pointed out to Parsons that he had too much riding on this week to risk getting into a fistfight with his employees."

That was why Greg had marched away, steam practically coming from his ears, Amanda decided. "But what about Julian and Marvin? They were at each other's throats after that disastrous first heat, but by the end of the day they were behaving as if they were candidates for the Kayaking Olympic Team."

Dane knew he was treading in dangerous waters again. He didn't want to lie to Amanda. But if he told her the truth about his conversation with the art director and head copywriter, she'd undoubtedly want to slug him again.

She'd also be furious that he'd interfered, little mind the fact that she'd needed some help at the time. Especially since her egocentric supervisor was obviously not only a bully, but an incompetent idiot to boot.

"I said pretty much the same thing to them I did to Parsons." He forced himself to meet her lovely, serious eyes. "I suggested this week was going to be long and tough enough to get through without complicating things with useless feuds.

"I also mentioned that since management, in its own ignorance, tended to take things like this ridiculous corporate challenge week seriously, it made sense to save their differences for the creative arena where it mattered, bury their individual hatchets and cooperate by trying to win the thing together."

"I'm impressed."

"It's not that big a deal."

It was the truth, so far as it went. What he'd failed to mention was that he'd also told the two combatants that if they didn't shape up and do their best to make this week a success, he'd throw them both off the cliff. Then drown them.

Although they'd resorted to bluster, from the uneasiness in their eyes, he realized that they'd half believed he might actually do it. And, although he wasn't violent, such behavior was undeniably tempting. If it helped Amanda.

Watching her today, seeing how seriously she took her work, understanding how important it was to her that she pull off this week, Dane knew that in order to get what *he* wanted, he would have to see that Amanda got what *she* wanted. And what she wanted, it seemed, was Greg Parsons's job. That being the case, he intended to move heaven and earth—and a portion of the Oregon coast, if necessary—to ensure her success.

"Believe me, Dane, it was a very big deal." Thinking back on what he'd done for her—for no other reason than that he'd wanted to help—Amanda felt guilty. "I'm sorry I hit you."

Her hand was on his arm. Dane covered it with his.

"You were right. I haven't exactly been the most forthright guy in the world the past couple of days. But I never meant to hurt you. Or to make you feel I was having fun at your expense."

His hand was darker than hers. Larger. And warmer. When she began imagining it moving over her body, touching her in places that were aching for just such a sensual touch, Amanda knew that no matter how hard she tried to deny it, Dane was right. Before this week was over, they would become lovers.

That idea was thrilling and terrifying at the same time.

"There's something I don't understand," she murmured.

"What's that?"

"What made you decide to buy the inn? After swearing that you couldn't wait to get away from Satan's Cove, I'm surprised to find you still here."

"Not still."

"Pardon me?"

"I said, I'm not still here. I'm back."

"Oh." That made a bit more sense, she supposed. "What did you do in between?"

Dane took encouragement from the fact that she cared about how he'd spent his life during those intervening years. "A little of this. A little of that."

"That's not very enlightening."

"I suppose not." He gave her a long look. "I guess I just can't figure out why you'd care. Since you've already said you haven't thought about me since that summer."

"I may have thought of you," she admitted, realizing that there was no way she'd be able to keep up the subterfuge. "From time to time."

Dane didn't answer. He just stood there, looking down at her, a frustratingly inscrutable look on his face, as the tension grew thicker and thicker between them.

"All right!" She threw up her hands in surrender. "I lied. I thought about you a lot, Dane. More than I should have. More than I wanted.

"Every man I've ever gone out with, I've ended up comparing to you. Once I dated a man for six months because, believe it or not, if I closed my eyes, his voice reminded me of yours.

"I go to work, and if I'm not careful, my mind will drift and I'll think of you and wonder where you are, and what you're doing. And at night—" On a roll now, she began to pace. "At night I'll lie in bed, and you'll be lying there beside me, kissing me, touching me, loving me.

"And then I'll wake up, and realize it was only a dream. But it doesn't seem like a dream, damn it. It seems real! And then, last night, I was tired and cranky, and worried, and all of a sudden I heard this voice I've dreamed about time and time again, and I turned around and there you were, and this time you weren't a dream.

"You were real. Wonderfully, marvelously real! And it was all I could do not to throw myself in your arms and beg you to make love to me—with me—for the rest of my life!

"So, there." She stopped in front of him, close enough that he could see the sheen of tears in her expressive blue eyes. "Now you know. Is that what you wanted to hear me say? Is your almighty male ego satisfied now?"

She was trembling. Once again the need to comfort

warred with the desire to seduce. Once again comfort won out. "Yes. It's what I wanted to hear."

He put his hands on her shoulders and drew her to him. And although she remained stiff, she wasn't exactly resisting, either.

He cupped her chin again. "But only because it's a relief to know that I wasn't the only one feeling that way."

Amanda read the truth in his warm, loving gaze and felt even more like weeping. Her emotions were in a turmoil. She couldn't think straight. She could only feel. She wrapped her arms around his waist and clung. "Really?"

"Really." His smile was that crooked, boyish one that had once possessed the power to make her young heart turn somersaults. It still did.

"And if you think it's dumb dating a guy for six months because he sounds like someone else, how about marrying someone because she has the same laugh as a girl you once loved?"

"You didn't!"

"Guilty." His grin turned sheepish. "I was young and determined to get you out of my system when I met Denise."

Denise. Dane had been married to a woman named Denise. A woman with her laugh. Amanda hated her. "What happened?"

"It's a long story."

"I'm not in any hurry to be anywhere." On the contrary, a very strong part of Amanda wished she could stop time and make this night last forever.

There'd been a moment, during her passionate speech about how many times she'd thought of him over the intervening years, that Dane had thought perhaps tonight would turn out to be the night he finally made love to Amanda. Now that he'd made the mistake of bringing up his ex-wife, he knew he'd have to remain patient a bit longer.

Reminding himself that Amanda was worth waiting for, Dane took her hand and led her over to a rowboat tied to the pier.

"We may as well get reasonably comfortable," he said. "Because this is going to take a while."

Chapter 7

Dane's fingers curved around her waist as he lifted her easily into the boat. Amanda sat down on the bench seat, leaned back against the bow and waited.

Dane sat down beside her. When he began talking, his words were slow and measured.

"I liked Denise from the moment I met her. Along with the all-important fact that she had your laugh, she was also beautiful and smart and sexy. And the only woman I'd ever met who was every bit as driven to succeed as I was."

"She sounds like an absolute paragon."

Dane would have had to be deaf not to hear the female jealousy in Amanda's dry tone. He chuckled as he put his arm around her shoulder, encouraged when she did not pull away.

"Unfortunately, except for our work, we didn't have a single solitary thing in common. Six months later, when neither of us had much to laugh about, we decided to call it quits before our disastrous marriage ruined a very good working relationship."

"I can't imagine working with an ex-husband."

Dane shrugged. "It hadn't been a typical marriage from the beginning. I'd married her to get over you and she married me on the rebound after her divorce from a miserable first marriage. Right before the split, I was promoted into a position that involved a lot of traveling. After a time, it was as if our marriage had never happened and we found we could be friends again. Two years ago, I introduced her to an old college friend of mine who's a stockbroker in San Francisco. They clicked right off the bat, got married, and I got a note from her last week announcing her pregnancy. So things worked out for the best."

"You said you were young?"

Dane sighed. Although he'd overcome any regrets he'd once harbored over his marriage, revealing such irresponsible behavior to the one woman he wanted to impress was proving more than a little embarrassing.

"I graduated from University of Oregon the summer after I met you," he said. "Mom was there, of course, along with Denise—who was my supervisor during my apprentice program at Whitfield. We went out to dinner, then after I took Mom back to her hotel, Denise invited me out for a drink to celebrate.

"One toast led to another, and another, and a few more, then we bought a bottle of champagne—a magnum—and the next thing I remember we were waking up in a motel room in Reno, Nevada.

"Denise couldn't remember much of anything, either, but the signed certificate from a justice of the peace on the dresser spoke for itself, so after several cups of strong coffee and a great many aspirin, we figured, since we'd always gotten along so well at the office, we might as well try to make a go of it."

Amanda didn't know which part of the story—so unlike the Dane she'd known who'd driven her crazy with his self-control—she found most amazing. "You actually married your boss?"

This time his grin was more than a little sheepish. "Women aren't the only ones who can sleep their way to the top of the company."

Since she knew he was joking, Amanda overlooked his blatantly chauvinistic remark. "She must have been older."

"About twelve years. But that didn't have anything to do with the breakup. We were just mismatched from the get-go."

In all his travels around the world, Dane had met a great many chic women, but none of them had oozed sophistication like his former wife. Denise preferred Placido Domingo to Garth Brooks, champagne cocktails at the symphony to hot dogs at the ballpark, and given the choice between spending an afternoon at a stuffy art museum with her uptown friends or fly-fishing on a crystal-clear Oregon river, she'd choose Jackson Pollack over rainbow trout any day.

Dane had often thought, over these past months since his return to Satan's Cove, that if he and Denise hadn't broken up that first year, they definitely would have divorced over his need to leave the city for this wildly beautiful, remote stretch of Oregon coast. Since there could have been children involved by this point, he was grateful they'd cut their losses early.

So stunned was Amanda by the story of Dane's marriage, it took a while for something else he'd said to sink in.

"You said she was your supervisor at Whitfield. Whitfield as in the Whitfield Palace hotel chain? 'When Deluxe Will No Longer Do'?" she asked, quoting the world-famous slogan. "*That's* where you were working?"

"I was in the intern program at Whitfield while I was in college and they hired me full-time after graduation."

This was more like it. This fit the burning need Dane had professed to escape Satan's Cove. This was the man, when she'd daydreamed about Dane, she'd imagined him to be. "What did you do there?"

"A bit of everything. Whitfield makes its managerial prospects start at the bottom and work in all the different departments. I was assigned to the custodial department my sophomore year at U of O, worked my way up to housekeeping my junior year, reservations my senior year, then spent the summer after graduation in the kitchen."

"That's the summer you were married." Even knowing that it hadn't worked out, Amanda realized that she hated the idea of any other woman sharing Dane's life. Let alone his bed.

It should have been her, Amanda thought with a surprisingly furious burst of passion. It could have been her, if her parents hadn't manipulated things to keep them apart. Or if her feelings hadn't been so wounded and his pride so stiff.

Unaware of her thoughts, Dane nodded. "That's it. By Christmas I was on my way to being single again."

Denise's petition for divorce—they'd agreed she'd

be the one to file—had arrived at his office on December 23. He'd spent the next two days in Satan's Cove with his mother.

The morning after Christmas, he was on a plane to Paris. And after that Milan. Then Zurich. And on and on until he was spending so much of his life at 30,000 feet, he'd often joked—not quite humorously—that he should just give the postal service his airline schedule.

"And then you began traveling." Amanda recalled the earlier condensed version. "Still for Whitfield?"

"When Denise and I split, I'd just gotten promoted to assistant director of guest relations, working out of the New Orleans headquarters. Essentially, it was my job to visit each hotel at least twice a year and pull a surprise inspection."

"You must have been popular," Amanda said dryly.

"I like to think I bent over backward to be fair. But I will admit to being tough. After all, guests pay big bucks to stay at a Whitfield Palace. It's important they feel they're getting their money's worth."

"I stayed at the Park Avenue Whitfield last month," Amanda revealed, "on a trip back to Manhattan. The New York agency handles their advertising account." With luck and Dane's help, Greg Parsons would soon be transferring to those renowned Madison Avenue offices. "It really was like being in a palace."

Although she'd grown up with wealth, Amanda hadn't been able to keep from staring at the sea of marble underfoot or the gleaming crystal chandeliers overhead. She'd had the impression that at any minute, a princess would suddenly appear from behind one of the gilded pillars.

"That's the point," Dane said.

"True." Whoever had named the worldwide hotel chain had definitely hit the nail right on the head.

Amanda also remembered something else about her stay at the flagship hotel. Her room, furnished with genuine antiques and boasting a view of the leafy environs of Central Park, had been comfortably spacious. And the marble bathrooms had an amazing selection of French milled perfumed soaps, shampoos and lotions. In addition, the staff had been more than accommodating. Still, even with all that, Amanda had felt vaguely uncomfortable during her three-day stay.

"You know," she said thoughtfully, "as luxurious as the Park Avenue Whitfield is, I like what you've done with Smugglers' Inn better. It's more comfortable. Cozier."

His slow, devastating grin reached his eyes. "That's the point." Dane was undeniably pleased that she understood instinctively the mood he'd wanted to create. "I'm also glad you approve."

"I really do." He was looking at her as if he wanted to kiss her again. Her heart leaped into her throat. Then slowly settled again. "It's lovely, Dane. You should be very proud."

The sea breeze fanned her hair, causing it to waft across her cheek. Dane reached out to brush it away and ended up grabbing a handful. "Speaking of lovely…"

He pulled her closer with a gentle tug on her hair.

"It's too soon," she protested softly.

Personally, Dane thought it was about ten years too late. "Just a kiss." His mouth was a whisper from hers. "One simple kiss, Amanda. What could it hurt?"

She could feel herself succumbing to the temptation in his dark eyes, to the promise of his silky breath against her lips, to the magic in the fingers that had slipped beneath her hair to gently massage the nape of her neck.

A simple kiss. What could it hurt?

"Just a kiss," she whispered in a soft, unsteady breath. Her lips parted of their own volition, her eyes fluttered shut in anticipation of the feel of his mouth on hers. "You have to promise."

He slid the fingers of his free hand down the side of her face. "I promise." He bent his head and very slowly, very carefully, closed the distance.

The stirring started, slow and deep. And sweet. So achingly, wonderfully sweet.

There was moonlight, slanting over the sea, turning it to silver. And a breeze, feathering her hair, whispering over her skin, carrying with it the salt-tinged scent of the sea. Somewhere in the distance a foghorn sounded; the incoming tide flowed over the rocks and lapped against the sides of the boat that was rocking ever so gently on the soft swells.

His lips remained night-cool and firm while hers heated, then softened. Amanda's hand floated upward, to rest against the side of his face as Dane drew her deeper and deeper into a delicious languor that clouded her mind even as it warmed her body to a radiant glow.

Although sorely tempted, Dane proved himself a man of his word, touching only her hair and the back of her neck. With scintillating slowness, and using only his mouth, he drew out every ounce of pleasure.

A soft moan slipped from between Amanda's heated lips. No man—no man except Dane—had ever been able to make her burn with only a kiss. He whispered words against her mouth and made her tremble. He murmured promises and made her ache.

Dane had spent most of the day hoping that he'd overreacted to last night's encounter. A man accustomed to thinking with his head, rather than his heart—or that other vital part of his anatomy that was now throbbing painfully—he'd attempted to make sense out of a situation he was discovering defied logic.

Despite all the intervening years, despite all the women he'd bedded since that bittersweet summer, Dane found himself as inexplicably drawn to Amanda as ever.

The first time they'd been together like this, his desire had been that of a boy. Last night, and even more so now, as he shaped her lips to his, forcing himself to sample their sweet taste slowly, tenderly, Dane knew that this desire was born from the age-old need of a man for his mate.

Because he could feel himself rapidly approaching that dangerous, razor-thin line between giving and taking, Dane lifted his head. Then waited for Amanda to open her eyes.

Those wide eyes he'd never been able to put out of his mind were clouded with unmistakable desire as she stared up at him in the moonlight.

He could have her, Dane knew. Right here, he could draw her into his arms and crush her mouth to his until she was senseless, until she couldn't speak, couldn't think, couldn't breathe. And couldn't run away.

Although he'd never considered himself a masochist, Dane fantasized about the way her body would feel next to his, beneath his, on top of his. He wanted her in every way possible.

The problem was, Dane realized with a stunned sense of awareness, he also wanted her forever.

She murmured a faint, inarticulate protest as he brushed one last quick kiss against her parted lips, then stood.

"Just a kiss," he reminded her, holding out his hand to help her to her feet.

Amanda needed all the assistance she could get. Her mind was still spinning from that devastating, heart-swelling kiss and she wasn't certain if her legs would hold her. She wanted Dane. Desperately. Worse yet, she needed him. Absolutely. For not the first time in her life, Amanda found herself damning his iron control.

"This is getting impossible," Amanda said.

Watching the myriad emotions storm in her eyes—desire, confusion, frustration—Dane vowed that there would be a time when he would take more. But for to-night, that kiss would have to be enough.

"What's that?" he asked mildly.

"You. Me. And what's happening between us. I had my life planned. I knew what I wanted. But ever since I arrived back in Satan's Cove, I can't understand what I'm feeling."

Sympathy stirred as the hair she'd ruffled with un-steady fingers fell back into place. "I think the prob-lem is that you understand exactly what you're feeling."

"All right," she said on a frustrated sigh. "You're right. I do know. But you have to understand that I'm not that silly teenager who threw herself at you ten years ago, Dane. I've worked hard to get where I am. My entire life, from the day I chose a major in college, has revolved around advertising."

Personally, Dane thought that was about the saddest

thing he'd ever heard, but not wanting to get into an argument over the art and artifice of the advertising marketplace, he kept silent.

"I've given up so many things, made so many sacrifices, not to mention plans—"

"They say life is what happens when you're making plans," he interjected quietly.

Amanda stared up at him and shook her head. "Yes. Well."

She, who'd always been so smug about her ease with words, could not think of a single thing to say. Still unnerved by the kiss they'd shared, and uneasy at the way he was looking down at her, so calm, so comfortable with who he was and where he was, Amanda dragged her gaze back out to sea. A boat drifted by on the horizon, the running lights looking like fallen stars on the gleaming black water.

They stood there, side by side, looking at the ocean, all too aware of the closeness of the other.

"Damn it," she said with a sudden burst of frustration. "You, of all people, should understand. You obviously didn't succeed at Whitfield because you married your supervisor. You had to have worked hard."

"Sixteen to eighteen hours a day," he agreed. "Which is one of the reasons I quit."

"Yet I'll bet there are still days when you put in that many hours."

"Sure." Dane thought about the hours he'd spent fixing up the tower room. Just for her. He'd told himself at the time that the work had been done out of ego, because he wanted her to see what a success he'd made of the place. But now Dane suspected that his motives had been far more personal.

"But I said long hours were *one* of the reasons I quit Whitfield," he reminded her. "There were others."

"Such as?" Amanda was genuinely interested in whatever roads Dane had taken that had led him all over the world before returning to Satan's Cove.

"I wasn't overly fond of corporate structure." That was the truth. "And corporate structure wasn't overly fond of me."

That was a major understatement. Fortunately, he'd been successful enough that the guys in the pin-striped suits in the executive towers had overlooked his independent streak. Most of the time.

Granted, he'd thoroughly enjoyed the work in the beginning. Especially the travel. For a young man who'd grown up in an isolated coastal town of less than two hundred people, his early years at the hotel chain had been an exhilarating, eye-opening experience.

But newness faded over time and the day he'd realized he was close to suffocating in the luxurious eighteenth-floor corner window suite of the glass tower that dominated New Orleans's central business district, he'd turned in his resignation.

Eve Whitfield Deveraux—who'd inherited control of the hotel chain from her father—had asked him to reconsider. Having married a maverick herself, the hotel CEO appreciated having someone she could always count on to tell her the truth. There were already too many sycophants around her, she'd told him on more than one occasion. What she needed was a few more rebels like Dane Cutter.

As much as he'd genuinely liked her, Dane couldn't stay. So he'd cashed in his stock options and his IRA, closed his money-market and checking accounts, and returned home.

Dane realized that while his mind had been drifting, Amanda had been quietly waiting for him to continue.

"Besides," he said, "working long hours these days is a helluva lot different. Because Smugglers' Inn is mine. It's not some trendy real-estate investment I plan to sell to some foreign development company in a few years for a quick profit.

"I've put more than money into the place, though to be truthful, it's just about cleaned out my bank account, which is the only reason I decided to take that money from your agency.

"But I don't really mind the broken heaters and clogged pipes and leaky roofs, because I'm building something here, Amanda. I'm building a home. For myself and my family.

"Because as much of a rush as it admittedly was at first, flying all over the world, staying in presidential suites, having everyone snap to attention the moment my car pulled up in front of a Whitfield Palace hotel, the novelty eventually wore off.

"That was when I realized that what I truly wanted, more than money, or power, or prestige, was someone to come home to at the end of the day.

"Someone to walk along the beach with in the twilight of our years. Someone who'll love me as much as I'll love her—and our children, if we're lucky enough to have them."

He'd definitely been on a roll. It was, Dane considered as he felt himself finally running down, probably the longest speech he'd ever given. And, he thought, perhaps his most important.

Amanda didn't speak for a long time. Dane's fervent declaration, while sounding well-thought-out, had definitely taken her by surprise. Since arriving at Smugglers' Inn, she'd been trying to make the various aspects of Dane mesh in her mind.

The young man she'd first fallen in love with had been the most driven individual she'd ever met. And that included her father, who was certainly no slouch when it came to workaholic, success-at-all-cost strategies.

Remembering all Dane's lofty dreams and plans and ambitions, when she'd mistakenly believed he'd never left Satan's Cove, she hadn't been able to understand how he could have failed so miserably in achieving his goals.

Then she'd discovered he actually owned the landmark inn. And, as lovely as it admittedly was, she couldn't help wondering how many people could so easily turn their back on power and prestige.

"That picture you're painting sounds lovely."

"You almost sound as if you mean that."

He wondered if she realized it was almost the exact same picture she'd painted for him so many years ago. It was, Dane considered, ironic that after all these years apart they were back here in Satan's Cove, still attracted to one another, but still at cross purposes. It was almost as if they'd entered a parallel universe, where everything—including their individual dreams and aspirations—was reversed.

"Of course I mean it. I also admire you for knowing yourself well enough to know what's right for you."

"I think I hear a *but* in there."

"No." She shook her head. "Perhaps a little envy."

"I don't know why. Seems to me you're in the catbird

seat, contessa. All you have to do is get Parsons out of your way and you're definitely back on the fast track."

"So why does it feel as if the lights at the end of the tunnel belong to an oncoming train?" She was not accustomed to revealing weakness. Not to anyone. But tonight, alone at the edge of the world with Dane, it somehow seemed right.

"Because you're tired." Dane couldn't resist touching her. "Because change is always disruptive," he murmured as he began kneading her tense, rocklike shoulders. "And with the takeovers and mergers, you've been going through a lot of changes lately.

"Not to mention the fact that Parsons is the kind of jerk who'd stress out Deepak Chopra. And along with trying to juggle this stupid corporate challenge week, you're being forced to confront feelings you thought you'd put behind you long ago."

His talented fingers massaged deeply, smoothing out the knots. "If I were a better man, I'd leave you alone and take a bit of the pressure off. But I don't think I'm going to be able to do that, Amanda."

She knew that. Just as she knew that deep down inside, she didn't really want Dane to give up on her.

"I just need a little more time." She was looking up at him, her eyes eloquently pleading her case. When she allowed her gaze to drift down to his mouth—which she could still taste—Amanda was hit with an arousal more primal and powerful than anything she'd ever known.

She imagined those firmly cut lips everywhere on her body, taking her to some dark and dangerous place she'd only ever dreamed about. "To think things through."

It wasn't the answer he wanted. Unfortunately, it *was* the answer he'd been expecting.

Dane's response was to cup the back of her head in his hand and hold her to a long, deep kiss that revealed both his hunger and his frustration. And, although she was too caught up in the fire of the moment to recognize it, his love.

"Think fast," he said after the heated kiss finally ended.

Still too aroused to speak, Amanda could only nod.

Chapter 8

Amanda was more than a little relieved when the next day began a great deal more smoothly than the previous day's kayak races. When team members woke to a cool, drizzling rain streaming down the windows that necessitated putting off the bike race until afternoon, she was prepared to switch gears.

Taking the indoor equipment from her store of supplies, she divided the teams into subgroups and put everyone to work building a helicopter from pieces of scrap paper, cardboard, rubber bands and Popsicle sticks. Although speed was of the essence, it was also important that the constructed vehicle manage some form of brief flight.

"I still don't get the point of this," Laura complained as yet another attempt fatally spiraled nosefirst into the rug.

"You're blending science and art," Amanda explained patiently yet again. "Advertising is a subtle, ever-changing art that defies formularization."

"That's what it used to be," Luke Cahill muttered as he cut a tail rotor from a piece of scarlet construction paper. "Until the invasion of the MBA's." A rumpled, casual man in his mid-thirties, he possessed the unique ability to pen a catchy tune and link it with an appealing advertising idea.

Amanda had always considered Luke to be the most easygoing person working at the agency. She realized the recent stress had gotten to him, as well, when he glared over at Don Patterson, the financially oriented marketing manager, who stopped remeasuring the length of the cardboard helicopter body to glare back.

"However much you artsy types would like to spend the day playing in your creative sandboxes, advertising is a business," Don countered. "I, for one, am glad to see this agency finally being run as a profit-making enterprise."

"You won't *have* any profits if the product suffers," Luke snapped back. "Advertising is more than numbers. It's our native form of American anthology."

"He's right," Marvin Kenyon said. "Advertising—and life—would be a helluva lot easier if it could be treated like science—A plus B equals C—but it can't.

"Life is about change, damn it. And advertising reflects that. The best advertising, the kind we *used* to do for C.C.C., can even act as an agent for change."

Greg, who was sitting off to the side, watching the group, applauded, somehow managing to make the sound of two hands coming together seem mocking.

"Nice little speech, Kenyon." He poured himself a

drink—his second of the morning—and took a sip. "But if you're not part of the solution you're part of the problem. If you can't get with the program, perhaps you don't belong in advertising."

"Not belong?" This from Julian. "You *do* realize that you're talking to a man who has twenty-nine years' experience creating witty, appealing, and totally original advertising that makes the sale through its ability to charm prospective buyers?"

As she heard the art director stand up for the head copywriter, Amanda felt a surge of excitement. As foolish as these games had seemed at first, something was happening.

Until the pressures brought about by first the mergers, then the takeover, C.C.C. had been viewed throughout the advertising world as a flourishing shop.

Unfortunately, because of the political machinations that were part and parcel of becoming a bigger agency, Marvin and Julian had started sniping at each other, causing morale to tailspin as sharply and destructively as Laura's failed helicopter model.

But now, thanks to Greg's threat, Julian had just felt the need to stand up for his former creative partner. And although she wondered if they'd ever regain the sense of "family" that had been the hallmark of Connally Creative Concepts, Amanda hoped such behavior was a sign that the creative members of the agency would resume encouraging each other, spurring their colleagues to even greater achievements, as they'd done in the past.

"We can't ignore the fact that we're in a service business," she said. "Unfortunately, no matter how creative our advertising is, if we don't possess the organization to effectively service our clients, we'll fail."

"That's what I've been trying to say," Don insisted.

"On the other hand," Amanda said, seeking a middle ground, "we could have the best media buying and billing system in the world but if creativity suffers because everyone's getting mired down in details, we won't have any clients to bill. And no profits. Which, of course, eventually would mean no salaries."

She reached out and picked up the helicopter the blue team had just finished and held it above her head. When she had their undivided attention, she let it go. The copter took off on a sure, albeit short flight, ending atop a bookcase.

"That was teamwork, ladies and gentlemen," she said with a quick, pleased grin. "Science and creativity, meshing into one efficient, artistic entity."

Dane had slipped into the back of the room during the beginning of the argument. He'd convinced himself that Amanda wasn't really happy in her work; that deep down inside, where it really counted, she was still the young girl who wanted to have babies and make a comfortable home for her family.

Now, having observed the way she'd deftly turned the discussion around, he was forced to admit that perhaps Amanda really did belong exactly where she was.

It was not a very satisfying thought.

Her spirits buoyed by the successful helicopter project, Amanda found herself thoroughly enjoying the excellent lunch of grilled sockeye salmon on fettucini, black bean salad, and fresh-baked sourdough bread, the kind that always reminded her of San Francisco's famed Fisherman's Wharf. Dessert was a blackberry cobbler topped with ice cream. The berries, Mary told the appreciative guests, had been picked from the bushes growing behind the inn; the ice cream, which was almost unbearably rich with the unmistakable taste of real vanilla beans, was homemade.

"It's a good thing I'm only spending a week here," Amanda said when she stopped by the kitchen to thank Dane's mother again for helping make the week a success.

"Oh?" With lunch successfully behind her, Mary had moved on to preparing dinner and was slicing mushrooms with a blindingly fast, deft stroke that Amanda envied, even as she knew she'd undoubtedly cut her fingers off if she ever dared attempt to duplicate it. "And why is that, dear?"

"Because I'd probably gain a hundred pounds in the first month." She still couldn't believe she'd eaten that cobbler.

"Oh, you'd work it all off," Mary assured her easily. "There's enough to do around here that burning calories definitely isn't a problem."

"I suppose you're right." Amanda had awakened this morning to the sound of hammering. Although the sun was just barely up, when she'd looked out her window she'd seen Dane repairing the split-rail fence that framed the front lawn and gardens. "Dane certainly seems to be enjoying it, though."

"He's happy as a clam."

"It's nice he's found his niche."

"It's always nice to know what you want out of life," Mary agreed easily. "Even nicer if you can figure out a way to get it."

"You must have been proud of him, though. When he was working for the Whitfield Palace hotel chain."

Amanda had the feeling that if she'd made the lifestyle reversal Dane had chosen, her father would have accused her of dropping out. Amanda's father remained vigilant for any sign that his daughter might be inclined to waver from the straight-and-narrow path he'd chosen for her—the one that led directly to an executive suite in some Fortune 500 company.

Never having been granted a son, Gordon Stockenberg had put all his paternal dreams and ambitions onto Amanda's shoulders. And except for that one summer, when she'd fallen in love with a boy her father had found totally unsuitable, she'd never let him down.

"I'd be proud of Dane whatever he chose to do." Mary piled the mushrooms onto a platter and moved on to dicing shallots. "But I have to admit that I'm pleased he's come home. Not only do I enjoy working with my son, it was obvious that once he became a vice president at Whitfield, he began feeling horribly constrained, and—"

"Vice president?"

"Why, yes." Mary looked up, seeming surprised that Amanda hadn't known.

"Dane was actually a vice president at Whitfield Palace hotels?" After last night's conversation, she'd realized he'd been important. But a vice president?

"He was in charge of international operations," Mary divulged. "The youngest vice president in the history of the hotel chain. He was only in the job for a year, and Mrs. Deveraux—she's the CEO of Whitfield—wanted him to stay on, especially now that she and her husband have begun a family and she's cut back on her own travel, but Dane has always known his own mind."

Once again Amanda thought of her boastful words about her window office and her lovely, expensive Italian-leather chair. Unfortunately, as much as she wanted to be irritated at Dane for having let her make a fool of herself, she reluctantly admitted that it hadn't really been his doing. She'd been so eager to prove how important she was....

A vice president. Of International Operations, no less. She groaned.

"Are you all right, dear?"

Amanda blinked. "Fine," she said, not quite truthfully. She took out her roll of antacids. Then, on second thought, she shook two aspirin from the bottle she kept in her purse.

Mary was looking at Amanda with concern as she handed Amanda a glass of water for the aspirin. "You look pale."

"I'm just a little tired." And confused. Not only did she not really know Dane, Amanda was beginning to wonder if she even knew herself.

"You're working very hard." The stainless-steel blade resumed flashing in the stuttering coastal sunlight coming in through the kitchen windows. "Dane told me how important this week is to you."

"It is." Amanda reminded herself exactly how important. Her entire career—her life—depended on the challenge week's being a success.

"He also told me you're very good at motivating people."

"Dane said that?" Praise from Dane Cutter shouldn't mean so much to her. It shouldn't. But, it did.

"I believe his exact words were, barring plague or pestilence, you'll have your promotion by the end of the week."

"I hope he's right."

Mary's smile was warm and generous. "Oh, Dane is always right about these things, Amanda. He's got a sixth sense for business and if he says you're going to win your creative director's slot, you can count on it happening."

It was what she wanted, damn it. What she'd worked for. So why, Amanda wondered as she left the kitchen to meet the members of the team, who were gathering in the parking lot for their afternoon bicycle race, did the idea leave her feeling strangely depressed?

The mountain bikes, like the team-challenge T-shirts and accompanying slickers, were red and blue.

"At least they look sturdy," Julian decided, studying the knobby fat tires.

"And heavy," Kelli said skeptically. "What's wrong with a nice, lightweight ten-speed?"

"Kelli has a point, Amanda," Peter interjected with what Amanda supposed was another attempt to make points with the sexy public-relations manager. "Why can't we just use racing bikes?"

"In the first place, you're not going to be sticking to the asphalt." Amanda handed everyone a laminated map of the course. "You'll need a sturdy bike for all the detours over gravel and dirt roads and creekbeds."

When that description earned a collective groan, Amanda took some encouragement from the fact that everyone seemed to share the same reservations. That, in its own way, was progress.

"Think of it as touring new ground," she suggested optimistically.

"That's definitely pushing a metaphor," Marvin complained over the laughter of the others.

Amanda's grin was quick and confident. "That's why I leave the copywriting to you."

She went on to explain the rules, which involved the riders leaving the parking lot at timed intervals, following the trail marked on the maps, then returning to the inn, hopefully in time for dinner. She would ride along as an observer and, if necessary, a referee. Once everyone was back, the collective times would determine which team had won.

"Any questions?" she asked when she was finished.

"I have one." Laura was adjusting the chin strap on her helmet with the air of someone who'd done this before. "Since it's obvious you can't be at every checkpoint, how are you going to ensure some people don't skip a segment?"

"Are you accusing people of not being honest?" Don complained.

"You're in advertising marketing, Don," Luke reminded. "I'd say a lack of forthrightness goes with the territory."

When everyone laughed, Amanda experienced another surge of optimism. Only two days ago, such a comment would have started a fight. Things were definitely looking up!

"Not that I don't trust everyone implicitly," Amanda said, "but now that you bring it up, there will be referees at all the checkpoints to stamp the appropriate section of your map." She had arranged with Dane to hire some of his off-duty employees.

"Is Mindy going to be one of those referees?" Peter asked hopefully.

"Mindy Taylor will be working the second segment," Amanda revealed.

"There go our chances," Don grumbled as he pulled on a pair of leather bicycle gloves. "Because with Miss America working the second checkpoint, Peter will never get to number three."

There was more laughter, and some good-natured teasing, along with the expected complaints from Peter, which only earned him hoots from his fellow teammates and the opposing team.

"Well," Amanda said, glancing down at her stopwatch, "if everyone's ready, we'll send off the first team."

"Oh, look!" Kelli exclaimed, pointing toward the inn. "Here comes Dane." Amanda found the public-relations manager's smile far too welcoming. "Hey, coach," Kelli called out, "any last advice?"

Since the course was easily followed and everyone knew how to ride a bike, Amanda had decided it wouldn't be necessary for Dane to come along. He was, however, scheduled to lead the upcoming backpacking trip and rock-climbing expedition.

"Just one." He rocked back on his heels and observed the assembled teams with mild amusement. "Watch out for logging trucks."

Marvin frowned. "I didn't realize they were logging this part of the coast."

"Well, they are. And those drivers aren't accustomed to sharing the back roads. Stay out of their way. Or die."

With that ominous warning ringing in everyone's ears, the teams pedaled out of the parking lot.

She was going to die. As she braked to a wobbly stop outside the inn, Amanda wondered if she'd ever recover the feeling in her bottom again.

"You made good time," Dane greeted her. He was up on a ladder, painting the rain gutter. He was wearing cutoff jeans and a white T-shirt. "Considering all the extra miles Kelli said you put in riding back and forth between teams."

"You'd think adults could conduct a simple bike race without trying to sabotage one another, wouldn't you?" Amanda frowned as she remembered the fishing line members of the blue team had strung across a particularly rocky stretch of path.

"You wanted them working together," he reminded her. "Sounds as if that's exactly what they were doing."

"I wanted them to cooperate," she muttered. "Not reenact Desert Storm." The red team had, naturally, sought to retaliate. "Thanks for the suggestion to take along the extra tire tubes. I still haven't figured out where they got those carpet tacks."

"I've got a pretty good guess." Dane had found evidence of someone having been in the workshop.

"Well, other than a few bumps and bruises, at least no one got hurt," Amanda said with a long-suffering sigh. "You were also right about those trucks, by the way. They're scary."

"Like bull elk on amphetamines." As he watched her gingerly climb off the bike, Dane wiped his hand over his mouth to hide his smile. "You look a little stiff."

How was it that she had no feeling at all in her rear, yet her legs were aching all the way to the bone? "That's an understatement." She glared at the now muddy mountain bike that had seemed such a nifty idea when the original challenge coach, who'd conveniently managed to avoid taking part in the week's activities, had first suggested it. "I swear that seat was invented by the Marquis de Sade."

"If you're sore, I can give you a massage. To get the kinks out," he said innocently when she shot him a stern look. "I've got pretty good hands. If I do say so myself." He flexed his fingers as he grinned down at her from his perch on the ladder.

Amanda had firsthand knowledge of exactly how good those hands were. Which was why there was absolutely no way she was going to take Dane up on his offer.

"Thanks, anyway. But I think I'll just take a long soak in a hot bath." Suddenly uncomfortably aware of how dirty and sweaty she must look, she was anxious to escape.

"Suit yourself." He flashed her another of those devastating smiles, then returned to his painting.

She was halfway up the steps when he called out to her.

"Yes?" She half turned and looked up at him. He was so damn sexy, with that tight, sweat-stained T-shirt and those snug jeans that cupped his sex so enticingly. He reminded her of the young Brando, in *A Streetcar Named Desire*. Rough and dangerous and ready as hell.

It crossed Amanda's mind that if Eve Deveraux had ever seen her vice president of international operations looking like this, she probably would have offered to triple his salary, just to keep him around to improve the scenery.

"If you change your mind, just let me know."

"Thank you." Her answering smile was falsely sweet. "But I believe that just might be pushing your hospitality to the limit."

"We aim to please." The devilish grin brightened his dark eyes. "Service With a Smile. That's our motto here at Smugglers' Inn."

She might be confused. But she wasn't foolish enough to even attempt to touch that line. Without another word, she escaped into the inn.

Enjoying the mental image of Amanda up to her neck in frothy white bubbles, Dane was whistling as he returned to work.

Chapter 9

After a long soak and a brief nap, Amanda felt like a new woman. During her time in the claw-footed bath-tub, she'd made an important decision. The next time Dane tried to seduce her, she was going to let him.

Having already spent too much time thinking of him, she'd come to the logical conclusion that part of her problem regarding Dane was the fact that they'd never made love.

Tonight, Amanda vowed as she rose from the per-fumed water, toweled off and began dusting fragrant talcum powder over every inch of her body, she was going to remedy that nagging problem.

She dressed carefully for dinner, in an outfit she'd providentially thrown into her suitcase at the last min-ute—a broomstick gauze skirt that flowed in swirls the color of a summer sunrise, and a matching scoop-necked top with crisscross lacing up the front. The bright hues brought out the heightened color in her cheeks.

She paused in front of the mirror, studying her reflection judiciously. Her freshly washed hair curved beneath her chin, framing her face in gleaming dark gold. Anticipation brightened her eyes, while the fullness of the skirt and blouse suggested more curves than she currently possessed.

"You'll do," she decided with a slow smile ripe with feminine intent. Spritzing herself one last time with scent, she left the tower room, heading downstairs to dinner. And to Dane.

He wasn't there! Amanda forced a smile and attempted to make small talk with the other people at her table as the evening droned on and on. On some level she noted that her meal of shrimp Provençal and tomato, mushroom and basil salad was excellent, but the food Mary Cutter had obviously labored over tasted like ashes in Amanda's mouth.

She wasn't the only person inwardly seething. Greg, who was seated at the neighboring table, did not even bother to conceal his irritation at the fact that Kelli was also absent from the dining room. He snapped at his table companions, glared at the room in general and ordered one Scotch after another.

Finally, obviously fed up, Miss Minnie marched up to the table and insisted that he display more consideration.

"This is, after all," she declared with all the haughty bearing of a forceful woman accustomed to controlling those around her, "supposed to be a civilized dining room."

Greg looked up at her through increasingly bleary

eyes. "In case it's escaped your notice," he said, the alcohol causing him to slur his words, "the firm of Janzen, Lawton and Young happens to have booked every room in this inn, with the exception of the suite occupied by you and your sister."

His jaw was jutted out; his red-veined eyes were narrowed and unpleasant. "That being the case, if you have a problem with my drinking, I would suggest that you just hustle your skinny rear end upstairs and order room service."

A hush fell over the dining room. Shocked to silence for what Amanda suspected was the first time in her life, Miss Minnie clasped a blue-veined hand to the front of her dove-brown silk dress.

Out of the corner of her eye, Amanda saw Mary emerging from the kitchen at the same time Mindy was entering from the lobby. Feeling somehow to blame—she was responsible for the horrid man having come to Smugglers' Inn, after all—Amanda jumped to her feet and went over to Greg's table.

"You owe Miss Minnie an apology, Greg," she said sternly. She bestowed her most conciliatory smile upon the elderly woman. "It's been a long day. Everyone's tired. And out of sorts."

"Don't apologize for me, Amanda," Greg growled, continuing to eye the elderly woman with overt contempt.

"But—"

"He's right," Miss Minnie agreed in a voice that could have slashed through steel. "There's no point in trying to defend such uncouth behavior. It would be like putting a top hat and tails on an orangutan and attempting to teach him how to waltz." She lifted her white head and marched from the room.

A moment later, Miss Pearl, who'd been observing the altercation from across the room, hurried after her sister, pausing briefly to place a plump hand on Amanda's arm.

"Don't worry, dear," she said. "My sister actually enjoys these little tiffs." Dimples deepened in her pink cheeks. "She insists it keeps her blood flowing." With that encouragement ringing in Amanda's ears, she left the room.

Perhaps Miss Minnie found such altercations beneficial, but this one had sent Amanda's blood pressure soaring. "That was," she said, biting her words off one at a time, "unconscionable behavior."

"Don't take that holier-than-thou tone with me, Amanda," Greg warned. "Because, in case it's escaped that empty blond head of yours, I can fire you. Like that." He attempted to snap his fingers, but managed only a dull rubbing sound that still managed to get his point across. Loud and clear.

"You're representing the agency, Greg. It seems you could try not to be such a bastard. At least in public."

"It's not *me* you need to worry about, sweetheart," he drawled as he twisted his glass on the tablecloth. "We both know that what's got you so uptight tonight is that our host is off providing personal service to the missing member of our challenge team."

No. As furious as she'd been at Dane, Amanda couldn't believe that the reason he hadn't come to dinner was because he preferred being with Kelli Kyle. Her eyes unwillingly whipped over to Laura—who was Kelli's roommate. When Laura blushed and pretended a sudden interest in the tablecloth, Amanda realized that about this, at least, Greg wasn't lying.

"You're wrong," she managed to say with a composure she was a very long way from feeling. "But there's nothing so unusual about that, is there? Since I can't think of a single thing you've been right about since you arrived in Portland.

"You're stupid, Greg. And mean-spirited. Not to mention lazy. And one of these days, Ernst Janzen is going to realize that nepotism isn't worth letting some incompetent bully destroy his empire."

Amazingly, the knot in her stomach loosened. She might have lost her job, but she'd finally gotten out feelings she'd been keeping bottled up inside her for too long.

When the other diners in the room broke out in a thundering ovation, she realized she'd been speaking for everyone. Everyone except, perhaps, the missing Kelli.

"And now, if you'll excuse me," she said, lifting her head, "I've another matter to take care of."

As fate would have it, Amanda passed Kelli coming into the inn as she was coming out.

"Hi, Amanda," Kelli said with her trademark perky smile. "Isn't it a lovely evening?"

Amanda was not inclined to bother with pleasantries. "Where's Dane?"

The smile faded and for a suspended moment, Kelli appeared tempted to lie. Then, with a shrug of her shoulders, she said, "On the beach."

Amanda nodded. "Thank you."

"Anytime."

Intent on getting some answers from Dane, as she

marched away, Amanda didn't notice Kelli's intense, thoughtful look.

She found Dane at the cave. The place where those long-ago pirates had allegedly stashed their treasure. The place she'd always thought of as *their secret sanctuary*. He'd lit a fire and was sitting on a piece of driftwood beside it, drinking a beer. The lipstick on the mouth of the empty bottle beside the log told its own story.

"Hello, contessa." His smile was as warm as any he'd ever shared with her. "I've been waiting for you."

As confused as Amanda had been about everything else, the one thing she'd thought she could believe for certain was that Dane was an honorable man. To discover otherwise was proving terribly painful.

"Why don't you tell that to someone stupid enough to believe you." She'd tried for frost and ended up with heat. Instead of ice coating her words, a hot temper made them tremble.

Amanda's bright gauze skirt was almost transparent in the firelight. Dane found it difficult to concentrate on her anger when his attention was drawn to her long, firm legs.

He slowly stood. "I think I'm missing something here."

"I can't imagine what." Amanda sent him a searing look. "Unless it's your scorecard." When he gave her another blank look, she twined her fingers together to keep from hitting him as she'd done the other night. "To keep track of all your women."

"What women? I don't—"

"Don't lie to me!" When he reached out for her, she gave him a shove. "I passed Kelli on the way down here." Her voice rose, shaky but determined. "She told me where to find you."

"I see." He nodded.

She'd hoped he would explain. On her way down the steps to the beach, she'd prayed that he would have some logical reason for being alone on a moonlit beach, or worse yet, in this cozy cave, with a woman like Kelli Kyle.

Her imagination had tossed up scenario after scenario—perhaps the faucet was dripping in Kelli's bathroom, or perhaps her shutters had banged during last night's brief storm. Perhaps...

Perhaps she'd decided that Dane would make a better lover than Greg Parsons.

Ignoring the anger that was surrounding Amanda like a force field, Dane put his hands on her shoulders. "I can explain."

"That's not necessary." She shrugged off his touch and turned away. "Since it's all perfectly clear. 'Service With a Smile.' Isn't that what you said?"

He spun her around. "Don't push it, Amanda."

Threats glittered in his dark gaze, frightening her. Thrilling her. "And don't *you* touch *me*."

She was still gorgeous. Still stubborn. And so damn wrong. "I'll touch you whenever I want."

"Not after you've been with her. But don't worry, Dane, I understand thoroughly. Kelli was just a fling for you. Like you would have been for me."

Temper, need, desire, surged through him. "You still know what buttons to push, don't you, sweetheart?"

Before she could answer, his head swooped down. Unlike the other times he'd kissed her over the past few days, this time Dane wasn't patient.

His mouth crushed hers with none of his usual tenderness. The hard, savage pressure of his lips and teeth grinding against hers was not a kiss at all, but a branding.

Fear battered, pleasure surged. She tried to shake her head, to deny both emotions, but his hand cupped the back of her head, holding her to the irresistible assault.

All the passions Amanda had suppressed, all the longings she'd locked away, burst free in a blazing explosion that turned her avid lips as hungry as his, had her tongue tangling with his, and had her grabbing handfuls of his silky hair as she gave herself up to the dark. To the heat. To Dane.

He pulled back, viewed himself in her passion-clouded eyes, then took her mouth again.

This time Amanda dived into the kiss, matching his speed, his power. She'd never known it was possible to feel so much from only a kiss. She'd never known it was possible to need so much from a man.

Having surrendered to the primitive urges coursing through her blood, she clung to Dane as she went under for the third time, dragging him down with her.

Somehow—later she would realize that she had no memory of it happening—they were on their knees on the blanket he'd laid on the sand when he'd first arrived at the cave, and his hand was beneath her skirt while she was fumbling desperately with the zipper at the front of his jeans.

Despite the danger of discovery—or perhaps, she would consider later, because of it—as those clever, wicked fingers slipped beneath the high-cut elastic leg of her panties, seeking out the moist warmth pooling between her legs, Amanda wanted Dane. Desperately.

There were no soft words. No tender touches. His hands were rough and greedy. And wonderful. As they moved over her body, creating enervating heat, Amanda gasped in painful pleasure, reveling in their strength, even as she demanded more.

A fever rose, rushing through her blood with a heat that had nothing to do with flames from the nearby fire. Her need was rich and ripe and deep, causing her to tear at his clothing as he was tearing at hers. She wanted— needed—the feel of flesh against flesh. Her skin was already hot and damp. And aching.

There was a wildness in Dane that thrilled her. A violence that staggered Amanda even as she strained for more. This was what she'd wanted. This mindless passion that she'd known, instinctively, only he could create.

She hadn't wanted gentle. Or tender. What she'd sought, what she'd been waiting for all of her life, was this heat. This madness. This glory.

Dane Cutter knew secrets—dark and dangerous secrets. Tonight, Amanda swore, he would teach them to her.

She was naked beneath him, her body bombarded by sensations her dazed mind could not fully comprehend. When his harshly curved lips closed over her breast, she locked her fists in his jet hair and pressed him even closer.

She said his name, over and over. Demands ripped from her throat. "Take me," she gasped, arching her hips upward as something dark and damning curled painfully inside her. "Now. Before I go mad."

She was wet and hot. Her flesh glowed in the flickering orange light from the flames. She looked utterly arousing.

She was not the only one about to go mad. His long fingers urgently stroked that aching, swollen bud between her quivering thighs with wicked expertise. Within seconds she was racked by a series of violent shudders that left her breathless.

Trembling, she stared up at Dane, momentarily stunned into silence, but before she could recover, his hands had grasped her hips, lifting her against his mouth. He feasted greedily on the still-tingling flesh. She was pulsing all over, inside and out. Amanda clung to Dane, unable to do anything else as he brought her to another hammering climax.

Her body was slick and pliant. His was furnace-hot. Dane wanted Amanda with a desperation like nothing he'd ever known. There was no thought of control now. For either of them.

Hunger had them rolling off the blanket and onto the sand, hands grasping, legs entwined, control abandoned. As the blood fired in his veins and hammered in his head, Dane covered her mouth with his and plunged into her, swallowing her ragged cry.

For a suspended moment as he encountered the unexpected barrier, Dane turned rigid, his burning mind struggling to make sense of the stunning message riveting upward from his pounding loins. But before he could fully decode it, a red haze moved over his eyes and he was moving against her, burying himself deep within her heat.

Sensations crashed into passion, passion into love, with each driving stroke. It was more than Amanda could have imagined, more than she'd ever dreamed.

The pain she'd expected never came. Instead, there was only glorious heat and dazzling pleasure.

She wrapped her legs around Dane's lean hips, pressed her mouth against his and hung on for dear life.

Just when she thought she couldn't take any more, he was flooding into her. Then entire worlds exploded.

Her mind was numb, her body spent. She lay in his arms, her hair splayed over his chest, her lips pressed over his heart, which seemed to be beating in rhythm with her own.

Although the stinging pulsating had begun to diminish, Amanda's entire body remained devastatingly sensitized. His hand, resting lightly at the base of her spine, seemed to be causing her body to glow from inside with a steady, radiant heat.

"Why the hell didn't you tell me?" Emotions churned uncomfortably inside Dane. Of all the stupid mistakes he'd made concerning this woman, this one definitely took the cake.

Amanda knew there was no point in pretending ignorance. She knew exactly what he was talking about. Besides, she'd made her decision and had no intention of apologizing for it.

"I didn't think it mattered." She closed her eyes and wished that this conversation could have waited until she was ready to return to the real world. And her real life.

"She didn't think it mattered." He grabbed hold of her hair—not gently—and lifted her composed gaze to his. "My God, Amanda, I practically raped you."

The fire was burning down, but there was still enough light for her to see the guilt in his dark eyes.

"It wasn't anything near rape." Amanda refused to

let Dane take away what he'd given her. Refused to let him reject what she'd given him.

"I sure as hell didn't use any finesse."

"I know." She stretched, enjoying the feel of his muscular legs against her thighs. "And it was wonderful." Actually, it was better than wonderful. But there were not enough words in all the world to describe what she was feeling.

"I was too damn rough." His dark eyes, already laced with chagrin, turned bleak with self-disgust. He frowned as he viewed the bruises already beginning to form on her arms, her hips, her thighs.

He brushed his knuckles over the tops of her breasts, which were also marred with angry smudges. "A woman's first time should be special." He touched the tip of his tongue to a nipple and heard her sigh.

"It *was* special." She lifted her hands to comb them through his hair, but a lovely lethargy had settled over her, infusing her limbs, and she dropped them back to her sides. "The most special thing that ever happened to me."

Her softly spoken words could not quite expunge his feelings of guilt. "It was too fast."

She laughed at that. The rich, satisfied sound of a woman in love. "Don't worry," she murmured against his neck as she pressed her body against his, rekindling cooling sparks. "We can do it again." She ran her tongue in a provocative swath down his neck. "And this time, you can take all night."

It was an offer he was not about to refuse. But having already screwed up what should have been one of the most memorable occasions of her life, Dane intended to do things right.

Wanting to set a more romantic stage—and on a practical level, wanting to wash off the sand he feared was embedded in every pore—he suggested moving to the house. To his room.

Amanda immediately agreed. "But I'd rather we make love in the tower room." Her smile, as she refastened the lacy bra he'd ripped off her, was as warm as any a woman had ever shared with any man. "It already has warm memories for me. I love the idea of making more."

He suddenly realized that he definitely wasn't pleased by the thought that she'd soon be leaving Satan's Cove. Whatever they did together tonight in the refurbished tower room would simply become another memory that she'd look back on with fondness over the coming years.

"Dane?" She witnessed the shadow moving across his eyes, watched his lips pull into a taut line. "Did I say something wrong? If I'm pushing you—"

"No." Her hands had begun to flutter like frightened birds. He caught them by the wrists, lifted them to his mouth and kissed them. "I want you, Amanda. I have from the moment you walked in the door. The problem is, I don't know what you want."

"I want you." The answer was echoed in the sweet warmth of her smile.

Dane couldn't help himself. He had to ask. "For how long?"

He could not have said anything worse. Amanda flinched inwardly even as she vowed not to let him see he'd scored such a direct hit. Obviously, she considered, now that he'd discovered she'd been a virgin, he was concerned she'd take what had happened between them, what was about to happen again, too seriously.

He'd already professed the belief that he should have done more—as if such a thing was humanly possible— to make her first lovemaking experience special. Now, it appeared he was afraid of becoming trapped in a permanent relationship he hadn't initially bargained for.

"If you're asking if I'm going to call my father and have him show up in Satan's Cove with a shotgun, you don't have to worry, Dane." She withdrew her hands from his and backed away, just a little.

As he watched her trying to relace the blouse he'd torn open, Dane experienced another pang of regret for having treated her so roughly.

"Just because I chose to make love with you, doesn't mean that I'm foolish enough to get all misty-eyed and start smelling orange blossoms and hearing Lohengrin." Her voice was remarkably calm, given the fact that she was trembling inside.

Once again he found himself missing the young girl who wanted nothing more from life than to spend her days and nights making babies with him. On the heels of that thought came another.

"Hell." This time he dragged both hands through his hair. "I didn't use anything."

He'd put the condoms in his pocket before coming down here, but then he'd gotten sidetracked by Kelli Kyle. Then, when Amanda had arrived, she'd been so busy spitting fire at him and had made him so angry, he'd completely forgotten about protection.

Smooth move, Cutter, he blasted himself. Even in his horny, hormone-driven teenage days, he'd never behaved so irresponsibly.

He looked so furious at himself, so frustrated by the situation, that Amanda wrapped her arms around his waist and pressed a brief kiss against his scowling mouth. "It's okay. It's a safe time of the month for me."

He'd heard that one before. "You know what they call people who use the rhythm method of family planning, don't you?"

She tilted her head back and looked up at him. "What?"

"Parents." He shook his head again, thinking that tonight was turning out to be just one disaster after another. "I'm sorry."

"I do wish you'd stop saying that," she said on a soft sigh. "Truly, Dane, it would take a miracle to get me pregnant tonight. And besides, it was only one time."

Dane wondered how many pregnant women had ended up reciting that old lament. "Things aren't the same as they were that summer, Amanda. There's a lot more to be worried about than pregnancy, as serious as that is."

His expression was so somber, Amanda almost laughed. "I don't need a lecture, Dane. I know the risks. But I also know you. And trust you."

"Sure. That's why you went ballistic when you realized I'd been drinking beer out here with Parsons's PR manager."

She'd been hoping that wouldn't come up. She still couldn't believe that she'd behaved like a teenager who'd just caught her date necking with another girl in the parking lot outside the senior prom.

"I *was* jealous," she admitted reluctantly.

"Join the club." He smiled and ran the back of his hand down the side of her face in a slow, tender sweep.

"When Jimmy was adjusting your bike pedals today, I just about saw red."

The Brad Pitt look-alike had been unusually attentive. At the time, Amanda had been flattered by his obvious admiration. Especially when the inn was overrun with young girls who could compete with Mindy for her Miss Satan's Cove crown.

"You're kidding."

"I'd already decided that if he touched your leg one more time, I'd fire him."

Amanda laughed at that, finding Dane's confession surprising and wonderful. "I suppose having a crush on an older woman is natural at nineteen."

"I wouldn't know." He gathered her close and kissed her smiling mouth. Lightly. Tenderly. Sweetly. As he'd planned to do all along. "When *I* was nineteen I was so bewitched by a sexy young siren, I wouldn't have thought of looking at anyone else."

It was exactly what she'd been hoping he'd say. Rising up on her toes, she twined her arms around his neck and clung.

"By the way," Dane said when the long, heartfelt kiss finally ended, "I had a life-insurance physical when I bought this place. You don't have to worry about any diseases."

"I wasn't worried." She watched him carefully put out the fire. When he crouched down, his jeans pulled tight against his thighs, making her all too aware of how wonderful those strong, firm legs had felt entwined with hers. "May I ask one question without sounding like a jealous bitch?"

"You could never sound like a bitch." Satisfied with his efforts, he stood again. "But shoot."

"What *was* Kelli doing down here?"

Dane shrugged. "Damned if I know." Seeing the disbelief on her face, he mistook it for another stab of feminine pique. "But if she was trying to lure me into her bed, she sure had a funny way of going about it."

"Oh?" Amanda believed that was exactly what Kelli had had in mind. Obviously she'd tired of Greg and was looking for some way to pass the time until returning to Portland. What better diversion than a man for whom the word *hunk* had been invented?

"She spent the entire time it took her to drink that beer talking about you," he revealed.

"Me?" That was a surprise. "Why on earth would she be interested in me? And what did she say?"

"It was more what she wanted me to say." He rubbed his chin thoughtfully. The conversation had seemed strange at the time. Looking back, it didn't make any more sense.

Unless, of course, Greg was using her to pump him to discover any flaws he might use against Amanda in their corporate warfare. "She asked a lot of questions about how I thought you were conducting the challenge week. If you'd mentioned your feelings about the value of the games. And whether or not you had discussed individual team members with me."

"That doesn't make any sense," Amanda mused. "Perhaps Greg's using her as a spy. To discover my weak points. And to find out if I'm trying to unseat him."

"That'd be my guess." Even as Dane agreed, he thought that although the explanation made sense, it hadn't seemed to fit Kelli Kyle's probing questions. Putting the nagging little problem away for now, he ran his hands through Amanda's tousled hair, dislodging silvery grains of sand.

"Are we through talking about business?"

"Absolutely." She beamed up at him. "Are you going to make love to me again?"

"Absolutely." And, after a long interlude spent beneath the shower in the bath adjoining the tower room, that's exactly what Dane did.

With a restraint that she never would have guessed possible, he kept the pace slow and this time when he took her, the ride was slow and long and heartbreakingly gentle. But no less dizzying.

Amanda had mistakenly believed that in that whirlwind mating in the cave, Dane had taught her everything he knew about love. Before the sun rose the following morning, she realized that she'd been wrong.

Her first heady experience, as dizzying as it had proved to be, had only been a prelude to the most glorious night any woman could have known.

A night she knew she would remember for the rest of her life.

Chapter 10

It was the coo of a pigeon sitting on her windowsill that woke her. Amanda stretched luxuriously and felt her lips curve into a slow, satisfied smile. For the first time in her life she knew exactly how Scarlett had felt the morning after Rhett had carried her up all those stairs.

Although she felt a pang of regret to find herself alone in bed, she decided that Dane must have slipped away to prevent gossip. Not that anyone would actually come all the way up here to the tower room. But it was thoughtful of him all the same.

It certainly wouldn't help matters to have the team members gossiping about her and Dane sleeping together. Not that either of them had gotten much sleep.

Besides, they both had a busy day today. Amanda was taking the team out on a deep-sea fishing trip, while Dane caught up on some much-needed grounds work.

She climbed out of the high log bed, aware of an unfamiliar stiffness. *To think you've wasted all that time on the stair stepper,* she scolded herself lightly. *When there are far better ways to work out.*

Perhaps, she considered with an inward grin, she should take Dane back to Portland with her at the end of the challenge. *Maybe, with the raise that comes with the creative director's slot, I could hire him to be my personal trainer.* And dear Lord, how *personal* he'd been!

Even as she found the idea more than a little appealing, it brought home, all too clearly, that their time together was coming to an end. If everything went according to plan, in two short days she'd be getting back on that bus and returning to Portland, where hopefully she'd move into Greg's office. While Dane would stay here, in Satan's Cove, living the bucolic life of a coastal innkeeper.

The thought of losing him, just when she'd found him again, was not a pleasant one. But unwilling to spoil what brief time they had left together, Amanda decided to take yet another page out of Scarlett O'Hara's story and think about that tomorrow.

She went into the adjoining bathroom, which was now overbrimming with memories of the long hot shower they'd taken together last night.

This morning, as she stood beneath the streaming water, she wondered if she'd ever be able to take a shower again without remembering the feel of Dane's strong, sure hands on her body, or the taste of his lips on hers, or the dazzling, dizzying way his mouth had felt when he'd knelt before her and treated her to lovemaking so sublime she'd actually wept.

When memories began flooding her mind and stimulating her body yet again, Amanda decided it was time to get to work. She turned off the water and slipped into the plush white robe—reminiscent of those favored by the Whitfield Palace hotels—hanging on the back of the door.

She found Dane pouring coffee. The scent of the rich dark brew, along with the aroma of Mary Cutter's freshly baked croissants, drew her like a magnet.

"You weren't kidding about special service."

"With a smile." He handed her a cup of steaming coffee, but before she could drink it, he bent his head and kissed her. "I knew it."

"What?" How was it that he could set her head spinning with a single kiss? Although she doubted they'd had more than three hours' sleep, Amanda had never felt more alive.

"That you'd be drop-dead gorgeous in the morning." His eyes took a slow tour of her, from her wet caramel-colored hair down to her toes, painted the soft pink of the inside of a seashell. Beads of water glistened on the flesh framed by the lapels of the bulky white robe. Dane was struck with an urge to lick them away.

"Flatterer." She laughed and dragged a hand through her damp hair. "And if you don't stop looking at me that way, I'll miss the fishing boat."

"If you've ever smelled a fishing boat, you'd know that would be no great loss." His own smile faded. "I've been thinking about the final challenge event."

Amanda nodded. It had been on her mind, as well. "The cliff climb."

"You realize there isn't much room for error in rock climbing."

"I know." She sat down at the skirted table and tore

off a piece of croissant. It was as flaky as expected, layered with the sweet taste of butter. "I trust you to keep things safe."

"I'm not in the survival business." He sat down as well, close enough that their knees were touching.

"I know that, too." After last night, Amanda couldn't find it in her to worry about anything. "But so far, you've done a wonderful job."

"You haven't been so bad, yourself, sweetheart. The way you've kept those team members from going for one another's throats would probably earn you a top-level job in the diplomatic corps, if you ever decide to give up advertising."

She wondered what he'd say if he knew she thought about exactly that on an almost daily basis lately. One of the things that had drawn her to advertising in the first place was that it was a service business, a business that prospered or failed on how it served its clients.

With all the recent megamergers, there seemed to be very little benefit to clients. In fact, more than one old-time C.C.C. client had proclaimed to be upset by a supposed conflict of interest now that the same huge agency was also handling their competitors' advertising.

"You know," she murmured, "a lot of people—mostly those in New York—used to consider C.C.C. old-fashioned. And perhaps it was." Which was, she'd often thought lately, one of the things she'd loved about Connally Creative Concepts. "But it was still an agency where clients' desires were catered to.

"These days, it seems that if you can't win new accounts by being creative, you buy them by gobbling up other, more innovative shops. But the forced combination inevitably fails to create a stronger agency."

"Instead of getting the best of both worlds, you get the worst of each," Dane guessed.

"Exactly." Amanda nodded. "Creativity becomes the last item on the agenda. And, although I hate to admit it, the advertising coming out of Janzen, Lawton and Young these days shows it. In the pursuit of profits, our clients have become an afterthought. They're getting lost in the shuffle."

"It's not just happening in advertising," Dane observed. "The workplace, in general, has become increasingly impersonal."

Which was another of the reasons he'd left the world of big business. Although, under Eve Whitfield Deveraux's guidance, the Whitfield Palace hotel chain routinely topped all the Best 100 Corporations to Work For lists, it was, and always would be, a profit-driven business.

"Every day I arrive at my office, hoping to rediscover the business I used to work in." Amanda had been so busy trying to keep things on an even keel at work, she hadn't realized exactly how much she'd missed the often-frantic, always-stimulating atmosphere of C.C.C. "But I can't. Because it's disappeared beneath a flood of memos and dress codes and constantly changing managerial guidelines."

She sighed again. "Would you mind if we tabled this discussion for some other time?" The depressing topic was threatening to cast a pall over her previously blissful mood.

"Sure." It was none of his business anyway, Dane told himself again. What Amanda chose to do with her life was no one's concern but her own. Knowing that he was utterly hooked on this woman who'd stolen his heart so long ago, Dane only wished that were true.

"May I ask you something?"

There was something in his low tone that set off warnings inside Amanda. She slowly lowered her cup to the flowered tablecloth. "Of course."

"Why me? And why now?"

Good question. She wondered what he'd say if she just said it right out: *Because I think—no, I know—that I love you.*

She put her cup down and stared out at the tall windows at the sea, which was draped in its usual silvery cloak of early morning mist.

"When I was a girl, I was a romantic."

"I remember." All too well.

"I believed that someday a handsome prince would come riding up on his white steed and carry me off to his palace, where we'd live happily ever after." Dane had had a Harley in those days instead of a white horse, but he'd fit the romantic fantasy as if it had been created with him in mind. He still did.

"Sounds nice," Dane agreed. "For a fairy tale." Speaking of fairy tales, he wondered what would happen if, now that he finally had her back again, he just kept Amanda locked away up here in the tower room, like Rapunzel.

"For a fairy tale," she agreed. "I also was brought up to believe that lovemaking was something to be saved for the man I married."

"A not-unreasonable expectation." Dane considered it ironic that he might have Gordon Stockenberg to thank for last night.

"No. But not entirely practical, either." She ran her

fingernail around the rim of the coffee cup, uncomfortable with this discussion. Although they'd been as intimate as two people could be, she was discovering that revealing the secrets of her heart was a great deal more difficult than revealing her body.

"If we'd made love that summer, I probably would have found it easier to have casual sex with guys I dated in college. Like so many of my friends.

"But you'd made such a big deal of it, I guess I wanted to wait until I met someone I could at least believe myself to be in love with as much as I'd been in love with you."

Which had never happened.

"Then, after I graduated, I was so busy concentrating on my work, that whenever I did meet a man who seemed like he might be a candidate, he'd usually get tired of waiting around and find some more willing woman."

"Or a less choosy one."

She smiled at that suggestion. "Anyway, after a time, sex just didn't seem that important anymore."

"You *have* been working too hard."

Amanda laughed even as she considered that now that she'd experienced Dane's magnificent lovemaking, sex had taken on an entirely new perspective.

"Anyway," she said with a shrug designed to conceal her tumultuous feelings, "perhaps it was old unresolved feelings reasserting themselves, but being back here again with you, making love to you, just felt so natural. So right."

"I know the feeling." He covered her free hand with his, lacing their fingers together. "You realize, of course, that you could have saved me a great many cold showers if you'd just admitted to wanting me that first night?"

The way his thumb was brushing tantalizingly against the palm of her hand was creating another slow burn deep inside Amanda. "Better late than never."

"Speaking of being late…" He lifted her hand to his lips and pressed a kiss against the skin his thumb had left tingling. "How much time do we have before you're due at the dock?"

She glanced over at the clock on the pine bedside table and sighed. "Not enough."

"I was afraid of that." He ran the back of his hand down her cheek. "How would you like to go into town with me tonight?"

The opportunity to be alone with Dane, away from the prying eyes of the others, sounded sublime. "I'd love to."

"Great. Davey Jones's Locker probably isn't what you're used to—I mean, the tablecloths are white butcher paper instead of damask and the wine list isn't anything to boast about. But the food's pretty good. And the lighting's dark enough that we can neck in the back booth between courses."

Her smile lit her face. "It sounds absolutely perfect."

Other than the fact that the sea had turned rough and choppy by midafternoon, and Dane had been right about the smell of fish permeating every inch of the chartered fishing boat, the derby turned out better than Amanda had honestly expected.

The teams seemed to be meshing more with each passing day, and at the same time the competitive viciousness displayed on the bike race had abated somewhat. At least, she considered, as the boat chugged its way into the Satan's Cove harbor, no one had thrown anyone overboard.

As team members stood in line to have their catch weighed and measured, Amanda noticed that Kelli was missing. She found her in the restroom of the charter office, splashing water on her face. Her complexion was as green as the linoleum floor.

"Whoever thought up this stupid challenge week should be keelhauled," the public-relations manager moaned.

Since the week had been Greg's idea, Amanda didn't answer. "I guess the Dramamine didn't work." Prepared for seasickness among the group, Amanda had given Kelli the tablets shortly after the boat left the dock, when it became obvious that the woman was not a natural-born sailor.

"Actually, it helped a lot with the seasickness. I think it was the smell of the fish that finally got to me." She pressed a hand against her stomach. "I'm never going to be able to eat salmon or calamari again."

"I'm sorry," Amanda said, realizing she actually meant it. "Is there anything I can do?"

"No." Kelli shook her head, then cringed, as if wishing she hadn't done so. "I just want to get back to the inn, go to bed, pull the covers over my head and if not die, at least sleep until morning."

"That sounds like a good idea. I'll ask Mary Cutter to fix a tray for you to eat in your room."

If possible, Kelli's complexion turned an even sicklier hue of green. "I don't think I could keep down a thing."

"You need something in your stomach. Just something light. Some crackers. And a little broth, perhaps."

Although obviously quite ill, Kelli managed a smile. "You know, everything I've been told about you suggests you're a dynamite advertising executive. Yet, sometimes, like during that stupid helicopter session, you seem to be a born diplomat."

"Thank you." Amanda was surprised to receive praise from someone so close to her nemesis.

"You don't have to thank me for telling the truth," Kelli said. "But there's another side to you, as well. A softer, nurturing side. So, what about children?"

The question had come from left field. "What about them?"

"Do you intend to have any?"

"I suppose. Someday."

"But not anytime soon?"

"Getting pregnant certainly isn't on this week's agenda," Amanda said honestly.

For some reason she could not discern, Kelli seemed to be mulling that over. Amanda waited patiently to see what the woman was up to.

"You don't like me much, do you?" Kelli asked finally.

"I don't really know you."

"True. And spoken like a true diplomat. By the way, Dane was a perfect gentleman last night."

"I can't imagine Dane being anything but a gentleman."

"What I mean is—"

"I know what you mean." Amanda didn't want to talk about Dane. Not with this woman.

Kelli reached into her canvas tote, pulled out a compact and began applying rose blush to her too-pale cheeks. "You love Dane, don't you?"

"I really don't believe my feelings are anyone's business but my own."

"Of course not," Kelli said quickly. A bit too quickly, Amanda thought. "I was just thinking that advertising is a very unstable business, and if you were to get involved with our sexy innkeeper, then have to move back East—"

"I doubt there's much possibility of that. Besides, as exciting as New York admittedly is, I'm comfortable where I am."

Kelli dropped the blush back into the bag and pulled out a black-and-gold lipstick case. "Even with Greg as creative director?"

She'd definitely hit the bull's-eye with that question.

"Greg Parsons isn't Patrick Connally," Amanda said truthfully. "And his management style is a great deal different." Sort of like the difference between Genghis Khan and Ghandi. "But, as we've pointed out over these past days, advertising is all about change."

"Yes, it is, isn't it?" Kelli looked at Amanda in the mirror. Her gaze was long and deep. Finally, she returned to her primping. After applying a fuchsia lipstick that added much-needed color to her lips, she said, "I suppose we may as well join the others."

As they left the restroom together, Amanda couldn't help thinking that their brief conversation wasn't exactly like two women sharing confidences. It had strangely seemed more like an interview. Deciding that she was reading too much into the incident, she began anticipating the evening ahead.

* * *

Amanda hadn't been so nervous since the summer of her fifteenth year. She bathed in scented water that left her skin as smooth as silk, brushed her newly washed hair until it shone like gold and applied her makeup with unusual care. Then she stood in front of the closet, wondering what she could wear for what was, essentially, her first real date with Dane.

She'd only brought one dress, and she'd already worn it last night. Besides, somehow, the front ties had gotten torn in their frantic struggle to undress. And although she had no doubt that the patrons of Davey Jones's Locker wouldn't complain about her showing up with the front of her blouse slit down to her navel, she figured such sexy attire would be overkill for Satan's Cove.

Although she'd been underage, hence too young to go into the bar/restaurant the last time she'd visited the coastal town, from the outside, the building definitely did not seem to be the kind of place where one dressed for dinner.

With that in mind, she finally decided on a pair of black jeans and a long-sleeved white blouse cut in the classic style of a man's shirt. Some gold studs at her ears, a gold watch, and a pair of black cowboy boots completed her ensemble.

"Well, you're not exactly Cinderella," she murmured, observing her reflection in the antique full-length mirror. "But you'll do."

So as not to encourage unwanted gossip, she'd agreed to meet Dane in the former carriage house that had been turned into a garage. As she entered the wooden building, his eyes darkened with masculine approval.

"You look absolutely gorgeous, contessa."

She was vastly relieved he hadn't seen her when she'd arrived from the boat, smelling of fish, her face pink from the sun, her nose peeling like an eleven-year-old tomboy's and her hair a wild tangle.

"I hope this is appropriate." She ran her hands down the front of her jeans. "I thought I'd leave my tiara at home tonight."

"All the better to mingle with your subjects," he agreed, thinking that although she'd cleaned up beautifully, he still kind of liked the way she'd looked when she'd returned from the fishing derby today.

He'd been in the garden, tying up his mother's prized tomato plants, when he'd seen her trying to sneak into the lodge, her complexion kissed by the sun and her tangled hair reminding him of the way it looked when she first woke up this morning after a night of passionate lovemaking.

"I got to thinking," he said, "that perhaps, after a day on a fishing boat, taking you out for seafood wasn't the best idea I've ever had."

"Don't worry about me." Her smile was quick and warm and reminded him of the one he'd fallen for when he was nineteen. "I've got a stomach like a rock. And I adore seafood."

"Terrific. Iris has a way with fried oysters you won't believe."

"I love fried oysters." She batted her lashes in the way Scarlett O'Hara had made famous and a fifteen-year-old girl had once perfected. "They're rumored to be an aphrodisiac, you know."

"So I've heard. But with you providing the inspiration, contessa, the last thing I need is an aphrodisiac."

He drew her into his arms and gave her a long deep

kiss that left her breathless. And even as he claimed her mouth with his, Dane knew that it was Amanda who was claiming him. Mind, heart and soul.

Satan's Cove was laid out in a crescent, following the curving shoreline. As Dane drove down the narrow main street, Amanda was surprised and pleased that the town hadn't changed during the decade she'd been away.

"It's as if it's frozen in time," she murmured as they drove past the cluster of buildings that billed themselves as the Sportsman's Lodge, and the white Cape Cod–style Gray Whale Mercantile. "Well, almost," she amended as she viewed a window sign on another building that advertised crystals and palm readings. A For Rent sign hung in a second-story window above the New Age shop.

"Nothing stays the same." Dane said what Amanda had already discovered the hard way at C.C.C. "But change has been slow to come to this part of the coast."

"I'm glad," she decided.

"Of course, there was a time when Satan's Cove was a boomtown. But that was before the fire."

"Fire?"

"Didn't you learn the town's history when you were here before?"

"I was a little preoccupied that summer," she reminded. "Trying to seduce the sexiest boy on the Pacific seaboard. Visiting dull old museums was not exactly high on my list of fun things to do."

Since he'd had far better places to escape with her than the town museum, Dane decided he was in no position to criticize.

"With the exception of Smugglers' Inn, which was located too far away, most of the town burned down in the early nineteen-thirties. Including the old Victorian whorehouse down by the docks. Well, needless to say, without that brothel, the fishermen all moved to Tillamook, Seaside and Astoria."

"Amazing what the loss of entrepreneurs can do to a local economy," she drawled sapiently. "So what happened? Didn't the women come back after the town was rebuilt?"

"By the time the city fathers got around to rebuilding in the mid-thirties, the prohibitionists had joined forces with some radical religious reformers who passed an ordinance forbidding the rebuilding of any houses of ill repute.

"After World War II, alcohol returned without a battle. And so did sex. But these days it's free." He flashed her a grin. "Or so I'm told."

Even though she knew their time was coming to an end, his flippant statement caused a stab of purely feminine jealousy. Amanda hated the idea of Dane making love to any other woman. But short of tying him up and taking him back to Portland with her, she couldn't think of a way to keep the man all to herself.

She was wondering about the logistics of maintaining a commuter relationship—after all, Portland was only a few hours' drive from Satan's Cove—when he pulled up in front of Davey Jones's Locker.

From the outside, the weathered, silvery gray building did not look at all promising. Once inside, however, after her eyes adjusted to the dim light, Amanda found it rustically appealing.

Fish, caught in local waters, had been mounted on the knotty-pine-paneled walls, yellow sawdust had been sprinkled over the plank floor and behind an L-shaped bar was a smoky mirror and rows of bottles.

"Dane!" A woman who seemed vaguely familiar, wearing a striped cotton-knit top and a pair of cuffed white shorts, stopped on her way by with a tray of pilsner glasses filled with draft beer. Her voluptuous breasts turned the red and white stripes into wavy lines. "I was wondering what it would take to get you away from that work in progress."

She flashed Dane a smile that belonged in a toothpaste commercial and her emerald eyes gleamed with a feminine welcome Amanda found far too sexy for comfort. Then her eyes skimmed over Amanda with unconcealed interest.

"Just grab any old table, you two," she said with an airy wave of her hand. "As soon as I deliver these, I'll come take your drink order."

With that, she was dashing across the room to where a group of men were playing a game of pool on a green-felt-topped table. The seductive movement of her hips in those tight white shorts was nothing short of riveting.

"Old friend?" Amanda asked as she slipped into a booth at the back of the room.

"Iris and I dated a bit in high school," Dane revealed easily. "And when I first returned to town. But nothing ever came of it. We decided not to risk a great friendship by introducing romance into the relationship."

Relief was instantaneous. "She really is stunning." Now that she knew the woman wasn't a threat, Amanda could afford to be generous.

"She is that," Dane agreed easily. "I've seen grown men walk into walls when Iris walks by. But, of course, that could be because they've had too much to drink."

Or it could be because the woman had a body any *Playboy* centerfold would envy. That idea brought up Dane's contention that she was too thin, which in turn had Amanda comparing herself with the voluptuous Iris, who was headed back their way, order pad in hand. The outcome wasn't even close.

"Hi," she greeted Amanda with a smile every bit as warm as the one she'd bestowed upon Dane. "It's good to see you again."

Amanda looked at the stunning redhead in confusion. "I'm sorry, but—"

"That's okay," Iris interrupted good-naturedly. "It's been a long time. I was waiting tables at Smugglers' Inn the summer you came for a vacation with your parents."

Memories flooded back. "Of course, I remember you." She also recalled, all too clearly, how jealous she'd been of the sexy redheaded waitress who spent far too much time in the kitchen with Dane. "How are you?"

"I'm doing okay. Actually, since I bought this place with the settlement money from my divorce, I'm doing great." She laughed, pushing back a froth of copper hair. "I think I've found my place, which is kind of amazing when you think how badly I wanted to escape this town back in my wild teenage days."

She grinned over at Dane. "Can you believe it, sugar? Here we are, two hotshot kids who couldn't wait to get out of Satan's Cove, back home again, happy as a pair of clams."

"Iris was making a pretty good living acting in Hollywood," Dane revealed.

"Really?" Although she'd grown up in Los Angeles, the only actors she'd ever met were all the wannabes waiting tables at her favorite restaurants. "That must have been exciting."

"In the beginning, I felt just like Buddy Ebsen. You know—" she elaborated at Amanda's confused look "—'The Beverly Hillbillies.' Movie stars, swimming pools... Lord, I was in hog heaven. I married the first guy I met when I got off the bus—an out-of-work actor. That lasted until I caught him rehearsing bedroom scenes with a waitress from Hamburger Hamlet. In our bed.

"My second marriage was to a director, who promised to make me a star. And I'll have to admit, he was doing his best to keep his promise, but I was getting tired of being the girl who was always murdered by some crazed psycho. There's only so much you can do creatively with a bloodcurdling scream.

"Besides, after a time, a girl gets a little tired of her husband wearing her underwear, if you know what I mean."

"I can see where that might be a bit disconcerting," Amanda agreed. She'd never met anyone as open and outgoing as Iris. She decided it was no wonder the woman had chosen to leave the art and artifice of Hollywood.

"After my second divorce, I got fed up with the entire Hollywood scene and realized, just like Dorothy, that there's no place like home."

"I just realized," Amanda said, "I've seen one of your films."

"You're kidding!"

"No. I went to a Halloween party a few years ago and the host screened *Nightstalker.*"

"You've got a good eye," Iris said. "I think I lasted about three scenes in that one."

"But they were pivotal," Amanda said earnestly, remembering how Iris's character—a hooker with a heart of gold—had grabbed her killer's mask off, enabling a street person rifling through a nearby Dumpster to get a glimpse of his scarred face. Which in turn, eventually resulted in the man's capture.

"I knew I liked you." Iris flashed a grin Dane's way. "If I were you, I'd try to hold on to this one."

"Thanks for the advice." Dane didn't add that that was exactly what he intended to do.

Chapter 11

Although the ambience was definitely not that of a five-star restaurant, and the food was not covered in velvety sauce or garnished with the trendy miniature vegetable-of-the-week, Amanda couldn't remember when she'd enjoyed a meal more.

There was one small glitch—when Julian, Marvin, and Luke Cahill had unexpectedly shown up. Fortunately, they appeared no more pleased to see her than she was to see them, and after a few stiltedly exchanged words, settled into a booth across the room.

Amanda wondered what the three were doing together. They could be plotting strategy, were it not for the fact that Marvin and Julian were on the blue team and Luke was on the red.

As much as she had riding on the corporate challenge, for this one night Amanda refused to think about her plan for success. After all, here she was, on her first real date with the man she'd always loved, and she wasn't going to spoil things trying to figure out this latest bit of corporate intrigue.

Instead, she took a sip of the house white wine, smiled enticingly over the heavy rim of the glass, and allowed herself to relax fully for the first time since arriving in Satan's Cove.

It was late when they returned to the inn. The moon and stars that had been so vivid the other night were hidden by a thick cloud of fog.

Someone—undoubtedly Mindy—had left a lamp in the downstairs reception parlor on; it glowed a warm welcome. The lights in the upstairs windows were off, revealing that the other guests had gone to bed.

Amanda didn't invite Dane up to her room. There was no need. Both of them knew how the night would end.

The elevator was cranking its way up to the third floor when Dane turned and took her in his arms. "I'd say tonight went pretty well," he murmured against her cheek. "For a first date."

"Better than well." She sighed her pleasure as she wrapped her arms around his waist. "I can't remember when I've enjoyed myself more."

"I'm glad." His lips skimmed up to create sparks at her temple. Dane didn't add that he'd worried she'd find Davey Jones's Locker too plebeian for her city tastes.

"And just think—" she leaned back a bit, sensual amusement gleaming in her eyes "—the night's still young."

Actually, that wasn't really the case. But Dane wasn't about to argue. After all the sleep he'd lost fixing up the inn, he wasn't about to complain about losing a bit more if it meant making love again to Amanda.

Lowering his head, he touched his lips to hers. At first briefly. Then, as he drew her closer, the kiss, while remaining tender, grew deeper. More intimate. More weakening.

Her limbs grew heavy, her head light. Amanda clung to him, wanting more. She'd never known an elevator ride to take so long.

The cage door finally opened. Hand in hand, they walked to the stairwell at the end of the hallway. It was like moving in a dream. A dream Amanda wished would never end.

They'd no sooner entered the tower room than Dane pulled her close and kissed her again. Not with the slow self-control of a man who knew how to draw out every last ounce of pleasure, but with the impatient demand of a lover who realized that this stolen time together was rapidly coming to an end.

With a strength and ease that once again bespoke the life of hard, physical work he'd chosen over shuffling papers, Dane scooped her up in his arms and carried her across the plank floor to the bed, which had been turned down during their absence. A mint, formed in the unmistakable shape of the inn, had been left on the pillow. Dane brushed it onto the floor with an impatient hand and began unbuttoning Amanda's blouse.

"No." It took an effort—her bones had turned to syrup—but she managed to lift her hands to his.

"No?" Disbelief sharpened his tone, darkened his eyes.

She laid a calming hand against his cheek and felt the tensed muscle beneath her fingertips. "It's my turn."

Unconsciously, she skimmed her tongue over her lips, enjoying the clinging taste of him. "To make love to you."

It was at that moment, when every atom in his body was aching to take Amanda—and take her now—that Dane realized he could deny this woman nothing.

His answering smile was slow and warm and devilishly sexy. "I'm all yours, contessa." He'd never, in all his twenty-nine years, spoken truer words.

He rolled over onto his back, spread out his arms and waited.

Never having undressed a man—last night's frantic coupling in the cave didn't really count, since Amanda still couldn't remember how they'd ended up naked—she was more than a little nervous. But, remembering how his bare torso had gleamed like bronze in the firelight, she decided to begin with his shirt.

With hands that were not as steady as she would have liked, she tackled the buttons one by one. She'd known he was strong—his chest was rock hard and wonderfully muscled. But it was his inner strength that continued to arouse her. Just as it was his loyalty, integrity and steely self-confidence that Amanda had fallen in love with.

When she reached his belt, she had two choices—to unfasten his jeans or tug the shirt free. Unreasonably drawn to the enticing swell beneath the crisp indigo denim of the jeans that had become his dress slacks when he'd changed lifestyles, Amanda stuck to her vow to keep things slow.

Dane was moderately disappointed when she took the easy way out and pulled his shirt free of his waistband—until she folded back the plaid cotton and pressed her silky lips against his bare chest. Her mouth felt like a hot brand against his flesh, burning her claim on him, just as she'd done so many years ago.

"I'm not very experienced." Her lips skimmed down the narrow arrowing of ebony chest hair, leaving sparks. "You'll have to tell me what you like." Retracing the trail her mouth had blazed, she flicked her tongue over a dark nipple. The wet heat caused a smoldering deep in his loins, which threatened to burst into a wildfire.

"That's a dandy start," he managed in a husky voice roughened with hunger.

"How about this?" She bestowed light, lazy kisses back down his chest, over his stomach.

"Even better," he groaned, when she dipped her tongue into his navel. His erection stirred, pushing painfully against the hard denim barrier. Realizing that it was important to cede control to Amanda, Dane ignored the ache and concentrated on the pleasure.

He could have cursed when she suddenly abandoned her seduction efforts. Relief flooded through him as he realized she was only stopping long enough to take off his shoes and socks.

For a woman who a little more than twenty-four hours ago had been a virgin, Amanda was definitely making up for lost time.

"I've never noticed a man's feet before," she murmured, running her hands over his. "Who could have guessed that a foot could be so sexy?"

He began to laugh at that outrageous idea, but when she touched her lips to his arch, lightning forked through him, turning the laugh into a choked sound of need.

"Lord, Amanda—" He reached for her, but she deftly avoided his hands.

She touched her mouth to his ankle, felt the thundering of his pulse and imagined she could taste the heat of his blood beneath her lips.

Realizing that she was on the verge of losing control of her emotions, Amanda shifted positions, to lie beside him. She returned her mouth to his face, kissing her way along his rigid jaw as her hands explored his torso, exploiting weaknesses he'd never known he possessed.

She left him long enough to light the fire he'd laid while she'd been out on the fishing boat. Then she proceeded to undress. She took as much time with her buttons as she had with his. By the time the white shirt finally fluttered to the floor, Dane had to press his lips together to keep his tongue from hanging out. As he observed her creamy breasts, unbearably enticing beneath the ivory lace bra, Dane discovered that ten years hadn't lessened his reaction to the sexy lingerie that had driven a sex-crazed nineteen-year-old to distraction.

She sat down in the wing chair beside the bed, stuck out a leg and invited him to pull off the glove-soft cowboy boot. Dane obliged her willingly. The left boot, then the right, dropped to the floor.

The jeans were even tougher to get off than the boots. "I should have thought this through better," she muttered as she tugged the black denim over her hips, irritated she'd lost the sensual rhythm she'd tried so hard to maintain.

"You certainly don't have to apologize, contessa." The sexy way she was wiggling her hips as she struggled to pull the tight jeans down her legs had Dane feeling as if he was about to explode. "Because it definitely works for me."

Their gazes touched. His eyes were dark with desire, but tinged with a tender amusement that eased her embarrassment.

She had to sit down in the chair again to drag the jeans over her feet, but then she was standing beside the bed, clad only in the lacy bra and panties. The soft shadow beneath the skimpy lace triangle between her thighs had Dane literally biting the inside of his cheek.

"Don't stop now."

Thrilled by the heat flashing in his midnight-dark eyes, along with the hunger in his ragged tone, Amanda leaned forward, unfastened the back hooks of the bra, then held it against her chest for a suspended moment. With her eyes still on his, she smiled seductively.

As she raised her hands to comb them through her hair in a languid gesture, the lace bra fell away.

Unbearably aroused, Dane drank in the sight of her creamy breasts. While not voluptuous, they were smooth and firm. He remembered, all too well, how perfectly they had fit in his hands. In his mouth.

Watching him watch her, Amanda experienced a rush of power—followed by a wave of weakness. Although far more nervous now than when she'd begun the impromptu striptease, Amanda was determined to see it through. She hooked her fingers in the low-cut waistband, drawing the lace over her hips and down her legs.

"You are absolutely gorgeous." The truth of his words was echoed in his rough voice.

"And you're overdressed." Returning to the bed, she knelt over him, struggling with his belt buckle for a few frustrating seconds that seemed like an eternity.

Success! She dragged his jeans and white cotton briefs down his legs, then kissed her way up again.

"You're killing me," he moaned as her hand encircled his erection.

"Now you know how I felt." His sex was smooth and hot. "Last night." She lowered her head, and her hair fell over his hips like a gleaming antique-gold curtain as she swirled her seductive tongue over him.

Curses, pleas, or promises, Dane wasn't sure which, were torn from his throat. For the first time in his life, he understood what it was to be completely vulnerable.

She touched. He burned.

She tasted. He ached.

Amanda straddled Dane, taking him deep inside her, imprisoning him willingly, wonderfully, in her warmth.

Their eyes locked, exchanging erotic messages, intimate promises that neither had dared put into words.

Then, because they could wait no longer, she began to move, quickly and agilely, rocking against him, driving him—driving herself—toward that final glorious crest.

Although their time together was drawing to an end, neither Amanda nor Dane brought up the subject of what would happen once the challenge week ended. By unspoken mutual agreement, they ignored the inevitable, intent on capturing whatever pleasure they could. Whenever they could.

On the overnight backpacking trip, while the others tossed and turned, unaccustomed to sleeping on the ground, Dane slipped into Amanda's tent. Their lovemaking, while necessarily silent, was even more thrilling because of the risk of discovery. And when she couldn't remain quiet at the shattering moment of climax, Dane covered her mouth with his, smothering her ecstatic cry.

Time passed as if on wings. On the day before she was scheduled to leave, while Dane was on the beach, preparing for the final event of the challenge week—the cliff climb—Amanda was alone in her room, her eyes swollen from the tears she'd shed after he'd left her bed.

The knock on her door had her wiping her damp cheeks. "Yes?"

"Amanda?" It was Kelli. "May I speak with you?"

Although they hadn't exchanged more than a few words since the fishing-boat incident, Amanda had gotten the impression that Kelli had been watching her every move, which had only increased her suspicions that the public-relations manager was spying for Greg.

"Just a minute." She ran into the adjoining bathroom, splashed some cold water on her face and pulled a brush through her hair. Then she opened the door.

"I'm sorry to bother you, but…" Kelli's voice drifted off as she observed Amanda's red-rimmed eyes. "Is something wrong?"

"No." When Kelli arched an eyebrow at the obvious lie, Amanda said, "It's personal."

Kelli's expression revealed understanding. "Love can be a real bitch, can't it?"

"Is it that obvious?" Amanda thought she and Dane had been so careful.

"Not to everyone," Kelli assured her.

Amanda decided it was time to get their cards on the table. "That's probably because not everyone has been watching me as closely as you."

If she'd expected Kelli to be embarrassed, Amanda would have been disappointed.

"That's true. But none of the others were sent here from Manhattan to evaluate the office."

"So you *are* a company spy?"

"*Spy* is such a negative word, don't you think?" Kelli suggested mildly. "I prefer to think of myself as a troubleshooter."

"Then you ought to shoot Greg Parsons," Amanda couldn't resist muttering.

"I've considered that. But my recommendation is going to be to fire him, instead."

"You're kidding!" Amanda could have been no more surprised than if Kelli had told her that Martians had just purchased the agency. "But he's family."

"Not for long," Kelli revealed. "It seems his wife has gotten tired of his philandering and is about to file for divorce. Obviously, Mr. Janzen isn't eager to employ the man who's broken his granddaughter's heart."

"It probably helps that he's incompetent to boot."

"That is a plus," Kelli agreed. "Which is, of course, where you come in." She paused a beat. For effect, Amanda thought. "You're the obvious choice to replace Greg as regional creative director."

"I'd hoped that was the case."

"I've already informed the partners that you'd be terrific at the job. But after receiving my daily emails, they've instructed me to offer you another position.

"You also know that all the recent mergers and downsizing has created a great deal of anxiety."

"Of course."

"Your Portland office is not unique. Janzen, Lawton and Young has been experiencing the same problems with all its new worldwide acquisitions. Which is why the partners have come up with the idea of creating the post of ombudsman. Which is where you come in.

"If you decide to accept the position, you'll achieve upper-management status and be required to travel between offices, creating the same good feeling and teamsmanship you've managed with this group."

"I'd rather have a root canal than repeat this challenge week."

Kelli grinned. "After that fishing trip, I'm in your corner on that one. Actually, the partners think the challenge week was overrated and undereffective. They believe that you could achieve the same results simply by visiting each office and employing your diplomatic skills to assure the employees that the mergers are in everyone's best interests."

"Even if I don't believe they are?" Amanda dared to ask.

"You're in advertising," Kelli reminded her with one of her perky trademark smiles. "Surely you're not averse to putting a positive spin on things. As you've done to get Marvin and Julian working together this week. You weren't lying when you stressed how important it was for the creative people and the accounting people to work together, were you?"

"Of course not, but—"

"Take some time to think it over," Kelli suggested. She went on to offer a salary that was more than double what Amanda was currently making. "Of course, you'll have a very generous expense account. Since image is important in advertising, all upper-level employees travel first class."

"It sounds tempting," Amanda admitted. She thought

about what her father would say when she called him
with the news.

"Believe me, you'll earn every penny."

"If I decide not to accept—"

"The job of creative director for the Northwest re-
gion is still yours."

"How much time do I have?"

"The partners would like your answer by the end of
next week. Sooner if possible."

With that, Kelli flashed another self-assured grin
and turned to leave. She was in the doorway when she
looked back. "I'd appreciate you not saying anything
about this to Greg."

"Of course not," Amanda murmured, still a bit
stunned by the out-of-the-blue offer. It was more than
she'd dared hope for. More than she'd dreamed of. So
why wasn't she ecstatic?

Chapter 12

The rock cliffs towered above the beach, looking cold and gray and forbidding.

"Who'll take care of my kids when I die?" Laura asked, her lack of enthusiasm obvious.

"No one's going to die," Dane assured her.

"This isn't fair to the women," Nadine complained. "I've seen rock climbers on the Discovery channel, and they're mostly all men."

"It's true that some climbing—like overhangs—requires strength in the shoulders and arms. But the fact that women aren't usually as strong in those areas isn't as important as you'd think," Dane said. "Since women tend to be smaller than men, they don't need as much strength. In fact, on the average, smaller people have a better strength-to-weight ratio, which is what's important in climbing."

"That's easy for you to say," Nadine muttered, casting a disparaging glance at Dane's muscular arms.

"It's true. Climbing is done primarily with the legs and feet because they're stronger. You can stand for hours at a time on your feet, but even the strongest man can only hang from his arms for a few minutes. The most essential element of climbing is balance."

While the group eyed the cliff with overt suspicion, Dane explained the basics of rock climbing. "One of the most important things to remember," he told the team members, "is that although the tendency is to look up for handholds, you should keep your hands below your shoulders and look down for footholds.

"Balance climbing, which is what you'll be doing, is like climbing stairs, although today you'll be climbing more sideways than vertically. You find a place for your foot, settle into a rest step, then make a shift of your hips and move on to the next step, always striving to keep your body poised over one foot.

"You can pause, or rest supported by both feet. You can also lift your body up with both legs, but never advance a foot to the next hold until you're in balance over the resting foot."

"What about ropes?" Laura, still unconvinced, asked.

"There's an old adage—'It's not the fall that hurts, it's the sudden stop.' If a rope stops a fall too fast, you can end up with a broken body. Or, a rope can pull loose and let you continue to fall. So, although you'll be equipped with a rope harness, since there are plenty of ledges and handholds, you shouldn't need to use the rope on this climb."

"We're not going to rappel?" Luke asked.

"Not today." Dane's assurance drew murmurs of relief.

After more explanation of terms and techniques, Dane climbed up the side of the cliff to set the woven climbing rope while the others watched.

"He makes it look so easy," Laura said.

"Kobe Bryant makes hoops look easy, too," Luke added. "But I wouldn't be stupid enough to play one-on-one with the guy."

"It's tricky," Kelli allowed. "But this cliff is only a grade one."

"What does that mean?" Julian asked. "And how do you know so much about it?"

"I've been climbing since my teens," she answered the second question first. "As for the rating, climbs are divided into grades from one to six. A grade one, like this one, will only have one to two pitches. A grade six, like some of the routes on El Capitan, can have more than thirty pitches."

"Terrific," Julian muttered. "The red team's brought in a ringer."

"I've already decided to take myself off the team," Kelli revealed, as Dane came back down the rocks with a deft skill that Amanda admired, even as her heart leaped to her throat.

"That's not necessary," Marvin said. "I've been climbing since college. And while I haven't done El Capitan, I think I can do my bit for the blue team."

With the competitive balance restored, the final challenge event began. To everyone's surprise, the climb went amazingly well. Even Laura, who'd sworn that she wouldn't be able to get past the first rest stop, managed to make her way to the top, then back down again.

The final participant was Julian, who was making record time when, eager to reach the top of the cliff, he leaned too far into the slope, pushing his feet outward, causing him to slip. Sensing he was about to slide, he grabbed for a handhold, causing a small avalanche of pebbles.

Everyone watching from below breathed a united sigh of relief as the rope looped around his waist held.

"There's a ledge six inches to the left of you," Dane called out. "Just stay calm. You can reach it with no trouble."

Dangling against the cliff, Julian managed to edge his left foot sideways until it was safely on the ledge.

"That's it," Dane said encouragingly. "Now, put the heel of your right foot on that outcropping just below where it is now."

Although he was trembling visibly, Julian did as instructed.

"It's going to be okay," Dane assured Amanda and the others. "He's not in any danger." He lifted his cupped hands again. "Now, all you have to do is come back down the way you went up and you're home free."

Later, Amanda would decide that the next moment was when Julian made his mistake. He looked down, viewed the gathered team members far below, realized exactly how close he'd come to falling—and literally froze.

Dane was the first to realize what had happened. He cursed.

"I'd better go bring him down."

"No," Marvin said. "He's my teammate. I can talk him the rest of the way up."

"It's just a game," Amanda protested. "Winning isn't worth risking anyone's life."

"I know that." Marvin gently pried her fingers off his arm. "But there's more at risk than winning, Amanda. Julian will never forgive himself if he gives up now."

That said, he repeated the ascent path he'd worked out the first time he'd scaled the cliff. Within minutes he was perched on a rock horn beside the art director and although it wasn't possible to hear what they were saying, it was obvious the two men were engaged in serious conversation.

When Julian looked down again, Amanda drew in a sharp breath, afraid that he'd panic and lose his balance again. But instead, he turned his attention back to the rock wall and began slowly but surely moving upward, with Marvin right behind him, offering words of encouragement and pointing out possible paths.

When Julian reached the top of the cliff, cheers rang out from the team members below.

"Talk about teamwork," Kelli murmured to Amanda. "You've definitely pulled it off, Amanda. I hope you're seriously considering the partners' offer."

"How could I not?" Amanda answered.

As Julian and Marvin made their way back down the cliff, Dane came over to stand beside Amanda. "I couldn't help overhearing Kelli. Congratulations. You'll be great."

She looked up at him with confusion. "You know?"

It was Dane's turn to be confused. "Know what? I assumed you'd been offered Parsons's job."

"I was." She glanced around, not wanting the others to hear. "But it's turned out to be a bit more complicated."

She didn't want to discuss the amazing offer with

Dane until they were alone and she could attempt to discern how he felt about her possibly moving to New York.

If he asked her to stay, she would. Already having missed one opportunity with this man, she was not about to blow another.

Something was wrong. Dane felt it deep in his gut. He was going to lose her again.

The ride back to the inn was a boisterous one. Although the blue team had won the week's event on points, even their opponents were fired up by Julian and Marvin's cooperative team effort. By the time the van pulled into the parking lot of the inn, everyone had decided to go into Satan's Cove to celebrate having ended the week on such a high note.

"Are you sure you don't want to come with us?" Kelli asked an hour later, after the trophies had been handed out.

"It's been a long day," Amanda demurred. "I have a lot to think about. I think I'll just stay here."

"If you're sure."

"I'm sure."

Kelli glanced at Dane, who'd come into the room during the awards ceremony, then back at Amanda. "It's a fabulous offer, Amanda."

"I know."

"But then again, men like Dane Cutter don't come into a girl's life every day."

"I know that, too." She'd had two chances with Dane. How many more would she be lucky enough to be given?

"Well, I don't envy you your choice, but good luck." Kelli left the room to join the others, who were gathering in the reception foyer for their trip to town.

Unbearably nervous, Amanda stood rooted to the spot as Dane walked toward her.

"Your hands are cold," he said as he took both of them in his.

"It's the weather." Rain streaked down the windows, echoing her mood. "It'll be good when you get the new furnace installed."

"Yes." It wasn't the chill outside that had turned her fingers to ice, but a nervousness inside, Dane decided.

"Would you like to talk about it?" he asked quietly.

Amanda swallowed past the lump in her throat. "Actually," she said, her voice little more than a whisper, "I would. But first I'd like to make love with you."

Dane needed no second invitation.

Alone in the tower room, Dane and Amanda undressed each other slowly, drawing out this suspended time together with slow hands and tender touches.

The candles she'd lit when they'd first entered the room burned low as they moved together, flowing so effortlessly across the bed, they could have been making love in an enchanted world beneath the sea.

Whispered words of love mingled with the sound of rain falling on the slate roof; soft caresses grew more urgent, then turned gentle again as they moved from patience to urgency, returning to tenderness, before continuing on to madness. All night long.

The candles stuttered out. The rain stopped, the moon began to set. And despite their unspoken efforts to stop time, morning dawned. Gray and gloomy.

Amanda lay in Dane's arms, feeling more loved than she'd ever felt in her life. And more miserable.

"Are you ready to talk about it?" he asked quietly.

As his thumb brushed away the errant tear trailing down her cheek, she squeezed her eyes tight and helplessly shook her head.

"We have to, Amanda." His voice was as calm and self-controlled as it had been ten years ago, making her feel like a foolish, lovestruck fifteen-year-old all over again. "We can't put it off any longer."

"I know."

With a long sigh, she hitched herself up in bed. Dane wondered if she realized how beautiful she was, with her face, flushed from making love, framed by that tousled dark gold cloud of hair. Her eyes were wide and laced with more pain than a woman who'd spent the night making mad, passionate love should be feeling. She dragged her hand through her hair. "I don't know where to start."

He sat up as well and put his arm around her shoulder. "How about at the beginning?"

This wasn't going to be good. Dane's mind whirled with possibilities, trying to get ahead of the conversation so he could supply an argument to any reason she might try to give for leaving.

"Kelli *is* a company spy. But not for Greg."

"She works for the home office." All the pieces of the puzzle that had been nagging at him finally fell into place.

"Yes."

"When did you find out?"

"Right before the rock climb. She told me Greg was going to be fired. And that his job was mine, if I wanted it."

"Which you do." Dane decided there were worse

things than commuter marriages. Portland wasn't that far away, and if her job made her happy…

"I thought I did." Her fingers, plucking at the sheets, revealed her nervousness. Dane waited.

"She offered me another position."

"Oh?" His heart pounded hard and painfully in his chest. "In Portland?"

Her words clogged her throat. Amanda could only shake her head.

"The job's in Manhattan," Dane guessed flatly.

"Yes." She shook her head again. "No."

"Which is it? Yes? Or no?" An impatience he'd tried to control made his tone gruff.

"My office would be in Manhattan. But I'd be traveling most of the time. In an ombudsman position."

It made sense. Having watched her in action, Dane knew she'd be a natural. And Lord knows, if the lack of morale the employees of the former C.C.C. agency had displayed when they'd first arrived at Smugglers' Inn was indicative of that of the international firm's other acquisitions, they were in desperate need of an effective ombudsman.

"That's quite an offer."

"Yes." Her voice lacked the enthusiasm he would have expected. "I think I could be good at it."

"I know you'd be great." It was, unfortunately, the absolute truth.

"And the salary and benefits are generous."

When she related them to Dane, he whistled. "That would definitely put you in the big leagues." Which was where her father had always intended her to be.

"I've dreamed of ending up on Madison Avenue,

of course," Amanda admitted. "But I never thought my chance would come this soon. My parents would probably be proud of me," she murmured, echoing his thoughts.

"They'd undoubtedly be proud of you whatever you did." It wasn't exactly the truth. But it should be.

Her crooked, wobbly smile revealed they were thinking the same thing.

"When do you have to give the partners your answer?"

"By the end of next week." *Tell me not to go,* she begged him silently.

Dane wanted to tell her to turn the offer down. He wanted to insist she stay here, with him, to make a home during the day and babies at night, as they'd planned so many years ago.

But, just as he'd had to do what was right for him, Dane knew that Amanda could do no less for herself.

"It's a terrific opportunity," he forced himself to say now. "I'm sure you'll make the right choice."

Because he feared he was going to cry, Dane drew her back into his arms, covered her mouth with his, and took her one last time with a power and a glory that left them both breathless.

Not wanting to watch Amanda walk out of his life for a second time, later that morning Dane went down to the beach, seeking peace.

In the distance, he heard the bus taking the corporate team—and Amanda—away.

He knew that Eve Deveraux would be happy to give him a job at the Park Avenue Whitfield Palace. But, although it would allow him to be with Amanda, Dane was honest enough with himself to admit that there was no way he could return to the rat race of the city.

During his last years at Whitfield, he'd become driven and impatient. He hadn't liked that hard-edged individual, his mother definitely hadn't, and he knew damn well that Amanda wouldn't, either. Which made his choice to go to Manhattan no choice at all.

He saw the words written in the sand from the top of the cliff, but the mist kept him from being able to read them.

As he climbed down the stone steps, the words became clearer.

Amanda loves Dane.

"I love you." The soft, familiar voice echoed her written words. Dane turned and saw Amanda standing there, looking like his every dream come true.

"We found something together the other night in the cave, Dane. Something that's far more valuable to me than any alleged pirate's treasure. I want to stay. Here, in Satan's Cove with you." Her heart was shining in her eyes. "If you'll have me."

As much as he wanted to shout out *Yes!,* Dane knew they'd never be happy if she felt her decision was a sacrifice.

"What about New York?"

"It's a great place to visit."

"But you wouldn't want to live there."

"Not on a bet."

He felt a rush of relieved breath leave his lungs. "What about the job of creative director?"

"You're not going to make this easy for me, are you?" she asked with a soft smile.

"I don't think a decision this important *should* be easy."

"True." She sighed, not having wanted to get into the logistics of her decision right now. "The problem is, if I move into Greg's job, I'd still be working for a huge agency. Which wasn't why I got into advertising in the first place.

"After you left the room this morning, I had some visitors. Marvin, Julian, and Luke. They've been as unhappy as I have with the profit craze that's taken over the industry lately. They also decided Satan's Cove was a perfect place to open a shop.

"They've arranged to lease the offices above the crystal store and asked me to join them." Her smile was beatific, reminding Dane of how she looked after they'd made love.

"As much as I love the idea of you staying here, with me," Dane said, "I have to point out there aren't many prospective accounts in Satan's Cove, sweetheart."

"They've already contacted former clients who are unhappy with the way things have been going, and want to sign on. A lot of our business can be done by phone and email, with the occasional trip into the city…. And speaking of local clients, I thought you might consider redoing your brochure."

"What's wrong with my brochure?"

"It's lovely. But it could use some fine-tuning. Why don't I give you a private presentation later?" She'd also come up with a nifty idea for Davey Jones's Locker she intended to run by Iris.

Putting advertising aside for now, Amanda twined her arms around Dane's neck and pressed her smiling lips to his.

As they sealed the deal with a kiss, the last of the fog burned off.

Amanda loves Dane.

The brilliant sun turned the love letter she'd written in the sand to a gleaming gold nearly as bright as Dane and Amanda's future.

* * * * *

Dear Reader,

I'm thrilled to have *Maid for the Millionaire* releasing this month. It's always fun to see a book get new life, but it's an honor to be in the same release as JoAnn Ross, one of my favorite authors. JoAnn's books are always populated by wonderful characters in a rich story of love and trouble.

Which makes one of her books perfect for pairing with *Maid for the Millionaire*. Cain and Liz had been married before and their romance ended badly. He was a workaholic who thought their lives were perfect. He didn't realize how lonely she was. Then a miscarriage showed her he would never be emotionally available, and she left.

Now, years later, his assistant inadvertently hires her company to clean his home, and their chance meeting causes him to see how much he hurt her. Determined to make up for the past, he never expects to fall in love again...and neither does she. But can they mend wounds so deep they cut to the very soul?

Healing wounds is also the theme of my upcoming release, *Daring to Trust the Boss*. Except Tucker Engle's wounds aren't caused by the heroine. A former foster child, Tucker doesn't believe he knows how to love, especially someone who's already been through one traumatic relationship with a man.

I hope you enjoy these stories. I'm so thrilled to be in a book with JoAnn...a talented writer and a truly wonderful person!

Susan Meier

MAID FOR THE MILLIONAIRE

Susan Meier

Special thanks to Denise Meyers,
who lets me talk out my ideas....

Chapter 1

Pink underwear?

Grimacing, Cain Nestor tossed his formerly white cotton briefs into the washing machine and slammed the door closed. Damn it! He should have stopped at the mall the night before and bought new ones, but it had been late when his private plane finally landed in Miami. Besides, back in Kansas he had done his own laundry plenty of times. He couldn't believe he'd forgotten so much in twelve years that he'd end up with pink underwear, but apparently he had.

Tightening the knot of the towel at his waist, he stormed out of the laundry room and into the kitchen just as the back door opened. From the pretty yellow ruffled apron that was the trademark of Happy Maids, he knew that his personal assistant, Ava, was one step ahead of him again. He'd been without a housekeeper since the beginning of February, three long weeks ago. Though Ava had interviewed, he'd found something wrong with every person she'd chosen—his maid lived in and a man couldn't be too careful about whom he let stay in his home—but the lack of clean underwear had clearly proven he'd hit a wall.

Leave it to his assistant to think of the stopgap measure. She'd hired a cleaning service.

Ready to make an apology for his appearance, Cain caught his once-a-week housekeeper's gaze and his heart froze in his chest. His breathing stopped. His thigh muscles turned to rubber.

"Liz?"

Though her long black hair had been pulled into a severe bun at her nape and she'd lost a few pounds in the three years since he'd seen her, he'd know those cat-like green eyes anywhere.

"Cain?"

A million questions danced through his head, but they were quickly replaced by recriminations. She'd quit a very good job in Philadelphia and moved with him to Miami when she'd married him. Now, she was a maid? Not even a permanently employed housekeeper. She was a fill-in. A stopgap measure.

And it was his fault.

He swallowed. "I don't know what to say."

Liz Harper blinked a few times, making sure her eyes were not deceiving her and she really was seeing her ex-husband standing wrapped in only a towel in the kitchen of the house that was her first assignment for the day. He hadn't changed a bit in three years. His onyx eyes still had the uncanny ability to make her feel he could see the whole way to her soul. He still wore his black hair short. And he still had incredible muscles that rippled when he moved. Broad shoulders. Defined pecs. And six-pack abs. All of which were on display at the moment.

She licked her suddenly dry lips. "You could start by saying, 'Excuse my nakedness. I'll just run upstairs and get a robe.'"

Remarkably, that made him laugh, and myriad memories assaulted her....

The day they'd met on the flight from Dallas to Philadelphia...

How they'd exchanged business cards and he'd called her cell phone even before she was out of the airport...

How they'd had dinner that night, entered into a long-distance relationship, made love for the first time on the beach just beyond his beautiful Miami home, and married on the spur of the moment in Las Vegas.

And now she was his housekeeper.

Could a woman fall any farther?

Worse, she wasn't in a position where she could turn down this job.

"Okay. I'll just—"

"Do you think—"

They stopped. The scent of his soap drifted to her and she realized he hadn't changed brands. More memories danced through her head. The warmth of his touch. The seriousness of his kiss.

She cleared her throat. "You first."

He shook his head. "No. Ladies first."

"Okay." She pulled in a breath. She didn't have to tell him her secrets. Wouldn't be so foolish again as to trust him with her dreams. If everything went well, she wouldn't even have to see him while she did her job. "Are you going to have a problem with this?"

He gripped his towel a little tighter. "You working for me or chatting about you working for me while I stand here just about naked?"

Her cheeks heated. The reminder that he was naked under one thin towel caused her blood to simmer with anticipation. For another two people that might be ridiculous three years after their divorce, but she and Cain had always had chemistry. Realistically, she knew it wouldn't simply disappear. After all, it had been strong enough to coax a normally sensible Pennsylvania girl to quit her dream job and follow him to Miami, and strong enough that a typically reclusive entrepreneur had opened up and let her into his life.

"Me working here for you until you hire a new maid." She motioned around the kitchen. The bronze and tan cut-glass backsplash accented tall cherrywood cabinets and bright stainless-steel appliances. "Is *that* going to be a problem?"

He glanced at the ceramic tile floor then back up at her. "I've gotta be honest, Liz. It does make me feel uncomfortable."

"Why? You're not supposed to be here when I am. In fact, I was told you're usually at the office by eight. It's a fluke that we've even run into each other. And I need this job!"

"Which is exactly why I feel bad."

That changed her blood from simmering with chemistry to boiling with fury. *"You feel sorry for me?"*

He winced. "Not sorry, per se—"

"Then sorry, per what?" But as the words tumbled out of her mouth she realized what was going on. Three steps got her to the big center island of his kitchen. "You think I fell apart when our marriage did and now I can only get a job as a maid?"

"Well—"

Three more steps had her standing in front of him. "Honey, I *own* this company. I am the original Happy Maid."

She was tall enough that she only had to tilt her head slightly to catch his gaze, but when she did she regretted it. His dark eyes told her their closeness had resurrected their chemistry for him, too. Heat and need tightened her insides. Her breathing stuttered out of her chest. The faint scent of soap she'd sniffed while at the door hit her full force bringing back wonderful, painful memories.

He stepped away and broke eye contact. "Nice try."

"Call your personal assistant." When her voice came out as a breathy whisper, Liz paused and gulped some air to strengthen it. "I'm the one she dealt with. I signed the contract."

"If you're the owner, why are *you* cleaning my house?" He stopped. His sharp black eyes narrowed. "You're spying."

"On you? Really? After three years?" She huffed out a sound of disgust and turned away, then whirled to face him again. "You have got to be the most vain man in the world! I was hired through your assistant. She didn't give me your name. She hired me to clean the house of the CEO of Cain Corporation. I never associated you with Cain Corporation. Last I heard your company name was Nestor Construction."

"Nestor Construction is a wholly owned subsidiary of Cain Corporation."

"Fantastic." She pivoted and walked back to the center island. "Here's the deal. I have six employees and enough work for seven. But I can't hire the people I need and work exclusively in the office until I get enough work for eight." She also wouldn't tell him that she was scrambling to employ every woman from A Friend Indeed, a charity that provided temporary housing for women who needed a second chance. He didn't understand charities. He most certainly didn't understand second chances.

"Then my profit margins will allow me to take a salary while I spend my days marketing the business and the expansions I have planned."

"Expansions?"

"I'm getting into gardening and pool cleaning." She combed her fingers through the loose hair that had escaped the knot at her nape. "Down the road. Right now, I'm on the cusp with the maid service. I seriously need thirty more clients."

He whistled.

"It's not such a stretch in a city like Miami!"

"I'm not whistling at the difficulty. I'm impressed. When did you get into this?"

She hesitated then wondered why. It shouldn't matter. "Three years ago."

"You decided to start a company after we divorced?"

She raised her chin. She would not allow him to make her feel bad for her choices. "No. I took a few cleaning jobs to support myself when I moved out and it sort of blossomed."

"I offered you alimony."

"I didn't want it." Squaring her shoulders, she caught his gaze. Mistake. She'd always imagined that if she ever saw him again, their conversation would focus on why she'd left him without a word of explanation. Instead the floodgates of their chemistry had been opened, and she'd bet her last cent neither one of them was thinking about their disagreements. The look in his dark eyes brought to mind memories of satin sheets and days spent in bed.

"In a year I had enough work for myself and another maid full-time. In six more months I had four employees. I stayed level like that until I hit a boom again and added two employees. That's when I realized I could turn this business into something great."

"Okay, then."

"Okay?"

"I get it. I know what it's like to have a big idea and want to succeed." He turned away. "And as you said, our paths won't cross."

"So this is really okay?"

"Yeah. It's okay." He faced her again with a wince. "You wouldn't happen to be doing laundry first, would you?"

"Why?"

"I sort of made fifty percent of my underwear pink."

She laughed, and visions of other times, other laughter, assailed her and she felt as if she were caught in a time warp. Their marriage had ended so badly she'd forgotten the good times and now suddenly here they were all at the forefront of her mind. But that was wrong. Six years and buckets of tears had passed since the "good times" that nudged them to get married the week they'd accompanied friends to Vegas for their elopement. Only a few weeks after their hasty wedding, those good times became few and far between. By the time she left him they were nonexistent.

And now she was his maid.

"Is the other fifty percent in a basket somewhere?"

"Yes." He hooked a thumb behind him. "Laundry room."

"Do you have about an hour's worth of work you can do while you wait?"

"Yes."

"And you'll go to your office or study or to your bedroom to do that."

"I have an office in the back."

"Great. I'll get on the laundry."

A little over an hour later, Cain pulled his Porsche into the parking space in front of the office building he owned. He jumped out, marched into the lobby and headed for the private elevator in the back. He rode it to the top floor, where it opened onto his huge office.

"Ava!"

He strode to his desk, dropping his briefcase on the small round conference table as he passed it. He'd managed not to think about Liz as she moved around his home, vacuuming while the washing machine ran, then the dryer. To her credit, she hadn't sauntered into his office and dumped a clean pair of tidy-whities on the document he was reviewing. She'd simply stepped into the room, announced that the laundry had been folded and now sat on his bed. But it was seeing the tidy stack on his black satin bedspread that caused unwanted emotions to tumble through him.

When they were married she'd insisted on doing laundry. She hadn't wanted a maid. She had stayed home and taken care of him.

As he'd stared at the neat pile, the years had slid

away. Feelings he'd managed to bury had risen up like lava. She'd adored him and he'd worshipped her. He hadn't slept with a woman before her or one since who had made him feel what Liz could. And now she was in his house again.

Which was wrong. Absolutely, totally and completely wrong. For a woman who'd adored him and a man who'd worshipped her, they'd hurt each other beyond belief in the last year of their marriage. She hadn't even left a note when she'd gone. Her attorney had contacted him. She hadn't wanted his money, hadn't wanted to say goodbye. She simply wanted to be away from him, and he had been relieved when she left. It was wrong— wrong, wrong, wrong—for them to even be in the same room! He couldn't believe he'd agreed to this, but being nearly naked had definitely thrown him off his game.

Underwear in his possession, he had dressed quickly, thinking he'd have to sneak out, wondering if it would be prudent to have Ava call her and ask her to assign another of her employees to his house. But as she promised, she was nowhere to be seen when he left.

"Just a bit curious, Ava," he said when his short, slightly chubby, fifty-something-assistant stepped into his office. "Why'd you choose Happy Maids?"

She didn't bat an eye. "They come highly recommended and they're taking new clients." She peered at him over the rim of her black frame glasses. "Do you know how hard it is to get a good maid in Miami?"

"Apparently very hard or I'd have one right now."

"I've been handling my end. It's you who—" Her face froze. "Oh." Her eyes squeezed shut. "You were there when the maid arrived, weren't you?"

"Naked, in a towel, coming out of my laundry room."

She pressed her hand to her chest. "I'm so sorry."

He studied her face for signs that she knew Liz was his ex-wife, but her blue eyes were as innocent as a kitten's.

"I should have realized that you'd sleep late after four days of traveling." She sank to the sofa just inside the door. "I'm sorry."

"It's okay."

"No. Seriously. I am sorry. I know how you hate dealing with people." She bounced off the sofa and scampered to the desk. "But let's not dwell on it. It's over and it will never happen again." Changing the subject, she pointed at the mail on his desk. "This stack is the mail from the week. This stack is the messages I pulled off voice mail for you. This stack is messages I took for you. People I talked to." She looked up and smiled. "And I'll call the maid and tell her not to come until after nine next week."

"She's fine." She was. Now that his emotions were under control again, logic had kicked in. The fact that she wasn't around when he left the house that morning proved she didn't want to see him any more than he wanted to see her. If there was one thing he knew about Liz, it was that she was honest. If she said he'd never see her, she'd do everything in her power to make it so. That, at least, hadn't changed. Though she was the one to leave, the disintegration of their marriage had been his fault. He didn't want to upset her over a non-problem. He'd upset her enough in one lifetime.

"No. No. Let me call," Ava chirped happily. "I know that you don't like to run into people. You don't like to deal with people at all. That's my job, remember?"

"I can handle one maid."

Her expression skewed into one of total confusion. "Really?"

The skepticism in her voice almost made him want to ask her why she'd question that. But she was right. Her job was to keep little things away from him. Not necessarily people, but nitpicky tasks. It was probably a mistake that she'd said people. But whatever the reason she'd said it, it was irrelevant.

"I won't have to deal with her. I'll be out of my house by seven-thirty next week. It won't be a problem."

"Okay." She nodded eagerly, then all but ran from the room.

As Cain sank into his office chair, he frowned, Ava's words ringing in his head. Had it been a mistake when she said she knew he didn't like dealing with people or was he really that hard to get along with?

Once again, irrelevant. He got along just fine with the people he needed to get along with.

He reached for the stack of mail. All of it had been opened by Ava and sorted according to which of his three companies it pertained to. He read documents, correspondence and bids for upcoming projects, until he came to an envelope that hadn't been opened.

He twisted it until he could read the return address and he understood why. It was from his parents. His birthday had come and gone that week. Of course, his parents hadn't forgotten. Probably his sister hadn't, either. But he had.

He grabbed his letter opener, slit the seal and pulled out four inches of bubble wrap that protected a framed picture. Unwinding the bubble wrap—his dad always went a bit overboard—he exposed the picture and went still.

The family photo.

He leaned back in his chair, rubbed his hand across his chin.

The sticky note attached to the frame said, *Thought you might like this for your desk. Happy birthday.*

He tried to simply put it back in the envelope, but couldn't. His eyes were drawn to the people posing so happily.

His parents were dressed in their Sunday best. His sister wore an outfit that looked like she'd gotten it from somebody's trash—and considering that she'd been sixteen at the time, he suspected she might have. Cain wore a suit as did his brother, Tom, his hand on Cain's shoulder.

"If you get into trouble," Tom had said a million times, "you call me first. Not Mom and Dad. I'll get you out of it, then we'll break the news to the wardens."

Cain sniffed a laugh. Tom had always called their parents the wardens. Or the guards. Their parents were incredibly kind, open-minded people, but Tom loved to make jokes. Play with words. He'd had the type of sense of humor that made him popular no matter where he went.

Cain returned the picture to its envelope. He knew what his dad was really saying when he suggested Cain put the picture on his desk. Six years had gone by. It was time to move on. To remember in a good way, not sadly, that his older brother, the kindest, funniest, smartest of the Nestors, had been killed three days before his own wedding, only three weeks after Cain and Liz had eloped.

But he wasn't ready.

He might never be.

Chapter 2

"Are you kidding me?" Carrying boxes of groceries up the walk to the entrance of one of the homes owned by A Friend Indeed, Ellie "Magic" Swanson turned to face Liz. Her amber-colored eyes were as round as two full moons.

"Nope. My first client of the day was my ex-husband."

She hadn't meant to tell Ellie about Cain, but it had slipped out, the way things always seemed to slip out with Ellie. She was a sweet, smart, eager twenty-two-year-old who had gotten involved with the wrong man and desperately needed a break in life. Liz had given her a job only to discover that it was Liz who benefited from the relationship more than Ellie did. Desperate for a second chance, Ellie had become an invaluable employee. Which is why Liz didn't merely provide cleaning services and grocery delivery services for A Friend Indeed, she also tried to give a job to every woman staying at the shelter homes who wanted one. She firmly believed in second chances.

Ellie shouldered open the back door, revealing the outdated but neat and clean kitchen. "How can that happen?"

"His assistant, Ava, hired us to clean the house of the CEO of Cain Corporation."

"And you didn't know your ex-husband was CEO of Cain Corporation?"

Liz set her box of groceries on the counter. "When we were married he only owned Nestor Construction. Apparently in three years he's branched out. Moved to a bigger house, too." In some ways it hurt that he'd sold the beach house they'd shared, but in others it didn't surprise her. He'd been so lost, so despondent after the death of his brother, that he'd thrown even more of himself into his work than before. The much larger house on the beach had probably been a reward for reaching a goal.

Ellie walked out of the pantry where she had begun storing canned goods, her beautiful face set in firm lines and her long blond curls bouncing. "I'll take his house next week."

"Are you kidding? He'll think I didn't come back because I was intimidated." She pointed her thumb at her chest. "I'm going. Besides, I have something else for you." She opened her shoulder-strap purse and rifled through its contents. After finding the employment application of a young woman, Rita, whom she'd interviewed the night before, she handed it to Ellie.

"What do you think?"

"Looks okay to me." She glanced up. "You checked her references?"

"Yes. But she's staying at one of our Friend Indeed houses. I thought you might know her."

Ellie shook her head. "No."

"Well, you'll be getting to know her next week. As soon as we're through here, we'll drop by the house she and her kids are using and tell her she's got the job and that she'll be working with you."

"You want me to train her?"

"My goal is to get myself out of the field and into the office permanently." Such as it was. The desk and chairs were secondhand. The air-conditioning rarely worked. The tile on the floor needed replacing. The only nice features of the crowded room were the bright yellow paint on the walls and the yellow-and-black area rug she'd found to cover most of the floor. But she was much better off than the women who came to A Friend Indeed, and working with them kept her grounded, appreciative of what she had, how far she'd come. It wasn't so long ago that her mom had run from her abusive father with her and her sisters. The second chance they'd found because of a shelter had changed the course of not just her mom's life, but also her life and her sisters'.

"To do that, I have to start teaching you to be my new second in command."

Pulling canned goods from the box on the counter, Ellie glanced up again.

Liz smiled. "The promotion comes with a raise."

Ellie's mouth fell open and she dropped the cans before racing to Liz to hug her. "I will do the best job of anybody you've ever seen!"

"I know you will."

"And seriously, I'll take your ex-husband's house."

"I'm fine. My husband wasn't abusive, remember? Simply distant and upset about his brother's death." She shrugged. "Besides, our paths won't cross. We'll be fine."

Liz reassured Ellie, but she wasn't a hundred percent certain it was true. Though she and Cain wouldn't run into each other, she'd be touching his things, seeing bits and pieces of his life, opening old wounds. But she needed the job. A recommendation from Cain or his assistant could go a long way to getting the additional clients she needed. She wanted to expand. She wanted to be able to employ every woman who needed a second chance. To do that, she had to get more business.

Liz and Ellie finished storing the groceries and made a quick sweep through the house to be sure it was clean. A new family would be arriving later that afternoon to spend a few weeks regrouping before they moved on to a new life.

Satisfied that the house was ready for its new occupants, Liz led Ellie through the garage to the Happy Maids vehicle. The walk through the downstairs to the garage reminded her that she was content, happy with her life. She was smarter now and more confident than she had been when she was married. Surely she could handle being on the periphery of Cain's life.

The following Friday morning when it was time to clean Cain's house again, she sat in the bright yellow Happy Maids car a few houses down from Cain's, telling herself it wouldn't matter what she found. If the cupboards were bare, she wouldn't worry about whether or not he was eating. She would assume he was dining out. If his mail sat unopened, she'd dust around it. Even if there were lace panties between the sheets, she would not care.

Fortified, she waited until he pulled his gorgeous black Porsche out of his driveway and headed in the other direction. But just as their encounter the week before had brought back memories of happier times, seeing him in the Porsche reminded her of their rides along the ocean. With the convertible top down. The wind whipping her hair in all directions.

She squeezed her eyes shut. Their marriage had been abysmal. He was a withdrawn workaholic. Though his brother's death had caused him to stop talking almost completely, she'd seen signs that Cain might not be as involved in their relationship as she was during their six-month courtship. Canceled plans. Meetings that were more important than weekends with her. It had been an impulsive, reckless decision to marry. When she was his girlfriend, he at least tried to make time for her when she visited from Philadelphia. When she became his wife, he didn't feel the need to do that and she'd been miserably alone. When they actually did have time together, he'd been antsy, obviously thinking about his company and the work he could be doing. He'd never even tried to squeeze her into his life. So why wasn't she remembering that?

Fortified again, she slid the Happy Maids car into his drive and entered his house. As she'd noticed the week before, there were no personal touches. No pictures. No awards. No memorabilia.

Glancing around, she realized how easy it would be to pretend it was the home of a stranger. Releasing any thought of Cain from her mind and focusing on doing the best possible job for her "client," she cleaned quickly and efficiently. When she was done, she locked up and left as if this job were any other.

The following week, she decided that her mistake the Friday before had been watching him leave for work, seeing him in "their" beautiful Porsche. So she shifted his house from the first on her list to the second, and knew he was already gone by the time she got there. As she punched that week's code into the alarm to disable it and unlocked the kitchen door, she once again blanked her mind of any thought of Cain, pretending this was the house of a stranger.

Tossing the first load of laundry into the washer, she thought she heard a noise. She stopped, listened, but didn't hear it again. She returned to the kitchen and didn't hear any more noise, but something felt off. She told herself she was imagining things, stacked dishes in the dishwasher and turned it on.

She spent the next hour cleaning the downstairs in between trips to the laundry room. When the laundry was folded, she walked up the cherrywood staircase to the second floor. Humming a bit, happy with how well she was managing to keep her focus off the house's owner, she shouldered open the master bedroom door and gasped.

Damn.

"Who is it?"

The scratchy voice that came from the bed didn't sound like Cain's at all. But even in the dim light of his room, she could see it was him.

"It's me. Liz. Cleaning your house."

"Liz?"

His weak voice panicked her and she set the stack of

clean laundry on the mirrored vanity and raced to the bed. His dark hair was soaked with sweat and spiked out in all directions. Black stubble covered his chin and cheeks.

"My *wife*, Liz?" he asked groggily.

"Ex-wife." She pressed her hand to his forehead. "You're burning up!"

Not waiting for a reply, she rushed into the master bathroom and searched through the drawers of the cherrywood vanity of the double sinks looking for something that might help him. Among the various toiletries, she eventually found some aspirin. She ran tap water into the glass and raced back to the bed.

Handing two aspirin and the water to him, she said, "Here."

He took the pills, but didn't say anything. As he passed the water glass back to her, he caught her gaze. His dark eyes were shiny from the effects of the fever, so she wasn't surprised when he lay down and immediately drifted off to sleep again.

She took the glass downstairs and put it in the sink. Telling herself to forget he was in the bedroom, she finished cleaning but couldn't leave in good conscience without checking up on him.

When she returned to the bedroom, Cain still slept soundly. She pressed her hand to his forehead again and frowned. Even after the aspirin, he was still burning up and he was so alone that it felt wrong to leave him. She could call his assistant but somehow that didn't seem right, either. An assistant shouldn't have to nurse him through the flu.

Technically an ex-wife shouldn't, either, but with his

family at least a thousand miles away in Kansas, she was the lesser of two evils.

Sort of.

Tiptoeing out of the room, she pulled her cell phone from her apron pocket and dialed Ellie.

"Hey, sweetie," Ellie greeted her, obviously having noted the caller ID.

"Hey, Ellie. Is Rita with you?"

"Sure is. Doing wonderfully I might add."

"That's good because I think I need to have her take over my jobs this afternoon."

"On her own?"

"Is that a problem?"

Ellie's voice turned unexpectedly professional. "No. She'll be great."

"Good."

"Um, boss, I know where you are, remember? Is there anything going on I should know about?"

"No. I'm fine. I just decided to take the afternoon off." Liz winced. She hadn't actually lied. She was taking time off; she simply wasn't going to do something fun as Ellie suspected.

"No kidding! That's great."

"Yeah, so I'll be out of reach for the rest of the day. Give the other girls a call and instruct them to call you, not me, if they have a problem."

"On it, boss!" Ellie said, then she laughed. "This is so exciting!"

Liz smiled, glad Ellie was enjoying her new responsibilities. "I'll see you tomorrow."

She closed her cell phone then ambled to the kitchen. She'd promised herself she wouldn't care if he had food or not, but with him as sick as he was, he had to at least have chicken broth and orange juice. Finding neither, she grabbed her purse and keys and headed to the grocery store where she purchased flu medicine, orange juice, chicken broth and a paperback book.

She put everything but the flu meds and book away, then she grabbed a clean glass from the cupboard and tiptoed upstairs again. He roused when she entered.

"Liz?"

"Yes. I have flu meds. You interested?"

"God, yes."

"Great. Sit up."

She poured one dose of the flu meds into the little plastic cup and held it out to him. He swallowed the thick syrup and handed the cup back before lying down again.

As she took the medicine to the bathroom, a bubble of fear rose up in her. Caring for him had the potential to go so wrong. Not because she worried that they'd get involved again. Tomorrow, she would forget all about this, if only because even pondering being involved with him would bring back painful memories.

But she knew Cain. He hated owing people, and if she stayed too long or did too much, he'd think he owed her. When he believed he owed somebody he could be like a dog with a bone. Being beholden made him feel weak. He was never weak. Which made her caring for him when he was sick a double threat. Not only had he been weak, but she'd seen him weak. He'd *have* to make this up to her.

Of course, with him as sick as he was, she could hope he wouldn't remember most of this in the morning.

Everything would be fine.

With a peek at the bed to be sure he was asleep, she

left the room and went to the Happy Maids car. In the trunk, she found a pair of sweatpants and a tank top. She changed out of her yellow maid uniform in one of the downstairs bathrooms then she took her book and a glass of orange juice into the study. Reclining on the sofa, she made herself comfortable to read.

She checked on him every hour or so. Finding him sleeping soundly every time, she slid out of the room and returned to the study. But just as she was pulling the door closed behind her on the fourth trip, he called out to her.

"Where are you going?"

She eased the door open again and walked over to the bed. "Cain? Are you okay?"

"I'm fine." He sat up. "Come back to bed."

Realizing the fever had him hallucinating or mixing up the past and present, she smiled and went into the bathroom to get him some water. She pressed the glass to his lips. "Sip."

As she held the glass to his mouth, he lifted his hand to the back of her thigh and possessively slid it up to her bottom.

Shock nearly caused her to spill water all over him. She hadn't even dated since she left him, and the feeling of a man's hand on her behind was equal parts startling and wonderful.

He smiled up at her. "I'm better."

Ignoring the enticing warmth spiraling through her, she tried to sound like an impartial nurse when she said, "You're hallucinating."

His hand lovingly roamed her bottom as his fever-glazed eyes gazed up at her longingly. "Please. I seriously feel better. Come back to bed."

His last words were a hoarse whisper that tiptoed into the silent room, the yearning in them like a living thing. She reminded herself that this wasn't Cain. The Cain she'd married was a cold, distant man. But a little part of her couldn't help admitting that this was the man she'd always wished he would be. Loving. Eager for her. Happy to be with her.

Which scared her more than the hand on her bottom. Wishing and hoping were what had gotten her into trouble in the first place—why she'd married him that impulsive day in Vegas. On that trip, he'd been so loving, so sweet, so happy that she'd stupidly believed that if they were married, if she didn't live a thousand miles away, they wouldn't have to spend the first day of each of their trips getting reacquainted. He'd be comfortable with her. Happy.

And for three weeks they had been. Then his brother had died, forcing him to help his dad run the family business in Kansas through e-mails and teleconference calls, as he also ran Nestor Construction. Their marriage had become one more thing in his life that he had to do. A burden to him.

That's what she had to remember. She'd become a burden to him.

She pulled away, straightening her shoulders. She wasn't anybody's burden. Not ever.

"Go back to sleep."

She returned to the study and her book, but realized that in her eagerness to get out of the room she'd forgotten to give him another dose of medicine. So she returned to his room and found him sleeping peacefully. Not wanting to disturb him, she took a seat on the chair by the window. The next time he stirred, she'd be there to give him the meds. She opened her book and began to read in the pale light of the lamp behind her.

Cain awakened from what had been the worst night of his life. Spasms of shivers had overtaken him in between bouts of heat so intense his pillow was wet with sweat. He'd thrown up. All his muscles ached. But that wasn't the half of it. He'd dreamed Liz had taken his temperature, given him medicine and walked him to and from the bathroom.

With a groan, he tossed off the covers and sat up in bed. He didn't want to remember the feeling of her palm on his forehead, the scent of her that lingered when she had hovered over him or the wave of longing that swept through him just imagining that she was back in his life. He pulled in a breath. How could he dream about a woman who'd left him without a word of explanation? A woman who was in his bed one day and gone without a word the next?

Because he'd been a fool. That's how. He'd lost her because he was always working, never had time for her, and grieving his brother. No matter how she'd left, he couldn't blame her. She was innocent of any wrongdoing…and that was why he still wanted her.

As his eyes adjusted, he noticed soft light spilling toward him from across the room. He must have left the bathroom light on. He looked to the left and saw Liz watching him from his reading chair.

He licked his dry lips. She was so beautiful. Silhouetted in the pale light from the bathroom, she looked ethereal. Her long black hair floated around her, accenting her smooth, perfect alabaster skin. She wore sweatpants and a tank top, and he realized she'd turned off the air-conditioning. Probably because of his shivering.

Still, her being in his bedroom didn't make sense. They'd divorced three years ago.

"Why are you here?" he demanded. "*How* are you here?"

"I'm your maid, remember?"

"My maid?"

"Your assistant hired Happy Maids to clean your house once a week—"

He closed his eyes and lay down again, as it all came back to him. "Yeah. I remember."

"You were pretty sick when I got here Friday morning."

"Friday morning?" He sat up again and then groaned when his stiff muscles protested. "What day is it?"

"Relax. It's early Saturday morning."

He peered over. "You've been here all night?"

She inclined her head. "You were very sick. I didn't feel comfortable leaving you."

He fell back to the pillow. "Honest Liz."

"That's why hundreds of people let me and my company into their homes every week to clean. My reputation precedes me."

He could hear the smile in her voice and fought a wave of nostalgia. "I guess thanks are in order."

"You're welcome."

"And I probably owe you an apology for fondling your butt."

"Oh, so you remember that?"

This time she laughed. The soft sound drifted to him, smoothed over him, made him long for everything he'd had and lost.

Which made him feel foolish, stupid, *weak*. She was gone. He had lost her. He could take total blame. But he refused to let any mistake make him weak.

"You know what? I appreciate all the help you've given me, but I think I can handle things from here on out."

"You're kicking me out?"

"I'm not kicking you out. I'm granting you a pardon. Consider this a get-out-of-jail-free card."

"Okay." She rose from the chair. Book under her arm, she headed for the door. But she stopped and glanced back at him. "You're sure?"

He'd expect nothing less from her than absolute self-lessness. Which made him feel like an absolute creep. He tried to cover that with a smile so she wouldn't even have a hint of how hard just seeing her was for him. "I'm positive. I feel terrific."

"Okay."

With that she opened the door and slipped out. When the door closed behind her, he hung his head. It had been an accident of fate that he'd gotten the flu the very day she was here to clean his house. But he wasn't an idiot. His reaction to her proved that having her back in his life—even as a temporary employee—wasn't going to work. The weeks it took Ava to find a permanent maid would be filled with a barrage of memories that would overwhelm him with intense sadness one minute and yearning for what might have been the next.

He should get rid of her. That's what his common sense was telling him to do. But in his heart he knew he owed her. For more than just staying with him while he was sick. He should have never talked her into marrying him.

Chapter 3

It was five o'clock when Liz finally fell into bed. Ellie called her around eleven, reminding her that they were taking Amanda Gray and her children, the family who had moved into the Friend Indeed house the weekend before, to the beach.

She slogged out from under the covers and woke herself up in the shower. She pulled a pair of shorts and a navy blue-and-white striped T-shirt over her white bikini, and drove to Amanda's temporary house. Ellie's little blue car was already in the driveway. She pushed out into the hot Miami day and walked around back to the kitchen door.

"Mrs. Harper!" Amanda's three-year-old daughter Joy bounced with happiness as Liz entered and she froze.

Liz had been part of the welcoming committee when

Amanda and her children had arrived at the house, but until this very second she hadn't made the connection that Joy was about the age her child would have been.

Her child.

Her heart splintered. She should have a child right now. But she didn't. She'd lost her baby. Lost her marriage. Lost everything in what seemed like the blink of an eye.

Swallowing hard, she got rid of the lump in her throat. The barrage of self-pity that assailed her wasn't just unexpected; it was unwanted. She knew spending so much time with Cain had caused her to make the connection between her baby and Joy. But that didn't mean she had to wallow in it. Her miscarriage had been three years ago. She'd had therapy. She might long for that child with every fiber of her being, but, out of necessity, she'd moved on.

Amanda, a tall redhead with big blue eyes, corrected her daughter. "It's Ms. Harper, not Mrs."

"That's okay," Liz said walking into the kitchen, knowing she had to push through this. If she was going to work in the same city as her ex, she might not be able to avoid him. She most definitely couldn't avoid all children the same age her child would have been. Being in contact with both might be a new phase of her recovery.

She could handle this. She *would* handle this.

"Smells great in here."

"I made French toast," Ellie said, standing at the stove. "Want some?"

"No. We're late." She peeked into the picnic basket she'd instructed Ellie to bring. "When we get to the beach, I'll just eat some of the fruit you packed."

"Okay." Ellie removed her apron and hung it in the pantry. "Then we're ready to go."

Amanda turned to the hall. "I'll get Billy."

Billy was a sixteen-year-old who deserted them the second the two cars they drove to the beach stopped in the public parking lot. Obviously expecting his desertion, Amanda waved at his back as he ran to a crowd of kids his own age playing volleyball.

Amanda, Ellie and Liz spent the next hours building a sand castle with Joy who was thrilled with all the attention. Around four o'clock, Ellie and Amanda left the sand to set up a picnic under their umbrella.

Joy smiled up at Liz. "Do you like sand?"

She gazed down at the adorable cherub. The wind tossed her thin blond locks. Her blue eyes sparkled. Now that Liz was over the shock of realizing Joy and her baby would have been close to the same age, she felt normal again. Strong. Accepting of that particular sadness in her life. That was the difference between her and Cain. She'd dealt with her loss. She hadn't let it turn her into someone who couldn't connect with people.

"I love the beach. I'm happy to have someone to share it with."

Joy nodded enthusiastically. "Me, too!"

They ate the sandwiches and fruit Ellie had packed for dinner, then Joy fell asleep under the umbrella. Obviously relaxed and happy, Amanda lay beside her daughter and closed her eyes, too.

"So what did you do yesterday?" Ellie singsonged in the voice that told Liz she knew something out of the ordinary had happened the day before.

Liz peered over at Ellie. Did the woman have a sixth sense about everything? "Not much."

"Oh, come on. You never take a day off. I know something happened."

Liz grabbed the bottle of sunscreen and put her attention to applying it. Knowing Ellie wouldn't let her alone unless she told her something, she said, "I was taking care of a sick friend."

Ellie nudged her playfully. "So? Who was this friend?"

"Just a friend."

"A man!"

"I said nothing about a man."

Ellie laughed. "You didn't need to. The fact that you won't give me a name or elaborate proves I'm right."

How could she argue with that?

Ellie squeezed her shoulder. "I'm proud of you."

"Don't make a big deal out of it."

Ellie laughed gaily. "Let's see. You not only took a day off, but you were with a man and I'm not supposed to make a big deal out of it?"

"No, you're not. Because I'm never going to see him again."

"How do you know?"

"Because I know."

"Okay, then." Ellie closed her eyes and her face scrunched comically.

"What are you doing?"

"Wishing that you'd see him again."

"You might not want to do that."

"Oh, I think I do."

"The man was my ex."

Ellie's eyes popped open. "Oh, Liz! Damn it. You should have told me that before I wished. You know how powerful my wishes can be."

"That's why I told you now. You need to take it back."

"I can't."

"Yeah, well, you'd better or you're going to break your record of wishes granted. Because I'm not going to see him again."

Stupidly, that made her sad. She'd loved Cain with her whole heart and soul, but his brother had died and he'd gone into his shell. She'd tried to hang in there with him, to be there when he reached the point that he could work through his pain and withdrawal, but he never had. And then one day she realized she was pregnant. She knew in her heart that Cain wasn't ready for a child, so she'd waited a few weeks, hoping that if she were further along the pregnancy would seem more real to him. Maybe even be a cause for joy.

But she'd miscarried before she'd had a chance to tell him and suddenly she was the one unable to function. She knew she needed help. At the very least she needed someone to talk to. She couldn't talk to Cain. She wouldn't have been able to handle it if he had dismissed the loss of the little life so precious to her. So she'd gone. Their marriage had been in shambles anyway. The miscarriage simply pointed out what she already knew. Cain wasn't emotionally available.

Ending their marriage had been the right thing to do. She'd gotten therapy, moved on and made a wonderful life for herself.

And he'd moved on. Achieved the success he'd always wanted.

There was nothing to be sad about.

She spent most of the rest of the day in the ocean with Joy, until all thoughts of her miscarriage and her ex-husband had receded. Through the week, occasionally something would remind her of her short pregnancy or her doomed marriage, but she ruthlessly squelched the urge to feel sorry for herself until by Friday, she didn't have a second thought about going to Cain's house to clean. The past was the past. She'd moved on, into the future.

Assuming he'd already gone to work, Liz simply pulled the Happy Maids car into his driveway, bounced out and let herself into his kitchen.

But when she turned from pulling her key from the door, she saw Cain standing over a tall stack of waffles.

"Good morning."

She froze.

They weren't supposed to run into each other. That was why she thought she could keep this job. But three of her four cleaning trips to his house, he'd been home. Without even knowing it, he'd dredged up memories that she'd had to deal with. Emotions she'd thought long dead. Now here he was again.

Still, she wouldn't make an argument of it. She could say a few words of casual conversation, as she walked to the door on the other side of the kitchen and slipped out of the room to clean another section of the house.

"You must be really hungry."

He laughed. "I am. But these are for you." He shrugged. "A thank-you for helping me last weekend."

She froze. She should have expected this. She *had* expected this. She knew he hated owing anyone.

She sucked in a quiet breath. Not only did she not want to spend time with him, but she hadn't eaten waffles since their fateful trip to Vegas. Mostly because she didn't want to remember that wonderful time. *That* Cain wasn't the real Cain. Neither was this guy who'd made her waffles. He didn't want to thank her as much as he felt guilty that she'd helped him the week before and wouldn't let that "debt" go unpaid.

"That's not necessary."

"I know it's not necessary, but I *want* to thank you."

"You did thank me. The words are enough."

He sighed. "Just sit down and have a waffle."

"No!" Because the single word came out so angrily, she smiled to soften it. "Thanks, but no."

Their gazes held for a few seconds. She read the confusion in his dark eyes. He didn't understand why she wouldn't eat breakfast with him. They'd been so happy the one and only time they'd had waffles together. And maybe that's why he'd chosen them?

Regret rose up in her, but regret was a foolish emotion. She couldn't change who he was. She couldn't change the fact that she'd lost their child. And she refused to be pulled into believing the nice side of him was in control. That would only lead to more heartache. Neither one of them wanted that.

She turned and walked away. "I'll get started upstairs while you eat."

Cain pretended her refusal to eat his thank-you waffles hadn't bothered him. Being incredibly busy at work, it was easy to block out the memory. But Saturday morning he took his boat out, and alone on the water with nothing to keep him company but his thoughts, he was miserable.

Liz was without a doubt the kindest woman in the world and he had hurt her. He'd hurt her enough that she couldn't even force herself to be polite and eat breakfast with him.

When she'd left him three years before, he'd experienced a bit of remorse, but mostly he was relieved. He'd quickly buried both emotions under work—as he always did. But sitting on the ocean, with the sun on his face and the truth stirring his soul, he knew he had to make it up to her. All of it. The quick marriage, the horrible three years together, the bitter divorce and probably the pain she'd suffered afterward.

He owed her. And he hated owing anyone. But her refusal had shown him that she didn't want a grand gesture. Hell, she didn't want any gesture at all. Still, he needed to ease his own conscience by doing something for her. And he would. He simply wouldn't let her know he was doing it.

On Sunday morning, he got her phone number from Ava and tried calling her. He needed no more than a ten-minute conversation with her. He was very, very good at figuring out what people wanted or needed. That was part of what had made him so successful at negotiating. In ten minutes, he could figure out what anyone wanted or needed and then he could use that knowledge to negotiate for what *he* wanted. The situation with Liz was no different. He wanted to ease his conscience and could do that by simply finding a need and filling it for her. Anonymously, of course. Then his conscience would be clear. He could fall out of her life again, and they both could go back to the new lives they'd created without each other.

His call went directly to voice mail, so he tried calling her on Monday morning. That call also went to voice mail. Not wanting to make a fool of himself by leaving a hundred unanswered messages, he waited for Friday to roll around. She might not take his calls, she might not have eaten the breakfast he'd prepared the week before, but she couldn't avoid him in his own house if he really wanted to talk to her.

And he did. In only a few minutes, he could ascertain what was important to her, get it and ease his conscience. If he had to follow her around while she dusted, he would.

Realizing she might not enter if she saw he was still home, Cain stayed out of sight until he heard the bip, bip, bip of his alarm being disabled. He waited to hear the back door open and close, then he stepped into the kitchen.

"Liz."

The woman in the yellow maid's apron turned. "Mr. Nestor?"

"Oh, I'm sorry."

Well, if that didn't take the cake! Not only had she refused his thank-you waffles and ignored his calls, but now she'd sent someone else to clean his house?

He sucked in a breath to control his temper so he could apologize again to Liz's employee, then he drove to his office. He was done with pussyfooting around. Now, she'd deal with him on his terms.

He kept the five o'clock space on his calendar open assuming she and her employees met back at her office for some sort of debriefing at the end of the work week. At the very least, to get their weekly paychecks. Ava gave him the business address she'd gotten for Happy Maids and he jumped into his black Porsche.

With traffic, the drive took forty minutes, not the twenty he'd planned on. By the time he arrived at the office building housing Happy Maids, he saw a line of women in yellow aprons exiting. He quickly found a parking place for his car, but even before he could shut off his engine, Liz whizzed by him in an ugly green car.

Damn it!

Yanking on the Porsche's gearshift, he roared out of the parking space. He wasn't entirely sure it was a good idea to follow Liz home. She might take that as an invasion of privacy, but right at this moment, with the memory of her refusal to eat his waffles ringing in his head, and his embarrassment when he realized she'd given the job of cleaning his house to one of her employees adding fuel to the fire, he didn't give a damn.

He wanted to get this off his conscience and all he needed was ten minutes. But she wouldn't even give him ten minutes. So he'd have to take them. He wasn't sure how he'd explain his presence at her door, but he suddenly realized he had the perfect topic of conversation. He could calmly, kindly, ask her why she'd left their marriage without a word. Three years had gone by. The subject wasn't touchy anymore. At least not for him. He knew why she'd left. He'd been a lousy husband. This should be something she'd want to discuss. To get off her chest.

He wouldn't be mean. He'd say the words women loved to hear. That he wanted to talk. To clean their slate. For closure. So they could both move on completely. Actually, what he was doing was giving her a chance to vent. She'd probably be thrilled for it.

He grinned. He was a genius. Mostly because Liz was the kind of woman she was. She didn't rant and rail. Or even get angry. She'd probably quietly tell him that she'd left him because he had been a nightmare to live with, and he would humbly agree, not argue, showing her he really did want closure. All the while he'd be processing her house, looking for clues of what mattered to her, what she needed. So he could get it for her and wipe this off his conscience.

He wove in and out of traffic two car lengths behind her, not surprised when she drove to one of Miami's lower-middle-class neighborhoods. She identified with blue-collar people. Which was one of the reasons their marriage had been so stressful. She'd been afraid to come out of her shell. Afraid of saying or doing the wrong thing with his wealthy friends. Afraid, even, to plan their own parties.

She pulled her car onto the driveway of a modest home and jumped out. As she ducked into the one-car garage and disappeared, he drove in behind her.

He took a second to catch his breath and organize his thoughts. First he would apologize for being presumptuous when he made the waffles for her. Then he'd give her the spiel about wanting a clean slate—which, now that he thought about it, was true. He was here to help them move on. Then he'd do what he did best. He'd observe her surroundings, really listen to what she said and figure out what he could do for her.

Taking a few measured breaths, he got out of his car and started up the cracked cement sidewalk. He was amazingly calm by the time a little girl of about three answered the door after he rang the bell.

"Mom!" she screamed, turning and running back into the dark foyer. "It's a stranger!"

Cain blinked. His mouth fell open. Then his entire body froze in fear. Liz had a child? A child old enough to be…well, *his?*

Oh, dear God. That would explain why she'd left without a word. Why she'd avoided him—

Liz and a red-haired woman Cain didn't recognize raced into the hall leading to the foyer. The red-haired woman pushed the little girl behind her in a move that very obviously said this was her child, not Liz's.

Chastising his overactive imagination, Cain forced his breathing back to normal but it wasn't so easy to get his heart rate off red alert.

And Liz still barreled up the hall, looking ready for a fight. She was only a few feet in front of him before she recognized him.

"Oh. It's you." Sighing heavily, she turned to the redhead. "This is my ex-husband, Cain."

Still coming down from the shock of thinking he was a dad, he quickly said, "I'm here to apologize about the waffles last week."

"Apology accepted. Now leave."

Wow. She was a lot quicker on her feet than he'd remembered. "No. I can't. I mean, you didn't have to send another employee to clean my house today." Embarrassment twisted his tongue. He wasn't saying any of this well. Where was the control that helped him schmooze bankers, sweet-talk union reps and haggle with suppliers?

Gone. That's where. Because Liz wasn't a banker, union rep or supplier. She was a normal person. His ex-wife. Now he understood Ava's comments the day he'd discovered Liz was his temporary maid. He wasn't good at ordinary conversation with ordinary people. Business was his element. That was why he didn't have a personal life.

Still, he needed to talk to her.

He rubbed his hand across the back of his neck. "Could you give me ten minutes?"

"For what?"

He smiled as charmingly as he could, deciding to pretend this was a business conversation so he'd get some of his control back. "Ten minutes, Liz. That's all I want."

Liz sighed and glanced at the woman beside her.

She shrugged. "You could go outside to the patio."

Cain blanched. "This isn't your house?"

"No."

He squeezed his eyes shut in embarrassment, then addressed the redhead. "I'm sorry. Ms.—"

"It's Amanda." She shrugged. "And don't worry about it. It's not really my house, either."

"Then whose house is it?"

Liz motioned for him to follow her down the hall and into the kitchen. "I'll explain on the patio."

The little girl with the big blue eyes also followed them to the sliding glass door. Liz stopped short of exiting, stooping to the toddler's level. "Joy, you stay with your mom, okay?"

Grinning shyly, Joy nodded.

Liz smiled and hugged her fiercely, before she rose. Something odd bubbled up inside Cain, something he'd never once considered while they were married. Liz would make a wonderful mom. He'd known she'd wanted children, but after his brother's death, they'd never again discussed it. Was that why she'd left him without a word? And if it was—if what meant the most to her was having a child—how could he possibly make *that* up to her?

Without looking at him she said, "This way."

She led him to a small stone patio with an inexpensive umbrella-covered table. There was no pool, no outdoor kitchen. Just a tiny gas grill.

She sat at the table and he did the same. "Whose house is this?"

"It's owned by a charity." Lowering her voice to a whisper, she leaned in closer so he could hear her. "Look, Cain, I really can't tell you much, except this house belongs to a charity for women who need a second chance. They stay at houses like this until they can get on their feet."

Cain didn't have to work hard to read between the lines of what she'd said. He frowned. "She's been abused?"

Liz shushed him with a wave of her hand and whispered, "Yes." Lowering her voice even more she added, "Look, we don't like talking about this when we're with the clients. We're trying to establish them as any other member of their community. Not someone being supported by a charity. We want them to think of us as friends, not benefactors."

Following her direction to keep the conversation more private, Cain leaned closer to Liz. The light scent of her shampoo drifted over to him. The smoothness of her skin called him to touch. Memories tripped over themselves in his brain until he remembered this was how she'd been the day he'd met her on the plane. Sweet. Kind. Shy. Reluctant to talk. He'd had to draw her out even to get her to tell him the simplest things about herself.

That day he hadn't been bad at normal conversation. He'd wanted to sleep with her enough that he'd pushed beyond his inability to chitchat.

He rubbed his hand across the back of his neck. That was a bad connection to make with her sitting so close, smelling like heaven, while his own blood vibrated through his veins with recognition that this woman had once been his.

He cleared his throat. "So, this is a charity?"

"Yes." She winced.

He glanced around, confused. "What are *you* doing here?"

"Happy Maids donates housecleaning services when one of the Friend Indeed houses becomes vacant. I also stock the cupboards with groceries and cleaning supplies. I'm part of the committee that welcomes a woman to her new house and stays in her life to help her acclimate."

"A Friend Indeed?"

She nodded.

Processing everything she'd told him, Cain stayed silent. He'd accomplished his purpose. A woman who not only donated the services of her business, but also bought groceries, was obviously committed to this charity. Anything he did for A Friend Indeed would be a kindness to her. Clearly, they'd won her heart. So all he had to do was make a big contribution, and his conscience would be clear.

But figuring that out also meant he had nothing more to say.

He could try to make up a reason to talk to her, but he'd already proven chitchat wasn't his forte. Plus, that would only mean staying longer with the woman whose mere presence made him ache for what they'd had and lost. There was no point wanting what he couldn't have. They'd been married once. It had failed.

Exhaling a big breath, Cain rose. "I'm sorry I bothered you."

Her brow puckering in confusion, she rose with him. "I thought you wanted to talk."

"We just did." Rather than return to the kitchen and leave through the front door, he glanced around, saw the strip of sidewalk surrounding the house that probably led to the driveway and headed off.

His conscience tweaked again at the fact that he'd confused her but he ignored it. The money he would donate would more than make up for it.

On Monday morning, he had Ava investigate A Friend Indeed. At first she found very little beyond their name and their registration as a charitable organization, then Cain called in a few favors and doors began to open. Though shrouded in secrecy, the charity checked out and on Friday morning Cain had Ava write a check and deliver it to the home of the president of the group's board of directors. She returned a few hours later chuckling.

"Ayleen Francis wants to meet you."

Cain glanced up from the document he was reading. "Meet me?"

She leaned against the door frame. "I did the usual spiel that I do when you have me deliver a check like this. That you admire the work being done by the group and want to help, but prefer to remain anonymous, et cetera. And she said that was fine but she wouldn't accept your check unless she met you."

Cain frowned. "Seriously?"

"That's what she said."

"But—" Damn it. Why did everything about Liz have to turn complicated? "Why would she want to meet me?"

"To thank you?"

Annoyed, he growled. "I don't need thanks."

Ava shrugged. "I have no idea what's going on. I'm just the messenger." She set the check and a business card on Cain's desk. "Here's the address. She said it would be wonderful if you could be there tonight at eight."

Cain snatched up the card and damned near threw it in the trash. But he stopped. He was *this* close to making it up to Liz for their marriage being a disaster. No matter how much he'd worked with his dad before he sold the family business in Kansas and retired, Cain had never been able to do enough to make up for his brother's death. His parents had accepted Tom's death as an accident and eventually Cain had, too. Sort of. As the driver of the car, he would always feel responsible. He'd never let go of that guilt. But he did understand it had been an accident.

But his troubled marriage wasn't an accident. He'd coerced Liz. Seduced her. More sexually experienced than she had been, he'd taken advantage of their chemistry. Used it. She hadn't stood a chance.

And he knew he had to make that up to her. Was he really going to let one oddball request stand in his way of finally feeling freed of the debt?

Chapter 4

Arranging her notes for the executive board meeting for A Friend Indeed held the first Friday of the month, Liz sat at the long table in the conference room of the accounting firm that handled the finances for the charity. The firm also lent them space to hold their meetings because A Friend Indeed didn't want to waste money on an office that wouldn't often be used. Their work was in the field.

Ayleen Francis, a fiftysomething socialite with blond hair and a ready smile who was the president of the board, sat at the head of the table chatting with Ronald Johnson, a local man whose daughter had been murdered by an ex-boyfriend. A Friend Indeed had actually been Ron's brainchild, but it took Ayleen's money and clout to bring his dream to fruition.

Beside Ron was Rose Swartz, owner of a chain of

floral shops. Liberty Myers sat next to Rose and beside Liz was Bill Brown. The actual board for the group consisted of sixteen members, but the six-person executive board handled most of the day-to-day decisions.

Waiting for Ayleen to begin the meeting, Liz handed the receipts for the groceries she'd purchased for Amanda and her kids to Rose, the group's treasurer, as well as a statement for cleaning services. Liz donated both the food and the services, but for accounting purposes A Friend Indeed kept track of what each cost.

"Thank you, Liz," Rose said, her smile warm and appreciative. But before Liz could say you're welcome, someone entered behind her and a hush fell over the small group.

Ayleen rose just as Liz turned to see Cain standing in the door way. "I'm assuming you're Cain Nestor."

He nodded.

Ayleen smiled and turned to the group. "Everyone, this is Cain Nestor, CEO of Cain Corporation. He's visiting us this evening."

Shock and confusion rippled through Liz. She hadn't seen Cain in three years, now suddenly he was everywhere! Worse, she'd brought him here. She'd given him the name of the group when he followed her to Amanda's. She couldn't believe he was still pursuing the opportunity to thank her for staying with him while he was sick, but apparently he was and she didn't like it. She was over him. She wanted to stay over him!

"Just take a seat anywhere." Ayleen motioned to the empty seats at the end of the table.

Cain didn't move from the doorway. "Ms. Francis—"

Ayleen smiled sweetly. "Call me Ayleen."

"Ayleen, could we talk privately?"

"Actually, I don't say or do much for A Friend Indeed without my executive board present. That's why I asked your assistant to pass on the message for you to meet me here. If you'll let me start the meeting, I'll tell the group about your donation—"

Liz frowned. He'd made a donation? To *her* charity?

"My assistant was also supposed to tell you that the donation was to be kept confidential."

"Everything about A Friend Indeed is confidential." She motioned around the room. "Nothing about the group goes beyond the board of directors. Some things don't go beyond the six people at this table. However, none of us keeps secrets from the others. But if you don't care to stay for the meeting, then I'll simply tell the group I'm refusing your donation."

Cain gaped at her. "What?"

"Mr. Nestor, though we appreciate your money, what we really need is your help." She ambled to the conference-room door. "As I've already mentioned, everything about A Friend Indeed is confidential. That's out of necessity. We give women a place to stay after they leave abusive husbands or boyfriends." She smiled engagingly as she slid her arm beneath Cain's and guided him into the room.

"For their safety, we promise complete anonymity. But because we do promise complete anonymity to our clients, we can't simply hire construction firms to come and do repair work on our houses. As a result, several of them are in serious disrepair."

Liz sat up, suddenly understanding the point Ayleen was about to make. The group didn't need money as much as they needed skilled, trustworthy volunteers.

"The amount of your check is wonderful. But what

we really need is help. If you seriously want to do something for this group, what we'd like is your time."

Cain glanced at Liz, then returned his gaze to Ayleen. "What are you saying?"

"I'm asking you to do some work for us."

He looked at Liz again. Her skin heated. Her heartbeat jumped to double-time. He was actually considering it.

For her.

Something warm and syrupy flooded her system. He'd never done anything like this. It was overkill as a thank-you for her helping him through the flu. Donating money was more within his comfort zone. Especially donating anonymously. A secret donation of money, no matter how big, was easy for him.

But A Friend Indeed didn't need his money as much as his help. And he was considering it.

Holding his gaze, Liz saw the debate in his eyes. He'd have to give up time, work with people. Ordinary people. Because someone from A Friend Indeed would have to accompany him. A stranger couldn't go to the home of one of their abused women alone.

But, his money hadn't been accepted. If he still wanted to do something nice for Liz, it would require his time. Something he rarely gave.

Continuing to hold Liz's gaze he said, "What would I have to do?"

Liz smiled. Slowly. Gratefully. She didn't care as much about a thank-you as she cared about A Friend Indeed. About the families in the homes that needed repairs. She'd been up close and personal with most of them, since her group was in charge of cleaning them for the families, and she knew just how bad some of the homes were.

Alyeen said, "Liz? What would he have to do?"

Liz faced Ayleen. "Cain paid his way through university working construction jobs in the summer. If he could spare the time, the house we moved Amanda into a few weeks ago has a lot of little things that need to be repaired."

"It's been years since I've done any hands-on construction. I can't make any promises without seeing the house."

Ayleen clapped her hands together with glee. "Understandable. I'll have Liz take you to Amanda's."

Liz's heart thumped. She wanted his help, the group *needed* his help, but she didn't want to have to be with him to get it.

"I'm not sure I can," Liz said at the same time that Cain said, "That's not necessary."

"You're a stranger to us," Ayleen firmly told Cain. "For the safety and assurance of our families, I want you with someone from the board at all times." She faced Liz. "Liz, you've been at Amanda's every weekend since she moved in anyway. And you obviously know Cain. You're the best person to accompany him to Amanda's tomorrow." She smiled at Liz. "Please."

Drat. She shouldn't have mentioned her knowledge about Cain's construction experience. But she had been amazed and grateful that he was willing to help. She'd be crazy or shrewish to refuse to do her part.

"Sure."

Ayleen maneuvered Cain into a seat, but not once did Liz even glance in his direction. It was one thing to appreciate the gift of his help, quite another to be stuck spending time with him. Worse, the whole idea that he'd be willing to actually work, *physically work*, to thank her for a few hours of caring for him gave her a soft fluttery feeling in her stomach.

She ignored it. They had to spend time together the next day. Maybe hours. She couldn't be all soft and happy—but she couldn't be angry with him, either. He was doing a huge favor for a charity that meant a great deal to her.

Of course he'd wanted to do it anonymously. Being with her probably wasn't a happy prospect for him any more than it was for her. With anybody else she'd be figuring out a way to make this deal palatable for them. So maybe that's what she needed to do with Cain. Find a way to make this easy for him, as if they were two friends working together for a charity.

The thought caused her brow to furrow. They'd never been friends. They'd been passionate lovers. A distant married couple. Hurt divorced people. But they'd never really been friends. They'd never even tried to be friends.

Maybe becoming friends was the real way for them to get beyond their troubled marriage? To pretend, even if only for a few hours, that the past was the past and from this point on they were two nice people trying to help each other.

Cain was already at Amanda's house the next morning when Liz arrived. Instead of his black Porsche, he waited for her in one of his Nestor Construction trucks. An old red one.

Keeping with her decision to treat him as she would

a friend, she smiled and patted the side of the truck bed. "Wow. I haven't seen one of these in years."

He walked around the truck and Liz's smile disappeared as her mouth fell open slightly. She'd already noticed his T-shirt, but for some reason or another, the jeans he wore caught her off guard. He looked so young. So capable. So…sexy.

She cleared her throat, reminding herself that this was a new era for her and Cain. Friends. Two nice people working together for a charity.

"Mostly, we use Cain Corporation trucks now." He grinned. "But when I ran Nestor Construction, this one was mine." He patted the wheel well. "She was my first."

"Ah, a man and his truck." Eager to get out of the sun and to the reason they were here, Liz turned to the sidewalk. "Come on. This way."

They walked to the front door and Liz knocked. Joy answered, but Amanda was only a few feet behind her. She grabbed the giggling three-year-old and hoisted her into her arms. "Sorry about that."

Liz laughed. "Good morning, Joy," she said, tweaking the little girl's cheek as she passed.

Joy buried her face in Amanda's neck. "Morning."

Amanda looked pointedly at Cain. "And this is Cain?"

Cain held out his hand for shaking. "Sorry about our first meeting."

Amanda smiled. "That's okay. Neither one of us was in good form that day. Can I get you some coffee?"

Cain peered over at Liz.

Liz motioned for everyone to go into the kitchen. "Of course, we'd love some coffee."

When Amanda walked through the swinging door out of sight, Liz caught Cain's arm, holding him back. "If she offers something, take it. A lot of the women who come to us have little to no self-esteem. It makes them feel good about themselves to have coffee or doughnuts to offer. Take whatever she offers and eat it."

Looking sheepish and unsure, he nodded and everything inside Liz stilled. For the first time in their relationship she knew something he didn't. He needed her.

Their gazes caught.

Liz smiled, downplaying the reversal of their roles and seeking to reassure him.

The corners of his mouth edged up slowly in response, and his entire countenance changed. Crinkles formed around dark eyes that warmed.

The hallway suddenly felt small and quiet. The memory of how much she'd loved this man fluttered through her. With one step forward she could lay her palm on his cheek. Touch him. Feel his skin again. Feel connected to him in the only way they'd ever been connected. Touch.

But one touch always led to another and another and another. Which was probably why making love was the only way they'd bonded. They'd never had a chance to be friends. Never given themselves a chance to get to know each other.

Sad, really.

Instead of stepping forward, she stepped back, motioning to the door. "After you."

He shook his head. His voice was rich, husky when he said, "No. After you."

He'd been as affected by the moment as she had been. For a second she couldn't move, couldn't breathe, as another possibility for why he'd been so insistent on thanking her popped into her head. He hadn't forgotten their sexual chemistry any more than she had. They hadn't been good as a married couple, but they had been fantastic lovers. What if he was being kind, using this "thank-you" as a first step to seducing her?

A sickening feeling rose up in her. He hadn't hesitated the first time. He'd done everything he'd had to do to get her to Miami, into his bed. Working for a charity was small potatoes compared to some of the things he'd done to woo her, including whisk her to Vegas and seduce her into marrying him.

Well, six years later she wasn't so foolish. So young. So inexperienced. If he dared as much as make a pass at her, he'd find himself with a new Friend Indeed employee as his liaison. He'd still have to fulfill his end of the bargain. He just wouldn't do it with her.

She headed for the swinging door. Cain followed. In the kitchen, Amanda already had three mugs of coffee on the table. The room was spotless and smelled of maple syrup. Amanda had the look of a woman who'd happily served her daughter breakfast.

Cain took a seat at the table. "We can use this time to talk about what you need me to do."

"You're doing the work?"

Liz caught Amanda's hand, forcing her gaze to hers for reassurance. "Yes. Cain worked in construction to put himself through university."

"And as a bartender and a grocery boy. I was also a waiter and amusement-park vendor." He smiled at Amanda as she sat. "School was four long years."

Amanda laughed.

Liz pulled her hand away. "So go ahead. Give Cain the list of things that need to be done."

"First, the plumbing."

He took a small notebook from his shirt pocket. "Okay."

"There are some places with missing baseboard."

"Uh-huh."

"The ceiling in the first bedroom has water marks."

Without looking up from his note taking, Cain said, "That's not good."

"And most of the walls need to be painted."

"You guys can help with that."

Liz hesitated. She didn't want to agree to time in the same room with him, but from the sounds of the list Cain's work here wouldn't be a few hours. He'd be here for days and Liz would be, too. If she had to be here to oversee things, she might as well have something to do. Plus, the more she did, the sooner her time with Cain would be over.

"Sure."

Because Amanda had stopped listing repair items, Cain finally glanced up. "That's it?"

"Isn't that enough?"

"It's plenty. In fact," he said with a wince, "if those water marks are roof leaks, we've got a problem."

"Why?"

Cain caught Liz's gaze and her insides turned to gelatin again. But not because of chemistry. Because of fear. His eyes were soft, his expression grave. He wanted to do a good job. But he also had to be honest.

She'd only seen him look this way once. When she'd told him she couldn't plan a huge Christmas party he'd wanted to host for his business associates. She'd been afraid—terrified really—that she'd do something wrong, something simple, but so awful that she'd embarrass them both. He'd been angry first, but that emotion had flitted from his face quickly and was replaced by the expression he now wore. It had disappointed him that she couldn't do what he needed, but he had to be honest and admit he still wanted the party. So he'd hired someone to plan it for him.

He'd moved beyond it as if it wasn't a big deal. But the disappointment he'd felt in her lingered. Even now it reminded her that he knew they weren't good for each other as a couple. They didn't match. He wouldn't want to start something with her any more than she'd want to start something with him. No matter how sexually compatible they were, he wasn't here to seduce her. She actually felt a little foolish for even thinking it.

"A roof isn't a one-man job. Even with a crew a roof takes a few days. At the very least a weekend." He looked at Amanda. "But I'll choose the crew with care."

Amanda looked at Liz.

"We'll talk it over with Ayleen, but we can trust Cain. If he says he'll figure out a way to keep all this confidential, he'll do it." When it came to work Cain was as good as his word. "Plus, if Cain's okay with it, we'll only work weekends and you can take the kids to the beach or something. Not be around. Just to be sure no one sees you."

Amanda nodded. "Okay."

"Okay." Cain rose. "Let me take a quick look at all these things then I'll make a trip to the building supply store."

"Toilets are fixed. Showers all work," Cain said, wiping his hands on a paper towel as he walked into the kitchen.

Amanda had made grilled cheese sandwiches and

tomato soup for lunch. Liz already sat at the table. Amanda was happily serving. He took a seat and Liz smiled at him. After walking through the house with him behaving like a contractor, not her ex-husband, not the man she shared unbelievable chemistry with, Liz was slightly annoyed with herself for even considering he was only here as part of a plan to seduce her. His work here might have begun as a way to thank her for caring for him, but now that he was here, he clearly wanted to do a good job. It almost seemed he'd forgotten their chemistry or that she had imagined his reaction as they stood in the hallway that morning.

Which was good. Excellent. And took her back to her plan of behaving like his friend.

"So this afternoon we paint?"

"I'd like to get the painting done before we put up new baseboards. With all the rooms that need to be painted, it's going to take a few days. So it would be best if we started immediately after we eat."

"Okay."

Liz took a sandwich from the platter Amanda passed to her and handed it to Cain. Things were good. Relaxed. The more she was in his company this way, the more confident and comfortable she felt around him.

"I'll do the ceilings," Cain said, taking three sandwiches. "You guys handle the walls."

Amanda grimaced. "I'm sorry. I scheduled a playdate for Joy. I didn't realize you'd need me this soon."

"It's all right," Liz said easily. "Cain and I will be fine."

She genuinely believed that, until Amanda and Joy left and suddenly she and Cain were alone with two gallons of paint, two paint trays and a few brushes and rollers. Why did fate always have to test her like this? Just because she'd become comfortable around him, that didn't mean she had to be tested an hour after the thought had formed in her brain.

"What's the protocol on this?" she asked, nervously flitting away from him.

"First, we put blue tape around the windows and doors and existing baseboards so we don't get any paint where we don't want it. Then I'll do the ceiling and you do the walls."

He went out to his truck and returned with a roll of blue tape. Swiftly, without a second thought and as if he weren't having any trouble being alone with her, he applied it on the wood trim around the windows.

"Wow. A person would never guess you hadn't done that in about ten years."

He laughed. "It's like riding a bike. It comes back to you."

He *was* at ease. He wasn't seeing her as anything but a work buddy. Surely, she could follow suit.

"I know but you really look like you were born to this. It's almost a shame you don't do it anymore."

"My end of things is equally important." He turned from the window. "Come here. Let me show you how simple it is."

She walked over to the window and he positioned her in front of it. Handing her the roll, he said, "Hook the end of the tape over the edge of the top molding and then just roll it down."

She did as he said but the tape angled inward and by the time she reached the bottom the edge was still bare.

"Here." Covering her hand with his, he showed her how to direct the roll as she moved it downward, so that the side of the woodwork was entirely covered by the tape.

Liz barely noticed. With his chest brushing her back and his arm sliding along her arm, old feelings burst inside her. The scent of him drifted to her and she squeezed her eyes shut. She had never met a man who caused such a riot inside her. She longed to turn around and snuggle into him, wrap her arms around him, simply enjoy the feeling of his big body against hers.

She stiffened. She had to get beyond this! If he could treat her like a coworker, she could treat him like a friend.

As if unfazed, he pulled away and walked to the paint. He poured some of the gray into one of the trays and white into the second one.

"Okay. I'm ceilings. You're walls. But first I'm going to do the edge where the wall meets the ceiling." He nodded at the tray of gray paint. "You take that and a roller and go nuts on the walls. Just stay away from the edges."

"With pleasure." She managed to make her voice sound light and friendly, but inside she was a mess. Especially since he seemed so cavalier. All this time she'd believed his attraction to her fueled her attraction to him. Now, she wasn't so sure. Oh, she still believed he was attracted to her. His attraction simply didn't control him.

And by God she wasn't going to let hers control her, either!

For the next ten minutes they were quiet. Cain took a brush and painted an incredibly straight, incredibly neat six-inch swatch at the top of the wall, ensuring that Liz wouldn't even accidentally get any gray paint on the ceiling.

Deciding she needed to bring them back to a neutral place or the silence would make her nuts by the end of the day she said, "How do you do that so fast, yet so well?"

"Lots and lots of practice," he said, preoccupied with pouring more white paint into his tray. "Don't forget I did this kind of work four summers in a row. That was how I knew I wanted to run a construction company. I learned to do just about everything and I actually knew the work involved when I read plans or specs."

"Makes sense." She rolled gray paint onto the far wall. She'd heard that story before, but now that she was a business owner she understood it and could respond to it.

"In a way, I got into cleaning for the same reason. Once I realized what would be required of my employees, it was easy to know who to choose for what jobs and also what to charge."

"And you did great."

His praise brought a lump to her throat. In the three years they were married he'd never praised her beyond her looks. He loved how she looked, how she smelled, how soft she was. But he'd never noticed her beyond that.

She cleared her throat. "Thanks."

Occupied with painting the ceiling, Cain quietly said, "You know this is going to be more than a one-day job."

"So you've said."

He winced. "More than a two-week job."

She stopped. "Really?"

"Because we can only work weekends, I'm thinking we're in this for a month. And we're kind of going to be stuck together."

"Are you bailing?"

"No!" His answer was sharp. He stopped painting and faced her. "No. But I have to warn you that I'm a little confused about how to treat you."

Relief stuttered through her. She didn't want him to seduce her, but she certainly didn't want to be the only one fighting an attraction. "I thought we were trying to behave like friends."

"I'm not sure how to do that."

"Most of the day you've been treating me like a co-worker. Why don't you go back to that? Forget I'm your ex-wife."

He glanced over at her and all the air evaporated from Liz's lungs. The look he gave her was long and slow, as if asking how he could forget that they'd been married, been intimate.

Maybe that was the crux of their problem? Every time she looked at him something inside her stirred to life. She'd lived for three years without thinking about sex, but put him in the room with her and she needed to fan herself. Worse, through nearly three years of a bad marriage, they'd already proven they could be angry with each other, all wrong for each other and still plea-sure each other beyond belief.

It was going to be difficult to pretend none of that mattered.

But they had to try.

She cleared her throat. "I could use a glass of water. Would you like one?"

"Please."

In the kitchen, she took two bottles of water from

the refrigerator. She pressed the cool container against her cheek. Late March in southern Florida could be hot, but being in the same room with Cain was turning out to be even hotter.

Still, A Friend Indeed needed his help. Amanda deserved a pretty home for herself and her kids. Liz was also a strong, determined businesswoman who had handled some fairly tough trials through the three years of running her company. One little attraction wasn't going to ruin her.

Feeling better, she walked back to the living room, but stopped dead in the doorway. Reaching up to paint the ceiling, with his back to her, Cain stretched his T-shirt taut against his muscles. His jeans snugly outlined his behind. She swallowed. Memories of them in the shower and tangled in their sheets flashed through her brain.

She pressed the water bottle to her cheek again, pushing the pointless memories aside, and strode up behind him.

"Here."

He turned abruptly and a few drops of paint rained on her nose.

"Oops! Sorry. You kind of surprised me."

"It's okay."

He yanked a work hanky from his back pocket. "Let me get that."

Enclosing her chin in his big hand to hold her head still, he rubbed the cloth against her nose. Memories returned full force. Times he'd kissed her. Laughing on the beach before running into the house for mind-blowing sex. Falling asleep spooned together after.

He blinked. His hand stilled. Everything she was feeling was reflected in his dark eyes.

The world stopped for Liz. Holding his gaze, knowing exactly what he was remembering, feeling the thrum of her own heart as a result of the memories that poured through her brain, Liz couldn't move, couldn't breathe.

For ten seconds she was absolutely positive he was going to kiss her. The urge to stand on her tiptoes and accept a kiss was so strong she had to fight it with everything in her. But in the end, he backed away, his hand falling to his side.

Turning to the wall again, he said, "Another twenty minutes and I'll have the ceiling done. If you want to go put blue tape around the windows in the dining room we could probably get that room done today, too."

She stepped back. "Okay." She took another step backward toward the door. "Don't forget your water."

He didn't look up. "I won't."

Relief rattled through her. He'd just had a golden opportunity to kiss her, yet he'd stepped away.

She definitely wasn't the only one who wanted them to be friends, not lovers, or the only one who'd changed.

When Liz was gone, Cain lowered himself to the floor. Leaning against the old stone fireplace, he rubbed his hand down his face.

He could have kissed her. Not out of habit. Not out of instinct driven by happy memories. But because he wanted to. He *longed* to. She'd hardly left the house for their entire marriage. Now she was a business owner, a volunteer for a charity, a confident, self-sufficient woman. This new side of Liz he was seeing was very appealing. When he coupled her new personality with his blissful sexual memories, she was damned near irresistible.

But the clincher—the thing that almost took him over the top—was the way she looked at him as if she'd never stopped loving him. As if she wanted what he wanted. As if her entire body revved with anticipation, the way his did. As if her heart was open and begging.

He'd always known he was the problem in their marriage. And now that he was older and wiser, he desperately wanted to fix things. But he didn't want to hurt her again. He saw the trust in her eyes. Sweet, innocent trust. She was counting on him to do the right thing.

Part of him genuinely believed the right thing was to leave her alone. Let her get on with her life. Become the success she was destined to be.

The other part just kept thinking that she was his woman, and he wanted her back.

But he knew that was impossible.

Chapter 5

While they worked, Amanda and Joy returned from Joy's playdate, and Amanda prepared a barbecue. Liz didn't realize she was cooking until the aroma of tangy barbeque sauce floated through the downstairs. Just the scent brought Liz to the patio. A minute later, Cain followed behind her.

"What is that smell?"

Amanda laughed. "It's my mother's special barbeque-sauce recipe. Have a seat. Everything's done."

A glance to the right showed the umbrella table had been set with paper plates and plastic utensils. A bowl of potato salad sat beside some baked beans and a basket of rolls.

Starving from all the work she'd done, Liz sat down without a second thought. Cain, however, debated. She couldn't imagine how a single man could turn down home cooking until she remembered their near miss with the kiss. Their gazes caught. He looked away.

She could guess what he was thinking. It was getting harder and harder to work together because the longer they were together the more tempted they were. But his stepping away from the kiss proved he was here to help, only to help, not to try to work his way back into her bed.

And that meant she was safe. But so was he. He simply didn't know that she was as determined as he was to get beyond their attraction. Perhaps even to be friends.

So maybe she had to show him?

"Come on, Cain. This smells too good to resist."

He caught her gaze and she smiled encouragingly. She tried to show him with her expression that everything was okay. They could be around each other, if he'd just relax.

He walked to the table. "You're right. Especially since I'd be going home to takeout."

He sat across the table from her, leaving the two seats on either side of her for Amanda and Joy.

She smiled. As long as they paid no attention to their attraction, they could work toward becoming friends. She would simply have to ignore the extreme sadness that welled in her heart, now that their glances would no longer be heated and they had both silently stated their intentions not to get involved again. Mourning something that hadn't worked was ridiculous. She didn't want to go back to what they had. Apparently neither did he. So at least trying to become friends would make the next few weeks easier.

"Where's Billy?"

"Beach with some friends," Amanda announced casually. Then she paused and grinned. "You can't believe how wonderful it feels to say that. We were always so worried about Rick's reaction to everything that most of the time we didn't talk. Telling him where Billy was was an invitation to get into an argument." She shook her head. "It was no way to live."

"No. It isn't."

That came from Cain and caused Liz's head to swivel in his direction. Not only was he not one to talk about such personal things, but his sympathetic tone was so unexpected she almost couldn't believe it was he who had spoken.

"Men who abuse anyone weaker than they are are scum." His voice gentled and he glanced at Amanda. "I'm glad you're safe."

Liz stared at him, suddenly understanding. He'd never been a bad person, simply an overly busy person who had never stopped long enough to pay attention to anything that didn't pop up in front of him. Amanda and her children were no longer an "issue" to him. They were people with names and faces and lives. It lightened Liz's heart that he didn't just recognize that; he genuinely seemed to care for them.

Still, the conversation could potentially dip into subjects too serious for Joy's ears. "Well, that's all over now," Liz said, turning to the little girl. "And how did you like your playdate?"

Joy leaned across the table. "It was fun. Maddie has a cat."

"A huge monster cat!" Amanda said, picking up the platter of chicken and spearing a barbecued breast. "I swear I thought it was a dog when I first saw it."

They laughed.

"Do you have a cat?" Joy asked Liz.

"No. No cat for me. I'm allergic."

"It means she can't be around them or she'll sneeze," Amanda explained to Joy as she passed the beans to Cain.

"I didn't know you were allergic to cats."

That was Cain. His words were soft, not sharp or accusatory, but trepidation rippled through her, reminding her of another reason she and Cain couldn't be more than coworkers. She had bigger secrets than an allergy to cats. From the day she'd met him she'd kept her father's abuse a secret. Plus, she'd never told him they'd created a child, and then she'd lost that child.

If they weren't with Amanda, this might have been the time to tell him. They'd had a reasonably pleasant afternoon. They'd both silently stated their intention not to get involved, but to try to be friends. That had created a kind of bond of honesty between them, which would have made this the perfect time to at least tell him about his child.

But they weren't alone.

Liz turned her attention to the platter of chicken that had come her way. "You didn't have a cat. I didn't have a cat. It never came up."

He accepted her answer easily, but shame buffeted her, an unexpected result of spending so much time in his company. With him behaving like a good guy, a normal guy, a guy who wanted to get beyond their sexual chemistry and be friends, the secrets she'd kept in their marriage suddenly seemed incredibly wrong.

She hadn't told him that her dad had abused her, her mom and her sisters because at the time she was working to forget that. To build a life without her other life hanging over her head. She hadn't told him about her miscarriage because she'd needed help herself to accept it. And she'd had to leave him to get that help.

But three years later, so far beyond both of those problems that she could speak about each without breaking down, she wondered about the wisdom of having kept her secrets from him.

Would their marriage have been different if she'd admitted that as a child she'd been poor, hungry and constantly afraid?

Would *he* have been different if she'd turned to him for comfort in her time of need?

She'd never know the answer to, either, but the possibility that she could have changed her marriage, saved it, with a few whispered words, haunted her.

Sitting at the kitchen table of Amanda's house the next morning, finishing a cup of coffee after eating delicious blueberry pancakes, Liz smiled shakily at Cain as he stepped into the room. "Good morning."

"Good morning."

She might have kept secrets but she and Cain were now divorced, trying to get along while they worked together, not trying to reconcile. For that reason, she'd decided that the story of her abusive father could remain her secret. But as she had paced the floor the night before, working all this out in her brain, she realized how much she wanted to tell him about their baby.

When they divorced, she had been too raw and too hurt herself to tell him. By the time she'd gotten herself together, their paths never crossed. But now that their paths hadn't merely crossed, they were actually intersecting for the next several weeks; she couldn't keep the secret from him any more. He'd created a child. They'd lost that child. He deserved to know. And she wanted to tell him.

Which left her with two problems. When she'd tell him and how she'd tell him. She might be ready to share, but he might not be ready to hear it. She had to be alert for another opportunity like the one the day before… except when they were alone, not with other people.

Amanda turned from the stove. "Are you hungry, Cain? I'm making blueberry pancakes."

It was clear that Amanda reveled in the role of mom. Without the constant fear of her abusive husband she had blossomed. Joy was bright-eyed and happy, a little chatterbox who had entertained Liz all through breakfast. Amanda's only remaining problem was Billy, her sixteen-year-old son. They hadn't been away from their violent father long enough for any one of them to have adjusted, but once they had, Liz was certain Amanda would think of some way to connect with her son.

As far as Amanda's situation was concerned, Liz could relax…except for Cain, who hesitated just inside the kitchen door. Had he figured out she'd kept secrets bigger than an allergy to cats? Was he angry? Would he confront her? She couldn't handle that. Telling him about their baby had to be on her terms. That would be better for both of them. It would be horrible if he confronted her now.

Finally he said, "I've already eaten breakfast."

Relief wanted to rush out of her on a long gust of air, but she held it back. She'd instructed him to take everything Amanda offered. The day before he could have easily begged off her barbecue by saying it was time to go home. But he couldn't so easily walk away from breakfast when he would be staying all morning.

Amanda said, "That's okay. Just have some coffee." She reached for a mug from the cupboard by the stove, filled it and handed it to him. "Sit for a minute."

He took the coffee and he and Amanda ambled to chairs at the table, as Amanda's sixteen-year-old son Billy stepped into the room, music headphones in his ears. Totally oblivious to the people at the table, he walked to the refrigerator and pulled out the milk.

Amanda cast an embarrassed glance at her son. "Billy, at least say good-morning."

He ignored her.

She rose, walked over to him and took one of the headphones from his right ear. "Good morning," she singsonged.

Billy sighed. "Morning."

"Say good morning to our guests."

He scowled toward the table. "Good morning."

Liz had seen this a million times before. A teenager embarrassed that he had to count on a charity for a roof over his head frequently acted out. Especially the son of an abusive father. Even as Billy was probably glad to get away from his dad, he also missed him. Worse, he could be wondering about himself. If he was like his dad.

Liz's gaze slid to Cain. Billy was the kind of employee Cain hated. Troubled. He wanted only the best, both emotionally and physically, so he didn't have to deal with problems. His job was to get whatever construction project he had done and done right. He didn't have time for employee problems.

But after the way he'd reacted to Amanda's comment the day before, Liz knew he'd changed. At least somewhat. And he did have a soft spot for Amanda and her family. Billy was a part of that family. He desperately needed a positive male role model. If Cain simply behaved as he had the day before when he showed her how to use the blue tape and paint, Billy might actually learn something.

Plus, she and Cain wouldn't have to be in the same room.

She didn't want to spend the day worrying about how and when she'd tell him about their child. She also couldn't simply blurt it out in an awkward silence, particularly since they might be alone in the room but they weren't alone in the house. She wanted the right opportunity again, but she also needed time to think it through so she could choose her words carefully. Not being around Cain would buy her time.

She took a breath then smiled at Billy. "We could sure use your help today. Especially Cain."

Amanda gasped and clasped her hands together. "What a wonderful idea! Do you know who Mr. Nestor is?"

Billy rolled his eyes. "No."

"He owns a construction company." Amanda all but glowed with enthusiasm. "I'll bet he could teach you a million things."

"I don't need to know a million things, Mom. Besides, I want to go to med school."

"And you're going to need money," Amanda pointed out. "Mr. Nestor put himself through university working construction."

Billy glared at Cain.

Cain shifted uncomfortably. "Construction isn't for

everyone," he said, clearly unhappy to be caught in the middle. "I was also a bartender."

"But you're here now," Liz said, unable to stop herself. Her gaze roamed over to Cain's. "And you could teach him so much."

She let her eyes say the words she couldn't utter in front of the angry teen who desperately needed to at least see how a decent man behaved.

Cain pulled in a slow breath. Liz held hers. He'd changed. She knew he'd changed just from the sympathy he'd displayed to Amanda the day before. He could do this! All he had to do was say okay.

She held her breath as she held his gaze. His steely eyes bore into hers, but the longer their connection, the more his eyes softened.

Finally, he turned on his chair, facing Billy. "What I'm doing today isn't hard. So it might be a good place for you to start if you're interested in learning a few things."

"There! See!" Amanda clasped Billy on the shoulder. "It will be good for you."

Cain rose and motioned for Billy to follow him out of the kitchen. Liz stared after them, her heart pounding. No matter how much she wanted to believe he'd done that out of sympathy for Amanda's situation, she knew he'd done it for her.

She turned back to her coffee, smiled at Amanda, trying to appear as if nothing was wrong. But everything was wrong. First, spending time with him had caused her to realize he deserved to know he'd created and lost a child. Now he was softening, doing things she asked.

For the first time it occurred to her that maybe he wasn't changing because of their situation but to please her.

And if he was…Lord help them.

Ten minutes later Cain found himself in the living room with an angry, sullen teenager. He debated drawing him into conversation, but somehow he didn't think the charisma that typically worked on egotistical bankers and clever business owners would work with a kid. And the chitchat he was forcing himself to develop with Amanda and Liz hadn't served him all that well, either. He and Billy could either work in silence, or he could hit this kid with the truth.

"You know what? I don't like this any more than you do."

Surprised, Billy looked over.

"But your mom wants you here and every once in a while a man has to suck it up and do what his mom wants." Technically, he and Billy were in the same boat. He was in this room, with this angry boy, because he hadn't been able to resist the pleading in Liz's eyes. And that troubled him. He was falling for her again. Only this time it was different. This time he had nothing to prove professionally. No reason to back away. No way to erect walls that would allow him to be in a relationship and still protect his heart. She'd broken it once. She could do it again.

"If you'd kept your mouth shut I could have gotten out of this."

"How? By being a brat? That's a skill that'll really help you in the real world."

"I don't care about the real world."

Cain snorted. "No kidding." He slid his tape measure from his tool belt and walked to the wall. Holding the end of the tape against the wall, he waved the tape measure's silver container at Billy. "Take this to the other end of the wall."

Billy sighed, but took the tape box and did as Cain requested.

"What's the length?"

"Ten feet."

"Exactly ten feet?"

"I don't know."

Exasperated, but not about to let Billy know that and give him leverage to be a pain all day, Cain said, "Okay. Let's try this again. You hold this end against the wall. I'll get the number."

Without a word, Billy walked the tape back to Cain and they switched places.

He measured the length, told Billy to let go of his end and the tape snapped back into the silver container. He reached for one of the long pieces of trim he'd purchased the day before. It bowed when he lifted it and he motioned with his chin for Billy to grab the other end. "Get that, will you?"

Billy made a face, but picked up the wood.

Cain carried it to the miter box. The tools he had in his truck were from nearly ten years before. Though they weren't the latest technology they still worked. And maybe teaching this kid a little something today might be the best way to get his mind off Liz. About the fact that he didn't just want her, he was doing crazy things for her. About the fact that if he didn't watch himself, he'd be in so far that he'd be vulnerable again.

"You know, eventually you'll have to go to somebody for a job. You're not going to get through school on your good looks."

Adjusting the wood in the box, Cain made his end cuts. He gestured for Billy to help him take the piece of trim to the wall again. He snapped it into place and secured it with a few shots from a nail gun.

"I was thinking maybe I'd try the bartending thing like you did."

Surprised, Cain glanced over. He cautiously said, "Bartending is good when classes are in session and working nights fits into your schedule. But summers were when I made my tuition. To earn that much money, you have to have a job that pays. Construction pays."

Billy opened his mouth to say something, but snapped it shut. Cain unexpectedly itched to encourage him to talk, but he stopped himself. If the kid wanted to talk, he'd talk. Cain had no intention of overstepping his boundaries. He knew that Liz had set Billy up with him to be a good example, but he wasn't a therapist. Hell, he wasn't even much of a talker. He couldn't believe this kid had gotten as much out of him as he had.

"My dad was—is—in construction."

"Ah." No wonder Liz thought this would be such a wonderful arrangement.

"Look, kid, you don't have to be like your dad. You can be anybody, anything, you want." He glanced around the room. "Doing stuff like this," he said, bringing his words down to Billy's level, "gives you a way to test what you're good at while you figure out who you are." He paused then casually said, "You mentioned that you wanted to go to med school."

"It's a pipe dream. No way I'll swing that."

"Not with that attitude."

Billy snorted. "My mom *can't* help."

"Hey, I made my own way. You can, too." Motioning for Billy to pick up the next board, he casually eased them back into conversation. "Besides, it's a good life lesson. The construction jobs I took to pay for tuition pointed me in the direction of what I wanted to do with my life."

Seeing that Billy was really listening, Cain felt edgy. It would be so easy to steer this kid wrong. He wasn't a people person. He didn't know anything about being raised by an abusive father. There were a million different ways he could make a mistake.

"I think I want to be a doctor, but I'm not sure."

"You'll work that out." He motioned for Billy to grab the tape measure again. "Everything doesn't have to be figured out in one day. Take your time. Give yourself a break. Don't think you have to make all your decisions right now."

Oddly, his advice to Billy also relaxed him about Liz. Every decision didn't have to be made in a day. That's what had screwed them up in the first place. They jumped from seat mates in a plane to dating to sleeping together in a matter of days. Melting and doing her bidding just because she turned her pretty green eyes on him was as bad as working to seduce her the first day he'd met her.

Somehow he had to get back to behaving normally around his wife.

Ex-wife.

Maybe the first step to doing that would be to remember falling victim to their sexual attraction hadn't done anything except toss them into an unhappy marriage.

* * *

Just outside the door, Liz leaned against the wall and breathed an enormous sigh of relief. Two minutes after she suggested Billy help Cain she remembered they'd be using power tools—potential weapons—and she nearly panicked. But it appeared as if Billy and Cain had found a way to get along.

She and Amanda began painting the dining room but at eleven-thirty, they stopped to prepare lunch. At twelve they called Cain and Billy to the kitchen table and to her surprise they were chatting about a big project Cain's company had bid on when they walked to the sink to wash their hands.

They came to the table talking about how Cain's job is part math, part hand-holding and part diplomacy and didn't stop except to grab a bite of sandwich between sentences.

Liz smiled at Cain, working to keep their "friendship" going and determined not to worry about her secret until the time to tell him materialized, but Cain quickly glanced away, as if embarrassed.

When they'd finished eating, Billy and Cain went back to their work and Liz and Amanda cleaned the kitchen then resumed painting.

At five, Liz's muscles were pleasantly sore. She did manual labor for a living, but the muscles required for painting were different than those required for washing windows, vacuuming and dusting. Amanda planned to take her kids out to dinner so Cain and Liz had decided to leave to give them time to clean up before going out.

Still, as tired and sore as she was, she couldn't let Cain go without telling him she was proud of him. Billy needed him and he had cracked some barriers that Amanda had admitted she couldn't crack. After his wary expression when he glanced at her at lunch, she had to tell him how much he was needed, how good a job he was doing.

Leaning against the bed of his truck, waiting as he said goodbye to Amanda and Billy, she smiled as he approached.

"I'm not sure if you're embarrassed because you didn't want to help Billy or embarrassed that you did such a good job."

He tossed a saw into the toolbox in the bed of his truck. "He's a good kid."

"Of course he is. He just spent the first sixteen years of his life with a man who gave him a very bad impression of what a man's supposed to do. You were a good example today."

"Don't toss my hat in the ring for sainthood."

She laughed.

"I'm serious. If Billy had been a truly angry, truly rebellious teen, I would have been so far out of my league I could have done some real damage."

She sobered. He had a very good point. "I know."

He made a move to open his truck door and Liz stepped away. "I'm sorry."

Climbing into the truck, he shook his head. "No need to apologize. Let's just be glad it worked out."

She nodded. He started his truck and backed out of the driveway.

Liz stared after him. She'd expected him to either be angry that she'd set him up or to preen with pride. Instead, he'd sort of acted normally.

She folded her arms across her chest and watched his truck chug out of the neighborhood and an unexpected question tiptoed into her consciousness. Was acting normally his way of showing her they could be friends… Or his way of easing himself back into her life?

After all, he didn't have to be here, repairing Amanda's house. He could have refused when Ayleen asked him.

He also hadn't needed to befriend Billy. Yet, he'd responded to her silent plea and then did a bang-up job.

He also didn't have to interact with her. She was only here as a chaperone of sorts. Now that the work was going smoothly, he could ignore her.

So what was he doing?

Chapter 6

"Happy Maids. Liz Harper speaking."

"Good morning, Ms. Harper. It's Ava from Cain Corporation. Mr. Nestor asked me to call."

Liz's heart did a somersault in her chest. Something was wrong. There was no reason for Cain to ask Ava to call except to reprimand her or fire her. Or maybe he'd finally found a full-time maid? It wasn't that she begrudged him help, but with Rita working now, bringing her staff up to seven, she needed every assignment she had and more.

"He's having some friends for a small dinner tonight—"

Liz's heart tumbled again and she squeezed her eyes shut. She wasn't fired. He was inviting her to a party! Oh God! He *was* trying to ease her back into his life.

"He's cooking."

Knowing Cain was very good at the grill, Liz wasn't

surprised. But she still didn't want to go to a party at his house. Not when she was just about certain he was trying to get them back together.

"So he won't have a caterer to clean up. He's going to need you to send someone tonight after the party to do that. He'll pay extra, of course."

Liz fell into her office chair, her cheeks flaming. So much for being invited to his party. He wanted her to *clean up.* She was his maid. Not a friend. Not a potential lover or date…or even an ex-wife. She was an employee.

He wasn't trying to ease her into his life. He wasn't even trying to show her they could be friends. He wasn't thinking that hard about it because in his mind there was no longer a question.

He didn't want her.

She swallowed again, easing the lump in her throat so she could speak. That was, after all, what she wanted.

"We'll be happy to clean up after the party."

"You'll only need one person."

No longer upset about the call itself, Liz noticed the pinched, tight tone of Ava's voice.

"It's a small party. Mr. Nestor and the partners of his new venture are gathering to have dinner before they sign a contract. He believes everyone will be gone by nine. Let me suggest you arrive around a quarter after nine."

The first time Liz had spoken with Ava, she'd been light, friendly, eager to get some housecleaning help for her boss. Today's stiff voice and formal tone puzzled Liz.

"A quarter after nine is fine."

She hung up the phone confused. Could Cain have told his assistant that Liz was his ex-wife? But why would he? What difference would it make? He never shared personal information with employees. Why start now?

Placing her fingers on her computer keyboard to begin inputting her workers' hours on a spreadsheet, she frowned. Even if he had told Ava that Liz was his ex-wife, why would that upset his assistant?

And was that why she hadn't received any referrals from Ava?

She'd expected at least one person to call and say they'd been referred. That was how it worked in Liz's business. Maids had to be trusted. A word-of-mouth recommendation worked better than cold advertising. Yet, she'd gotten no recommendation from Cain.

She shook her head, dislodging those thoughts and getting her mind back on work. She didn't want to waste this precious time she had to do her paperwork fuming and speculating. With Rita working, Liz could now spend afternoons in the office and she basked in having evenings off.

She frowned again. She wouldn't have tonight off. She couldn't ask one of her employees to work on such short notice; all of them had children. Evening work meant extra child-care expenses. Besides, Cain's house was back to being her assignment. After he'd been angry that she'd sent someone else after the waffle debacle, she'd taken the job back herself.

She sighed. She'd have to go to his house tonight.

But maybe that was good?

If nothing else, she had her perspective back. They were divorced, not trying to reconcile, and she had something to tell him. Alone in his house tonight, they could be honest with each other.

A mixture of fear and relief poured through her. Though telling him about the miscarriage would be difficult, it had to be done. He deserved to know.

She finished her paperwork around five and raced home to shower and change to have dinner with Ellie. She didn't mention that she had to work that night—

Or the odd tone in Ava's voice—

Or her realization that they hadn't gotten *one* referral from Cain—

Or that this might be the night she told Cain the secret she'd kept from him.

All of that would put Ellie on edge. Or cause her to make one of her powerful wishes. Instead, Liz listened to Ellie chatter about the Happy Maids employees. From the sparkle in Ellie's amber eyes it was clear she enjoyed being everyone's supervisor. Not in a lord-it-over-her-friends way. But in almost a motherly way. Which made Liz laugh and actually took her mind off Cain. Ellie was twenty-two. Most of the women she now supervised were in their thirties or forties, some even in their fifties. Yet Ellie clucked over them like a mother hen. It was endearing.

Because they talked about work most of the meal, Liz paid for dinner, calling it a business expense, and parted company with Ellie on the sidewalk in front of the restaurant. When she slid behind the steering wheel of her car and saw the clock on the dashboard her mouth fell open. It was nearly nine. No time to go home and change into a Happy Maids uniform.

She glanced down at her simple tank top and jeans. This would do. No matter how messy his house, she couldn't damage a tank top and jeans.

Worry over being late blanked out all of her other

concerns about this job until she pulled into Cain's empty driveway. Ava had been correct. Cain's guests hadn't lingered. But suddenly she didn't want to see him. She really wasn't ready with the "right words" to tell them about their baby. She wasn't in the mood to "play" friends, either, or to fight their attraction. Their marriage might be over, but the attraction hadn't gone. And that's what made their situation so difficult.

If they weren't so attracted to each other there would be no question that their relationship was over and neither of them wanted to reopen it. But because of their damned unpredictable attraction, she had to worry about how *she* would react around him. Not that she wanted to sleep with him, but he'd seduced her before. And they were about to spend hours alone. If she was lucky, Cain would already be in the shower.

She swallowed. Best not to think about the shower.

But as she stepped out of her car into the muggy night, she realized it was much better to think of him being away from her, upstairs in his room, ignoring her as she cleaned, rather than close enough to touch, close enough to tempt, close enough to be tempted.

Cain watched her get out of her car and start up the driveway and opened the front door for her. "Come in this way."

She stepped into the echoing foyer with a tight, professional smile.

She was wary of him. Well, good. He was wary of her, of what was happening between them. It was bad enough to be attracted to someone he couldn't have. Now he was melting around her, doing her bidding when she looked at him with her big green eyes. He'd already decided the cure for his behavior around her was to treat her like an ex-wife. But he knew so little about her—except what he knew from their marriage—that he wasn't quite sure how to do that, either.

When he'd finally figured out they needed to get to know each other as the people they were now, he'd had Ava call with the request that Liz clean up after his dinner party. Maybe a little time spent alone would give them a chance to interact and she'd tell him enough about herself that he'd see her as a new person, or at least see her in a different light so he'd stop seeing the woman he'd loved every time he looked at her.

"Most of the mess is in the kitchen," he said, motioning for her to walk ahead of him. He didn't realize until she was already in front of him that that provided him with a terrific view of her backside and he nearly groaned, watching her jean-clad hips sway as she walked. This was why the part of him that wanted her back kept surfacing, taking control. Tonight the businessman had to wrestle control away.

"And the dining room." He said that as they entered his formal dining room and the cluttered table greeted them.

"I thought you were eating outside?"

"My bragging might have forced me to prove myself to the partners by being the chef for the steaks, but it was a formal meeting."

"Okay." She still wouldn't meet his gaze. "This isn't a big deal. You go ahead to your office or wherever. I can handle it. I've been here enough that I know where to put everything."

He shook his head. If they were going to be around each other for the next few weeks, they had to get to know each other as new people. Otherwise, they'd always relate to each other as the people they knew from their doomed marriage.

"It's late. If you do this alone, it could take hours. I'll help so you can be out of here before midnight."

The expression on her face clearly said she wanted to argue, but in the end, she turned and walked to the far side of the table, away from him. "Suit yourself."

She began stacking plates and gathering silverware at the head of the table. Cain did the same at the opposite end.

Though she hadn't argued with his decision to help her, she made it clear that she wasn't in the mood to talk. They worked in silence save for the clink and clatter of silverware and plates then he realized something amazing. She might be wary of him, but she wasn't afraid of his fancy silverware anymore. Wasn't afraid of chipping the china or breaking the crystal as she had been when they were married.

Funny that she had to leave him, become a maid, to grow accustomed to his things, his lifestyle.

"It seems weird to see how comfortable you are with the china."

She peeked up at him. "Until you said that, I'd forgotten how *uncomfortable* I had been around expensive things." She shrugged. "I was always afraid I'd break them. Now I can twirl them in the air and catch them behind my back with one hand."

He laughed, hoping to lighten the mood. "A demonstration's not really necessary."

She picked up a stack of dishes and headed for the kitchen.He grabbed some of the empty wineglasses and followed her. If discussing his china was what it took to get her comfortable enough to open up, then he wasn't letting this conversation die. "I never did understand why you were so afraid."

"I'd never been around nice things."

"Really?" He shook his head in disbelief. "Liz, your job took you all over the place. You yourself told me that you had to wine and dine clients."

"In restaurants." She slid the glasses he handed her into the dishwasher. "It's one thing to go to a restaurant where somebody serves you and quite another to be the one in charge."

"You wouldn't hesitate now."

"No. I wouldn't. I love crystal and china and fancy silver."

The way he was watching her made Liz self-conscious, so embarrassed by her past that she felt the need to brag a little.

"I'm actually the person in charge of A Friend Indeed's annual fund-raiser." Her attention on placing dishes in the dishwasher, she added, "When we were married, I couldn't plan a simple Christmas party, now I'm in charge of a huge ball."

"There's a ball?"

Too late she realized her mistake. Though she wanted him to know about her accomplishments, she wasn't sure she wanted him at the ball, watching her, comparing her to the past. As coordinator for the event, she'd be nervous enough without him being there.

"It's no big deal," she said, brushing it off as insignificant. "Just Ayleen's way of getting her rich friends together to thank them for the donations she'll wheedle out of them before the end of the evening."

She straightened away from the dishwasher and headed for the dining room and the rest of the dirty dishes.

He followed her. "I know some people who could also contribute." He stopped in front of the table she was clearing and caught her gaze. "Can I get a couple of invitations to this ball or is it closed?"

Liz stifled a groan, as his dark eyes held hers. There was no way out of this.

"As someone working for the group, you're automatically invited. You won't get an invitation. Ayleen will simply expect you to be there."

But he would get invitations to Joni's barbecue and Matt's Christmas party. As long as he volunteered for A Friend Indeed, he'd be connected to her. She had to get beyond her fear that he would be watching her, evaluating her, remembering how she used to be.

The room became silent except for the clang of utensils as Liz gathered them. Cain joined in the gathering again. He didn't say anything, until they returned to the kitchen.

"Are you going to be uncomfortable having me there?"

She busied herself with the dishwasher to cover the fact that she winced. "No."

"Really? Because you seem a little standoffish. Weird. As if you're not happy that I want to go."

Because her back was to him, she squeezed her eyes shut. Memories of similar functions they'd attended during their marriage came tumbling back. Their compatibility in bed was only equaled by how incompatible they'd been at his events. A Friend Indeed's ball would be the first time he'd see her in his world since their divorce. She'd failed miserably when she was his wife. Now he'd see her in a gown, hosting the kind of event she'd refused to host for him.

"This *is* making you nervous." He paused, probably waiting for her to deny that. When she didn't he said, "Why?"

She desperately wanted to lie. To pretend nothing was wrong. But that was what had gotten her into trouble with him the first time around. She hadn't told him the truth about herself. She let him believe she was something she wasn't.

She sucked in a breath for courage and faced him. "Because I'll know you'll be watching me. Looking for the difference in how I am now and how I was when we were married."

He chuckled. "I've already noticed the differences."

"All the differences? I don't think so."

"So tell me."

"Maybe I don't want to be reminded of the past."

"Maybe if you told me about your past, you wouldn't be so afraid. If what you're fearing is my reaction, if you tell me, we'll get it out of the way and you won't have anything to fear anymore."

He wasn't exactly right, but he had made a point without realizing it. Maybe if she told him the truth about her humble beginnings and saw his disappointment, she could deal with it once and for all.

She returned to the dining room and walked around the table, gathering napkins as she spoke, so she wouldn't have to look at him.

"When I was growing up my mom just barely made enough for us to scrape by. I'd never even eaten in a restaurant other than fast food before I left home for university. I met you only one year out of school. And though by then I'd been wining and dining clients, traveling and seeing how the other half lived, actually being dumped into your lifestyle was culture shock to me."

"I got that—a little late, unfortunately—but I got it. We were working around it, but you never seemed to adapt."

"That's because there's something else. Something that you don't know."

Also gathering things from the table, he stopped, peered over at her.

Glad for the distance between them, the buffer of space, she sucked in a fortifying breath. "I…um…my parents' divorce was not a happy one."

"Very few divorces are."

"Actually my mom, sisters and I ran away from my dad." She sucked in another breath. "He was abusive."

"He hit you?" Anger vibrated through his words, as if he'd demand payback if she admitted it was true.

"Yes. But he mostly hit my mom. We left in the night—without telling him we were going—because a charity like A Friend Indeed had a home for us hundreds of miles away in Philadelphia. We changed our names so my dad couldn't find us."

He sat on one of the chairs surrounding the table. "Oh." Processing that, he said nothing for a second then suddenly glanced up at her. "You're not Liz Harper?"

"I am now. My name was legally changed over a decade ago when we left New York."

"Wow." He rubbed his hand along the back of his neck. "I'm sorry."

"It's certainly not your fault that my father was what he was or that I lived most of my life in poverty, always on the outside looking in, or that I didn't have the class or the experiences to simply blend into your life."

"That's why you're so attached to A Friend Indeed."

She nodded. "Yes."

A few seconds passed in silence. Liz hadn't expected him to say anything sympathetic. That simply wasn't Cain. But saying nothing at all was worse than a flippant reply. She felt the sting of his unspoken rejection. She wasn't good enough for him. She'd always known it.

"Why didn't you tell me before?"

She snorted a laugh. "Tell my perfect, handsome, wealthy husband who seemed to know everything that I was a clueless runaway? For as much as I loved you, I never felt I deserved you."

He smiled ruefully. "I used to think the same thing about you."

Disbelief stole her breath. Was he kidding her? She'd been the one with the past worth hiding. He'd been nothing but perfect. Maybe too perfect. "Really?"

"I would think why does this beautiful woman stay with me, when I'm an emotional cripple." He combed his fingers through his hair as if torn between the whole truth and just enough to satisfy her openmouthed curiosity. Finally he said, "The guilt of my brother's death paralyzed me. Even now, it sometimes sneaks up on me. Reminding me that if I'd left a minute sooner or a few seconds later, Tom would still be alive."

"The kid who hit you ran a red light. The accident wasn't your fault."

"Logically, I know that. But something deep inside won't let me believe it." He shook his head and laughed miserably. "I'm a fixer, remember. Even after Tom's death, it was me Dad turned to for help running the business and eventually finding a replacement he could trust with his company when he wanted to retire. Yet, I couldn't fix that accident. I couldn't change any of it."

"No one could."

He snorted a laugh. "No kidding."

A few more seconds passed in silence. Fear bubbled in her blood. She had no idea why he'd confided in her, but she could see the result of it. She longed to hug him. To comfort him. But if she did that and they fell into bed, what good would that do but take them right back to where they had been? Solving all their problems with sex.

She grabbed her handful of napkins and walked them to the laundry room, realizing that rather than hug him, rather than comfort him, what she should be doing is airing all their issues. This conversation had been a great beginning, and this was probably the best opportunity she'd ever get to slide their final heartbreak into a discussion.

She readied herself, quickly assembling the right words to tell him about their baby as she stepped out of the pantry into the kitchen again.

Cain stood by the dishwasher, arranging the final glasses on the top row. She took a deep breath, but before she could open her mouth, he said, "Do you know you're the only person I've ever talked about my brother's accident with?"

"You haven't talked with your family?"

He shrugged and closed the dishwasher door. Walking to the center island, he said, "We talk about Tom, but we don't talk about his accident. We talk about the fact that he's dead, but we never say it was my fault. My family has a wonderful way of being able to skirt things. To talk about what's palatable and avoid what's not."

Though he tried to speak lightly, she heard the pain in his voice, the pain in his words, the need to release his feelings just by getting some of this out in the open.

This was not the time to tell him about their baby. Not when he was so torn up about the accident. He couldn't handle it right now. Her brain told her to move on. She couldn't stand here and listen, couldn't let him confide, not even as a friend.

But her heart remembered the three sad, awful years after the accident and desperately wanted to see him set free.

"Do you want to talk about it now?"

He tossed a dishtowel to the center island. "What would I say?"

She caught his gaze. "I don't know. What would you say?"

"Maybe that I'm sorry?"

"Do you really think you need to say you're sorry for an accident?"

He smiled ruefully. "I guess that's the rub. I feel guilty about something that wasn't my fault. Something I can't change. Something I couldn't have fixed no matter how old, or smart or experienced I was."

"That's probably what's driving the fixer in you crazy."

"Yeah."

"It's not your fault. You can't be sorry." She shook her head. "No. You *can* be sorry your brother is gone. You can be sorry for the loss. But you can't take the blame for an accident."

"I know." He rubbed his hand along the back of his neck. "That was weird."

"Talking about it?"

"No, admitting out loud for the first time that it wasn't my fault. That I can't take the blame." He shook his head. "Wow. It's like it's the first time that's really sunk in."

He smiled at her, a relieved smile so genuine that she knew she'd done the right thing in encouraging him to talk.

The silence in the room nudged her again, hinting that she could now tell him about their baby, but something about the relieved expression on his face stopped her. He'd just absolved himself from a burden of guilt he never should have taken up. What if she told him about her miscarriage and instead of being sad, he got angry with himself all over again?

She swallowed, as repressed memories of the days before she left him popped up in her brain. All these years, she'd thought she'd kept her secret to protect herself. Now, she remembered that she'd also kept it to protect him. He had a talent for absorbing blame that wasn't really his.

If she told him now, with the conversation about his brother still lingering in the air, he could tumble right back to the place he'd just escaped. Surely he deserved a few days of peace? And surely in those days she could think of a way to tell him that would help him to accept, as she had, that there was no one to blame.

"We're just about finished here." She ambled to the dining room table again and brought back salt-and-pepper shakers. "I'll wash the tablecloth and wait for the dishwasher, but you don't have to hang around. I brought a book to read while I wait. Why don't you go do whatever you'd normally do?"

"I should pack the contracts we signed tonight in my briefcase."

"Okay. You go do that." She smiled at him. "I'll see you Friday morning."

He turned in the doorway. "I'm not supposed to be here when you come to the house, remember?"

She held his gaze. "I could come early enough to get a cup of coffee."

Surprise flitted across his face. "Really?" Then he grimaced. "I'm leaving town tomorrow morning. I won't be back until Friday night. But I'll see you on Saturday."

Another weekend of working with him without being able to tell him might be for the best. A little distance between tonight's acceptance that he couldn't take blame for his brother's accident and the revelation of a tragedy he didn't even know had happened wouldn't be a bad thing.

"Okay."

He turned to leave again then paused, as if he didn't want to leave her, and she realized she'd given him the wrong impression when she'd suggested they have coffee Friday morning. She'd suggested it to give herself a chance to tell him her secret, not because she wanted to spend time with him. But he didn't know that.

She turned away, a silent encouragement for him to move on. When she turned around again, he was gone.

He could have brought her into his world, shown her his lifestyle and gradually helped her acclimate. Instead, he'd fallen victim to the grief of his brother's death and missed the obvious.

He wanted to be angry with himself, but he couldn't. Just as he couldn't bear the burden of guilt over his brother's death, he couldn't blame himself for having missed the obvious. Blaming himself for things he couldn't change was over. But so was the chance to "fix" their marriage.

Somehow or another, that conversation over his dirty dishes had shown him that he and Liz weren't destined for a second chance. He could say that without the typical sadness over the loss of what might have been because he'd decided they hadn't known each other well enough the first time around to have anything to fix. What they really needed to do was start over.

He went through the back door into Amanda's kitchen, got a drink of water and then headed upstairs to assess what was left to be done, still thinking about him and Liz. The question was…what did start over mean? Start over to become friends? Or start over to become lovers? A couple? A *married* couple?

He'd been considering them coworkers, learning to get along as friends for the sake of their project. But after the way she'd led him out of his guilt on Wednesday night, his feelings for her had shifted in an unexpected way. He supposed this was the emotion a man experienced when he found a woman who understood him, one he'd consider making his wife. The first time around his idea of a wife had been shallow. He'd wanted a beautiful hostess and someone to warm his bed. He'd never thought he'd need a confidante and friend more.

Now he knew just how wrong he'd been.

And now he saw just how right Liz would have been for him, if they'd only opened up to each other the first time around.

So should he expand his idea from experimenting with getting to know each other in order to become friends, to experimenting with getting to know each other to see if they actually were compatible? Not in the shallow ways, but in the real ways that counted.

Just the thought sent his head reeling. He didn't want to go back to what they'd had before…but a whole new relationship? The very idea filled him with a funny, fuzzy feeling. Though he didn't have a lot of experience with this particular emotion…he thought it just might be hope.

They couldn't fix their past. But what if they could have a future?

Shaking his head at the wonder of it all, Cain ducked into the first bedroom, the room with the most ceiling damage. He pulled a small notebook and pen from his shirt pocket and began making notes of things he would do the next day, Sunday. His crew would have the new roof far enough along that he could fix this ceiling and then the room could be painted. Because Amanda couldn't be there when any work crew was on site—to keep her identity safe—Liz would paint this room herself. The following weekend he and Billy could get to work on the baseboards and trim.

Proud of himself, Cain left the first room and walked into the second. This room still needed the works: ceiling, paint job, trim. He ducked out and into the bathroom, which was old-fashioned, but in good repair because he had fixed both the commode and shower the first week he'd been here. He dipped out and headed for the biggest bedroom, the one Amanda was using.

He stepped inside, only to find Liz stuffing a pillow into a bright red pillowcase.

"What are you doing here?"

Hand to her heart, she whipped around. "What are you doing down here! You're supposed to be on the roof."

"I'm making a list of things that need to be done tomorrow and next weekend."

"I'm surprising Amanda. I dropped her and her kids off at the beach, telling them I'd be back around six."

He leaned against the doorjamb. This room hadn't sustained any damage because of the bad roof. At some point during the week, Liz and Amanda had already painted the ceiling and walls. At the bottom of the bed were packages of new sheets and a red print comforter. Strewn across a mirror vanity were new curtains—red-and-gold striped that matched the colors in the comforter—waiting to be installed.

"By giving her a whole new bedroom?"

"Having a bedroom that's a comfortable retreat is a simple pleasure." Shaking a second pillow into a pillowcase, she smiled. "Women like simple pleasures. Bubble baths. A fresh cup of coffee. A good book."

"And a pretty bedroom."

She nodded. "And before you ask, Amanda's favorite color is red. I'm not going overboard."

"I'm glad because another person might consider this whole system a bit bright."

"This from a man with a black satin bedspread."

He laughed. "Point taken."

"How's the roof going?"

"It'll be done tomorrow night. That's the good thing about these houses. Small, uncomplicated roofs."

"Good."

With the pillows now on the bed and the fitted sheet in place, Liz grabbed the flat sheet, unfurling it over the bed.

Cain strode over and caught the side opposite her. "Here. Let me help."

"Thanks."

"You're welcome." He paused then added, "You know I'm really proud of you, right?"

"You don't have to say that."

"I think I do. Wednesday night, we sort of skipped from your childhood to my brother's death and never got back to it."

"There's no need."

"I think there is." He hesitated. In for a penny, in for a pound. "I'd like to know more." He shook his head. "No. That's not right. You said it's not something you want to talk about." In three years of living together, he'd bet she'd shown him signs of her troubles, but he'd never seen. He regretted now that he'd never seen her pain. Deeply. Wholeheartedly. If he'd noticed, he could have asked her about it at any time in their marriage. Now he knew she wanted it to be put behind her. If he really wanted a clean slate, he had to accept what she wanted, too.

"What I'm trying to say is that I want you to know that I get it. I understand. And maybe I'm sorry."

He still wasn't sure what he intended to do. If he should trust that funny feeling in the pit of his stomach that told him he should pursue this. Mostly because she was so different now that he had to treat her differently. She had goals and dreams. The first time they'd met he'd pulled her away from everything she had and everything she wanted. He wouldn't do that to her this time.

And maybe that was the real test of whether or not they belonged together. If he could coexist without taking over, and if she could keep her independence without letting him overpower her, then maybe they did belong together.

He nearly snorted with derision. That was a tall order for a man accustomed to being the boss and a woman so obviously eager to please.

"You don't have to be sorry."

"Well, I am. I'm sorry I didn't put two and two together. I'm sorry I made things worse."

They didn't speak while finishing the bed. Liz couldn't have spoken if she'd tried. There was a lump in her throat so thick she couldn't have gotten words past it.

When the bed was all set up, he said, "I better get back to the roof."

Liz nodded, smiling as much as she could, and he left the room. She watched him go then forced her attention on the bed she'd just made. She'd missed another really good opportunity to tell him. But his apology about her situation with her dad had left her reeling. She hadn't wanted to be overly emotional when she told him about their lost child. She wanted to be strong. So he could be sad. She wanted to keep the focus of the discussion on the loss being a loss…not someone's fault.

Still, she'd better pick a time…and soon. With two honest discussions under their belts, he'd wonder why she'd kept her most important secret to herself when she'd had opportunities to tell him.

* * *

The following weekend and the weekend after, Liz found herself working primarily with Amanda. With the roof done, Amanda and Billy didn't need to be off premises, and both were eager to get back on the job. Cain and Billy did the "man's work" as Billy called it, and Amanda and Liz painted and then made lunches. There was never a time when she and Cain were alone.

Their final Sunday of work, with the roof replaced, the rooms painted, the plumbing working at peak efficiency, and shiny new baseboard and crown molding accenting each room, Amanda had wanted to make a big celebration dinner, but Cain had a conference call and Liz had begged off in favor of a cold shower. She kissed Amanda, Joy and Billy's cheeks as Cain shook hands and gave hugs, then both headed for their vehicles.

"That was amazing," Cain said when they were far enough from Amanda's house that she couldn't hear.

Liz blew out a breath of relief. "Dear God, yes. Finishing is amazing!"

He shook his head. "No. I'm talking about actually doing something for someone." He sighed, stopping at the door to his truck. "You know that I give hundreds of thousands of dollars away a year, so you know I'm not a slouch. But giving is one thing. Working to help make a real person's life better is entirely different."

"No kidding!"

"I don't think you're hearing what I'm telling you. I feel terrific."

She laughed. "You've got charity worker's high."

He shook his head again. "No. It's more than that. I feel like I've found my new calling."

Shielding her eyes from the sun, she peeked up at him, finally getting what he was telling her. "Really?"

"Yes."

"You know A Friend Indeed has other houses."

"Yes."

"You can call Ayleen and I'm sure she'll let you fix any one of them you want."

He caught her gaze. "Will you help?"

Her heart stopped. Spend another several weeks with him? "I don't know." She pulled in a breath. When he looked at her with those serious eyes of his, she couldn't think of saying no. Especially since he'd been so happy lately. And especially since she still had something to tell him and needed to be around him.

But she didn't really want to connect their lives, and working together on another project more or less made them a team.

"Okay, while you think about that, answer this. I'm considering hiring Billy to be my assistant on these jobs. I know I'll have to clear it with Ayleen, but before I talk to her I'd like a little background. Just enough that I don't push any wrong buttons."

"As long as you don't hit his mother, I think you'll be fine."

"That bad, huh?"

Liz sighed. "I think the real problem might be getting him to accept a job."

"Really? Why?"

"He might think it's charity."

"I never thought of that."

"He's got a lot of pride."

Cain snorted a laugh. "No kidding. But we made

headway working together." He grinned at her. "I think he likes me."

Liz rolled her eyes. "He admires you."

"So I'll use that. I'll tell him he's getting a chance to work with the big dog. Learn the secrets of my success."

She laughed and an odd warmth enveloped her. Talking with him now was like talking with Ellie. Casual. Easy. Maybe they really had become friends?

"Hey, you never know. It might work."

She grimaced. "I'm sure it will work." She finished the walk to her car. She didn't mind being friends with him, but she also didn't want to risk the feeling going any further.

As she opened the door, Cain called after her, "So, are you going to help me?"

That was the rub. If she agreed to work with him, they really would become friends. And she'd probably have plenty of time not only to tell him her secret, but also to help him adjust to it. On the flip side, if things didn't go well, she'd have plenty of time to see him angry, to watch him mourn, if he didn't handle the news well.

"I'm going to think about it."

Liz slid into her car and drove away. Cain opened his truck door. He'd expected her to be happier that he wanted to work on more houses. But he supposed in a way he understood why she wasn't. The very reason he wanted her to work with him—to be together, to spend time together so they could get to know each other and see if they shouldn't start over again—might be the reason she didn't want to work with him. Their marriage had been an abysmal failure. She didn't want to be reminded and she didn't want to go back.

If he was considering "fixing" their marriage, he'd be as negative as she was. But he didn't want to fix their marriage. He wanted them to start over again.

Unfortunately, he wasn't entirely sure how.

Tuesday, Cain spoke with Ayleen and got approval to hire Billy. Actually, he got gushing glowing praise on the job he had done and his generosity in taking Billy under his wing. Then he got the address of the next house he was to repair and the suggestion that he might want to start that Saturday.

So he drove to Amanda's and offered Billy a job, which Billy happily accepted, especially after Cain mentioned his salary.

High on the success of the first part of his plan, Cain called Liz the minute he returned to his house.

She answered on the first ring. "Happy Maids."

"You really should have a personal cell phone."

"Can't afford it. What do you want, Cain?"

"Is that any way to talk to the man who's offering you a ride to our job site on Saturday? I'm already stopping for Billy—one more will fit into the truck."

"You got Billy to take a job?"

"I made him an offer he couldn't refuse."

"That's great! Amanda will be so thrilled."

"I'm glad to be able to do it." He paused. "So what do you say? Want a ride?"

"I haven't even agreed to work with you yet."

He could have threatened her with calling Ayleen and forced her hand. He could have said, "Please," and maybe melted her the way she could melt him. Instead he said nothing, letting the decision be her own, following his own directive that this relationship would be totally different. Fresh. New.

"Okay. But I'll meet you there." Her answer was cool, businesslike, but he didn't care. They'd had a crappy marriage. He'd hurt her. But more than that, he'd pulled her away from her dreams. He had to accept that she'd be wary of him. Then he had to prove to her she had no reason to be. They were starting over.

Peggy Morris had chosen not to be home when Cain and company did the work on her house. Liz had said she would get the keys and be there when Cain and Billy arrived. As Cain opened the back door into the kitchen, she turned from the sink. When she saw the picnic basket Billy carried, she grinned.

"Your mom's a saint."

Billy frowned. "Why?"

"For making lunch."

"I made that," Cain said. "Well, actually, I had Ava call a deli and place an order. I've got sandwiches, soda, bottled water, dessert… The cheesecake you like."

She groaned. "Oh, Cain! I can't have cheesecake! I'll be big as a house."

He laughed. She might have groaned about the cheesecake, but she accepted that he'd brought lunch. It was a good start. "You've lost weight since we were married."

Billy glanced from Cain to Liz. "You two were married?"

Cain said, "Yes."

Liz said, "A long time ago."

Billy shook his head. "You don't look like married people to me."

Liz walked over and put her hand on Billy's forearm. "Your parents' situation wasn't normal, Billy."

"Yeah, but even my friends' parents argue all the

time. You two get along." He looked from Cain to Liz again. "So why'd you get divorced?"

"Long story," Liz said.

"I was too busy," Cain countered.

Before Billy could say anything more about them, Liz turned him in the direction of the door again. "You don't need to know about this. It's ancient history, and we do need to get started on what we came here to do." She pointed at the door. "I'm guessing Cain's got about ten cans of paint in his truck. Let's go get them."

The three of them made a good team. Liz jumped into the truck bed and handed paint gallons, brushes, trays and other equipment to Cain and Billy who carted everything into the garage.

When the supplies were on the garage floor, Cain took charge again. "We're starting at this house because essentially everything is in good repair. When Ayleen brought me over this week to check things out, I noticed a few of the walls and ceilings need to be mended and there's also some work in the bathroom." He pointed at a new shower head and some unidentifiable plumbing equipment in another package. "I'll do all that. You guys can paint. I thought we'd start upstairs and work our way downstairs."

Liz said, "Okay."

Billy said, "I already know how to paint. I want to help with the repair work."

"The thing about construction is that you have to do whatever needs to be done. You don't get to pick your job." He handed Billy two gallons of beige paint. "Eventually you'll demonstrate that you have a strength or two like electrical or plumbing, and you'll be considered the expert and get to do those jobs whenever they come up. But if there's no electrical or plumbing, you'll paint."

Billy grumbled, but Cain pretended not to notice. Hiding a smile, Liz picked up some paint trays, brushes and rollers and followed Billy to the door into the kitchen.

He waited until Billy was through the door before he called her back. "Liz?"

She turned, her eyes wide and round, as if afraid of what he might say.

He wanted to tell her thanks. He wanted to say she looked pretty that morning. Because she appeared to be afraid of him and his motives, he handed the blue tape to her. "You're not a good enough painter to forget the blue tape."

She didn't have a free hand, so he tossed it onto a paint tray, then turned and picked up the bag of plaster.

Liz spent an enjoyable morning painting with Billy. A few times Cain came into the room and either pulled Billy to show him something about the repair work he was doing on the ceiling or in the bathroom, or to praise them for the good job they were doing. Billy blossomed under Cain's attention. He even chattered to Liz about the toilet tank "guts" exchange that Cain had explained to him.

"Because it's normal for commodes to need these kinds of repairs," Billy repeated Cain's comments verbatim. "My mom might need me to do that one day."

Though Liz was tempted to laugh, she held it back. "That's right. If you learn enough with Cain, you'll be able to fix things as they break at home."

"I know," Billy said seriously, sounding proud and responsible.

Liz ruffled his hair. "Get your paintbrush. We've got hours of this ahead of us."

Lunch was fun and relaxing. Billy had a million questions for Cain and he happily answered them. Having completed the repair work to the walls and ceilings, Cain joined the painting in the afternoon.

At five, Liz suggested they begin cleaning up.

"I could go for another hour or two, how about you, Billy?"

"I'm cool."

Liz shook her head. "The family has to come home sometime. Because Peggy is new and doesn't know any of us, Ayleen doesn't want her to find us here when she returns."

"Oops." Cain laughed. "Forgot."

Leaving the paint and supplies in the garage, Cain and Billy piled into his truck again. Liz walked to her car.

"See you tomorrow?"

She faced the truck. "Yeah."

Cain grinned at her. "Okay."

She climbed into her car with the same strange feeling she'd had at Amanda's about Cain being normal. Wondering if he was working to make her a friend or trying to ease her back into a relationship. But this time it was slightly different. Dealing with him today had been like dealing with a new friend. A *new* friend. Which was odd.

She knew their discussion about his brother had released him from the burden of guilt that had held him back emotionally. He was happy now. Easygoing. Which was probably why he seemed like a new person to her. She was also grateful that she had helped him. But something new was entering their equation. A question. A problem.

What if she told him about their baby and it threw him into a tailspin again?

She turned and watched his truck as it roared down the road. Billy sat in the passenger's side, his elbow out the open window. Cain sat in the driver's side, his elbow out the open window. They could be friends. Older and younger brother.

The truck turned right and disappeared down the street. Liz watched after it. He couldn't fake what he felt for Billy. The boy was just a tad too inquisitive for an impatient man like Cain to fake patience. He was the happiest she'd ever seen him. And her secret could ruin that.

The next morning Cain arrived at the house with Billy in tow and another picnic basket stuffed with food. Eager for lunch, Billy went straight to work. He'd become so good at painting and had such a steady hand that Cain suggested he paint the line bordering the ceiling and around the windows and trim.

Proud of himself, Billy continued to blossom under the praise.

But Liz found herself watching Cain, watching his patience with Billy, watching his commitment to doing a good job for A Friend Indeed, watching the way he treated her. Not as an ex-wife, not as a woman he was pursuing, but as a coworker.

In a lot of ways that was weird.

"Get the lead out, Harper. If you keep repainting the same wall, we'll be here again next weekend."

"Got it. Sorry."

"If you're tired, take a break."

She faced him. "A break? What's a break? Billy, do you know what a break is?"

"Not hardly."

She laughed and went back to painting, but Cain sighed. "All right. We'll all take ten minutes then we have to get back to it."

Liz didn't need to be told twice. After using the bathroom, she jogged down the stairs and into the garage, where Cain had stored a cooler with bottled water and soft drinks. She took a can of diet cola, snapped open the lid and drank.

"Sorry about that."

Lowering the can from her mouth, she turned and saw Cain walking into the garage. "You don't have to go overboard with being nice."

"I'm not."

"Sure you are. I'll bet you wouldn't apologize to your workers if you got so wrapped up in a job you forgot to give them a break."

"Probably not."

"So why treat me and Billy any differently?"

"Maybe because I'm having trouble finding a happy medium."

"Billy's a good kid who needs to be in the real world. And that might include a boss who forgets to give him a break."

"I'm not having trouble figuring out how to deal with Billy."

Right. She got it. She was the problem. Their feelings around each other had gone up and down, back and forth and sideways. Plus they had a past. Even as objective as she tried to be, sometimes that past snuck up on her.

"Maybe that's because we shouldn't be working together."

Just when she thought he'd admit he'd made a mistake in asking for her help, he surprised her. "We both like Billy. We both recognize that if somebody doesn't grab hold of him right now God only knows what he'll get into." He caught her gaze. "We can do this, Liz. We can help him. Save him. Don't you even want to try?"

She swallowed. "Actually, I do." And for the first time since she'd seen him standing in only a towel in his kitchen, she wanted to tell *him* she was proud of *him*. She wanted to say it so much that she suddenly understood what he'd been going through every time he'd seen one of the changes she'd made since their marriage.

The feeling was nearly overwhelming.

"You know I'll help Billy. I'll do everything I can."

He smiled at her, a smile so warm and open, she could only stare at him. The spark was back in his dark brown eyes. His hair fell boyishly to his forehead. But that smile. Oh, that smile. She would have done anything to see that smile three years ago. It seemed to say that he was different. Happy. Easy to be around. If they didn't have a past, if she didn't have a secret, Cain would be the man she would actually consider giving her heart to.

But they did have a past. And she did have a secret.

She chugged her soda and headed into the house just as Billy came out.

"Hey! I didn't even get a drink."

"Go ahead and get one. I'm ready to get back to work, so I'm going in. You and Cain take all the time you need."

Chapter 8

Cain jumped into his Porsche and punched the address on the invitation in his hand into his GPS unit. He'd been invited to a party being hosted by one of the women who'd been helped by A Friend Indeed. In a few minutes, he found himself driving down the street of the middle-class, blue-collar neighborhood.

He hadn't wanted to attend this party. But it had been a real stretch for him to volunteer to help with the Friend Indeed houses and an even bigger stretch to have taken Billy under his wing and those things had worked out amazingly well. So attending an event for the families involved with the charity was simply another level of change for him. Especially since it would involve chit-chat. No bankers or businessmen to schmooze. No business talk tonight. Somehow or other he'd have to be… well, normal.

But he'd decided to once again push beyond his own inadequacies to attend tonight because he couldn't stop thinking about something Liz had told him. When he'd first arrived at Amanda's, Liz had instructed him to accept anything any client offered because this might be the first time in a long time they'd had something to offer. He'd finally wrapped his head around just how demoralized and demeaned these women had been and then his thoughts had segued to the fact that Liz and her family had been abused.

Liz had been a child in a family just like this one. Alone. Scared. Usually hungry. He couldn't bear the thought.

But that also meant he couldn't refuse an invitation to anything connected to Liz. He didn't want her to feel rejected by him, or that somehow she and her friends weren't good enough. They were. He was the socially awkward one. So to protect her, here he was, driving in an unfamiliar section of the city, about to attend a gathering with people he didn't know.

He parked on the street and headed up the sidewalk to Joni Custer's house. As he climbed the stairs to the front door, he held back a wince of pain. He'd been so busy proving himself to Liz and enjoying doing the work he loved—the work that had nudged him in the direction of success and riches—that he'd forgotten he wasn't eighteen anymore. Billy was probably stronger. And maybe he should be the one hefting boxes of hardwood, while Cain stuck to measuring and fitting.

He found the bell and within two seconds, the bright red front door opened. Liz stood on the other side. Dressed in shorts and a halter top, she looked amazing. Comfortable. Confident. Relaxed.

Their gazes caught and she smiled sheepishly. His heart did a cartwheel. She was smiling at him now, like a real person, not a person she was forced to socialize with, not a person she had to pretend to like. Her smile was genuine.

"Come on. Everybody's outside on the patio." She took a look at his attire and winced. "Somebody should have told you dress was informal."

Cain immediately reached for his tie. Walking into the foyer, he yanked it off and stuffed it in his jacket pocket. "I can make do." He removed his jacket and tossed it over a hook on a coat tree in the foyer. Following Liz to a sliding glass door at the back of the house, he rolled up the sleeves of his white shirt. "See, now I'm dressed appropriately."

"Well, not exactly appropriately." She turned and gave him another smile. "But better."

"How about a little background before I go out there into a sea of people I don't know."

"Joni is one of the first women we helped. Every year she hosts a barbecue. Most of the people attending are also A Friend Indeed women, but some are parents and friends of the clients." She hooked her arm in the crook of his elbow and headed for the door again. "I'll introduce you around, but then you're on your own."

It felt so good to have her at his side that it disappointed him that she wouldn't stay with him, but he understood. If they had just met, they'd still be in a friend stage, not behaving like a couple. He had to accept that.

"I appreciate the introductions."

She hesitated another few seconds at the door. "You might get a critique or two of the work you've done."

"Hey, you helped!" He opened the sliding glass door. "If I'm going down in flames, you're going with me."

She laughed and the second they stepped onto the stone floor of the small patio, Liz said, "Hey, everybody, this is Cain. He's the new board member who's been fixing up houses."

A general round of approval rippled through the crowd.

Liz leaned in and whispered, "Get ready. Any second now you'll be surrounded."

Her warning didn't penetrate. He was too busy analyzing whether it was good or bad that she hadn't introduced him as her ex-husband. On the one hand it did point to the fact that she saw their association as being a new one. On the other, she could be embarrassed about having been married to him. So it took him by surprise when a middle-aged man approached him and extended his hand for shaking.

"You did Amanda's house?"

"That was mostly painting," Cain said, snatching Liz's hand, holding her in place when it appeared she would desert him. "And Liz and I were equal partners on that one."

"Don't be so modest," Ayleen said, ambling up to them. "I hear the whole house is to die for."

"It is." Amanda walked over. She unexpectedly hugged Cain. "Thanks again."

Embarrassment flooded him at her praise. What he'd done was so simple, so easy for him. Yet it had meant the world to Amanda. "I guess that means you like the house?"

"*Like* is too simple of a word," she said with a laugh.

Liz shook her hand free of his, as if eager to get away. "How about if I get us a drink? What would you like?"

Not quite sure what to say, Cain raised his eyebrows in question. "What do they have?"

"What if I get us both a cola?"

"Sounds great."

The second Liz left, he began fielding questions about the work he'd done on Amanda's house and the four houses he still planned to repair.

Eventually he and the middle-aged man who introduced himself as Bob, Joni's dad, wandered over to the grill.

"This is my grandson, Tony." Bob introduced Cain to the man flipping burgers.

Cain caught a flash of yellow out of his peripheral vision before a tall blonde grabbed his forearm and yanked him away from the grill. "Sorry, guys. But he's mine for a few minutes." She smiled at him. "I'm Ellie. My friends call me Magic."

"Magic? Like Magic Johnson, the basketball player?"

"No, magic as in my wishes generally come true and I can also pretty much figure out somebody's deal in a short conversation."

"You're going to interrogate me, aren't you?"

"I know who you are."

"Who I am?"

"You're Liz's ex. She hasn't said anything, but for her to be introducing you around, I'm guessing she likes you again."

He paused. His heart skipped a beat. Her wariness around him took on new meaning. He'd been so careful to behave only as a friend that she might not understand his feelings for her now ran much deeper. She might think he didn't like her "that" way anymore. But he did. And if she wanted more, so did he.

"Really?"

Ellie sighed. "Really. Come on. Let's cut the bull. We both know you're cute. We both know she loved you. Now you're back and she's falling for you. If she's holding back, I'm guessing it's only because she thinks you don't want her."

Cain couldn't help it; he smiled.

Ellie shook her head with a sigh. "Don't be smug. Or too sure of yourself. As her friend, I'm going to make it my business to be certain you don't hurt her again."

"You don't have to make it your business. You have my word."

She studied his face. "Odd as this is going to sound, I believe you."

Liz walked over with two cans of cola. "Ellie! What are you doing?"

"Checking him out," Ellie said without an ounce of shame in her voice. "I'm going to help Joni with the buns and salads."

Liz faced him with a grimace. "Sorry about that."

"Is she really magic?"

Liz laughed. "Did she tell you that?"

"Yes."

"Then she likes you and that's a big plus."

Liz casually turned to walk away, but Cain caught her arm. "So these people are your friends?"

"Yes."

He expected her to elaborate, but she didn't. She eased her arm out of his grasp and walked away. Ten minutes ago, that would have upset him. Now, Ellie's words repeated in his head. "If she's holding back I'm guessing it's only because she thinks you don't want her."

He glanced around and frowned. They were with her friends. He couldn't make a move of any kind here. That much *he* was sure of. But soon, very soon, he was going to have to do something to test Ellie's theory.

Cain went back to the group of men at the grill and in seconds he felt odd. Not exactly uncomfortable. Not exactly confused. But baffled, as if something important sat on the edge of his brain trying to surface but it couldn't.

The conversation of the men around him turned to children, house payments and job difficulties. He couldn't identify with anything they were discussing. He didn't have kids or a mortgage or job difficulties. So, he didn't say a word, simply listened, putting things in context by remembering the things he'd learned working with Billy and for Amanda, and then he suddenly understood why he felt so weird.

It wasn't because Liz's magical friend had basically told him that Liz cared for him. It was because Liz had left him alone with her friends. Alone. Not monitoring what he said. Not anxious or fearful that he'd inadvertently insult someone.

She trusted him.

She *trusted* him.

Just the thought humbled him. But also sort of proved out Ellie's suspicion that Liz liked him again as more than a friend. A woman didn't trust the people she loved to just anyone.

When the burgers were grilled to perfection, Cain scooped them up with a huge metal spatula and piled them on a plate held by Bob. When everything was on the table, he took a seat at the picnic table where Liz sat. He didn't sit beside her. He didn't want to scare her, but he did like being around her. And Ellie's comment that Liz was falling for him again was beginning to settle in, to give him confidence, to make him think that maybe it was time to let her know he was feeling the same way she was.

Not that it was time to get back together, but to start over.

The group at each table included adults of all ages and varieties and their children. They ate burgers, discussed football and fishing, and when everyone had eaten their fill, they played volleyball—in spite of Cain's Italian loafers. When the sun set, the kids disappeared to tell ghost stories in the dark, humid night and the adults congregated around the tables again, talking about everything from raising kids to the economy.

All in all it was a very relaxing evening, but an informative one, as well. Liz fit with these people. Easily. Happily.

And he had, too.

It was time for him to get their relationship on track. And since they were doing things differently this time around, he wouldn't slyly seduce her. He intended to actually tell her he wanted to be more than her friend, ask her if she agreed. To give her choices. To give her time.

Exactly the opposite of what he'd done when he met her six years ago.

The back door slid open. A little kid of about six yelled, "Hey! There's a jacket in here that's buzzing."

Everybody laughed.

An older girl raced up behind the kid. "Somebody's

cell phone is vibrating. It's in the pocket of a jacket hanging on the coat tree."

Cain rose. He'd been so caught up in being with Liz that he'd forgotten his cell phone, hadn't cared if he missed a call. "I think that's mine." He glanced at Joni with a smile. "It's time for me to be going anyway. Thank you very much for inviting me."

Joni rose. "Thank you for coming. It was nice to meet the guy who's stirred up so much gossip!"

Not exactly sure how to take that, Cain faced Liz, who also rose. "She means about fixing the houses." She slid her hand in the crook of his elbow. "I'll walk you to the door."

Liz waited as Cain said his good-nights. Together they walked into the house and to the foyer. He lifted his suit jacket from the coat tree and the phone buzzed again. He silenced it without even looking at caller ID.

She nearly shook her head in wonder. She'd been worried about how he'd handle this party, how he'd get along with her friends, and she needn't have given it a second thought.

He opened the front door. "Walk me to my car?"

Her breath stuttered in her chest. If they hadn't had such a nice evening, she might have thought this was her perfect opportunity to tell him about their baby. But they had had a nice evening. A quiet, comfortable, relaxing time. She'd seen how hard he worked to get along with her friends. And she'd appreciated that. Her sad revelation was for another time.

She pulled her keys from her pocket. "How about if you walk *me* to *my* car?"

He smiled. "Sure. I just thought you'd be going back in."

"Nope."

"You know Ellie's going to give you the third degree. Might as well get it over with tonight."

"Not necessary. She'll call me before I even get home."

He laughed. Her chest constricted with happiness as unexpected feelings rippled through her. She hadn't fully admitted to herself how important it was to her that he like her friends. But it had been. Seeing him interacting with the Friend Indeed people had filled her with pride. She couldn't remember a time when he'd ever been this relaxed and she knew she'd had something to do with that. She'd helped him get beyond his guilt and helped him acclimate at A Friend Indeed, and in the end he'd become the man she'd always known he could be. Warm. Caring. Wonderful.

When they reached her atrocious little green car, she turned and faced him. Their gazes met and clung and she suddenly realized asking him to walk her to her car might have seemed like an invitation for him to kiss her good-night.

Her heart stilled. Her breathing stalled in her chest. Part of her screamed for her to grab the door handle and get the hell out of here. The other part was melting into soft putty. She'd loved this man with her whole heart and soul. He'd suffered the torment of the damned and she'd had to stand by helplessly. Now he was back. Almost normal, but better.

Was it so wrong to want one little kiss?

As his head slowly descended, she had a thousand chances to change her mind. A million cautions pirouetted through her brain. Every nerve ending in her body flickered with something that felt very much like fear.

But when their lips met, it was like coming home. The years melted away and he was the Cain she'd fallen in love with. Cain before he'd been burdened by guilt over his brother's death or the drive to succeed to bury that guilt.

The Cain she knew loved her.

He was *her* Cain.

Her lips came to life slowly beneath his. His hands slid to her upper arms, to her back and down her spine. She stepped closer, nestling against him. For the three years of their marriage she'd longed for this feeling. For the three years they'd been separated, she'd tried to forget this feeling. The warmth, the connection, the spark of need that ignited in her and heated her blood. Nobody had ever made her feel what Cain made her feel.

And she was finally discovering part of the reason was that she didn't want anybody else to make her feel what Cain could. She wanted Cain.

He pulled away slowly. She blinked up at him.

"Good night."

His voice was a soft whisper in the warm summer night. Her lips curved upward slowly. A kiss. Just a kiss. He hadn't pushed for more, hadn't asked her to follow him home, or if he could follow her. He'd simply wanted a kiss.

"Good night."

"I'll call you."

"Okay."

She opened her car door and slid inside. He stepped back, out of the way, as she pulled her gearshift into Drive and eased out into the night.

A little voice inside her head told her not to be so happy, because she hadn't yet been totally honest with him.

But she would be.

Soon.

For now though she wanted to bask in the warmth that flooded her because he'd kissed her.

Cain couldn't remember ever feeling so good or so hopeful about his life. It wasn't simply because Liz had feelings for him and had admitted them in the way she kissed him. He was also a changed man. He hadn't pretended to like her friends. He liked her friends. He hadn't been bored, nervous, or eager to get away to get back to work. Somehow or another over the past weeks, his longing to make up to Liz for their horrible marriage had reordered his priorities. He'd done what he felt he needed to do to pay penance for their bad marriage and as a result learned to work with Billy and for a cause that genuinely needed him.

And when the dust settled, he was changed. When he looked ahead to their future, he could see them making it work this time.

Driving home with the top down, thinking about some of the brighter days in their marriage, he almost didn't hear his cell phone ring. He'd shifted it from vibrate to ring when he directed the last call to voice mail as he'd walked Liz to her car. Though it had taken a few rings, eventually the low sound penetrated his consciousness and he grabbed the phone. Somebody had been trying to get a hold of him for the past hour, but he hadn't even cared enough to check caller ID.

If that didn't prove he'd changed, nothing did.

He glanced at the small screen and saw his sister's phone number.

His sister? What would be so important that she'd

call at least three times on a Sunday night? He frowned and clicked the button to answer.

"What's up, sis?"

"Cain. Thank God you finally answered. Dad's on his way to the hospital. Mom thinks he had a heart attack. It's pretty bad."

All the good feelings welled in his belly turned into a rock of dread. Even if the words hadn't penetrated, the shiver in his sister's voice had.

"I'm on my way."

Without another thought, he pressed speed dial for Ava. Her voice groggy with sleep, she said, "Cain?"

"Sorry to wake you. My dad had a heart attack. I need to get to Kansas tonight. Can you wake Dale?" he asked, referring to his pilot.

"I'm on it," Ava said sounding awake and alert. "You just get yourself to the airport."

Chapter 9

Liz's cell phone was ringing when she awoke the next morning. She reached over and pawed the bedside table to snag it. When she saw the name on caller ID, her breath stuttered out.

Cain.

He'd kissed her the night before. She'd wanted him to. Her insides tightened at the memory. She'd always loved him and now he was behaving as if he loved her, too. Doing things for her. Caring about the cause she cared about. Easing his way into her life.

Part of her wanted it. All of it. The attention, the affection, the connection. The other part of her was scared to death. They'd made a mistake before.

Her phone rang again and she pressed the button to answer. Her voice was soft and uncertain when she said, "Good morning, Cain."

"Good morning."

His greeting was rough, tired, as if he hadn't slept all night. And not for good reasons.

She scrambled up in bed. "What's wrong?"

"My dad had a heart attack yesterday. I'm in Kansas."

She flopped back onto her pillow. "Oh, God. I'm so sorry. Is there anything I can do?"

"No, I just—" He paused. "I just—"

He paused again and Liz squeezed her eyes shut. She got it. He'd called her for support, but he couldn't say it. Didn't know how. He'd never asked anyone for support or help before.

Tears filled her eyes and her heart clenched. She'd longed for him to reach out to her in the three years of their marriage, but he hadn't been able to. Now, after coming to terms with his brother's death, after spending some time with her, he was finally turning to her.

How could she possibly not respond to that?

"Would you like me to fly to Kansas?"

He sucked in a breath. "No. You have a business to run and things here are out of our control. There's nothing you could do."

"I could hold your hand."

She said the words softly and wasn't surprised when he hesitated before he said, "Right now I'm holding my mother's hand."

"She needs you, Cain." And he hadn't thought twice about flying out to be with her. At his core, he'd always loved his family. He simply felt he'd let them down. "Is there anything I can do for you here?"

"You could call Ava, let her know there's no news but that I arrived safely."

She smiled. That little kindness was also something she wouldn't have expected from him three years ago—or three weeks ago.

"I'll be glad to." She paused then said, "If you'll call me any time there's news, I'll call her and keep her posted."

"Okay."

"Okay." She wanted to tell him she loved him. The words sat on her tongue aching to jump off. He needed to hear it. She longed to say it. But what would happen when his dad was better and he came home? Would those three little words cause awkwardness, or push them beyond where they should be in this relationship they seemed to be building? Would it cause another mistake? Especially since love hadn't been enough the first time.

"I'll call you."

"Lucky for you you only have to remember one cell number."

He laughed. "Goodbye, Liz."

"Goodbye." She disconnected the call then sat staring at the phone. She'd said and done all the right things. She'd been supportive. He'd accepted her support. But they hadn't gone too far.

But he'd called *her*. Not his assistant. He'd been vulnerable with her in a way he'd never been before. He'd even asked her to make his phone call to Ava for him.

He was definitely different.

And she had a lot of thinking to do.

At noon, Ellie dropped into the Happy Maids' office with iced tea and sandwiches. "So dish! What happened?"

Liz looked up from the spreadsheet she was reading, as Ellie set the iced tea and sandwiches on her desk. "What happened when?"

"Last night. With your ex. I know you told me he was withdrawn after his brother's death, but it looks like he's getting over it and…" She nudged Liz across the desk. "He wants you back. Why else would a man play volleyball in those shoes he had on?"

Liz pulled in a big breath. "That's actually the problem. I think he does want us to get back together."

Ellie sat. "You say that as if it's bad."

"It was a crappy marriage. We both walked away hurt."

"Because he was closed off after his brother's death," Ellie insisted as she opened the bag and pulled out the sandwiches.

Accepting hers from Ellie, Liz said, "There's a lot more to it than that. I didn't fit in with the businessmen and their wives that he socialized with. I couldn't plan his parties." Even as she said the words, Liz realized that would no longer be true. Just as she'd explained to Cain as they were cleaning up after his dinner party, she had grown. Changed. "And he had a tendency to disappear when he had an important project. I spent a lot of those three years alone."

"Things would be different this time," Ellie said before she bit into her sandwich. "Even a person without magic could see that. He's different. Involved. Interested." She peered across the desk at Liz. "And you're different."

"Which sort of makes my point. We're so different that we'd actually have to get to know each other all over again."

"But that's good," Ellie said with a laugh. "Since the two people you were couldn't exactly make a marriage work before." She patted Liz's hand. "Trust me. Needing to get to know each other all over again is a good thing."

"The only thing we have in common is sex."

Ellie laughed. Then she said, "And A Friend Indeed. He's really involved and he wants to stay involved."

"Yeah, but I think he only went to work for A Friend Indeed to get to me."

"At first, maybe. But I watched him last night. He was sincere in getting to know our people. He's actually mentoring Billy. He's volunteered to do more work. This guy is in for the long haul."

Until the first crisis with his own company came along. Until a business acquaintance was more important than Billy. Until she was back in his bed and he considered that to be enough time spent with her.

She squeezed her eyes shut. There were just too many variables.

Cain called her every day, and every day she phoned Ava. "He's coming home on Friday morning," she told Ava the following Monday morning. "His dad is recovering well from the surgery, but he wants to stay the extra four days to be sure. His mother is calm. His sister is there for both of them."

The relief was evident in Ava's voice when she said, "That's great." She paused then asked, "Did he say if he's coming to work on Friday?"

"He didn't say."

"I'll have things ready just in case."

"Great."

"Great."

There was an awkward silence before Liz said, "Goodbye, then."

But instead of saying goodbye, Ava said, "He doesn't really turn to people, you know?"

Not quite sure what Ava was driving at, Liz said simply, "I know."

"So it's kind of significant that he turned to you."

Liz swallowed. Now she understood. The fact that Cain had Liz touch base with his PA for him proved that Cain and Liz had a connection. Ava was probing and hinting right now because she didn't want to see Cain hurt.

"I'll call you if he calls again," Liz said lightly, trying to get off the phone without the serious discussion Ava wanted to have. Then she said goodbye, hung up the phone and put her head in her hands.

No one knew better than Liz that it was significant that Cain had reached out to her. But she couldn't just jump off the deep end and let herself fall head over heels in love. She had to be careful. She had to be smart. Somehow or other *he* had to prove that if she let herself fall in love with him, things really would be different this time.

Cain called Liz with a glowing report of his dad's prognosis when he returned on Friday. It was already noon, so she'd long ago finished cleaning his house and was on to her second house of the day. He'd asked her to come over, but Friday was the one day that she had an entire eight hours' worth of houses to clean. She begged off and he accepted her refusal easily, saying he was going to take a dip in his pool before he checked in with Ava.

"I'll see you tomorrow morning, then."

"Fran Watson's house?"

"Yes. That's the house I talked about with Ayleen."

She hadn't thought he'd jump into A Friend Indeed work so quickly, except she knew the physical activity relaxed him. So the next morning she woke early, put on her jeans and tank top and headed for Fran Watson's house.

Because the entire house needed new floors, Liz expected to see rolls of discounted carpeting and padding extending from the back of Cain's truck when she pulled into the driveway. At the very most, inexpensive tile or linoleum. Instead, she found Cain and Billy unloading boxes of oak flooring.

"Oh, Cain! This is too much."

"Not really." He heaved a box out of the truck. Though Liz tried not to look, she couldn't help herself. His muscles shifted and moved beneath his T-shirt, reminding her of times they'd played volleyball by the ocean, laughing, having a good time.

She turned away. She had to stop noticing things, remembering things and begin to look in earnest for some kind of proof that these changes in him were permanent. That he wouldn't hurt her or desert her after he married her. That he really wanted a second chance.

He headed for the kitchen where he and Billy began stacking boxes of flooring. When he returned outside, he wiped sweat off his neck with a red handkerchief.

Expecting him to say something about his dad or to be uncomfortable about the fact that the last time they'd seen each other, he'd kissed her, Liz was surprised when he said, "I got the hardwood at a discount supply store."

She almost couldn't believe this was the same man

who had called her every day with reports on his dad, the guy who'd wanted to spend Friday afternoon with her. He seemed so distant, so cool.

Of course, they were working—and Billy was only a few feet away in the kitchen.

"Enough for the whole house?"

"I'm going to do the kitchen in a tile of some sort. If you've got kids in a kitchen, it's best to stay away from wood. Then I'm putting carpet in the bedrooms." He caught her gaze. "Personally, I like the soft feeling of carpet when I first roll out of bed."

Unwanted memories surfaced again. He'd always loved soft carpet, soft towels, soft pajamas. Especially hers. He'd said that was part of why he liked her. She didn't just wear soft clothes. *She* was incredibly soft. The softest woman he'd ever held. Even years later, she could remember the warmth of happiness from his compliment. And a glance in Cain's eyes told her that was why he'd said it.

Billy walked by with a box of wood on his shoulder. "I think we should listen to him. He's pretty smart."

Cain winced at the praise, but Liz laughed, grateful Billy had brought them back where they belonged.

When the kitchen door closed behind Billy, she turned to Cain. "I think he's officially your number-one fan."

"I just don't want him to be too big of a fan. One mistake and I can undo every good thing we've accomplished by being friends."

"Just keep teaching him and you'll be fine." She glanced in the back of the truck, at the stacks of boxes of wood and the table saw. "What am I going to do?"

"I pretty much figure you'll be our cutter."

She studied the wicked-looking blade on the table saw then gaped at him. "I'm going to use *that?*"

"I need Billy's strength for the rubber mallet. I'm going to be the one on the nail gun. That leaves the saw for you."

"Oh, good grief!"

"You can do it. It's not nearly as complicated as it looks."

As it turned out, most of the morning was spent ripping out the old flooring in their target rooms, and carting it to the Dumpster Cain had arranged to have in Fran's backyard. He'd brought safety glasses, gloves and all the equipment they'd need, plus lunch, because Fran also didn't want to be in the house while they worked.

"How did you have the time to get all this together?"

"I didn't stay at work yesterday. I handled the important messages, then told Ava to arrange for the lunch and the things we'd need like safety glasses, then I headed to the building supply store."

"You did this yesterday?"

"Yes."

She wanted to ask, "After spending an entire week out of the office, you weren't clamoring to get back to work?" But she didn't. His actions spoke louder than any words he could have said.

When they began installing the new floors, Liz did some of the cutting, but Billy did his share, too. He'd paid attention as Cain showed Liz how to use the saw and easily stepped into the role. He and Cain worked like a team that had been together for decades, not a few weeks, and Liz marveled at their connection. She marveled at Cain's easy patience with the boy, and even the way he tempered his reactions to her around Billy.

There was no mention of the kiss. No mention of the way he'd called her for support. But there was something about the way he looked at her that said more than words could that his feelings for her had grown, sharpened. When their hands accidentally brushed, he would let his fingers linger, as if he wanted the contact but knew it wasn't the place or time.

At the end of the day, he and Billy gathered the saw and tools for installing the floors and stowed them in his truck. "One more day and the hardwood's in. Next week we lay carpet. The week after, we get the linoleum in the kitchen. Piece of cake."

As he said all that, he punched notes into his BlackBerry. Probably a summary for Ayleen of what they'd accomplished that day.

He jumped into the truck. On the passenger's side, Billy followed suit. With a flick of a key, his truck's engine roared to life.

Liz stepped back, out of his way, then she ambled to her car and slid inside. When Cain's truck rolled out of the driveway and into the street, she laid her head on her steering wheel in dismay.

She finally understood why he hadn't made a big deal out of calling her or even out of kissing her the night of Joni's barbecue. This life they were building had become normal to him. Working with her on the Friend Indeed houses, mentoring Billy, calling her to talk about his family, even kissing her had become routine for him. He was different, eased into an entirely different way to live, and he was easing her in, too. And the next time they were alone she had no doubt he'd suggest a reconciliation.

She lifted her head and started her car. She hadn't

forgotten that she had something she needed to tell him. She'd been waiting for the right time. But she finally saw the right time wasn't going to magically materialize. And even if it did, he might take hold of the conversation and she'd lose the chance to tell him about their baby.

She had to visit him, at home, and get the final piece of their past out in the open.

Chapter 10

Monday morning, when Ava paged Cain on the intercom to tell him he had a call from Liz, he dropped to his desk chair and grabbed the phone. "Liz?"

"You know your assistant hates me, right?"

"Ava? She doesn't hate anybody." He paused. "But I'm glad you called."

She sighed. "You don't even know why I'm calling."

He was hoping that she'd missed him. Hoping she wanted to see him outside of work or A Friend Indeed. He'd settle for her simply wanting to talk to him. "I'm hoping you wanted to talk to me."

"I do. But privately. Would you have a few minutes to see me tonight?"

Privately? He fell back in his chair in disbelief. Then he scrambled up again. "Sure."

"I'll be over around six. Right after work."

"Great."

He hung up the phone. "Ava! I'm going to need a bottle of champagne and some fresh flowers for the house."

She walked to his office door and leaned against the jamb. "And why would you need that?"

"I'm having a guest tonight."

Her eyes narrowed. "The Happy Maids woman?"

Ah. So Liz wasn't so far off the mark after all. Ava didn't like her. "Am I sensing a bit of a problem?"

"Cain, you're a rich guy. You don't like little people, remember? It amazed me that you were working for A Friend Indeed, then I remembered how pretty Liz Harper is."

"Why do you care?"

"I worry about you because you're doing so many things out of character lately that you're scaring me." Sounding very much like his mother, she pushed away from the doorjamb and came into the room. "How do you know she's not after your money?"

"Because she refused alimony when we divorced."

Ava looked aghast. "She's your ex-wife."

"I probably should have told you that before this."

Ava studied him with narrowed eyes. "Getting involved with an ex is never a good idea."

He forced his attention back to the work on his desk. "I don't want to get involved with my ex." He *didn't* want to get involved with his *ex*. The old relationship hadn't worked. He wanted something new. Something better. He wanted something with the new Liz.

"Then why the champagne and flowers?"

Trying to ignore her, he tapped his pen on his desk. He and Ava had never really had a personal conversation. Even though she'd handled every nitpicky need in his life and knew him as much as anybody could, she'd kept the line of propriety with him. He couldn't believe she was walking over it now.

She took a few more steps into the room. "Cain, I know you well enough to know that you're up to something. Why not just tell me? Maybe I can help?"

Help? He wasn't the kind of man to confide about things like relationships with anyone let alone someone he worked with. But he'd ruined his marriage by being clueless. And right now he might be making progress with Liz, but he knew one wrong word could ruin everything.

Maybe he could use some help?

He *did* trust Ava. Plus, he would do anything, even ask for help, to figure out the best way to start over again with Liz.

"I don't want to get involved with my ex-wife because I want us to start over again."

"There's a difference?"

"Liz is different." He leaned back in his chair and tossed his pen to his desk. "I'm very different. I want our relationship to be different."

Ava walked closer to the desk. "You're serious."

"Never more serious. She's the only woman I've ever really loved. Our marriage got screwed up when my brother died." He wouldn't tell her the whole story. Just enough that she'd understand Liz wasn't at fault in their bad marriage. "I withdrew and I basically left her alone. I wasn't surprised when she left. She's one of the most kind, most honest, most wonderful people I've ever met. Another woman would have been gone after six months. She stayed three long years. And I hurt her." He pulled in a breath. "She shouldn't want me back."

"But you think she does?"

"I think she still loves me."

"Wow."

"So now I want her back and I have no idea how to go about getting her back."

"You're sure this is the right thing?"

"Absolutely."

"You're not going to hurt her again?"

Cain laughed. Leave it to Ava to so quickly take Liz's side now that she knew Cain had been at fault.

"I swear."

"Okay, then for starters, I wouldn't do the things you did the last time around."

"That's the problem. The last time I wined and dined her. Swept her off her feet." He half smiled at the memory. "If I don't wine and dine her—" He caught Ava's gaze. "How is she going to know I'm interested?"

"Lots of ways. But you don't want to use champagne and flowers. That would be too much like the past. Plus she's a businesswoman now." Her face scrunched as she thought for a second, then she said, "What time is she coming?"

"Six. Right after work."

"Feed her dinner." She sat on the seat in front of Cain's desk. "Trust a working woman on this one. Be practical."

"I've spent the past few weeks being practical. Pretending we were work buddies at A Friend Indeed." He wouldn't mention the kiss after the barbecue. The sweet memory might linger in his mind, but spending the following two weeks in Kansas had wiped away any opportunity he might have had to talk about it or expand on it with Liz. When he returned home, they'd had to pretend to be just friends in front of Billy. Private time was at a premium and he didn't want to waste it.

"This might be my only chance to be romantic."

"I didn't say you couldn't be romantic. I just said be practical first. Feed her. Have a normal conversation. Then do whatever it is you want to do romantically."

Cain's mouth twisted with a chagrined smile. What he wanted to do and what he had finally figured out was appropriate for a first date were two totally different things. Still, this might be his only shot. He had to play by the rules.

"All right. I'll try it your way."

Ava rose. "We should talk more often. Makes me feel like you're almost human."

He laughed. "Trust me. I'm fully human." Otherwise, Liz wouldn't have been able to break his heart the last time around. He also wouldn't be worried that she could very well break it this time, too.

At a quarter to six that night, with steaks sizzling on the grill and his refrigerator stocked with beer, Ava's words repeated themselves in Cain's head. The first time around he'd done his damnedest to impress Liz. He hadn't been practical at all. His head had been in the clouds. This time around he would be better, smarter.

The doorbell sounded just as the steaks were ready to come off the grill. He raced through his downstairs, opened the door and pulled her inside. "Steaks have to come off the grill. Follow me."

"I didn't want you to cook dinner!"

"I like to grill." He did and she knew that, so that eased them past hurdle one.

She followed him through the downstairs into the

kitchen and toward the French doors to the patio. "I still didn't want you to cook for me. I can't stay that long."

"You can stay long enough to eat one measly steak."

He said the words stepping out onto the cool stone floor of his patio.

Liz paused on the threshold. "This is beautiful."

He glanced around at the yellow chaise lounges, the sunlight glistening off the blue water in the huge pool and the big umbrella table with the white linen table-cloth rustling in the breeze coming off the water just past his backyard. He hardly noticed how nice it was. With the exception of grilling and sometimes using the pool, he was never out here. In the past six years, he hadn't merely worked too much, he missed too much. He didn't enjoy what he had. Or the people in his life.

Maybe that's what Ava meant when she told him to be practical. To be normal.

"There's beer in the fridge."

She stopped midstep. "Beer?"

"Yes. Get me one and one for yourself, while I get these steaks off."

"Sure."

By the time she returned, he had the steaks on two plates, along with foil-wrapped potatoes and veggies, both of which he'd also cooked on the grill.

Studying the food he'd prepared, she handed him a beer. "This looks great."

He shrugged and motioned for her to take a seat. "All easy to do on a grill."

"I'm impressed."

He sat across from her. "I don't want you to be impressed. I want you to eat."

She unwrapped her potato and reached for the butter

and sour cream. "I think you really were serious about seeing me put on some weight."

He laughed. "I like you just the way you are." His compliment didn't surprise him as it popped out of his mouth. Ava wanted him to behave normally, which he took to mean behave as his real self, and that was how he felt. But the compliment embarrassed Liz. Her cheeks reddened endearingly.

He wanted to tell her how beautiful she was but Ava's words rang in his head again. *Be practical.* He hadn't been practical the first time and as a result they'd never gotten to know each other. They'd each married a stranger.

"So tell me about your family."

She peeked up at him. "I did, remember?"

"You told me about your dad…about your past. I'm interested in your family now. You said you had sisters."

She licked her lips, stalling, obviously thinking about whether or not she should speak, what she should say, if she should say anything at all. Cain's heart nearly stopped. This was it, the big test of whether or not she was interested in a real relationship, and she was hesitating over the easy questions.

Could he have read this whole situation wrong? The kiss before he left for Kansas? The lifeline she'd been while his father was sick? The heated looks and lingering touches at the Friend Indeed houses?

"My mom works as a nurse."

Relief poured through him. "No kidding?" Feigning nonchalance he didn't feel, he unwrapped the foil around his veggies. He had to be comfortable if he wanted her to be comfortable. "What about your sisters? What do they do?"

"My older sister is a physician's assistant. My younger sister is a pharmaceutical sales rep."

"Interesting. Everybody's in medicine in some way." He took a bite of broccoli.

Liz cut a strip off her steak. "Except me."

"You're still helping people."

"Yeah, but my degree's in business. I didn't get the nerves of steel my mother had. I couldn't have gone into medicine. I'm the family rebel."

"Me, too. My dad owned a chain of hardware stores. And here I am in Miami, running three companies that use hardware but aren't in the hardware business."

"I always wondered why you didn't just stay in Kansas and join the family business."

"When it was time for me to go to school, the stores hit a rough patch. That's why I put myself through university." He shook his head. "But what a backhanded lucky break. It led me to the work I love."

"You *were* lucky."

The second the words were out of her mouth, Liz regretted them. Cain might have been lucky in business but he hadn't been lucky in life. He'd suffered a horrible tragedy in the loss of his brother, particularly since he'd been the driver of the car. Their marriage had failed. Now she was here to tell him of another heartbreak. The conversation had been going in the absolute right direction until she'd made her stupid comment about him being lucky.

"I was lucky, but not entirely. Once I figured out what I wanted to do with my life I had to work hard to make it happen."

She nearly breathed a sigh of relief that he hadn't

taken her comment the wrong way and challenged it as he could have. "True."

He slid his hand across the table. "And that's why I'm glad you wanted to talk tonight." He pulled in a breath, reached for her fingers. Before Liz could stop him he had his hand wrapped around hers. "I know I'm going to say this badly, but I can't go on the way we have been over the past few weeks." He caught her stunned gaze. "I don't want a reconciliation. Neither one of us wants to go back to what we had." He brought her fingers to his lips and kissed them. "But there's no law that says we can't start over. We're both different—"

Liz's breath froze in her lungs. She was too late! She loved him and now he was falling for her. She'd thought she'd fallen first and maybe too fast because Cain was so different that it was easy for her to see that and respond to it. But he was right with her. Falling as fast and as hard as she had been. Now she had to scramble to set things right.

Only with effort did she find the air and ability to speak. "Oh, Cain, we can't pretend we don't have a past."

"Sure we can."

"We can't!" She sucked in a breath, calmed herself. For weeks she'd been waiting for the right time to tell him her secret. She'd hesitated when she should have simply been brave and told him. She couldn't let another opportunity pass. "Cain, I can't forget the past and neither can you. We have to deal with it. I left you because I had a miscarriage. I needed help. Real help to get beyond it."

His face shifted from happy to shocked. "You were pregnant?"

"Yes."

"And you didn't tell me?" He let go of her hand and combed his fingers through his hair.

"I *couldn't* tell you—"

Music suddenly poured from Liz's cell phone. She pulled it from her jeans pocket, hoping that a glance at caller ID would allow her to ignore it. When she saw it was Ayleen, she almost groaned. She couldn't ignore a call from A Friend Indeed.

She glanced at Cain in apology, but opened her phone and answered. "Hey, Ayleen. What's up?"

"We got an emergency call tonight. Is the old Rogerson place clean?"

An emergency meant a woman had suddenly run from her husband or boyfriend. She could be hurt. Mentally and physically. She could have kids with her.

Liz sat up, coming to attention, breaking eye contact with Cain. "Yes. It's ready."

Ayleen breathed a sigh of relief. "Great. Can you be there to meet the family?"

"Absolutely." Once again, she didn't hesitate but she caught Cain's gaze. "I can be there in a half an hour."

"No rush. The family's in transit. Their estimated arrival time is forty minutes."

"Ten minutes to spare." Ten minutes to talk Cain through this. "I'll call you later, after they're settled." She snapped her phone closed. Her gaze still clinging to Cain's, she said, "I'm sorry."

"For a miscarriage that wasn't your fault? For not telling me you were pregnant? Or for leaving me now before I can even wrap my head around it?"

"For all three."

He rubbed his hand across the back of his neck, and

turned away. Fear trickled down her spine. Not for herself, for him. She didn't want him to blame himself. Or be angry with himself.

"I know you have questions. I'm not sure I can answer them all, but I'll try."

He faced her again. "You know what? I get it." He shrugged. "We were both in a bad place. You did what you had to do. I'm stunned about losing a baby, but I can deal with that."

Her phone rang. She longed to ignore it, but knew what happened when A Friend Indeed was in crisis mode. The troops rallied. They called each other, making arrangements for what each would do. She couldn't ignore a call.

She flipped open her phone. "Hello."

"It's me, Ellie. Who's getting the groceries for the Rogerson house? You or me?"

"Could you do it?"

"Sure. See you, boss."

Warring needs tore her apart as she closed her phone. She wanted to be here for Cain, but he seemed to be handling this well. Three years had passed. Though she was sure he'd mourn the loss, it wasn't the same as actually going through it.

And the woman racing to the Friend Indeed house needed her. This was what she was trained to do.

Before she could speak, Cain did. "Go. I'm fine."

Liz studied his face and he smiled weakly. "Seriously, I'm fine. I'll call you."

His smile, though shaky, reassured her.

She rose. Her voice carried a gentle warning when she said, "If you don't call me, I'm calling you."

He smiled again. This time stronger. "Okay."

She turned and walked back into the house, through the downstairs and to the front door. On her way to her car she stopped and glanced back.

He'd taken that so well that maybe, just maybe, they really could have the new beginning he wanted.

Chapter 11

Walking into the shower the following Saturday, Cain cursed himself. He'd hardly slept since Monday night, and, when he had, he'd dreamed about things that made him crazy. The smoothness of Liz's perfect pink skin. The way her green eyes smoldered with need in the throes of passion. The feeling of her teeth scraping along his chest.

He shouldn't want her. *Shouldn't.* He was smarter than to want somebody who didn't want him.

She'd been so hesitant about spending time with him, to befriend him, to even consider anything romantic between them, yet he'd been oblivious to what her behavior was telling him. Just as he had been in their marriage. Now that he knew the real reason she'd left him, her not wanting anything to do with him made perfect sense.

He ducked his head under the spray, trying to rid

himself of the overwhelming shame that wanted to strangle him, but he couldn't. After his three years of guilt over his brother's death, he knew he couldn't assume responsibility for something that had been out of his control. And if her secret had simply been a matter of a miscarriage, he probably could have absolved himself. But how could he forgive himself for being so self-absorbed that his wife couldn't tell him she was pregnant? How could he forgive himself when her telling him about their baby might have been the thing that brought him back to life, bridged their marital gap, kept them together?

Stepping out of the shower, he grabbed a towel, telling himself to stop thinking about it. Running it over and over and over in his head wouldn't change anything. But memories of those final few months together had taken on new meaning and they haunted him.

And he could not—he would not—forgive himself.

At Amanda's house, Cain told Billy to take his time, hoping to delay seeing Liz. He hadn't called her as he told her he would but she also hadn't called him. He suspected she'd been busy with the new family moving into the Friend Indeed house. And for that he was grateful. He'd wanted to be alone. He didn't want to talk this out with her. Worse, he didn't want her to tell him it was "okay" that he hadn't been there for her. It wasn't "okay." It was abysmal—sinful—that he'd been so oblivious that his wife had to suffer in silence.

But the bad thing about avoiding her all week was that Billy would now witness their first meeting since she told him about their baby.

He pulled his truck into Fran's empty driveway. "No Liz," he mumbled, hardly realizing he was talking.

Billy pushed open the truck door. "Isn't there some kind of big party tonight?"

Cain turned to Billy. "Yes." How could he have forgotten? "A Friend Indeed's fund-raiser." On top of the new family that had moved in on Monday night, Liz had probably been occupied all week with last-minute details for the ball.

Billy jumped out of the truck. "And she's the boss of the whole deal, right?"

Cain nodded.

"So she's not going to be here." Billy slammed his door closed.

Cain's entire body sagged with relief. Until he remembered that he'd see her that night at the ball—

Unless he didn't go.

All things considered, that might be the right thing to do. Not for himself, but for her. This was her big night. He didn't want to ruin it. And seeing him sure as hell could ruin it for her. He'd been a nightmare husband. And when they'd "met" again in his kitchen when she came to work as his maid, she hadn't wanted to be around him. Yet he'd forced himself back into her life. He couldn't even imagine the pressure she'd endured for the weeks they'd worked together, the weeks he'd insinuated himself into A Friend Indeed. Not going would be a kindness to her.

For the next eight hours, he kept himself busy so he didn't have to think about Liz or the fund-raiser ball or their god-awful marriage. But at the end of the day he remembered that he'd promised Ayleen he would mingle with the guests, talking about the work he'd done, hoping to inspire other contractors and business owners to get involved in a more personal way. So if he didn't show, Ayleen would get upset and then Liz would worry about him.

He didn't want Liz to have to worry about him anymore. He wasn't her burden. He'd fulfill his responsibility and go to the ball, but he'd let her alone.

Liz had spent all day at the home of Mr. and Mrs. Leonard Brill, the couple who had volunteered their mansion for the ball for A Friend Indeed. After seeing to all the last-minute deliveries and details, she'd even dressed in one of their myriad spare bedrooms.

The event itself wasn't huge. Only a hundred people were attending. That was why the Brill mansion was the perfect choice. It was big enough to be luxurious, but not so large that the fund-raiser lost its air of intimacy. But the ball didn't need to be immense. All the people invited were big contributors. Liz expected to beat last year's donations by a wide margin, especially with the new guests Cain invited.

Walking into the empty ballroom ten minutes before the guests were due to arrive, she pressed her hand to her stomach. *Cain.* Just thinking his name gave her butterflies. He hadn't called her as he had promised, but she'd been overwhelmed with the ball, the new family in the Rogerson house and Happy Maids. He probably knew that and didn't want to add any more stress to her week.

But she remembered the expression on his face when she left, the calm way he'd taken the explanation of why she'd ended their marriage, and she not only knew she'd done the right thing by telling him, she also knew they were going to be okay.

Maybe better than okay.

"You look fabulous!" Wearing a peach sequined gown Ayleen floated across the empty dance floor to Liz, who pirouetted in her red strapless gown.

"Wow." Ellie joined them. "You two are going to be the talk of the town."

Liz laughed at Ellie, who looked like a vision in her aqua halter-top gown, her blond hair spilling around her in a riot of curls. "I think *you're* going to be the talk of the town."

She laughed. "Maybe we should all just settle for making our special men drool."

"My husband's past drooling," Ayleen said with a laugh, but just as quickly she frowned and her eyes narrowed at Liz. "I know Ellie is dating that lifeguard, but I've heard nothing about a special man in *your* life."

Liz felt her face redden and suspected it was probably as bright as her dress.

"Oh, come on!" Ellie chided. "Tell her about Cain."

Ayleen's eyebrows rose. "Our Cain?"

Ellie leaned in conspiratorially. "He was Liz's Cain long before he was A Friend Indeed's. He's her ex."

Ayleen's mouth dropped open. "No kidding."

"And I have a feeling," Ellie singsonged, "that they're not going to be exes long."

"Is that true?" Ayleen asked, facing Liz.

Liz sighed. "I have no idea."

Ellie playfully slapped her forearm. "You need to be more confident. That man loves you. I can see it in his face."

"But we have issues."

"Oh, pish posh!" Ayleen said. "Do you love him?"

"I don't ever think I ever stopped." As the words came out of her mouth, Liz realized how true they were. That was why she'd been so afraid to tell him about the miscarriage. She didn't want to hurt him or lose him. Which was why she was so grateful he'd reacted as well as he had to the news. She loved him. She always had and now that her secret had been confessed, they could finally move on with their lives.

"Then trust our magic friend. If she says he loves you, he loves you." She patted her hand. "You need to relax."

Cain strode up the stone sidewalk to the elaborate entrance of the Brill mansion. Twin fountains on both sides of the walk were lit by blue-and-gold lights. At the top of ten wide stone steps, columns welcomed guests to a cut-glass front door.

He could see why A Friend Indeed had chosen the Brill residence for their ball. It was one of Miami's most beautiful mansions. Plus, it was small enough to create an intimate atmosphere for guests. The kind of atmosphere that would allow Ayleen to personally walk among the guests and gather checks. Cain himself had an obscenely large check in his pocket. He wanted Liz to succeed.

Liz.

He could picture her now, excited about being pregnant and not being able to tell him. Then devastated by the loss and not being able to depend on him.

He cursed himself in his head for remembering, just as Leonard opened the front door.

"Cain! Welcome."

Cain pasted on a smile and stepped into the foyer. "Good evening, Mr. Brill."

"Call me Leonard, please," the older, gray-haired gentleman said as he directed Cain to the right. "Everyone's in the ballroom."

Nerves jangled through Cain as he entered the grand room. His eyes instantly scanned the crowd milling around the room, looking at artwork that had been donated for a silent auction that was also part of the event. A string quartet played in a corner as a dance band set up across the room.

He didn't see Liz, but he knew she was here and his heart began to hammer in anticipation. He shook his head. He had to get over this. Let her go. Let her find somebody worthy of her love.

Plus, he had a job at this fund-raiser. Ayleen had assigned him the task of walking around, talking about what he'd done for the houses so he could generate support and bigger contributions.

But only ten minutes into a conversation with a potential contributor he spotted Liz. As he spoke to Brad Coleman, his eyes had been surreptitiously scanning the room and he saw her standing with a small group of women, engaged in lively conversation.

He'd missed seeing her before because her beautiful black hair wasn't cascading over her shoulders, in a bouncy ponytail or even pulled back into a Happy Maids bun. It had been swept up into an elegant hairdo that gave her the look of a princess or aristocrat.

He let his eyes move lower and his breath whooshed from his lungs. Her dress was red—strapless—and didn't so much cling to her curves as gently caress them. He swallowed hard just as she turned and noticed him. She smiled hesitantly and his heart swelled with something that felt very much like love. But he stopped that, too.

He didn't deserve her. He never had.

"Why didn't you tell me that you and Liz had been married?"

Cain spun around and saw that Brad had deserted him and Ayleen had taken his place.

"It didn't seem relevant."

She laughed. "Men. You never know what's relevant."

Since he was the one so distant his own wife couldn't tell him she was pregnant, Cain couldn't argue that.

"She looks very beautiful tonight, doesn't she?"

Cain's gaze followed the direction of Ayleen's. Taking in the way her gown clung to her curves, and the sparkle in her brilliant green eyes, his blood raced in his veins, but his chest tightened in sadness. He had to walk away from her. Give her a chance for a real life.

"Yes. She is beautiful."

"You should ask her to dance."

"I don't think so. In fact," he said, reaching into his jacket pocket and producing his check, "I'll just give this to you."

Ayleen glanced at the check, then up at him. "This is the second time you've tried to give A Friend Indeed a check without going through the proper channels."

"I thought you were the proper channel."

"And I thought you'd want to give it to your ex-wife, so she could be impressed and proud of you."

He reared back as if she'd physically slapped him. If there were two things Liz should never be of him, they were proud or impressed.

He pressed the check into Ayleen's hand. "You take it."

She studied his face. "So you don't have to speak

with her?" She smiled ruefully. "Cain, this is wrong. She's excited to see you tonight and you're running?"

"Believe me. This is for her benefit, not mine." He lifted his eyes and luckily saw one of the guests he'd had Ayleen invite. "And before you ask why, I see one of my contributors." He slid away. "I'll see you later."

Liz shifted through the crowd, pausing to speak with people, asking if there was anything anyone needed, wishing everyone a good time. The dance band had been playing for about an hour. Dancers swayed and gyrated around the room. The silent auction proceeded as planned. Still, she walked around, introduced herself, saw to every tiny detail.

After another hour of pretending it didn't matter that Cain had ignored her when she'd smiled at him, she couldn't lie to herself anymore. He'd chosen not to speak with her. He hadn't said hello. Hadn't even returned her smile.

Pulling in a breath, she greeted a passing couple who praised her for the beautiful ball. But questions about why Cain wouldn't talk to her raced through her head. What if Cain hadn't taken her news as well as he'd seemed to? What if he'd been pretending? Or what if he was angry with her for not telling him she was pregnant?

It could be any of those things or all of them. She longed to find him and simply ask him, but she had a job to do. As if to punctuate that thought, a woman caught her hand and asked her a question about the auction. An elderly gentleman handed her a check. She couldn't walk two feet without someone stopping her.

The band took a break and the auction results were

announced by Ayleen, with Liz by her side on the small elevated platform that acted as a stage for the band.

"Those are our winners," Ayleen finally said, having given the final name on the list of those who'd won the bids. "You know where the checks go," she added with a laugh. "Thank you very much for your participation in this event. A Friend Indeed couldn't exist without you and on behalf of the women we've helped, I thank you."

The group broke into a quiet round of applause and after a reasonable time Ayleen raised her hand to stop them.

"I'd also like to thank Liz Harper for all of her hard work, not just on this ball but also for the group on a daily basis."

The crowd applauded again.

When they were through, Ayleen said, "And special thanks to Cain Nestor. He's been renovating the houses. Donating both his time and the materials to make the homes of our women some of the prettiest houses in their neighborhoods."

The crowd erupted in spontaneous, thunderous applause, and Liz felt such a stirring of pride for Cain, tears came to her eyes. He never saw what a wonderful person he was. But she did. And she'd made another huge mistake with him. She should have told him about their baby sooner.

Lost in her thoughts, she wasn't prepared when Ayleen caught her hand and pulled her forward, toward the microphone again.

"What most of you don't know though is that Liz has been helping Cain. At first she acted as A Friend Indeed's liaison, but then she picked up a paintbrush and threw herself into the work, too. Cain and Liz are an unbeatable team."

She hugged Liz in thanks then turned away, scanning the room. "Cain? Where are you? How about if you and Liz get the next set of the dancing started, so everyone can see who you are?"

Liz's mouth fell open in dismay. Ayleen had probably noticed Cain hadn't even spoken to her and was playing matchmaker. She didn't know Cain was upset about their child and he didn't want to talk with her. Liz had only figured it out herself. But there was nothing she could do to get out of this without embarrassing herself or Cain.

With her heart hammering in her chest, Liz looked down off the makeshift stage and searched the crowd for Cain. She found him in the back in a corner, watching her. Their gazes locked. She waited for him to look away. He didn't. She told herself to look away and couldn't. He walked out of the crowd to her.

Cain swallowed the last of the champagne in his glass and dropped it on the tray of a passing waiter. He wouldn't embarrass Liz by publicly refusing to dance with her. But he also knew this was as good of a time as any to get their relationship on track. She didn't want a second chance with him. He didn't deserve one. But they both worked for A Friend Indeed. So they had to spend time together. They couldn't ignore each other forever.

The whole room stilled as he and Liz met in the center of the dance floor. He pulled her into his arms, and the band began to play a waltz. Forcing himself to focus on the music, he tried to ignore her sweet scent, but it swirled around them like the notes of the song, tempting him. Especially when she melted against him. Not in surrender, but in acknowledgment. They would always have chemistry. But sometimes that wasn't enough.

He wasn't enough. She was worthy of someone much, much better.

The music vibrated around them as other dancers eased onto the floor. In minutes they were surrounded by a happy crowd. Not the center of attention, anymore. Not even on anyone's radar. He could slip away.

Just as he was ready to excuse himself and end the dance, she pulled back. Her shiny green eyes searched his.

"Are you okay?"

"I'm fine." He said the words casually then twirled her around to emphasize his lightness. He'd never make her feel responsible for him again.

She pulled back again. "But you're angry with me."

He laughed. "No, Liz. If there's one thing I'm not, it's angry with you."

"You have every right to be. I should have told you about our baby sooner."

The hurt in her voice skipped across his nerves like shards of glass. As if it wasn't bad enough he had to walk away from her, she was taking it all wrong.

"And I'm sorry. I'm very, very sorry."

He nearly squeezed his eyes shut in misery. He was the one who hadn't been there for her. Yet she was apologizing to him?

He stopped dancing, tugged his hand away from hers. "Stop."

"No. You told me on Monday night that you wanted to start over. I think we could—"

Other dancers nearly bumped into them. He caught her by the waist and hauled her against him, spinning them into the crowd again. "Don't say it," he said, nearly breathless from her nearness. They couldn't go on like this. And he'd made it worse by mentioning starting over before he knew just how bad he'd been as a husband. Now, in her innate fairness, or maybe because she was so kind, she was willing to try again. But he couldn't do that to her.

And if the only way to get her away from him, off the notion that somehow they belonged together, was to hurt her, then maybe one final hurt added to his long list of sins wouldn't matter.

"I made a mistake the other night when I mentioned reconciling. I was a lousy husband. You never should have married me. It's time we moved on. Time we let go. Time *you* let go."

With that he released her. The horrified expression on her face cut to his heart, but he ignored it, turned and walked off the dance floor. Letting her go was for the best. Even if it did break his heart.

Stunned, Liz turned and scanned the great room, until she found Ellie. She raced over. "I have to go."

Ellie's face fell. "What?"

"I'm sorry," she said, pulling Ellie with her as she ran through the foyer to the front door. "Everything's done, except the final goodbye and thank-you. Ayleen has already done the official thank-you. All you need to say is thank-you and good-night. Can you do that?"

Ellie said, "Sure, but—"

Liz didn't give her the chance to finish. She raced out the door and down the stone steps. The tinkling of the fountains followed her and the silver moon lit the way as she raced down the driveway to her car. The only thing missing from the scene was a pair of glass slippers.

Because like Cinderella, she'd lost her prince.

Again.

The old Cain was back. And the worst of it was Liz had brought him back. He'd pretended to take the news of their baby well, but the truth was he'd tumbled back into the horrible place where he'd lived the three years of their marriage. There had been no help for it. She couldn't have entered into a relationship with a secret hanging over them.

But she'd hurt him. More this time than she had by walking away from their marriage without a word.

He'd never forgive her.

She'd never forgive herself.

Balling up the skirt of her gown, she slid into her car and a horrible thought struck her. They had to work together in the morning. After the way he'd rejected her, dismissed her, she had to go to Fran's house in the morning and pretend nothing had happened.

Chapter 12

The next morning, Cain nearly called Ayleen and begged off his work on Fran's house. He hadn't wanted to hurt Liz, but he'd had to to force her to get on with her life. So he didn't really want to spend eight hours with her, seeing her hurt, knowing he'd hurt her and knowing he really would spend the rest of his days without the one woman he wanted in his life. All because he could never see her needs. She might be right for him, but he most certainly wasn't right for her and he had to let her go.

But in the end he conceded that bailing on Fran's house wasn't the thing to do. He had made a commitment to A Friend Indeed. Fran shouldn't have to wait for her house to be finished because he and Liz shouldn't be working together.

He rolled his truck to a stop in front of Fran's garage but didn't immediately open his truck door. Stuck in his thoughts, he stared at the empty space beside his truck.

"She'll be here," Billy said, undoubtedly assuming Cain was wondering where Liz was. "She never lets anybody down. Just ask my mom."

The kid's voice held the oddest note of both trust in Liz and scorn. It might have been simple teenage angst or it could have been that something had happened that morning to make him angry. Cain couldn't tell. Sooner or later, he'd get it out of him, but right now Cain's mind was still on Liz. About how his next step would have to be getting her off his work crew.

He shoved his truck door open and jumped out just as her little green car chugged into the driveway. He rushed back to his truck bed and immediately reached for the cooler and picnic basket. Intense and primal, the desire rose in him to get away before the need to talk to her, to touch her, became a hungry beast he couldn't control. He would have done anything, given anything, if there would have been a way they could start over, but they couldn't. He wouldn't do that to her. He would not ruin her life a second time.

Stepping out of her car, Liz saw the picnic basket and smiled shakily. "You brought lunch again."

He almost groaned. Even sweet Liz shouldn't be able to forgive him for how he'd rejected her the night before. Yet, here she was trying to get along, giving him the damned benefit of the doubt.

"Yes. I brought lunch." He turned away, taking the cooler and stowing it in the garage before he hauled the picnic basket into the kitchen.

Following him, she said, "What are we doing today?"

"We're finishing the carpet in the bedrooms." And it wasn't a three-person job. He and Billy had handled it alone the day before. This was his out, his way to save her, his way to save himself from the misery of being within arm's distance of the woman he'd always loved, but never deserved.

He faced her. "This is actually a two-person job. Billy and I can handle it. I know you're probably tired from all the work you did for the ball yesterday." Casually, as if nothing were wrong, he leaned against the counter. "So why don't you go on home?"

She took a step back. "You want me to leave?"

"Yes." The wounded look in her eyes made him long to tell her he was sorry that he hadn't been there for her. To tell her how much he wished he could make all his misdeeds up to her. To tell her he wished there was a way they didn't have to give up on their relationship.

But he couldn't do that. The only honorable thing for him to do would be to sacrifice his own needs, so that she'd find someone who really would love her.

She stared at him, as if waiting for him to change his mind. As the clock above the sink ticked off the seconds, her eyes filled with tears. Without a word, she turned and raced out the door before Cain could even say goodbye.

Billy shook his head in wonder. "Are you nuts?"

Before he could stop himself, Cain said, "Trust me. This is for her own good."

It might have been for her good, but the sadness that shivered through him told Cain that he wouldn't ever get over this. Forcing her to find a better man was the best thing for her, but it was the worst that could happen to him.

In her office that morning and afternoon, Liz kept herself so busy catching up on the work she'd ignored while she worked on the ball that she didn't have time to think about Cain.

She knew telling him about their lost baby had caused him to close himself off. But this time he didn't seem to be closing himself off from the world. Only from her.

She refused to let herself think about any of it, and instead worked diligently in her office until it was dark. Then she walked to her car, head high, breaths deep and strong. She'd lost him twice now. But this time she'd lost him honestly. She'd lost him because she wouldn't start a relationship while hiding a secret. She'd done the right thing. She'd simply gotten the wrong result.

And now she would deal with it.

In her condo, she tossed her keys to the table by the door and reached for the hem of her T-shirt as she walked back to the shower. She might have lost him honestly but she'd still lost him, and it hurt so much even the soothing spray of her shower didn't help. She'd lost Cain's love, the affection she craved from him, but more than that she would have to live with the knowledge that he would torment himself for the rest of his life.

She knew he was a good man. If only he could forgive himself and live life in the now, he could be free. But he couldn't, not even for her. Not even for *them*.

After her shower, she wrapped herself in a robe and headed out to the kitchen to make herself some cocoa. She reached into the cupboard for a mug just as her cell phone rang. For the second time in as many weeks, she wished she could ignore it. She wanted to weep, not for herself but for Cain. For as much as it hurt her to lose him, she knew he suffered the torment of the damned. He'd never be happy.

But as an integral part of a charity that didn't sleep, she couldn't ignore any call. She reached over and picked up her phone. Seeing that the caller was Amanda, she said, "Hey, Amanda. What's up?"

"Liz! Liz! Billy is gone!"

"What do you mean gone?"

"We had a fight this morning that we didn't get to finish because Cain came to get him for work. When he got home this afternoon he tried to act as if nothing happened, but I picked up right where we left off." Amanda burst into tears. "I'm so sorry. I was so stupid. But I'm so afraid he'll turn out like his dad that I go overboard. And now he's gone. He just walked out, slamming the door. Before I could go after him he was gone. I didn't even see if he turned right or left. It was like he disappeared." She took a shuddering breath. "I've looked everywhere I know to look. He's nowhere."

Liz's own breath stuttered in her chest. Fear for Billy overwhelmed her. "Don't worry. We'll find him."

"How? I've looked everywhere. And it's too soon to call the police. They make you wait twenty-four hours." She made a gurgling sound in her throat. "By the time twenty-four hours pass, anything could happen!"

"Okay, I'm calling Cain—" She made the offer without thinking. Even Amanda was surprised.

"Cain?"

"They talk a lot as they're working, Amanda. There's a good chance he'll know where Billy is."

Amanda breathed a sigh of relief. "Okay."

But Liz's breath froze when she realized what she'd

done. Now she had to call Cain. "You sit tight. I'll call you back as soon as I talk to him."

"Okay."

Liz clicked off and immediately dialed Cain's cell phone. She wouldn't let herself think about the fact that he hated her now. Wouldn't let herself consider that he might ignore her plea for help.

"Liz?"

Relieved that he'd answered, Liz leaned against her counter and said simply, "Billy's gone."

"Gone?"

"He had a fight with Amanda. She says she knows she pushed a bit too hard, and he flew out of the house and was gone before she could even see what direction he ran in."

A few seconds passed in silence before Cain said, "Look, Liz, I'm going to be honest. I think I know where Billy is, but you can't come with me."

"Like hell I can't!" He might have been able to kick her off the job site that morning, but Billy was her responsibility, and she wasn't letting Cain push her out of finding him.

"I think he's gone to his father's. If he has, this could be dangerous."

"I get that. But I'm trained for this! *You* aren't. If either one of us goes, it should be me."

There was a long pause. Finally Cain blew his breath out on a sigh. "I can't let you go alone, so we have to go together. Be ready when I get to your apartment." He stopped. "Where is your apartment?"

She gave him the address and, as he clicked off, she raced into her bedroom and pulled on jeans and a tank top. By the time he arrived in front of her building, she was already on the sidewalk.

She jumped into his Porsche and he raced away. The humid Miami air swirled around her as they roared down the street. With Cain's attention on driving, Liz glanced around at the car she'd loved when they were married. Memories of driving down this very highway in this very car, six years ago, before all their troubles, assailed her. They were so sweet and so poignant that part of her longed to pretend that everything was okay between them.

But that was their biggest problem. When things weren't working out, they'd tried to pretend they were. She was done with that and Cain was, too. She had to accept that they were over.

Cain tried not to think about Liz sitting next to him as he drove to Billy's old house, the house he and Amanda had lived in with an abusive father. He prayed that Billy hadn't been so angry with his mom that he told his father the location of their safe house. If they didn't get to Billy on time, Billy's dad could be on his way to Amanda's before they could warn her.

He pressed his gas pedal to the floor. Billy's dad lived far enough away that Billy would have had to take a bus. Cain didn't know the schedule, but he prayed Billy hadn't been lucky enough to walk out onto the street and hop on a bus. If he'd had to wait that bought him and Liz time to get to him. So there was still hope. Slim hope. But hope.

Nearing Billy's old neighborhood, Cain also prayed that if Billy had made it to his dad's and had had the gumption to refuse to tell his dad where his mom and sister were that his dad hadn't taken his fists to him.

A sick feeling rose up in him. There were too many ways this night could end badly.

Because he didn't have an exact address, Cain slowed his car. When he did, he heard Liz suck in a breath.

He automatically reached for her hand. "Don't worry. We'll do this."

The feeling of her hand in his brought an ache to his chest. He knew he shouldn't have touched her. But she looked so sad and he was so scared that it came automatically to him. She smiled at him across the console and his heart constricted. He'd give anything to deserve the trust she had in him.

He glanced away, at the area around them.

"Billy talked about a bar that was two buildings down from his house and going to the convenience store across the street." Cain let his Porsche roll along slowly as he and Liz scanned the area.

"There's the bar," Liz shouted, pointing. "And the convenience store."

"And Billy," Cain said, pointing at the kid sitting on the curb in front of a little blue house.

He found a parking space, and they pushed their way out of the car and raced up to Billy.

"Hey, Liz." Billy's eyes roved from Liz to Cain. "Hey, Cain."

"Hey." The kid's mood was sad more than upset, so Cain took a cue from him. Not caring about his gray trousers, he casually sat on the curb beside Billy. Liz sat on the other side. "Your mom is worried."

He snorted a laugh. "My mom is always worried."

"Looks like she's got good reason this time," Liz

said, turning and gesturing at the house behind them. "Is that your old place?"

Billy nodded.

"Dad not home?"

"He might be. I don't know."

Cain sat back, letting Liz take the lead in the conversation. She was the one who had been trained for this.

"You didn't go in?"

"I sorta feel like I'm doing that cutting off my nose to spite my face thing my mom talks about."

Cain chuckled and Liz out-and-out laughed. He could hear the relief in her voice. He felt it, too. Billy had run, but he couldn't take the final steps. He probably liked his new life. Even if his old life sometimes seemed like a way out of his troubles, he really didn't want to go back.

"Yeah. That's probably accurate." She waited a few seconds then said, "Do you want to talk about it?"

Billy shrugged. "Same old stuff."

"I'm not familiar with the stuff, so you'll have to fill me in."

"She's afraid of everything."

Liz's eyebrows rose. "She has good reason, Billy."

"I'm not my dad and I'm tired of paying for his mistakes."

Cain got a sudden inspiration and before Liz could reply, he said, "How does she make you pay?"

"She yells at me. I have a curfew."

"That's not paying for your dad's mistakes, Billy. That's her guiding you, looking out for your welfare, being a mom."

Billy looked at him sharply. "No one else I know has a curfew."

"Maybe that's why half your friends are in trouble."

Cain sighed and shifted on the curb, glancing at Liz who only gave him a look with her eyes that encouraged him to continue.

"Look, trust isn't handed out like hall passes in school. You have to earn it."

Unexpectedly, he thought of Liz, of all the ways he'd failed her and yet she trusted him. She trusted him when he didn't trust himself. Liz had always believed in him. Even when he let her down, she believed he'd do the right thing the next time.

Hooking his thumb toward the house behind them, he said, "Earning trust isn't easy, but running back to the past isn't the alternative. It's just a way of staying right where you are. Never learning from your mistakes. Never having what you want." A strange feeling bubbled up in him as he said that. As if he wasn't talking to Billy but to himself.

He cleared his throat. "But that means you're going to have to do a thing or two to earn your mom's trust."

"Like what?"

"Like not arguing about the curfew and coming in on time. Like telling her where you're going." He gave Billy a friendly nudge with his shoulder. "Like getting your grades up in school."

Billy snorted a laugh.

"So it sounds as if you agree that there's room for improvement."

"I guess."

Cain clasped his hand on Billy's shoulder. "Let's get you back to your mom."

Billy rose. "Okay."

Liz rose, too.

"But first let's go across the street and get a gallon of ice cream. What kind does your mom like?"

Billy blinked. "Chocolate. Why?"

"It never hurts to bring a present when you've made a mistake."

When Liz, Cain and Billy walked in the kitchen door of Amanda's house, Amanda burst into tears.

Billy held out a brown bag to his mom. "I'm sorry, Mom. I shouldn't have been mad. I know all your rules are to protect me. I'll do better."

Amanda took the bag and set it on the table without looking at it so she could grab Billy in a hug. Sobbing out her fear, she clung to him and wept.

Liz caught Cain's gaze and motioned that they should leave. He hesitated, but she headed for the door and he followed her.

The strangest feelings assaulted him. By punishing himself for something so far in the past he couldn't change it, he wasn't moving on. And he also wasn't learning any lessons. He was losing the one thing he'd always wanted—Liz. She was never the one to condemn him. He continually condemned himself. What if she was correct. What if—for once in his life—he gave himself a break?

She stepped out onto the sidewalk, walked to the driveway and got into his car.

Their car.

He squeezed his eyes shut and pressed his lips together. She wanted to forgive him. Was it so wrong to want to forgive himself?

Chapter 13

The next morning, Liz lay on her sofa, wrapped in a blanket, drinking hot cocoa, even though the temperature outside had long ago passed eighty.

She had awakened so sad and lonely, after a sleepless night, that she considered it a real coup that she'd made it to the couch. She'd seen the best of Cain the night before when he'd talked Billy into going home and even paid for the ice cream to take to his mother. Yet she knew he didn't see any goodness in himself. And because of that he couldn't forgive himself for the mistakes in their marriage. And because he couldn't forgive himself, he was letting her go. Freeing her.

She loved him with her whole heart and soul but if he didn't want her, then maybe it was time she got the message. She couldn't go on always being alone. Ellie dated. Her friends had gotten married. Yet she was still mourning a marriage that was over.

A soft rap on her door got her head off the back of the sofa. She didn't intend to answer it, but the knock sounded again. This time stronger.

Whoever it was wasn't going away, so she might as well answer. Rising from the sofa, she wrapped herself in her security blanket. When she reached the door, she tugged the soft fleece more securely around herself before she grabbed the knob and opened the door.

Cain smiled at her. "You know, last night when I got home I thought about the things I said when I was counseling Billy, and it occurred to me that I was actually pretty good at talking to people." He pulled in a breath. "Everybody but you."

She snorted a laugh.

"So I'm going to give this a shot. This past week, I've hated myself for being such a terrible husband to you."

"Oh, Cain!"

"Let me finish. I really let you down and I had every right to be angry with myself. But I also can't wallow in that."

Hope filled Liz's heart. Could he really be saying what she thought he was saying? She opened the door a little wider and invited him inside. "Why don't we have this discussion inside?"

He walked into her small living room. His eyes took note of the neat and tidy room. He smiled sheepishly at her. "How am I doing so far?"

She laughed. Please, please, please let him be headed in the direction that she thought he was headed. "So far you're doing fairly well."

"Okay, then." He drew in a breath and caught her gaze. "I love you and I want to remarry you. I can't change who I was. But I sure as hell don't intend to be that guy anymore."

"Now you're doing fabulously."

This time he laughed. "I was so miserable, so angry with myself, until I remembered what I said to Billy. Suddenly I realized that just like him I had a chance to move on, but I wouldn't if I didn't stop reaching back to the past. Punishing myself. Wallowing in grief."

"Cain, what I told you wasn't easy news," she whispered, so hopeful her voice rattled with it. "I think you deserved a week of confusion."

"I don't want to lose you because of things that happened in the past. We're different. Different enough that this time we can work this out."

"I think so."

"Good. Because I've got some plans." He tugged on her hand, bringing her against him.

Liz smiled up at him. He gazed down at her. And as always happened when they truly looked at each other, the unhappy six years between his brother's death and the present melted away. He looked young and happy, as he had on the flight from Dallas. His eyes had lost the dull regret they'd worn all through their marriage. He really was *her* Cain.

She couldn't pull her gaze away. Not even when his head began to lower and she knew—absolutely knew in her woman's heart—he was going to kiss her.

His lips met hers as a soft brush. It felt so good to be kissed by him, touched by him, that she kissed him back. For three years of being married to him she'd longed for this. Not the passion they'd had in their six-month long-distance relationship. They'd never lost that. But they had lost the need to be together, to connect. They lost happy, joyful, thankful-to-have-each-other kisses. And that's what this was. A happy kiss. An I'm-glad-I-know-you kiss.

He pulled away slowly. "I swear I will never hurt you again."

"I know." Tears flooded her eyes but she blinked them away. This was not the time for tears. Not even happy tears. "So where do you think we should start with this new relationship of ours?"

"At the beginning." He turned her in the direction of her bedroom. "How about if I make you something to eat while you get dressed? Then we can go out on the boat for a while? Just like normal people dating."

"Dating?"

"It's a little something people who like each other do to see if they should be married or not. It's a step we seemed to have missed."

She laughed. "All right."

He made lunch. Cheese sandwiches and soup. She changed into shorts and a tank top and they went out on the ocean for the rest of the day. The next weekend and every weekend after that for the next six months, they worked on A Friend Indeed houses during the day and attended Cain's myriad social engagements at night. They spent Christmas with her mother and sisters in Philadelphia and New Year's with his parents in Kansas.

When they returned on January second, he lured her back down the hall to his office and sat her on the edge of his desk.

Laughing, she waited while he opened the bottom drawer of his desk and pulled out a jeweler's box. "Open it."

Obedient, but cautious since he'd already given her

a Christmas present, she lifted the lid on the little box and her eyes widened. The diamond on the engagement ring inside was huge.

"This is too big!"

He laughed. "In the crowd we run in five carats is about average size."

"The crowd *we* run in is very different from the crowd *you* ran in. We have all kinds of friends now. But I like the ring." She peeked at him. "I'm going to keep it."

"Is that a yes?"

"I don't recall you actually asking me a question."

He got down on one knee and caught her fingers. "Will you marry me?"

Unable to believe this was really happening, she pressed her lips together to keep herself from crying before she said, "On two conditions."

"I'm listening."

"We have a real wedding."

He nodded his agreement.

"And we stay who we are."

He grinned. "I sort of like who we are."

She laughed. Her heart sang with joy that communication could be so easy between them. That they could say so much with so few words, and that they really were getting a second chance.

"Then you are one lucky guy."

He stood up, bent down and kissed her. "You better believe it."

He broke the kiss and Liz noticed an odd-shaped manila envelope stuffed with bubble wrap in the drawer. She kicked it with the toe of her sandal. "What's that?"

"I don't know."

* * *

Cain sat on his desk chair and reached down to lift out the fat envelope. He pulled out the bubble wrap and unwound it.

"That's gotta be from your dad. He's the only person I know who goes overboard with bubble wrap."

Cain laughed, but when he finished unwinding, he found the family photo his dad had sent him the weekend Liz had come back into his life.

"What is it?"

He inclined his head, waiting for sadness to overwhelm him. It didn't. "It's my family's last picture together."

She plucked it from his hands. "Very nice. But your sister looks like a reject from a punk band."

He laughed. "I know."

She turned and set the photo in front of his desk blotter. "I think it should go right here. Right where you can see it every day and be thankful you have such a great family."

Cain smiled. She'd turned his life around in the past few months. She'd brought him out of his shell, got him working for a charity and made him happy when he wasn't really sure he could ever be happy again.

How could he argue with success? Especially when she'd said she'd marry him. Again.

"I think you're right."

Epilogue

Cain and Liz's wedding day the following June turned out to be one of the hottest in Miami's history, making Liz incredibly glad she'd chosen a strapless gown.

On the edge of a canal, in the backyard of the Brill mansion, they toasted their future among family and friends this time. Liz's mom and sisters finally met Cain's parents and sister. The two families blended together as if they'd known each other forever.

Cain's parents were overjoyed that he'd gotten involved in A Friend Indeed and loved that the board of directors from the group *and* many of the women the charity had helped attended the wedding.

Though Liz's mom was happy to see Liz remarrying the man she'd always loved, she was more proud of her daughter's successful business. Her sisters were bridesmaids with Ellie and Amanda. Billy, the surprise best man, lived up to the role with a funny and sentimental toast to the two people who helped him grow from a boy with little to no prospects for the future to a guy who now believed the sky was the limit.

When it was finally time, Cain whisked Liz away. Driving with the top down in "their" beloved Porsche, he took a few turns and got them on the road to his house.

"Why are we going back to the house?"

"It's a surprise."

Wind blowing her veil in a stream behind her, she laughed. "Do we have time for this?"

"It's not like the pilot's going to leave without us, since he has no other passengers." He snuck a glance at her. "Plus, I sign his paycheck."

"True enough." She laughed again and within minutes they were at Cain's front door.

"Is this surprise bigger than a bread box?" she asked as he opened the door and led her inside.

"You'll see." He directed her up the steps.

Raising her full tulle skirt, she raced ahead eager to see what he'd done. "I knew there was a reason you only wanted to sleep at my condo these past few weeks."

"Here I thought I'd pulled a fast one on you."

She turned around and placed a smacking kiss on his lips. "Not hardly."

He laughed and pointed her in the direction of one of his empty bedrooms. He opened the door for her and let her walk inside.

"Oh, Cain!" Staring at the beautiful nursery she could hardly take it all in. "Did you do this?"

"I hired a designer."

"It's gorgeous." She faced him. "But we're not…well, you know. We're not pregnant."

He pulled her into his arms. "I know. I just don't ever want there to be any doubt in your mind again that I'm with you this time. A hundred percent. I want little girls with your eyes and little boys to take fishing."

He kissed her and what started off as something slow and dreamy quickly became hot and steamy.

Just when she thought he'd lower them to the floor, he whispered in her ear, "We have a perfectly good shower in the master suite. We can kill two birds with one stone."

"Two birds?"

"Yeah, we can make love and take a shower before we change into clothes to wear on the trip to Europe."

"I thought we were supposed to change on the plane."

He nibbled her neck. "Plans change."

"And Dale won't mind?"

"Dale is a very patient, understanding man."

He swept her off her feet and carried her to their bedroom, while she undid his tie. He set her down and she tossed his tie to the dresser, as he unzipped her dress. It puddled on the floor and she stepped out of it.

She stood before him in her white lace bra and panties and he sucked in a breath. "You're beautiful."

She kissed him before undoing the buttons of his shirt. "You're not so bad yourself."

He finished undressing and carried her to the shower.

And Dale the pilot got comfortable on the sofa in the office in the hangar housing Cain's private plane, smiling because he had a sneaking feeling he knew why his boss and his new bride had been delayed.

* * * * *

We hope you enjoyed reading

IT HAPPENED ONE WEEK

by *New York Times* bestselling author
JOANN ROSS and

MAID FOR THE MILLIONAIRE

by reader-favorite author SUSAN MEIER.

Both were originally Harlequin® series stories!

Escape with romances featuring real, relatable
women and strong, deeply desirable men.
Experience the intensity, anticipation and sheer
rush of falling in love with Harlequin® Romance!

Look for four new romances every month
from Harlequin® Romance!

Available wherever books are sold.

NYTHR0314

Enjoy this sneak preview of
STOLEN KISS FROM A PRINCE, the sparkling new
Harlequin Romance story from Teresa Carpenter!

"So wise." He kissed the back of her hand, the heat of his breath tickling over her skin making her shiver, distracting her for a moment. The old-fashioned gesture was definitely not meant to be shared between employer and nanny. And then he turned her hand over and kissed the palm.

Her breath caught. *Oh, my.*

He regained her attention when he framed her face in two large hands and lifted her gaze to his.

"Thank you." His thumbs feathered over her cheeks collecting the last of her tears. "You are a very giving woman."

"No one should be alone at such a time." She lifted her right hand and wrapped her fingers around one thick wrist, not knowing if she meant to hold him to her or pull him free.

"It's a dangerous trait." The thumb of the hand she held continued to caress her cheek, though he seemed almost unaware of the gesture.

"Why?" she breathed.

"Someone may take advantage of you."

A knot clenched in her gut. Someone had. The harsh memory threatened to destroy the moment. She should step back, return to her duties. But she didn't. Because of the glint of vulnerability in his eyes.

Instead she bit her bottom lip and stayed put. For the first time she successfully shushed it. Perhaps because she needed this moment as much as he did.

HREXP0314

"There is only you and me here." She blinked, noting the look in his eyes had changed. The pain lingered but awareness joined the grief. "Are you going to take advantage?"

"Yes." He lowered his head. "I am." And he pressed his mouth to hers. He ran his tongue along the seam of her lips then nipped her bottom lip. "You tempt me so when you torture this lip."

She opened her mouth to protest, but he took full advantage, sealing her mouth with his. Heat bloomed, senses taking over as sensation ignited passion. Large and warm, he dwarfed her, his strong body a shelter against the craziness of the past few days. He drew her closer, aligning her curves with his hard contours and taking the sensual escape to deeper levels.

For long moments she surrendered to his touch, to his heat, to his need. Lifting onto tiptoes she looped her arms around his neck and got lost with him in a world without loss, without hurt, without protocol.

She cleared her throat. "I should check on Sammy."

He nodded and crossed his hands behind his back in a formal pose. To remind himself of duty, or to keep his hands to himself? "I suppose we're going to allocate this to comfort, as well."

"It would be best," she agreed, knowing as she did there'd be even less chance of forgetting these moments in his arms than their last embrace.

Don't miss STOLEN KISS FROM A PRINCE
by Teresa Carpenter, available April 2013!

⬢HARLEQUIN®

Romance

Save $1.00 on the purchase of

STOLEN KISS
FROM A PRINCE

by Teresa Carpenter,

available April 2014
or on any other Harlequin® Romance book.

Available wherever books are sold, including most bookstores,
supermarkets, drugstores and discount stores.

Save
$1.00

on the purchase of
STOLEN KISS FROM A PRINCE
by Teresa Carpenter
available April 2014
or on any other Harlequin® Romance book.

Coupon valid until June 4, 2014. Redeemable at participating retail outlets
in the U.S. and Canada only. Limit one coupon per customer.

® and TM are trademarks owned and used by the trademark owner and/or its licensee.
© 2014 Harlequin Enterprises Limited

NYTCOUP0314

ReaderService.com

Manage your account online!

- Review your order history
- Manage your payments
- Update your address

We've designed
the Harlequin® Reader Service
website just for you.

Enjoy all the features!

- Reader excerpts from any series
- Respond to mailings and special monthly offers
- Discover new series available to you
- Browse the Bonus Bucks catalog
- Share your feedback

Visit us at:
ReaderService.com